Kingdoms

A Biblical Epic

Valley of Dry Bones

ZONDERVAN®

Valley of Dry Bones
Copyright © 2008 by Lamp Post, Inc.

Requests for information should be addressed to:

Zondervan, *Grand Rapids, Michigan 49530*

CIP applied for
ISBN: 978-0-310-71356-2

This book published in conjunction with Lamp Post, Inc.; 8367 Lemon Avenue, La Mesa, CA 91941

Series Editor: Bud Rogers
Cover Illustration: Mat Broome
Managing Art Director: Merit Alderink

Printed in the United States of America

08 09 10 11 12 13 • 8 7 6 5 4 3 2 1

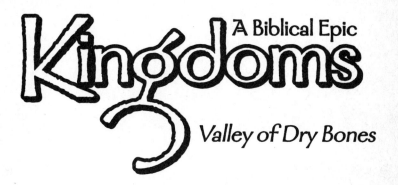

Kingdoms
A Biblical Epic
Valley of Dry Bones

Series Editor: Bud Rogers
Story by Ben Avery
Art by Gary Shipman
Created by Brett Burner

ZONDERVAN®

ZONDERVAN.com/
AUTHORTRACKER
follow your favorite authors

CHAPTER ONE

"The Messenger"

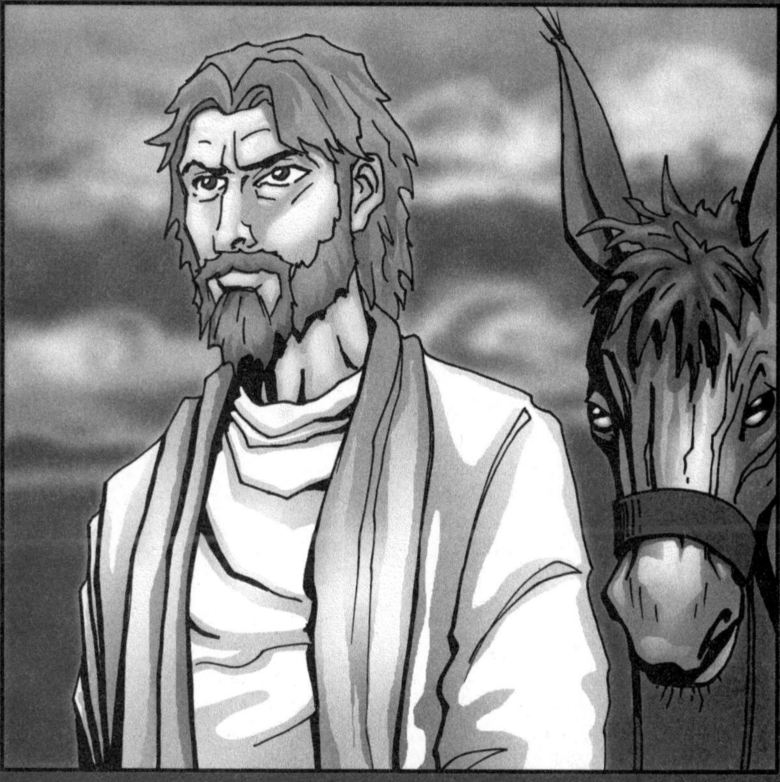

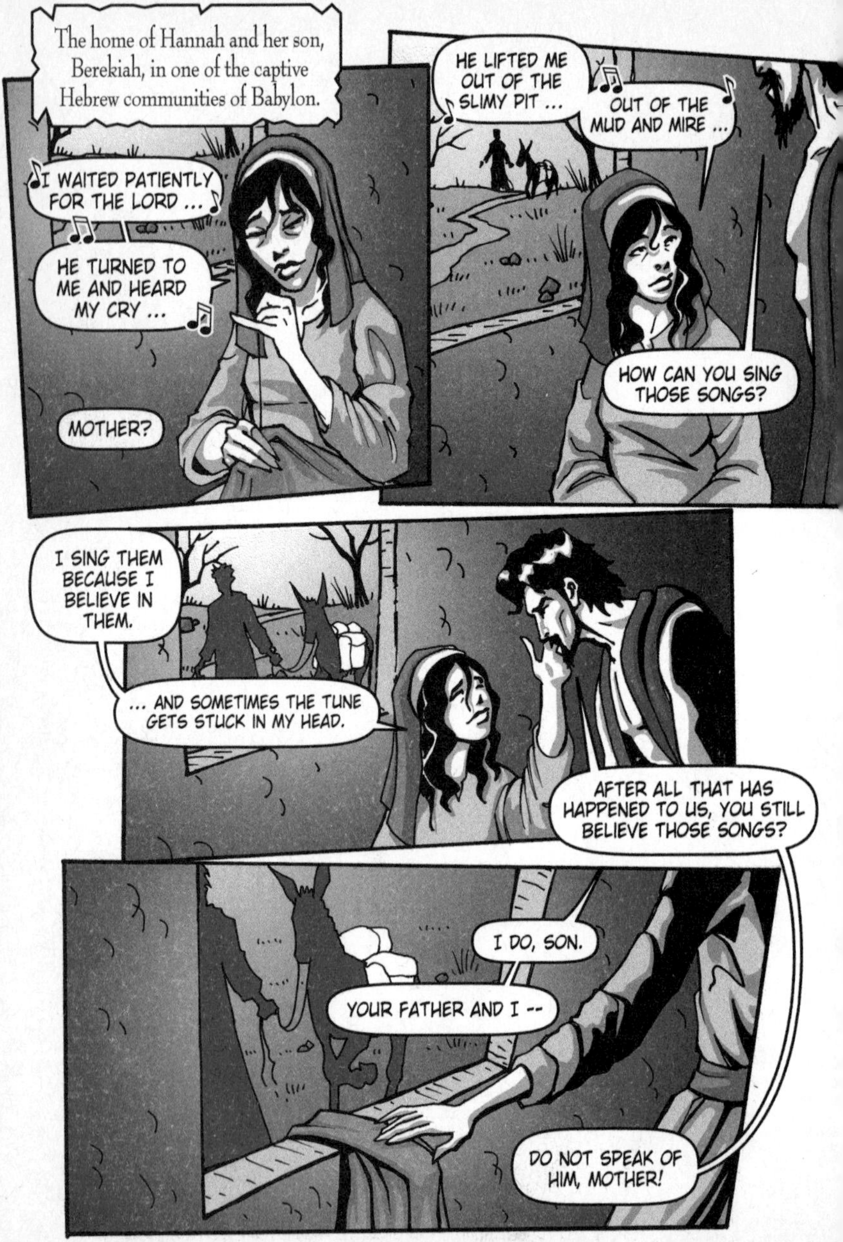
The home of Hannah and her son, Berekiah, in one of the captive Hebrew communities of Babylon.
I WAITED PATIENTLY FOR THE LORD ...
HE TURNED TO ME AND HEARD MY CRY ...
MOTHER?
HE LIFTED ME OUT OF THE SLIMY PIT ...
OUT OF THE MUD AND MIRE ...
HOW CAN YOU SING THOSE SONGS?
I SING THEM BECAUSE I BELIEVE IN THEM.
... AND SOMETIMES THE TUNE GETS STUCK IN MY HEAD.
AFTER ALL THAT HAS HAPPENED TO US, YOU STILL BELIEVE THOSE SONGS?
I DO, SON.
YOUR FATHER AND I --
DO NOT SPEAK OF HIM, MOTHER!

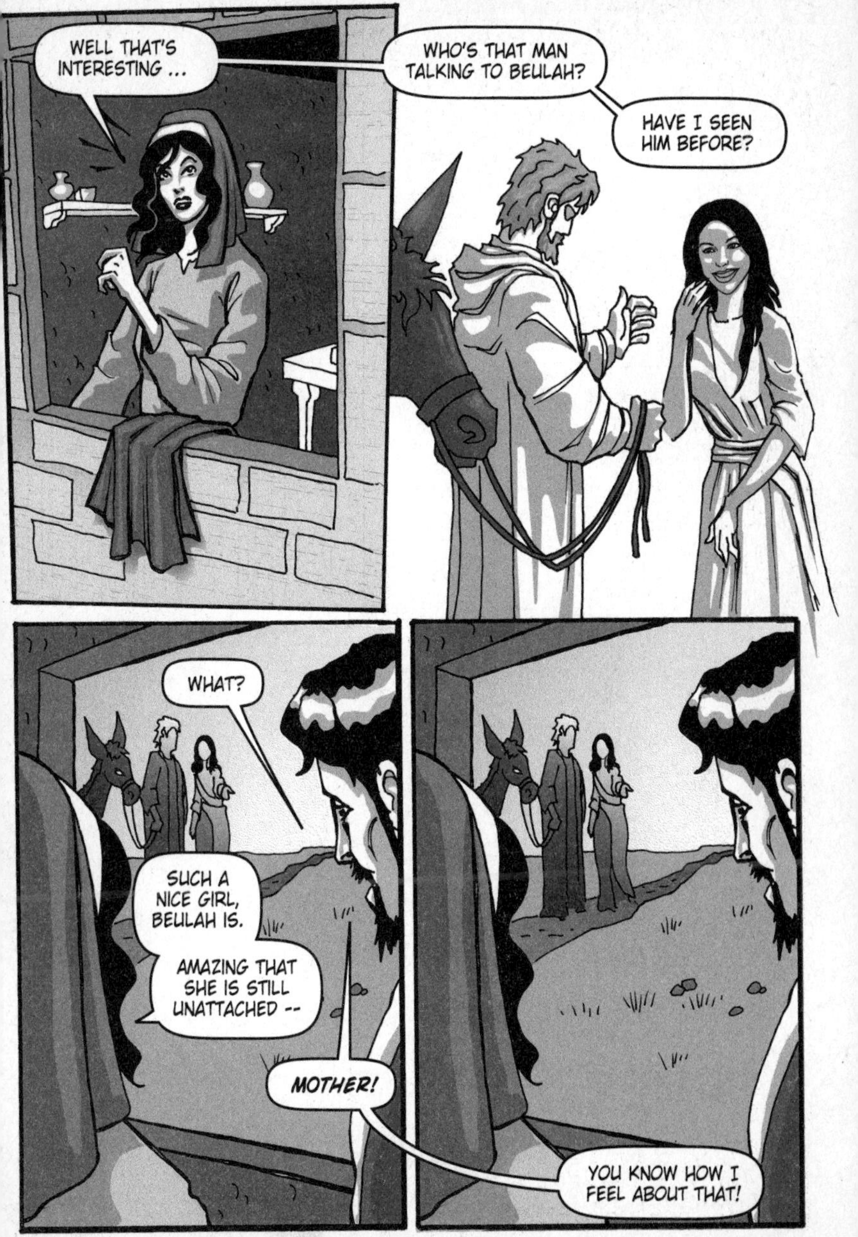
WELL THAT'S INTERESTING ...
WHO'S THAT MAN TALKING TO BEULAH?
HAVE I SEEN HIM BEFORE?
WHAT?
SUCH A NICE GIRL, BEULAH IS.
AMAZING THAT SHE IS STILL UNATTACHED --
MOTHER!
YOU KNOW HOW I FEEL ABOUT THAT!

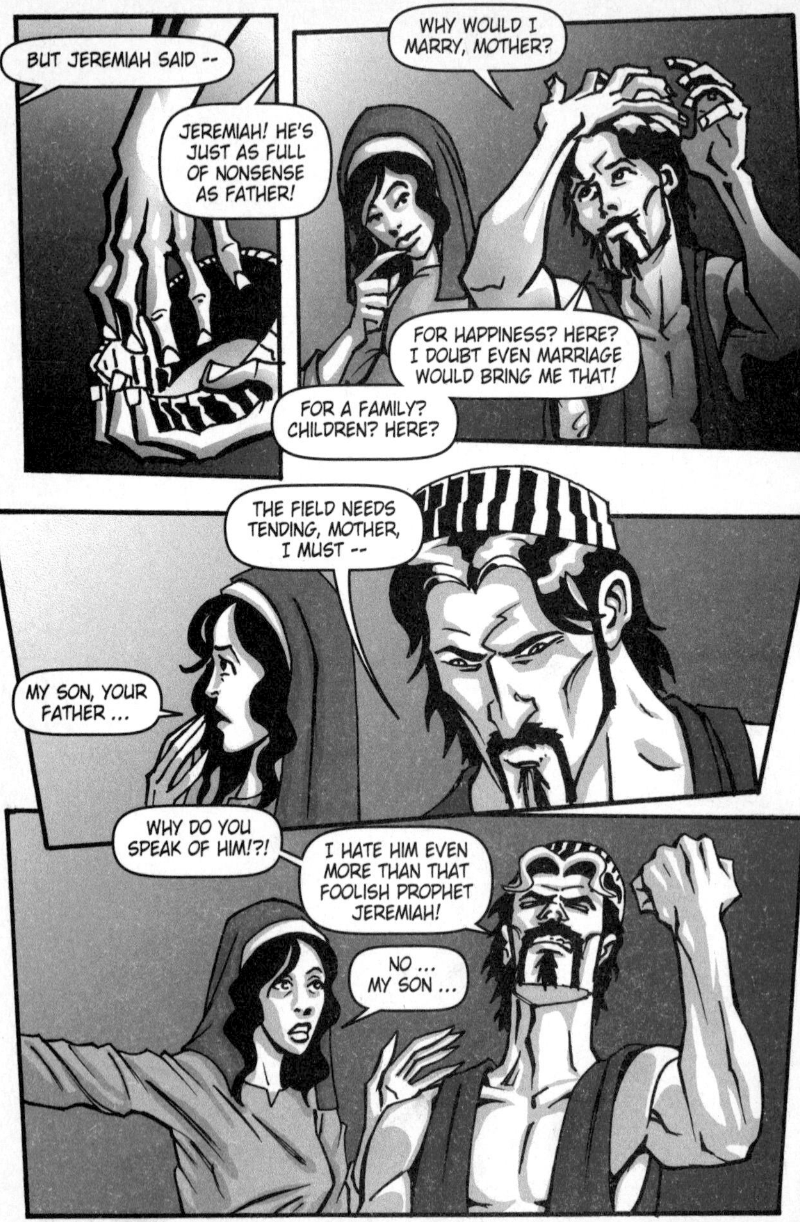
BUT JEREMIAH SAID --
JEREMIAH! HE'S JUST AS FULL OF NONSENSE AS FATHER!
WHY WOULD I MARRY, MOTHER?
FOR HAPPINESS? HERE? I DOUBT EVEN MARRIAGE WOULD BRING ME THAT!
FOR A FAMILY? CHILDREN? HERE?
THE FIELD NEEDS TENDING, MOTHER, I MUST --
MY SON, YOUR FATHER ...
WHY DO YOU SPEAK OF HIM!?!
I HATE HIM EVEN MORE THAN THAT FOOLISH PROPHET JEREMIAH!
NO ... MY SON ...

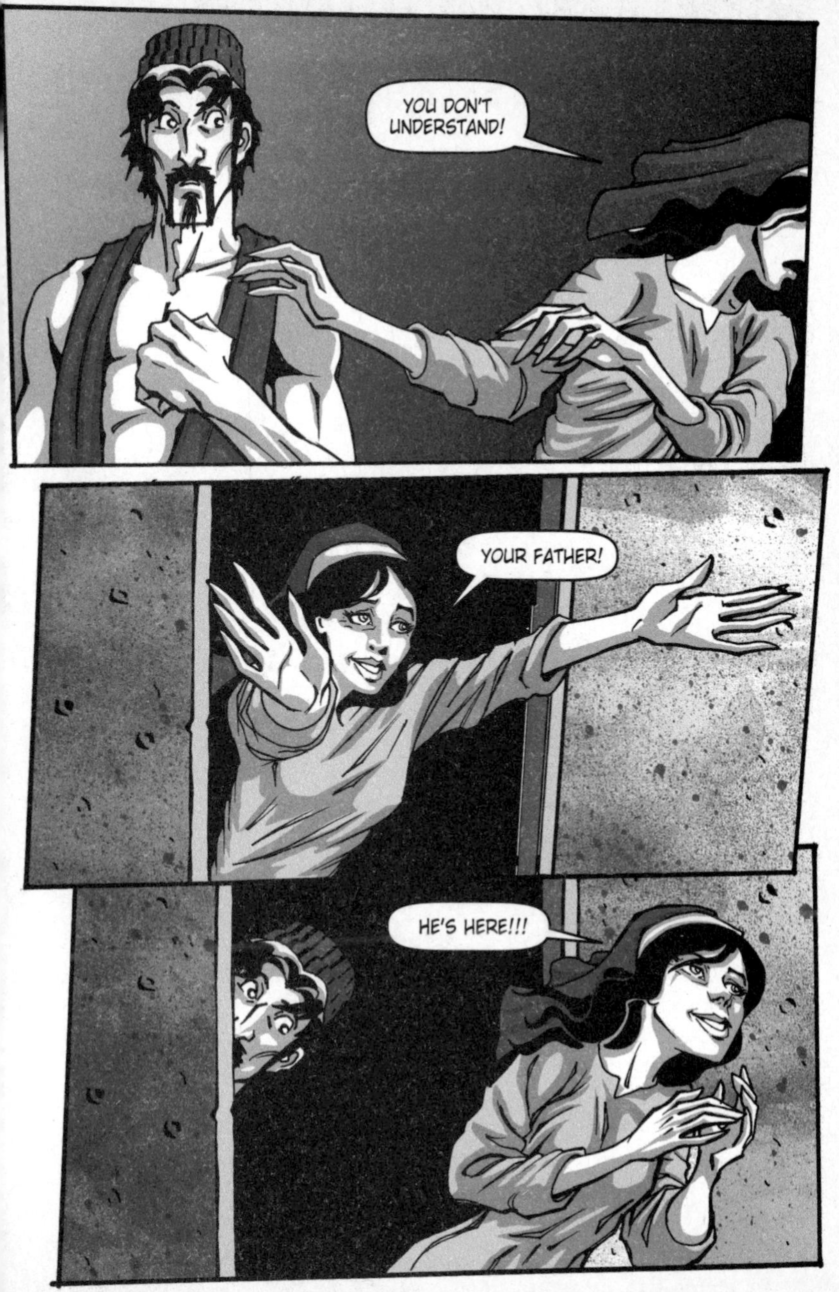
YOU DON'T UNDERSTAND!
YOUR FATHER!
HE'S HERE!!!

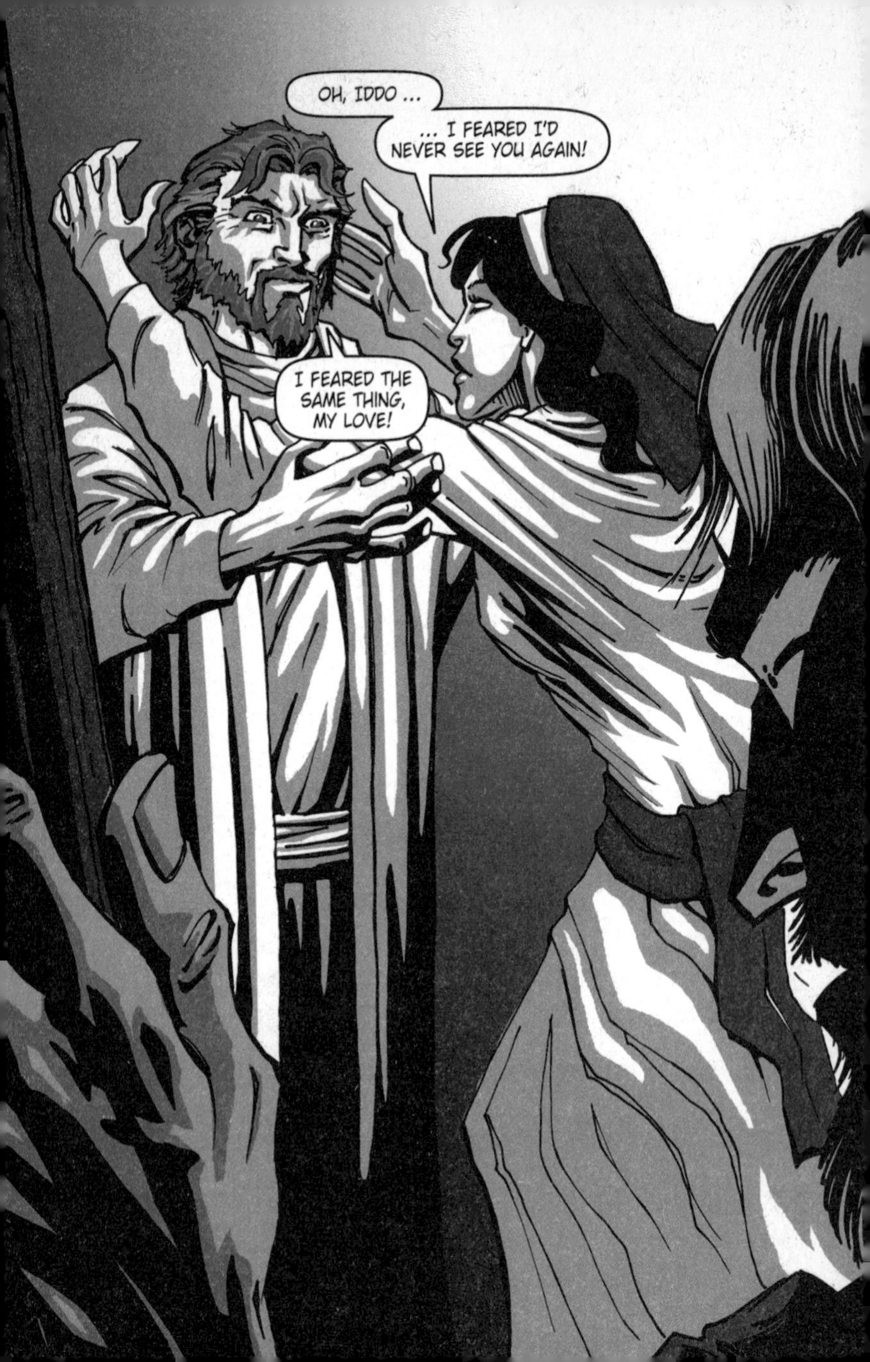
OH, IDDO ...
... I FEARED I'D NEVER SEE YOU AGAIN!
I FEARED THE SAME THING, MY LOVE!

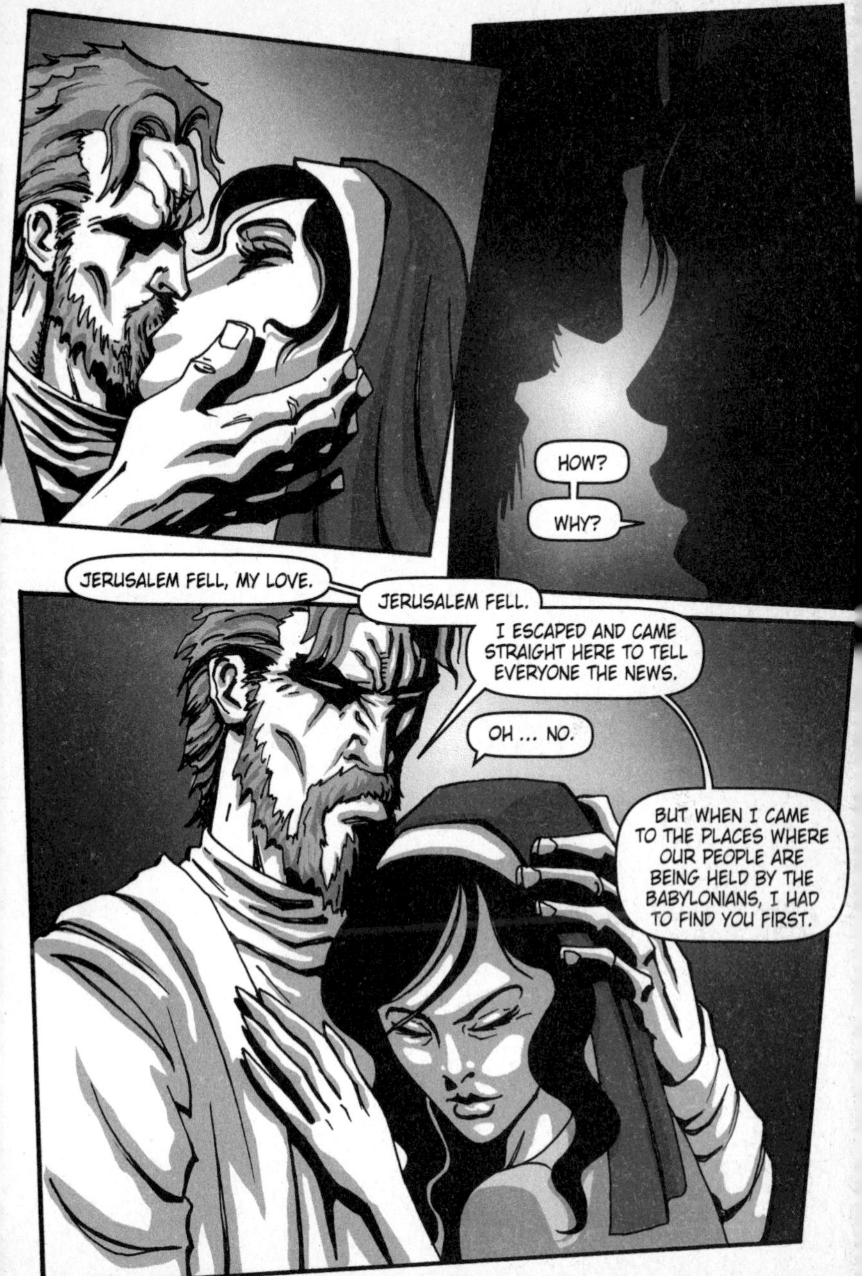
HOW?
WHY?
JERUSALEM FELL, MY LOVE.
JERUSALEM FELL.
I ESCAPED AND CAME STRAIGHT HERE TO TELL EVERYONE THE NEWS.
OH ... NO.
BUT WHEN I CAME TO THE PLACES WHERE OUR PEOPLE ARE BEING HELD BY THE BABYLONIANS, I HAD TO FIND YOU FIRST.

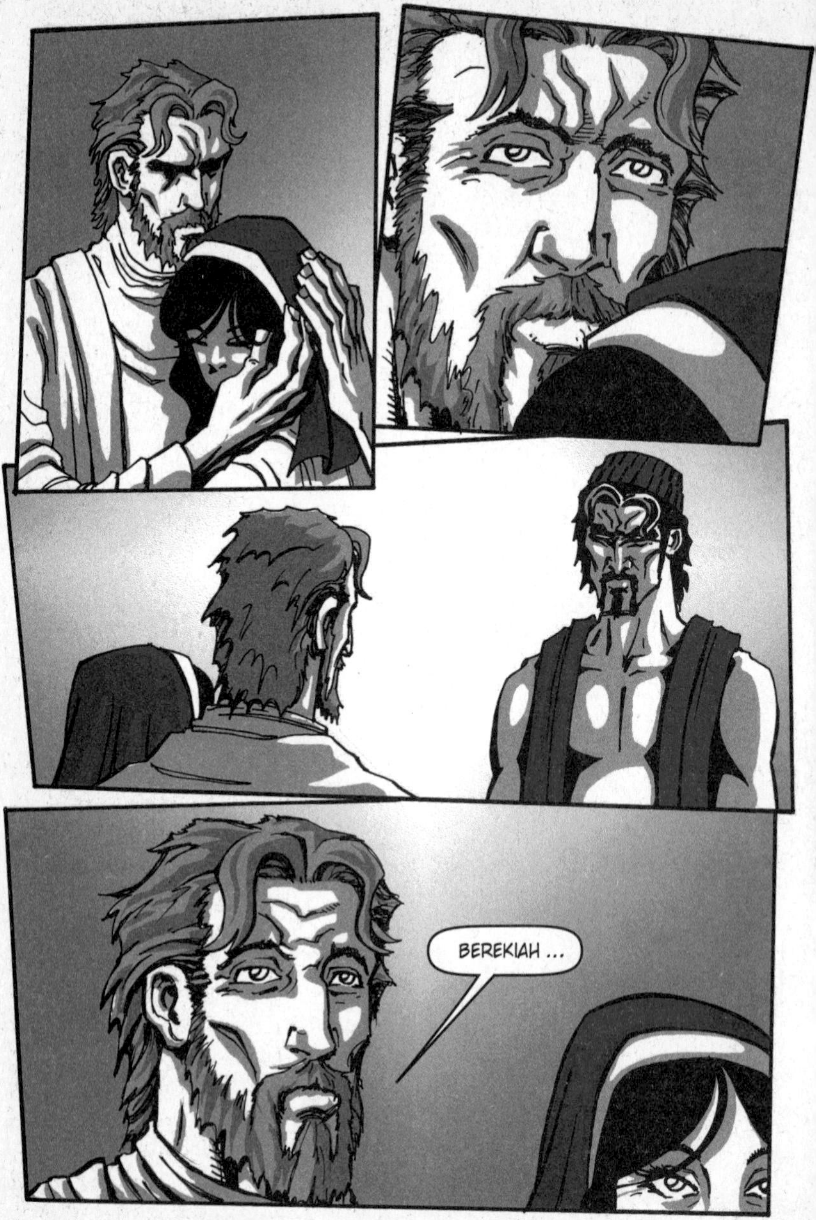
BEREKIAH ...

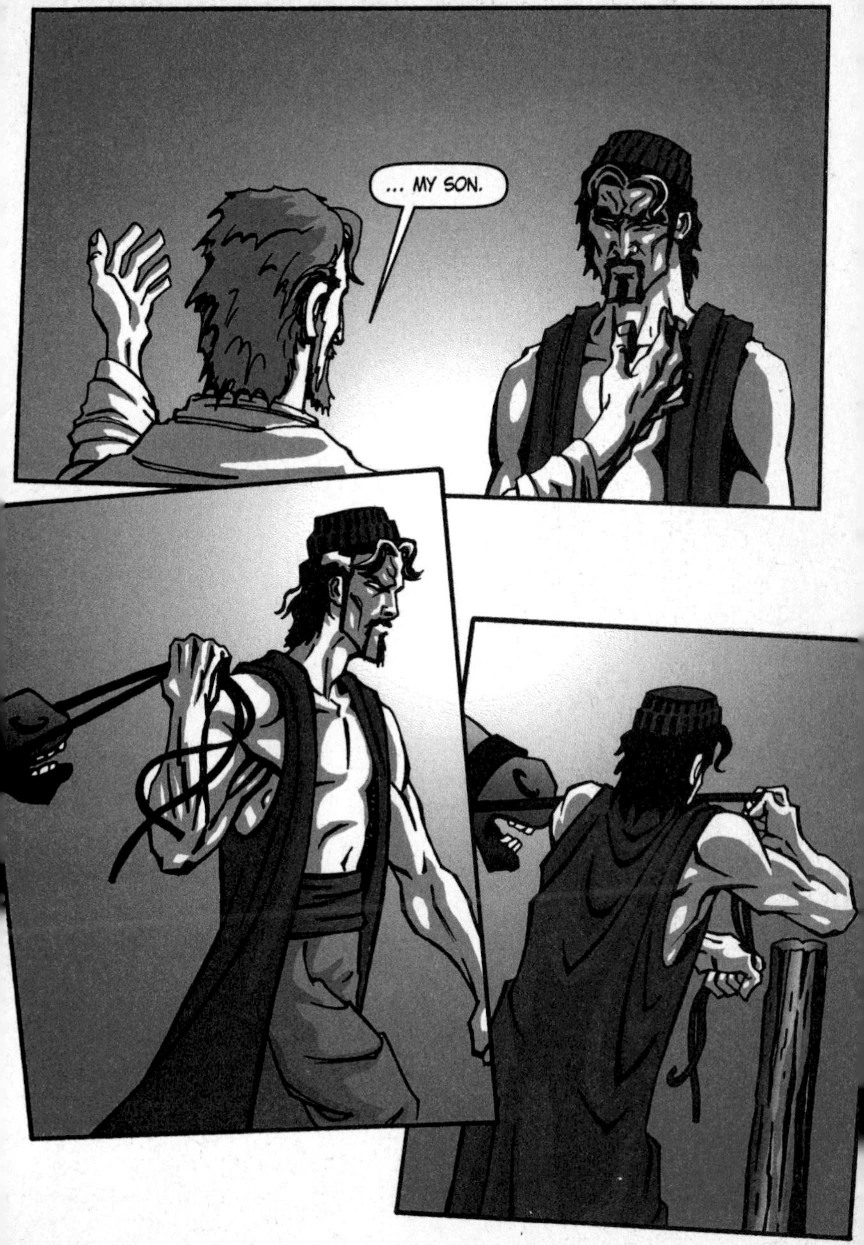
... MY SON.

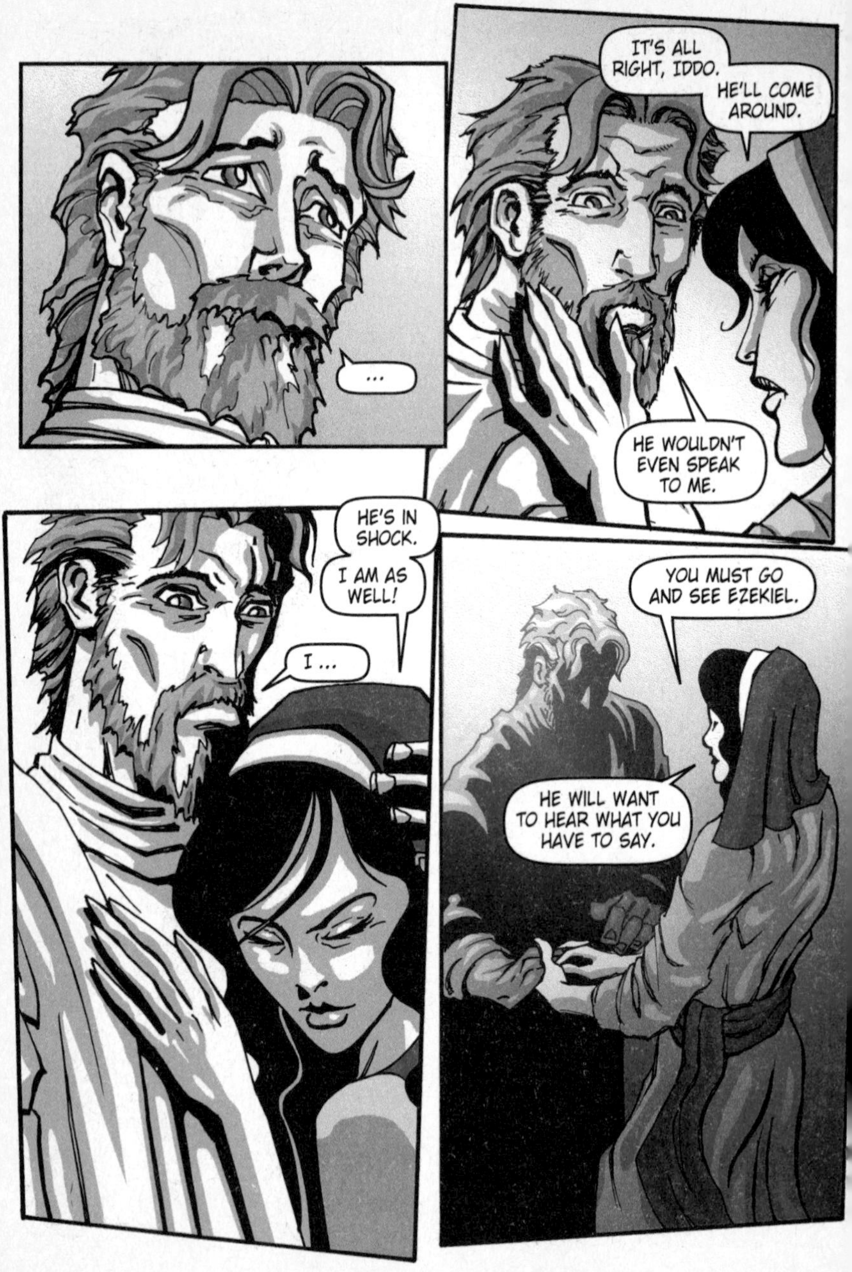
...
IT'S ALL RIGHT, IDDO.
HE'LL COME AROUND.
HE WOULDN'T EVEN SPEAK TO ME.
HE'S IN SHOCK.
I AM AS WELL!
I ...
YOU MUST GO AND SEE EZEKIEL.
HE WILL WANT TO HEAR WHAT YOU HAVE TO SAY.

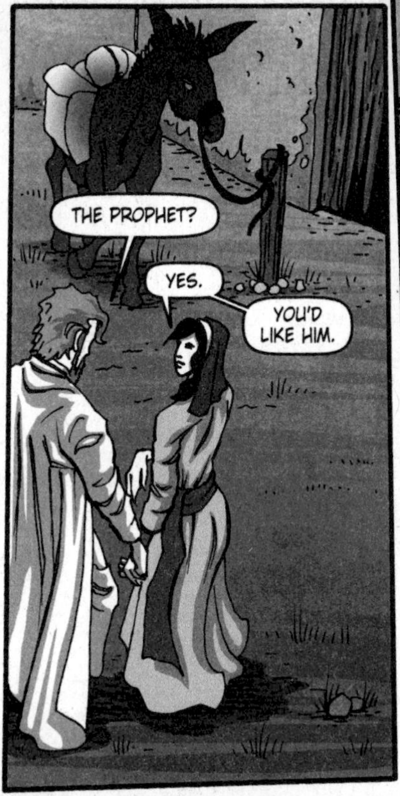
THE PROPHET?
YES.
YOU'D LIKE HIM.

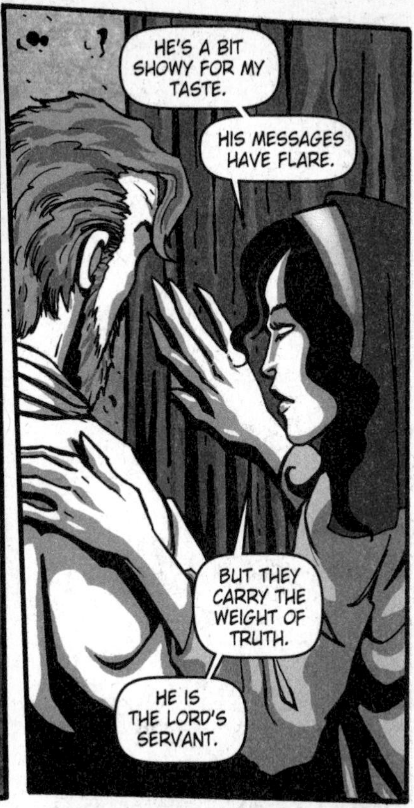
HE'S A BIT SHOWY FOR MY TASTE.
HIS MESSAGES HAVE FLARE.
BUT THEY CARRY THE WEIGHT OF TRUTH.
HE IS THE LORD'S SERVANT.

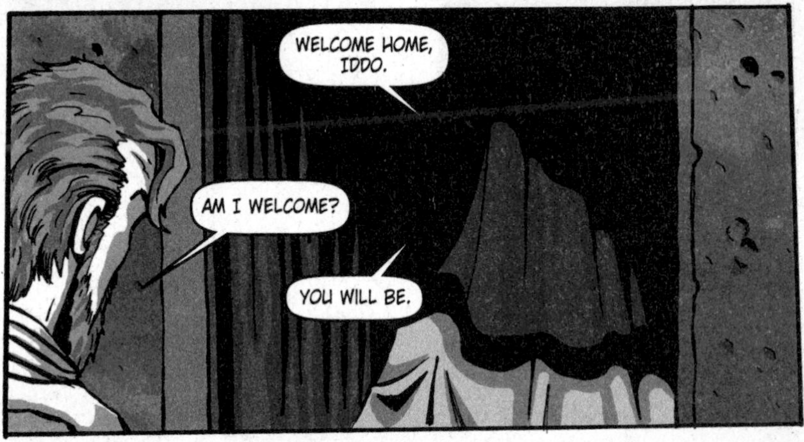
WELCOME HOME, IDDO.
AM I WELCOME?
YOU WILL BE.

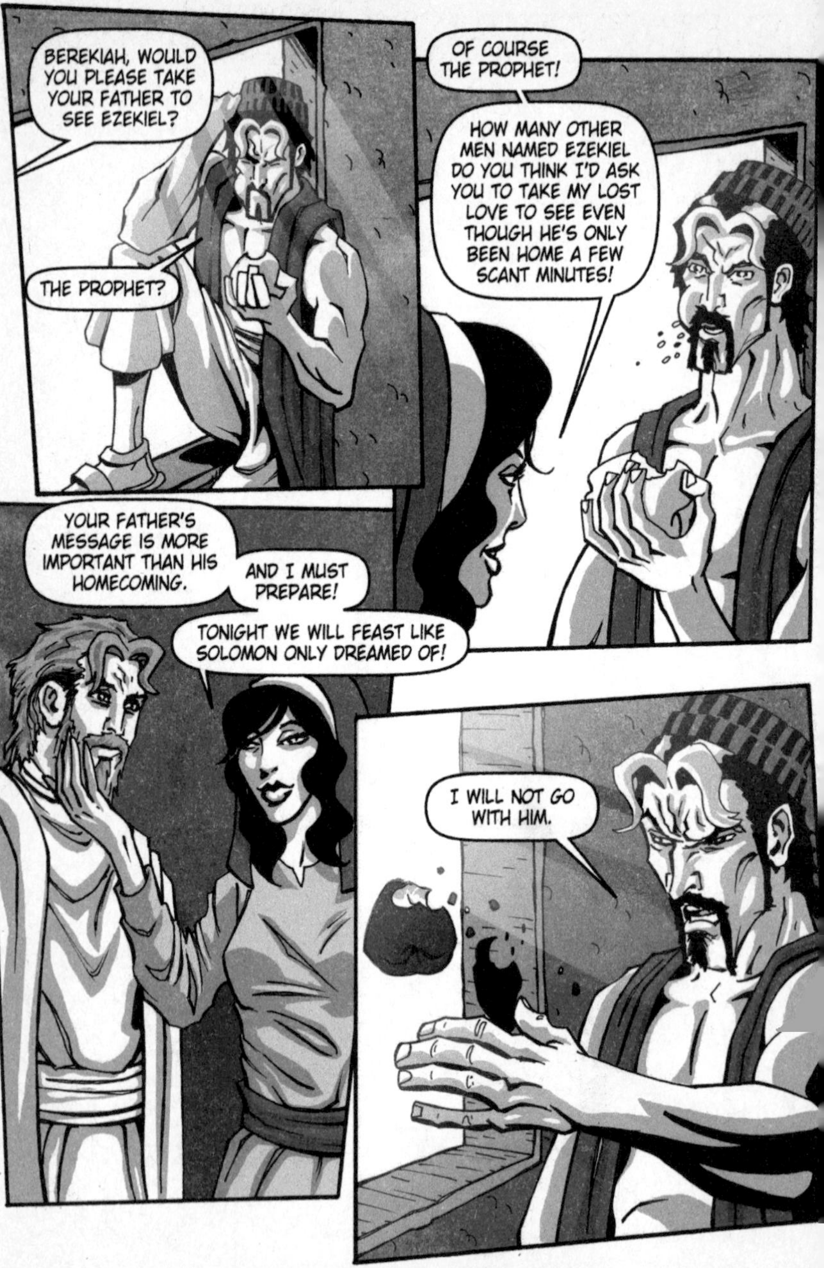
BEREKIAH, WOULD YOU PLEASE TAKE YOUR FATHER TO SEE EZEKIEL?
THE PROPHET?
OF COURSE THE PROPHET!
HOW MANY OTHER MEN NAMED EZEKIEL DO YOU THINK I'D ASK YOU TO TAKE MY LOST LOVE TO SEE EVEN THOUGH HE'S ONLY BEEN HOME A FEW SCANT MINUTES!
YOUR FATHER'S MESSAGE IS MORE IMPORTANT THAN HIS HOMECOMING.
AND I MUST PREPARE!
TONIGHT WE WILL FEAST LIKE SOLOMON ONLY DREAMED OF!
I WILL NOT GO WITH HIM.

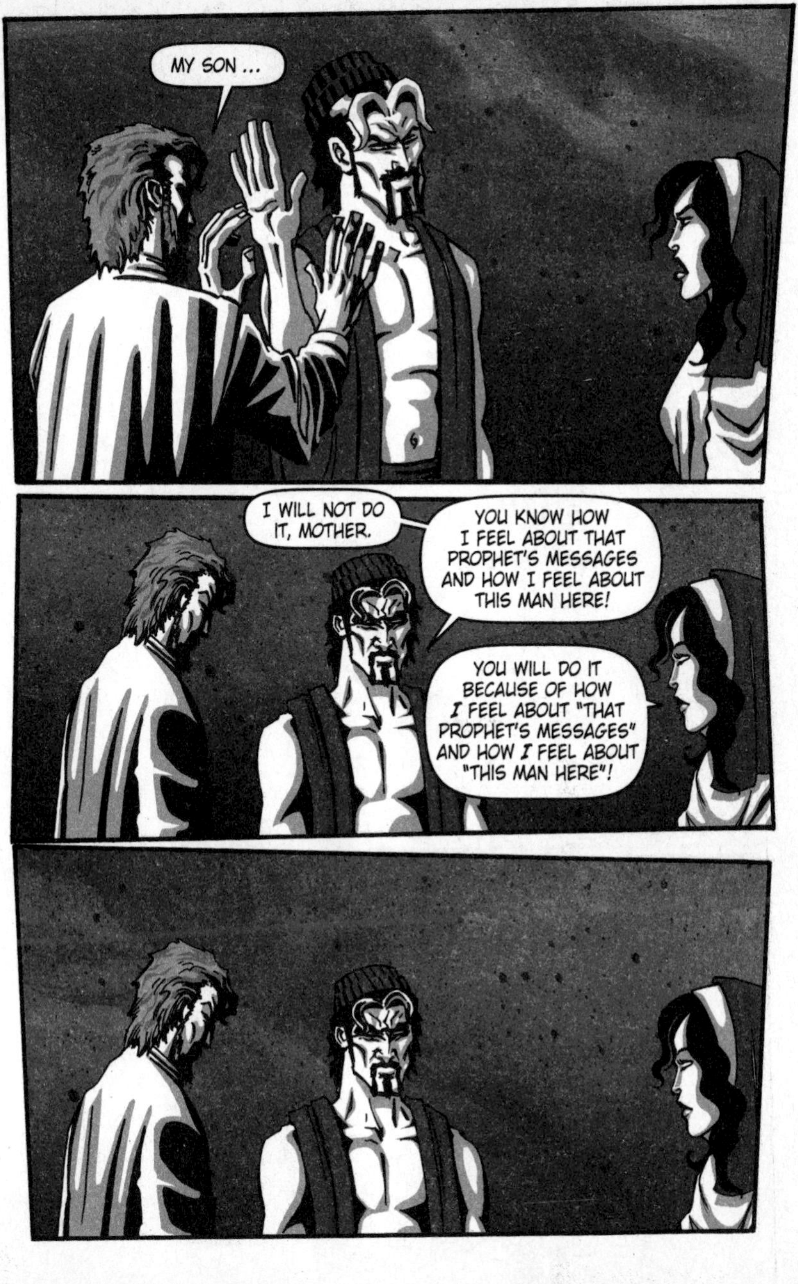
MY SON ...
I WILL NOT DO IT, MOTHER.
YOU KNOW HOW I FEEL ABOUT THAT PROPHET'S MESSAGES AND HOW I FEEL ABOUT THIS MAN HERE!
YOU WILL DO IT BECAUSE OF HOW *I* FEEL ABOUT "THAT PROPHET'S MESSAGES" AND HOW *I* FEEL ABOUT "THIS MAN HERE"!

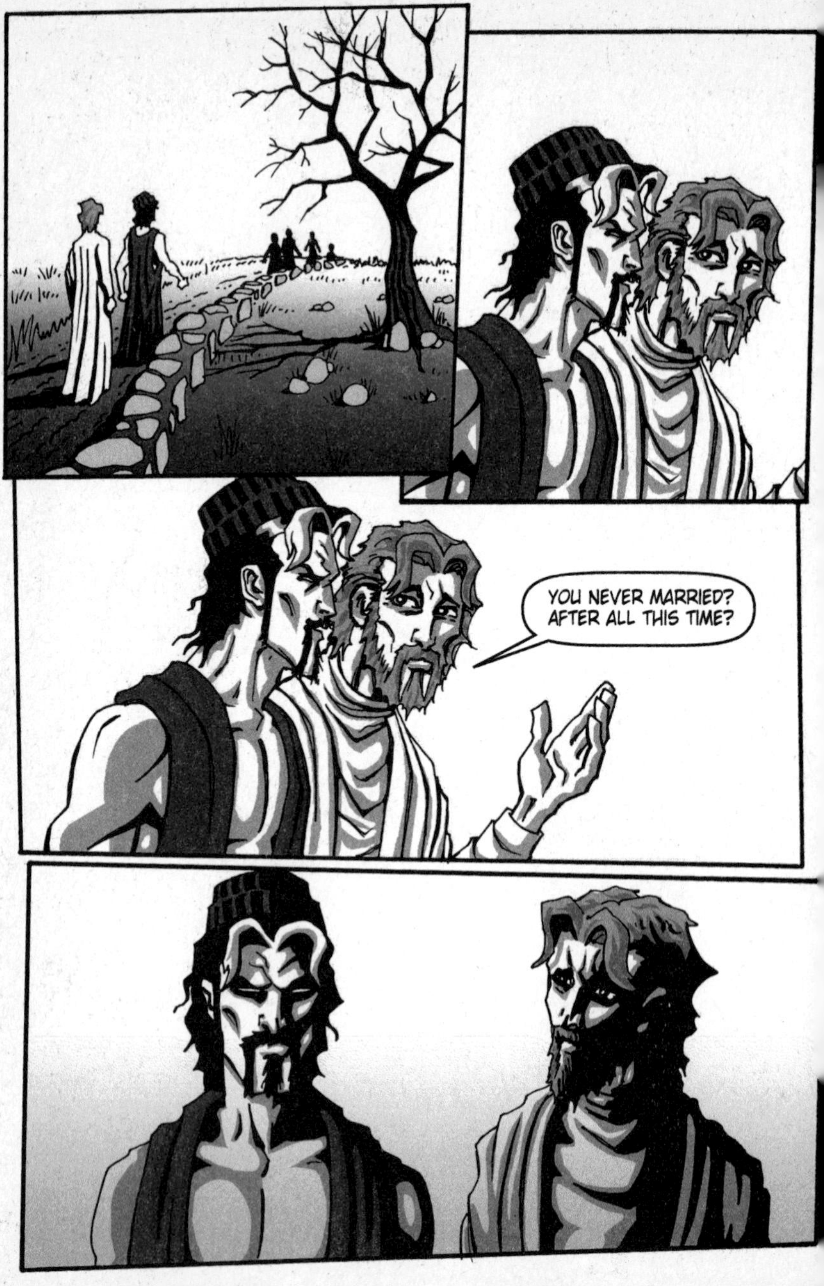
YOU NEVER MARRIED? AFTER ALL THIS TIME?

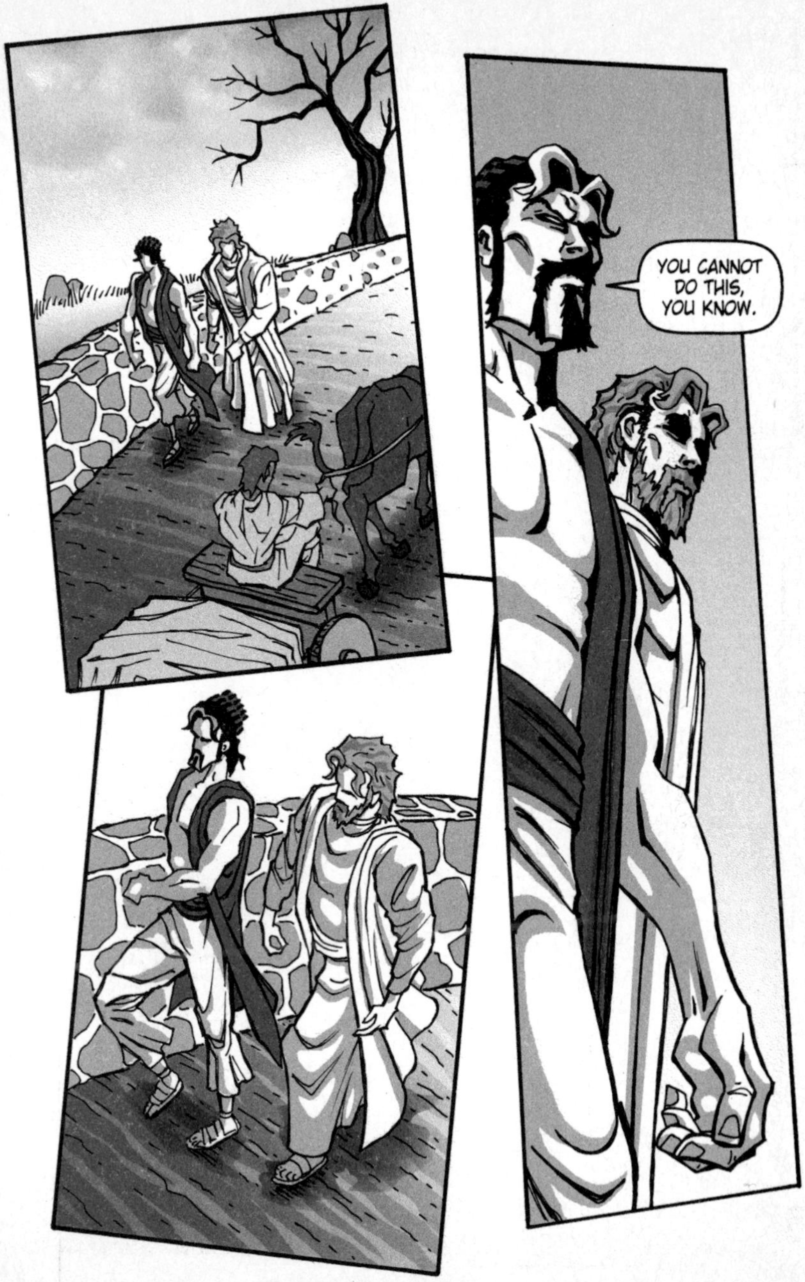
YOU CANNOT DO THIS, YOU KNOW.

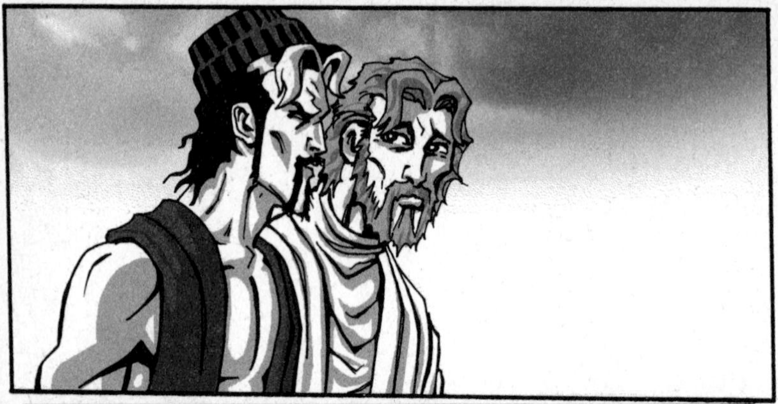

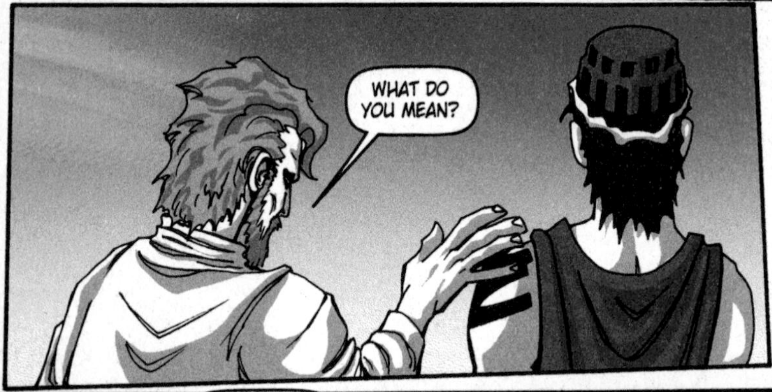

WHAT DO YOU MEAN?

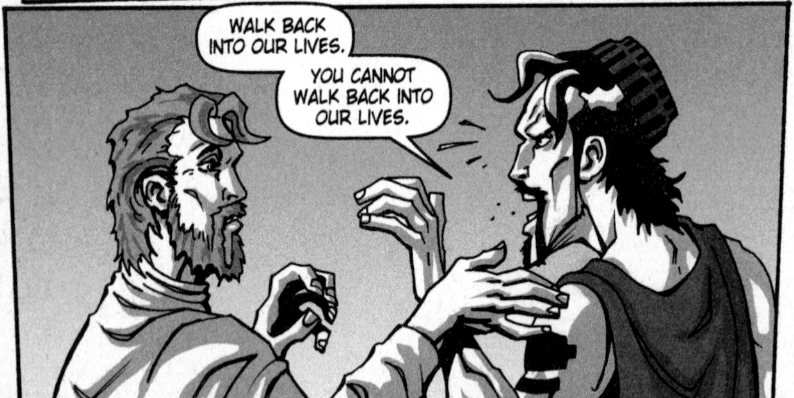

WALK BACK INTO OUR LIVES.
YOU CANNOT WALK BACK INTO OUR LIVES.

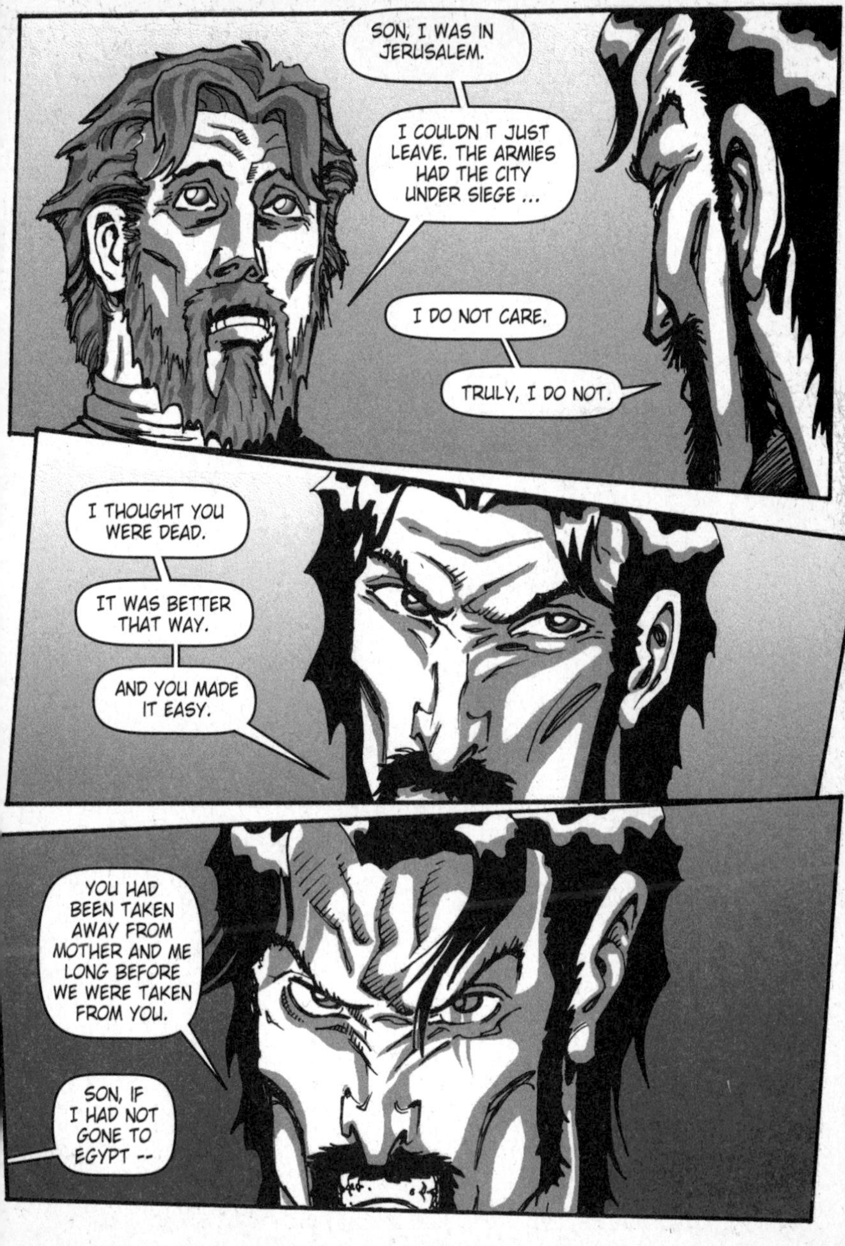
SON, I WAS IN JERUSALEM.
I COULDN T JUST LEAVE. THE ARMIES HAD THE CITY UNDER SIEGE ...
I DO NOT CARE.
TRULY, I DO NOT.
I THOUGHT YOU WERE DEAD.
IT WAS BETTER THAT WAY.
AND YOU MADE IT EASY.
YOU HAD BEEN TAKEN AWAY FROM MOTHER AND ME LONG BEFORE WE WERE TAKEN FROM YOU.
SON, IF I HAD NOT GONE TO EGYPT --

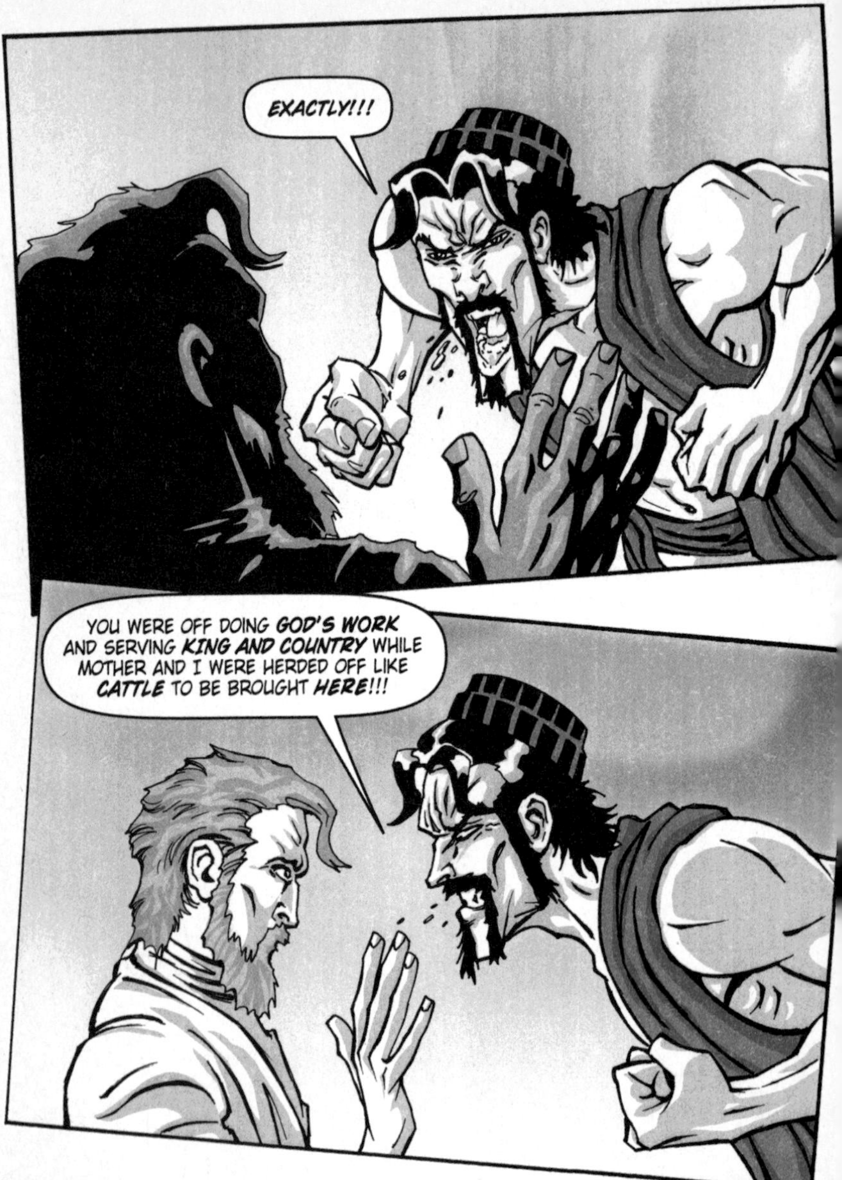
EXACTLY!!!
YOU WERE OFF DOING GOD'S WORK AND SERVING KING AND COUNTRY WHILE MOTHER AND I WERE HERDED OFF LIKE CATTLE TO BE BROUGHT HERE!!!

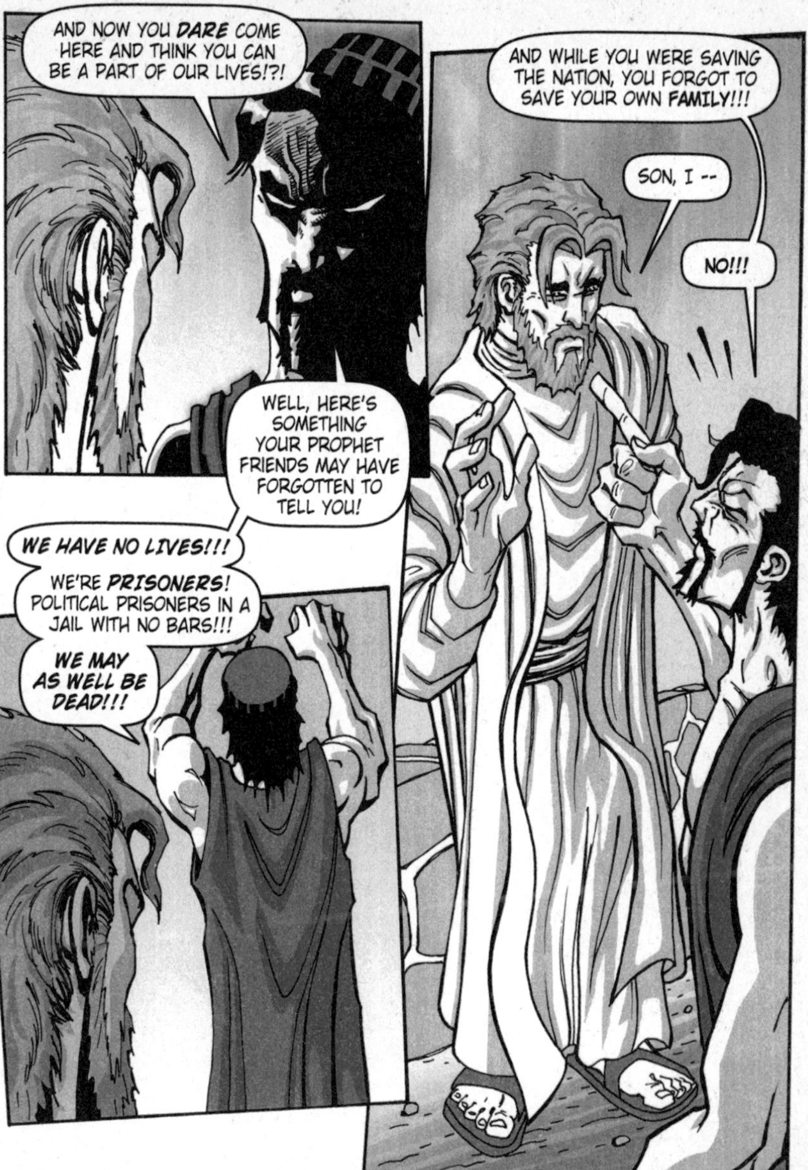
AND NOW YOU DARE COME HERE AND THINK YOU CAN BE A PART OF OUR LIVES!?!
WELL, HERE'S SOMETHING YOUR PROPHET FRIENDS MAY HAVE FORGOTTEN TO TELL YOU!
WE HAVE NO LIVES!!!
WE'RE PRISONERS! POLITICAL PRISONERS IN A JAIL WITH NO BARS!!!
WE MAY AS WELL BE DEAD!!!
AND WHILE YOU WERE SAVING THE NATION, YOU FORGOT TO SAVE YOUR OWN FAMILY!!!
SON, I --
NO!!!

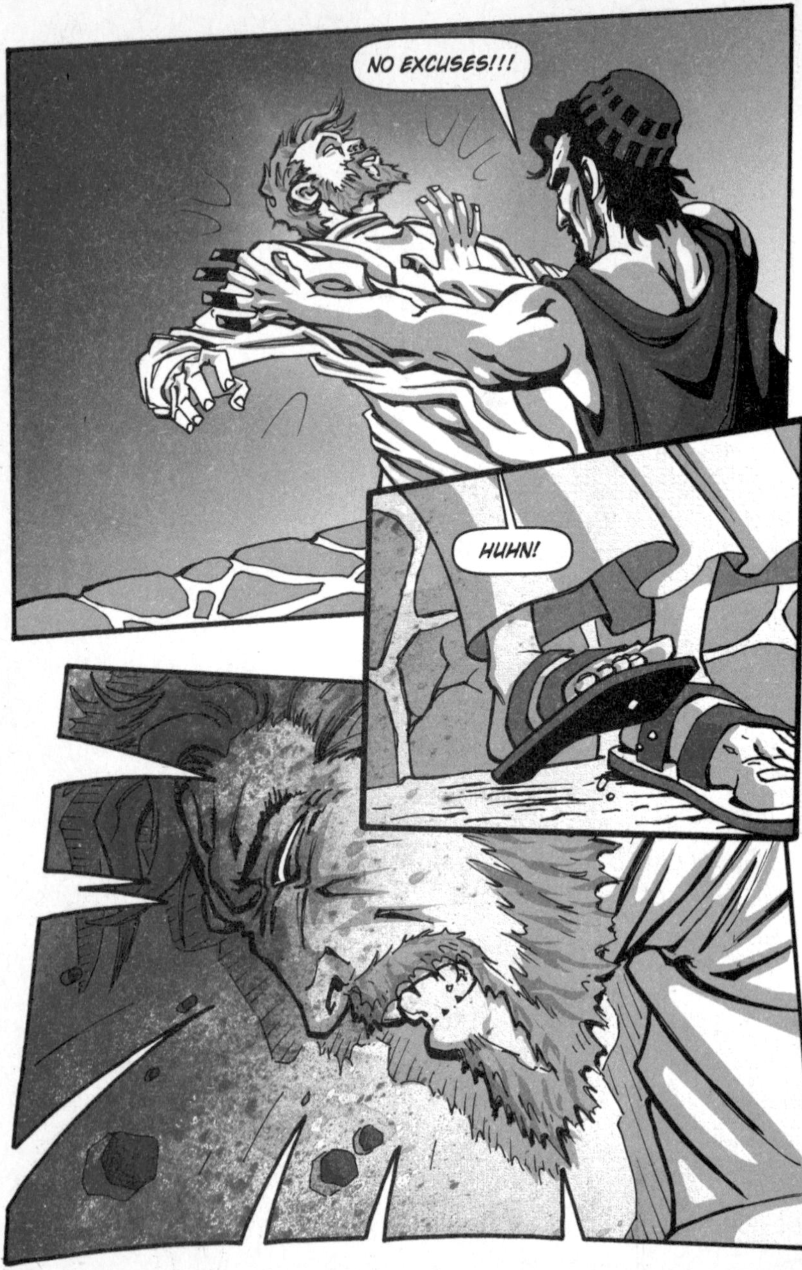
NO EXCUSES!!!
HUHN!

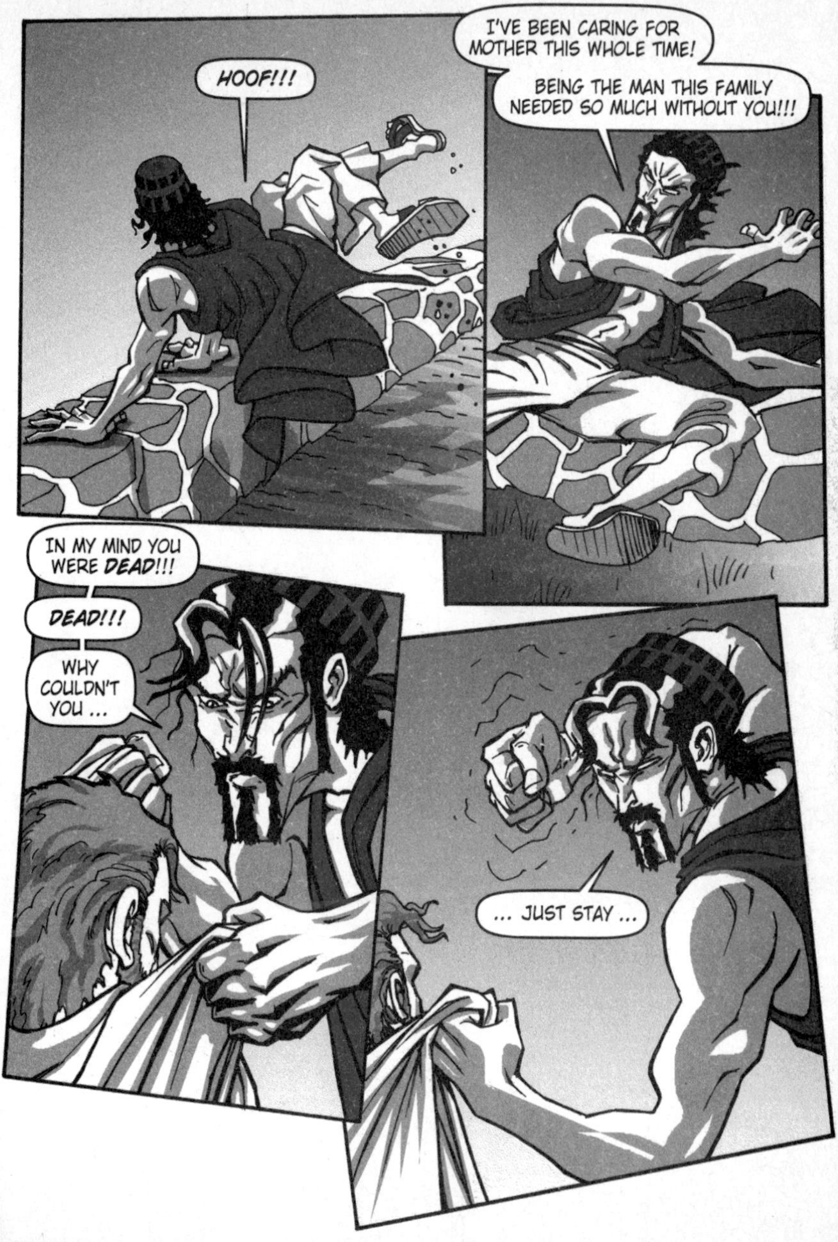
HOOF!!!
I'VE BEEN CARING FOR MOTHER THIS WHOLE TIME!
BEING THE MAN THIS FAMILY NEEDED SO MUCH WITHOUT YOU!!!
IN MY MIND YOU WERE DEAD!!!
DEAD!!!
WHY COULDN'T YOU ...
... JUST STAY ...

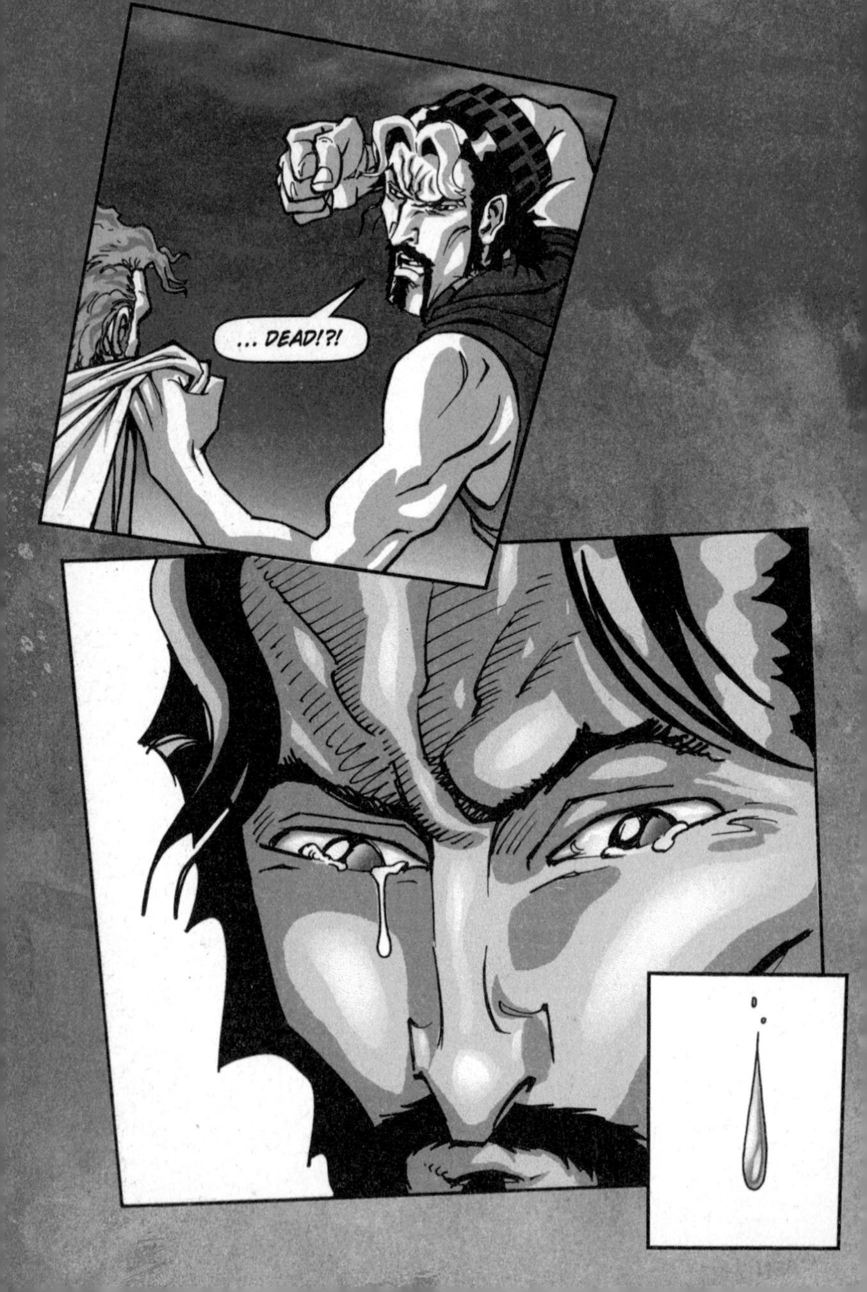
... DEAD!?!

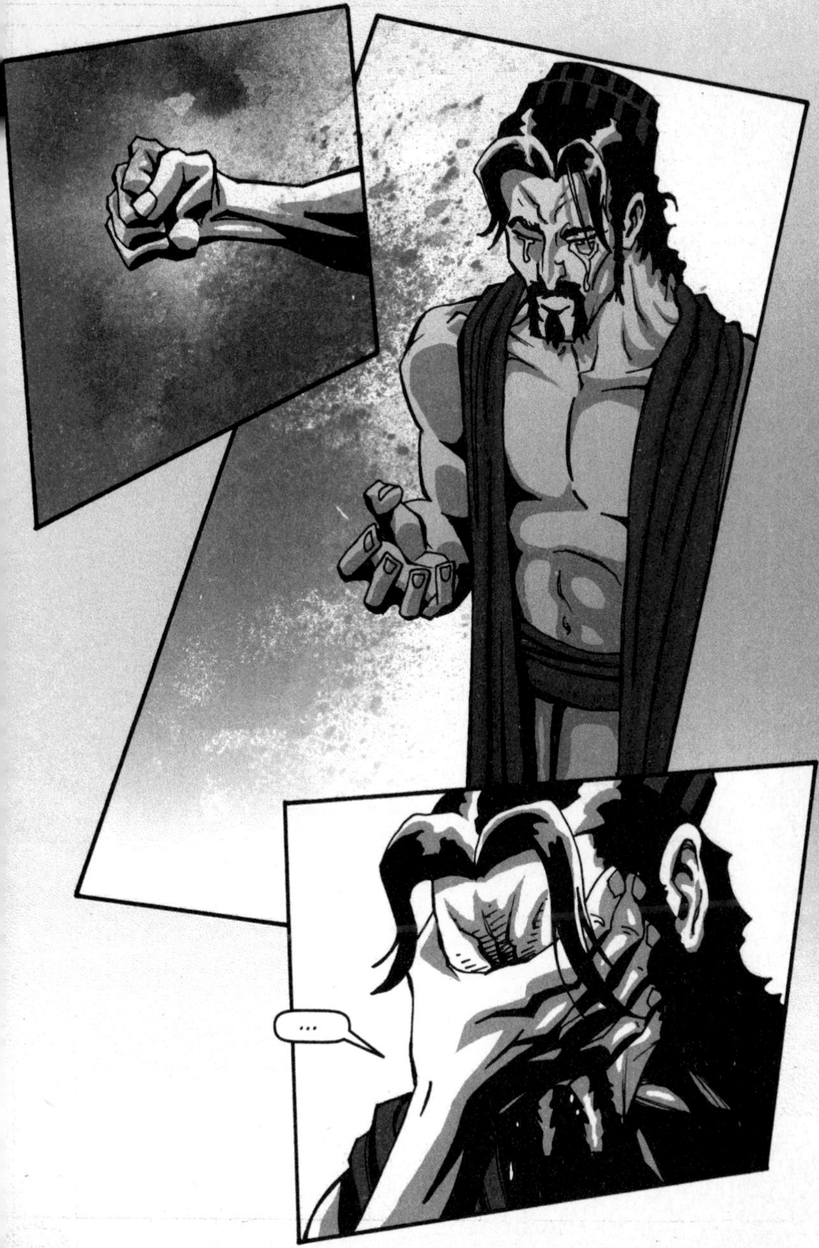
...

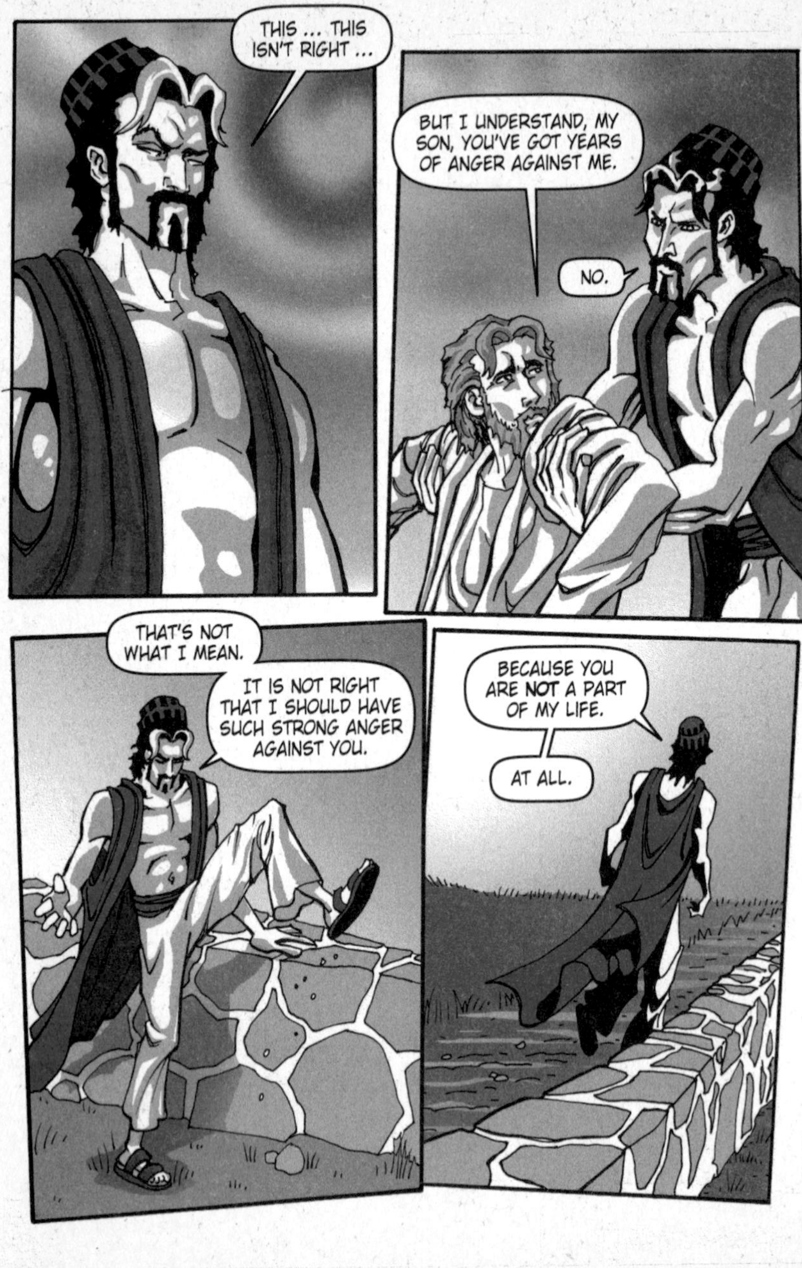
THIS ... THIS ISN'T RIGHT ...
BUT I UNDERSTAND, MY SON, YOU'VE GOT YEARS OF ANGER AGAINST ME.
NO.
THAT'S NOT WHAT I MEAN.
IT IS NOT RIGHT THAT I SHOULD HAVE SUCH STRONG ANGER AGAINST YOU.
BECAUSE YOU ARE NOT A PART OF MY LIFE.
AT ALL.

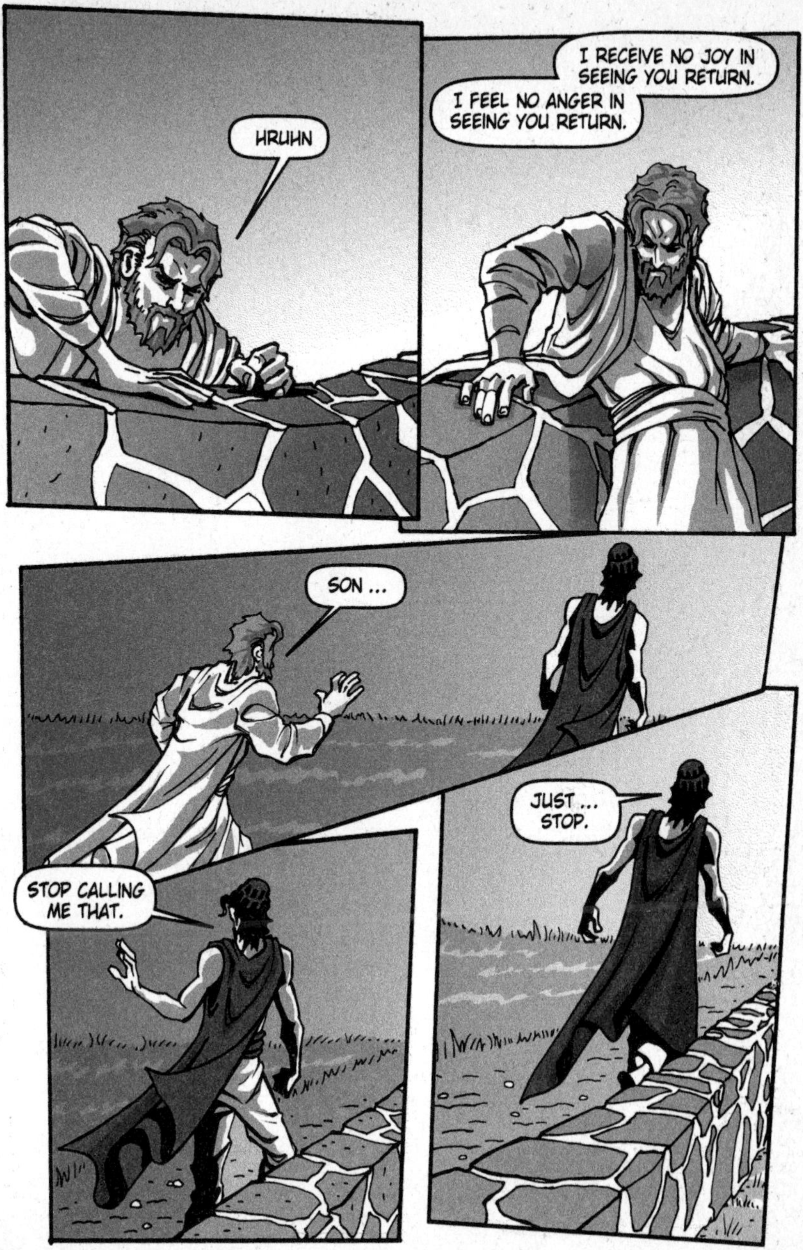
HRUHN
I RECEIVE NO JOY IN SEEING YOU RETURN.
I FEEL NO ANGER IN SEEING YOU RETURN.
SON ...
STOP CALLING ME THAT.
JUST ... STOP.

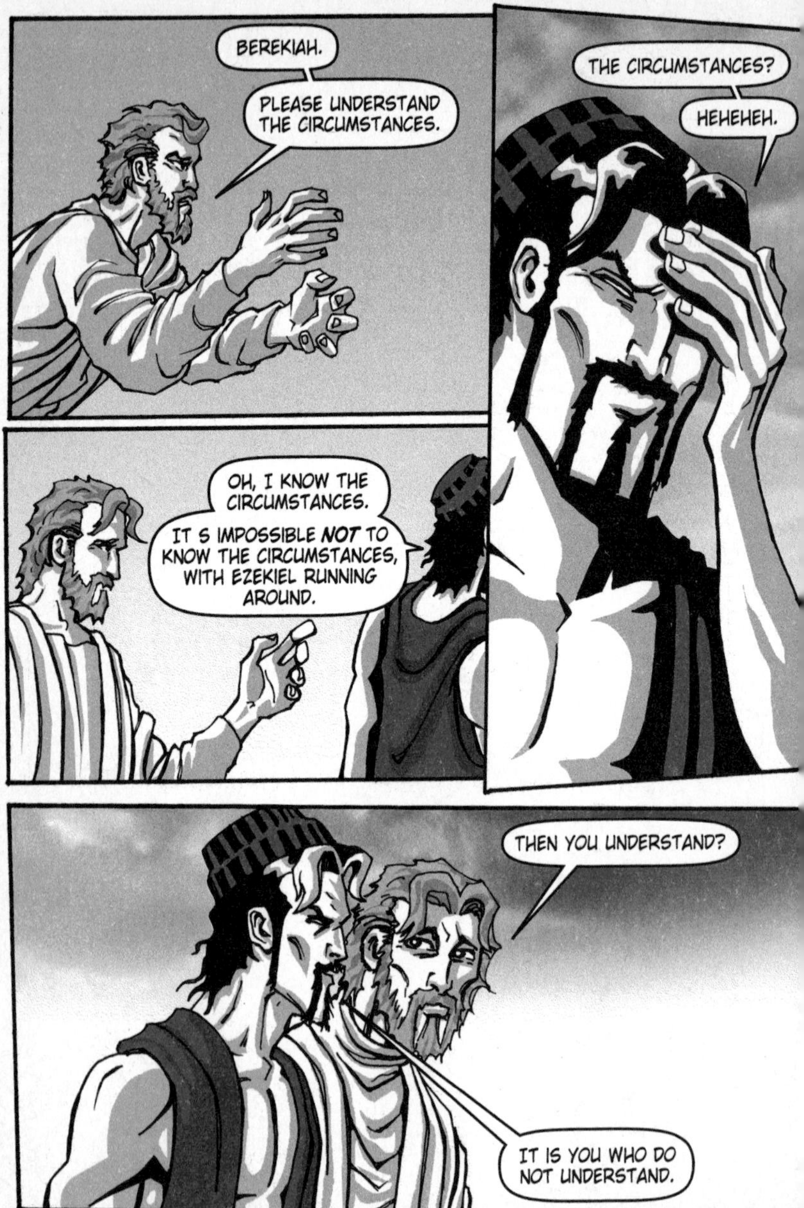
BEREKIAH.
PLEASE UNDERSTAND THE CIRCUMSTANCES.
OH, I KNOW THE CIRCUMSTANCES.
IT S IMPOSSIBLE ***NOT*** TO KNOW THE CIRCUMSTANCES, WITH EZEKIEL RUNNING AROUND.
THE CIRCUMSTANCES?
HEHEHEH.
THEN YOU UNDERSTAND?
IT IS YOU WHO DO NOT UNDERSTAND.

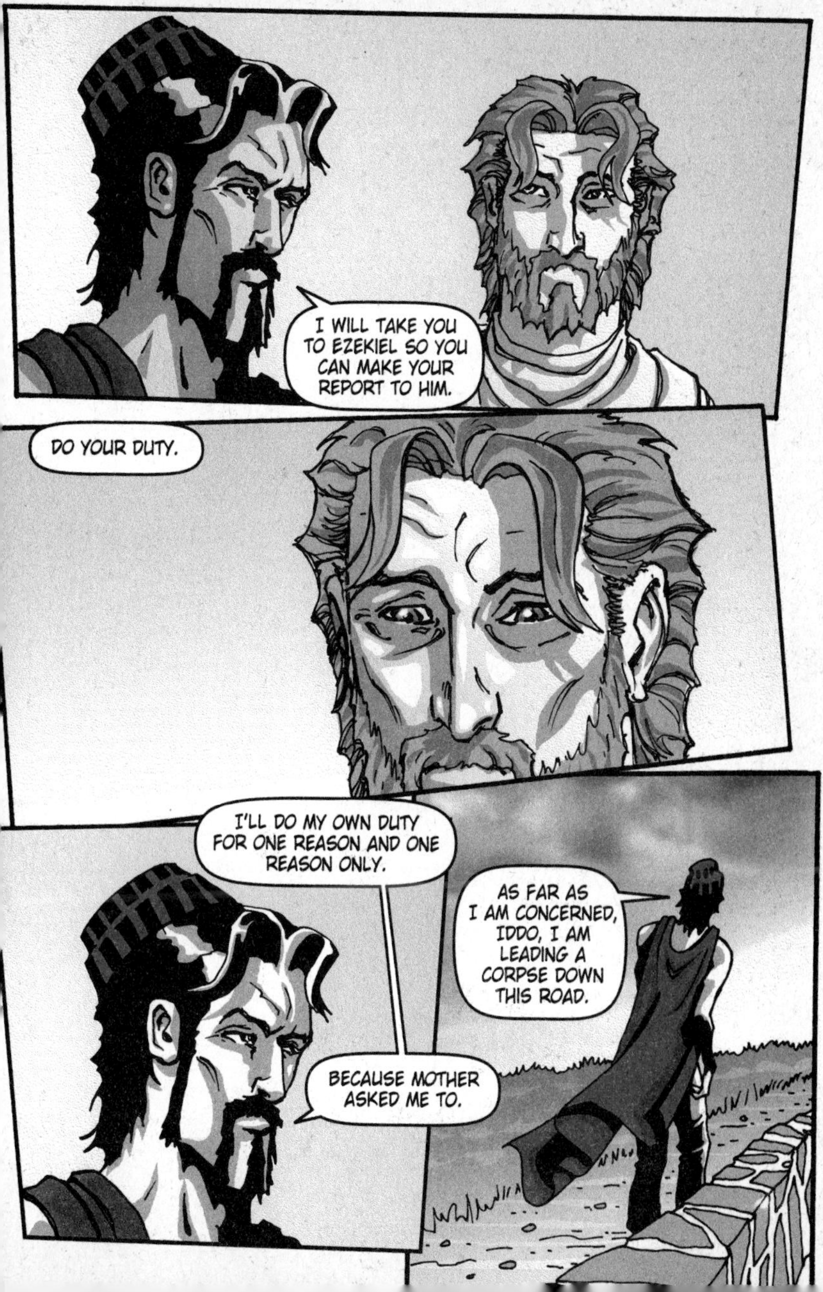
I WILL TAKE YOU TO EZEKIEL SO YOU CAN MAKE YOUR REPORT TO HIM.
DO YOUR DUTY.
I'LL DO MY OWN DUTY FOR ONE REASON AND ONE REASON ONLY.
BECAUSE MOTHER ASKED ME TO.
AS FAR AS I AM CONCERNED, IDDO, I AM LEADING A CORPSE DOWN THIS ROAD.

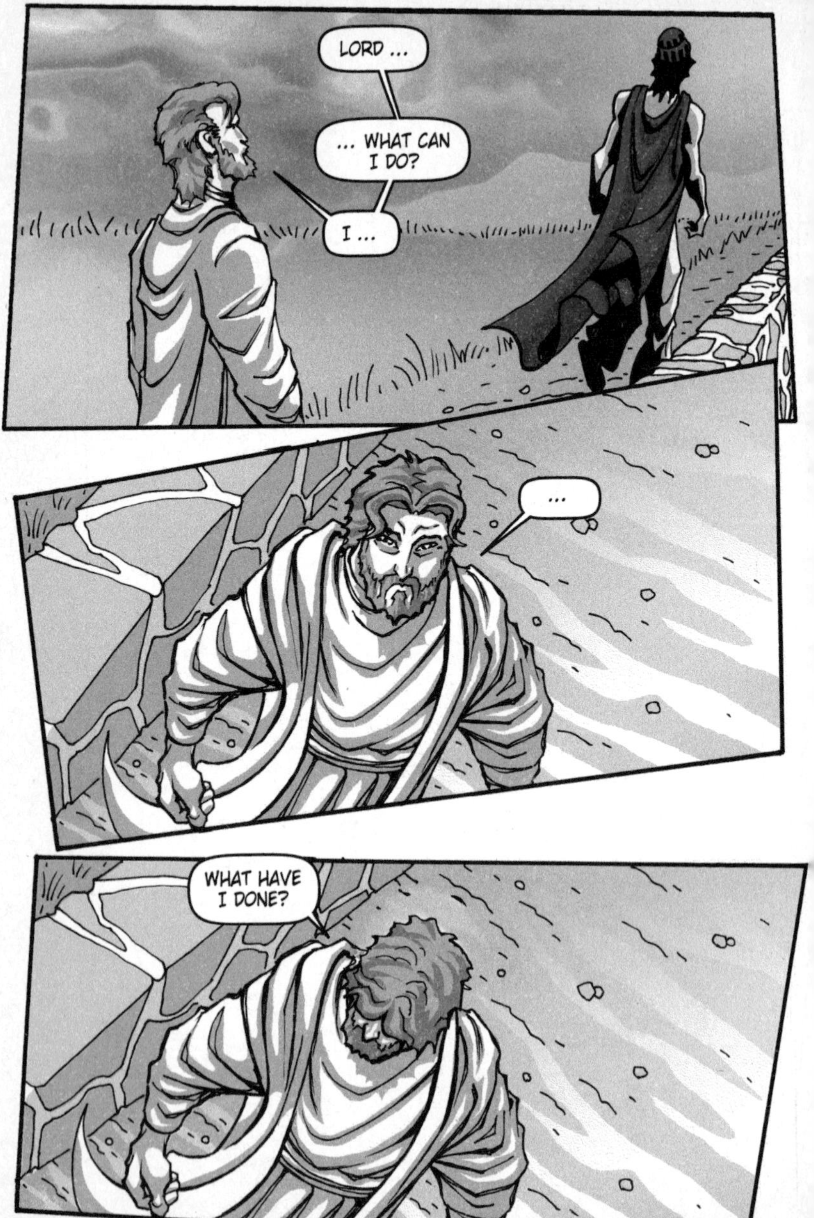
LORD ...
... WHAT CAN I DO?
I ...
...
WHAT HAVE I DONE?

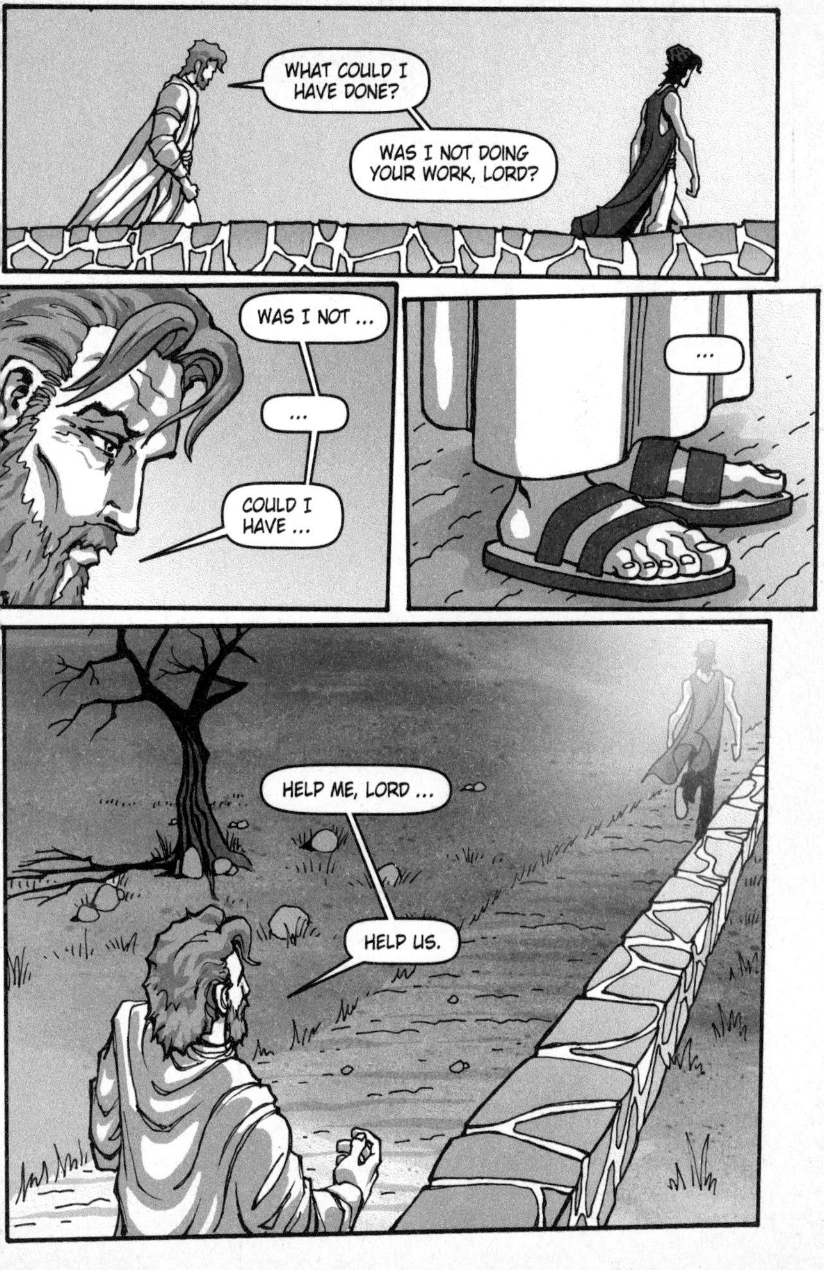
WHAT COULD I HAVE DONE?
WAS I NOT DOING YOUR WORK, LORD?
WAS I NOT ...
...
COULD I HAVE ...
...
HELP ME, LORD ...
HELP US.

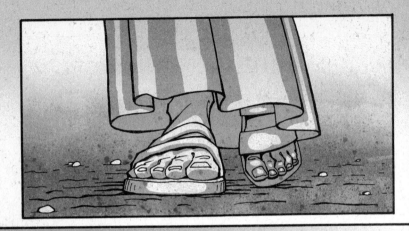

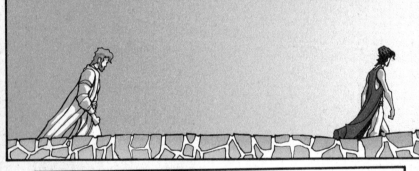

CHAPTER TWO
"The Prophet"

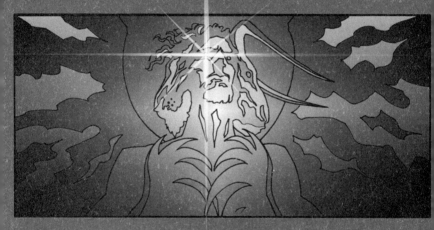

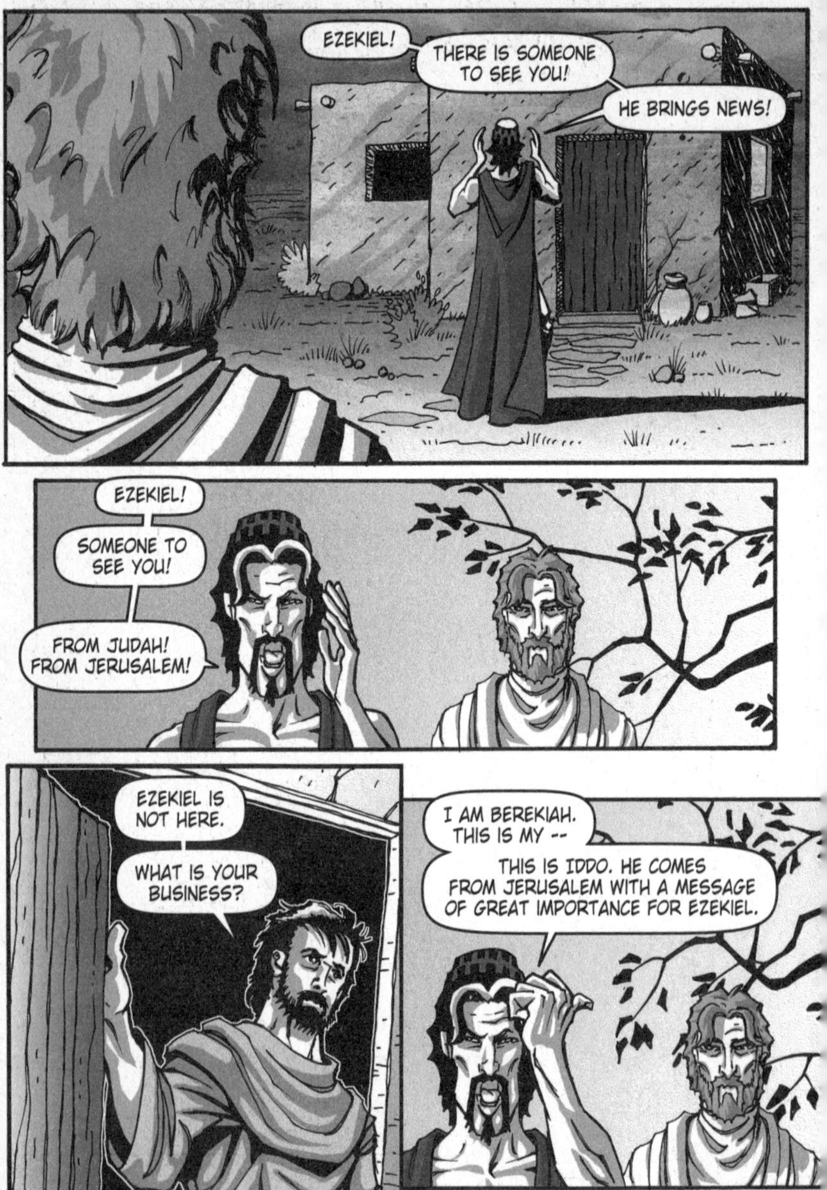
EZEKIEL!
THERE IS SOMEONE TO SEE YOU!
HE BRINGS NEWS!
EZEKIEL!
SOMEONE TO SEE YOU!
FROM JUDAH! FROM JERUSALEM!
EZEKIEL IS NOT HERE.
WHAT IS YOUR BUSINESS?
I AM BEREKIAH. THIS IS MY --
THIS IS IDDO. HE COMES FROM JERUSALEM WITH A MESSAGE OF GREAT IMPORTANCE FOR EZEKIEL.

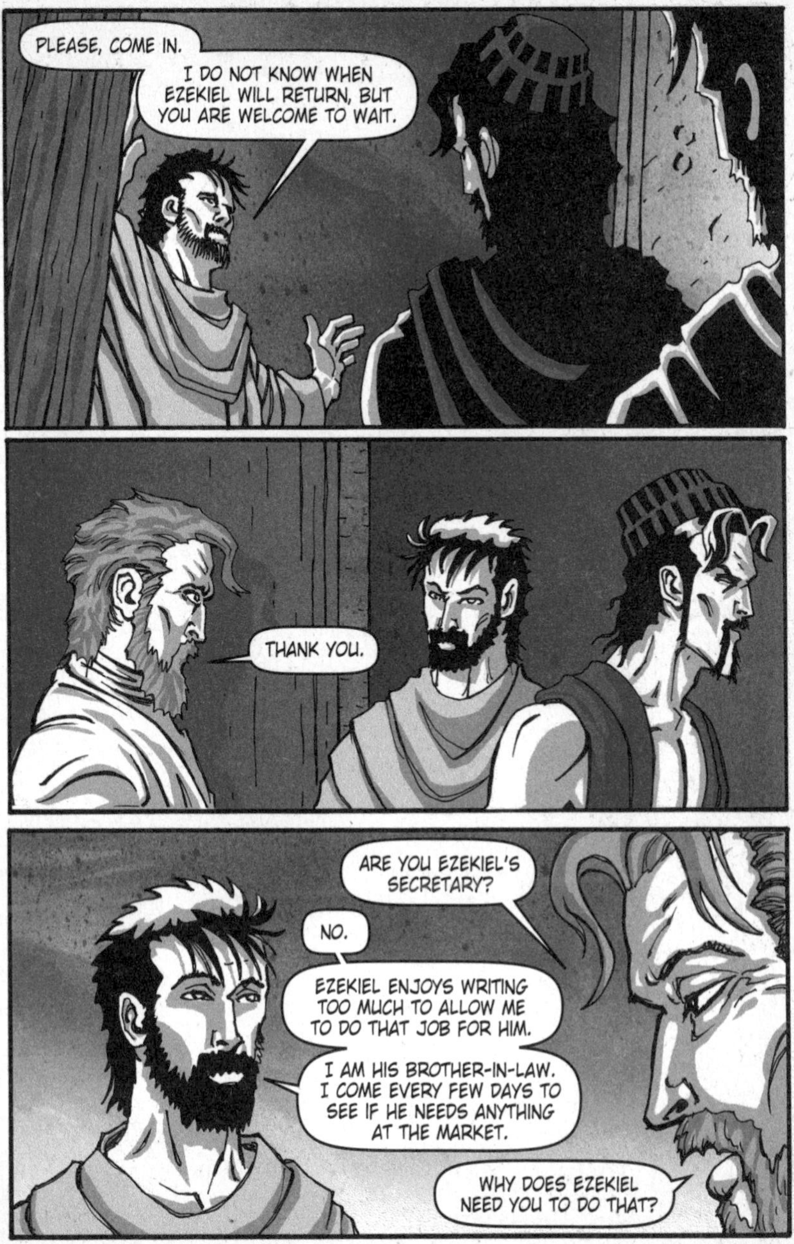
PLEASE, COME IN.
I DO NOT KNOW WHEN EZEKIEL WILL RETURN, BUT YOU ARE WELCOME TO WAIT.
THANK YOU.
ARE YOU EZEKIEL'S SECRETARY?
NO.
EZEKIEL ENJOYS WRITING TOO MUCH TO ALLOW ME TO DO THAT JOB FOR HIM.
I AM HIS BROTHER-IN-LAW. I COME EVERY FEW DAYS TO SEE IF HE NEEDS ANYTHING AT THE MARKET.
WHY DOES EZEKIEL NEED YOU TO DO THAT?

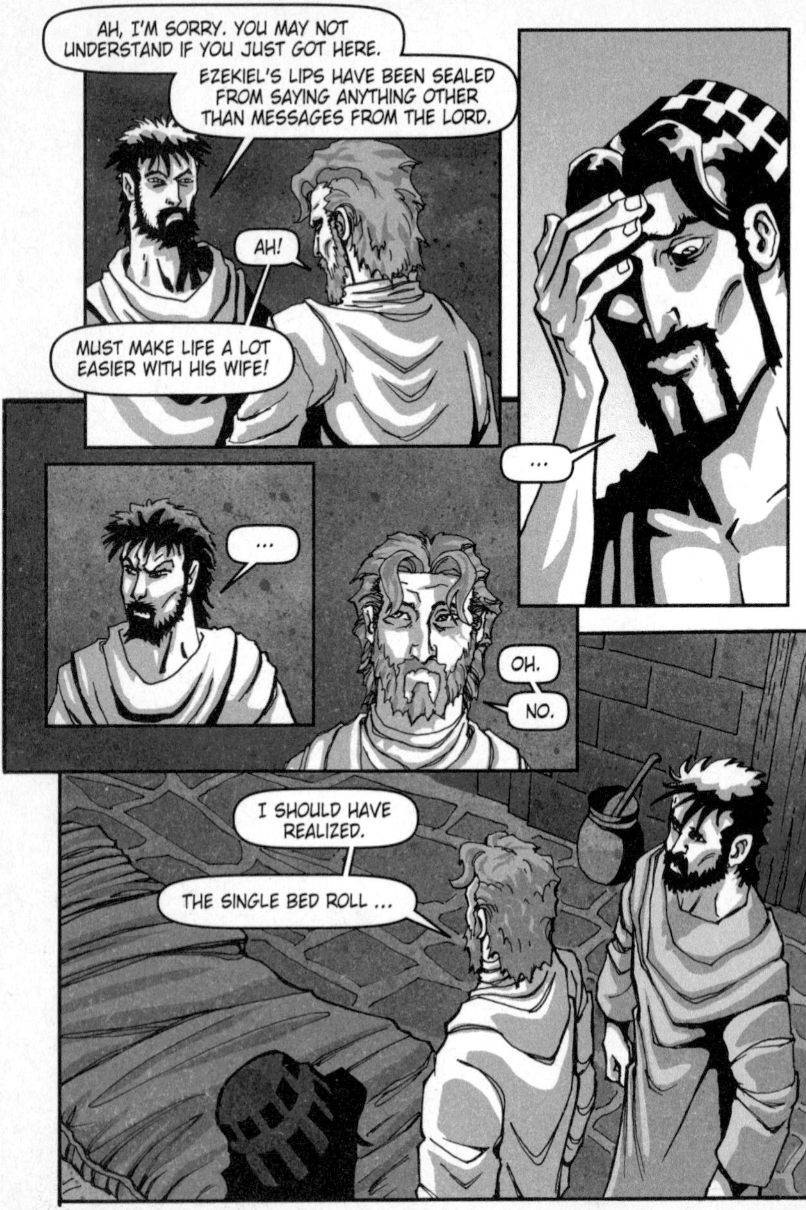
AH, I'M SORRY. YOU MAY NOT UNDERSTAND IF YOU JUST GOT HERE.
EZEKIEL'S LIPS HAVE BEEN SEALED FROM SAYING ANYTHING OTHER THAN MESSAGES FROM THE LORD.
AH!
MUST MAKE LIFE A LOT EASIER WITH HIS WIFE!
...
OH.
NO.
...
I SHOULD HAVE REALIZED.
THE SINGLE BED ROLL ...

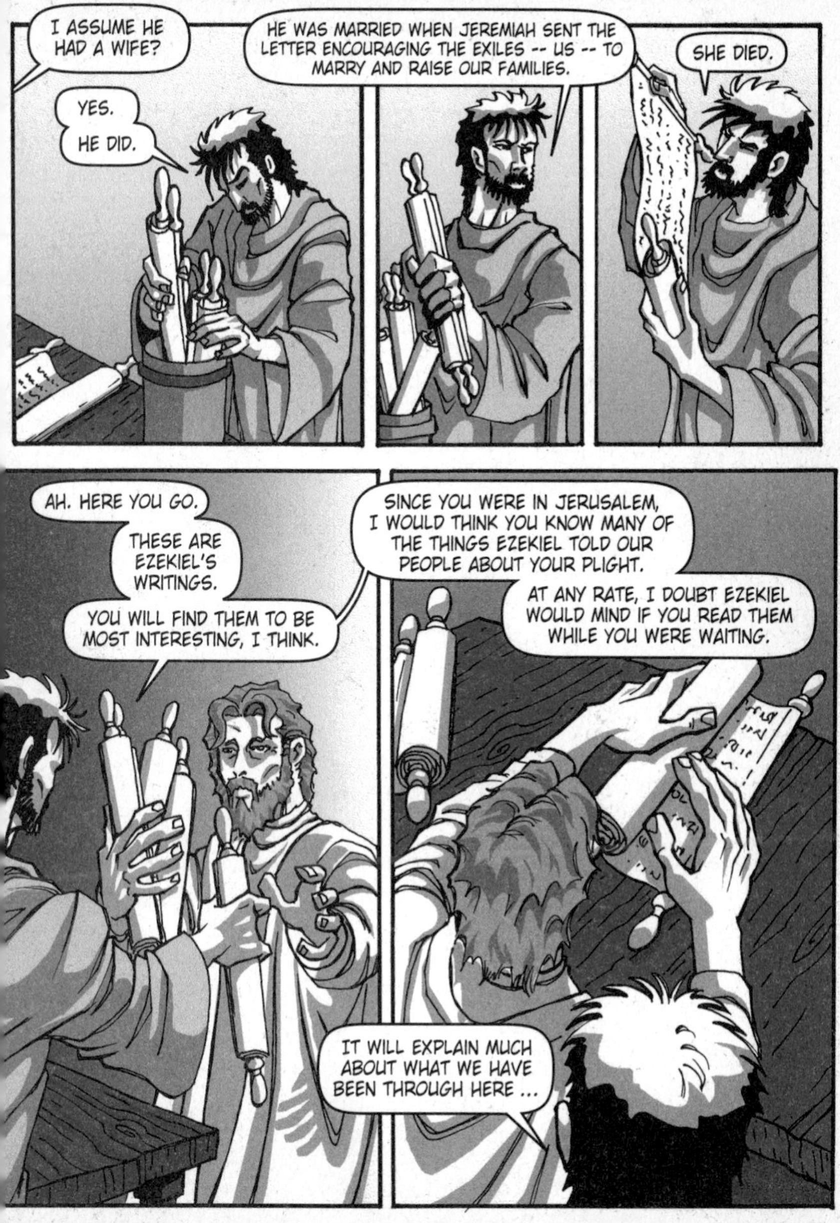
I ASSUME HE HAD A WIFE?
YES.
HE DID.
HE WAS MARRIED WHEN JEREMIAH SENT THE LETTER ENCOURAGING THE EXILES -- US -- TO MARRY AND RAISE OUR FAMILIES.
SHE DIED.
AH. HERE YOU GO.
THESE ARE EZEKIEL'S WRITINGS.
YOU WILL FIND THEM TO BE MOST INTERESTING, I THINK.
SINCE YOU WERE IN JERUSALEM, I WOULD THINK YOU KNOW MANY OF THE THINGS EZEKIEL TOLD OUR PEOPLE ABOUT YOUR PLIGHT.
AT ANY RATE, I DOUBT EZEKIEL WOULD MIND IF YOU READ THEM WHILE YOU WERE WAITING.
IT WILL EXPLAIN MUCH ABOUT WHAT WE HAVE BEEN THROUGH HERE ...

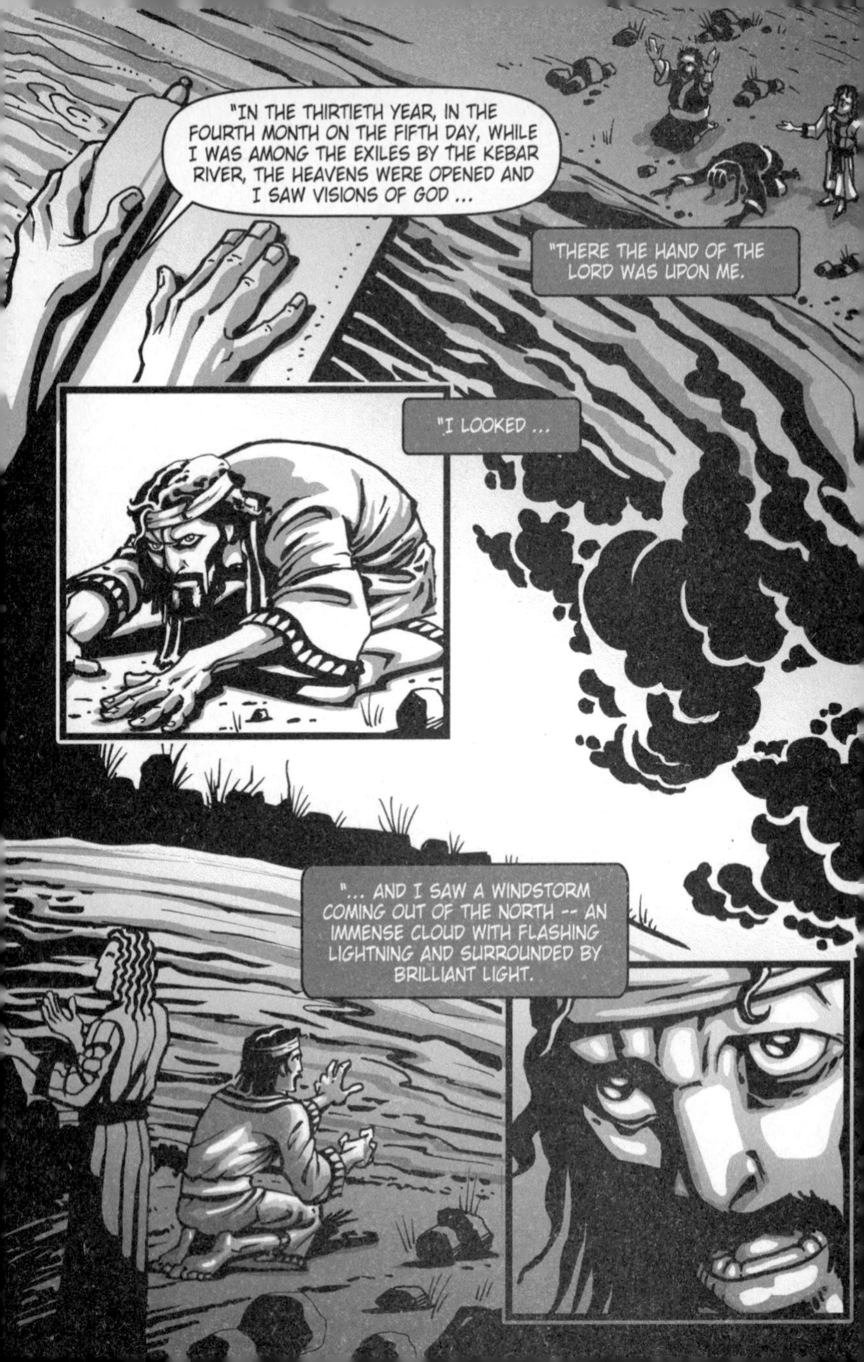
"IN THE THIRTIETH YEAR, IN THE FOURTH MONTH ON THE FIFTH DAY, WHILE I WAS AMONG THE EXILES BY THE KEBAR RIVER, THE HEAVENS WERE OPENED AND I SAW VISIONS OF GOD ...
"THERE THE HAND OF THE LORD WAS UPON ME.
"I LOOKED ...
"... AND I SAW A WINDSTORM COMING OUT OF THE NORTH -- AN IMMENSE CLOUD WITH FLASHING LIGHTNING AND SURROUNDED BY BRILLIANT LIGHT.

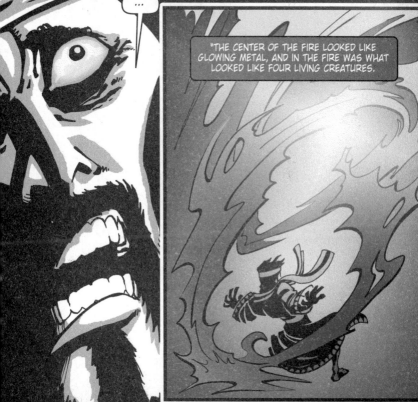

"THE CENTER OF THE FIRE LOOKED LIKE GLOWING METAL, AND IN THE FIRE WAS WHAT LOOKED LIKE FOUR LIVING CREATURES.

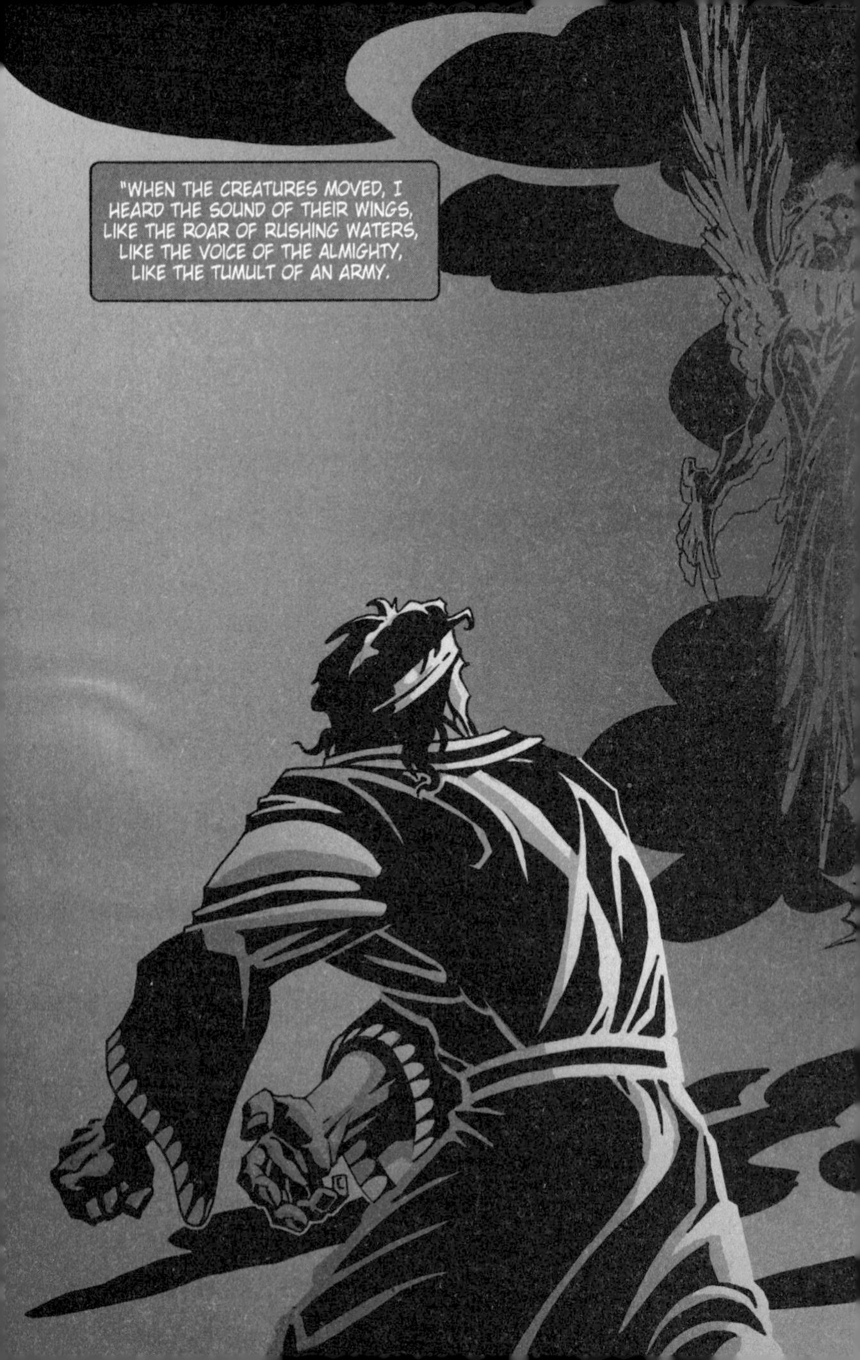
"WHEN THE CREATURES MOVED, I HEARD THE SOUND OF THEIR WINGS, LIKE THE ROAR OF RUSHING WATERS, LIKE THE VOICE OF THE ALMIGHTY, LIKE THE TUMULT OF AN ARMY.

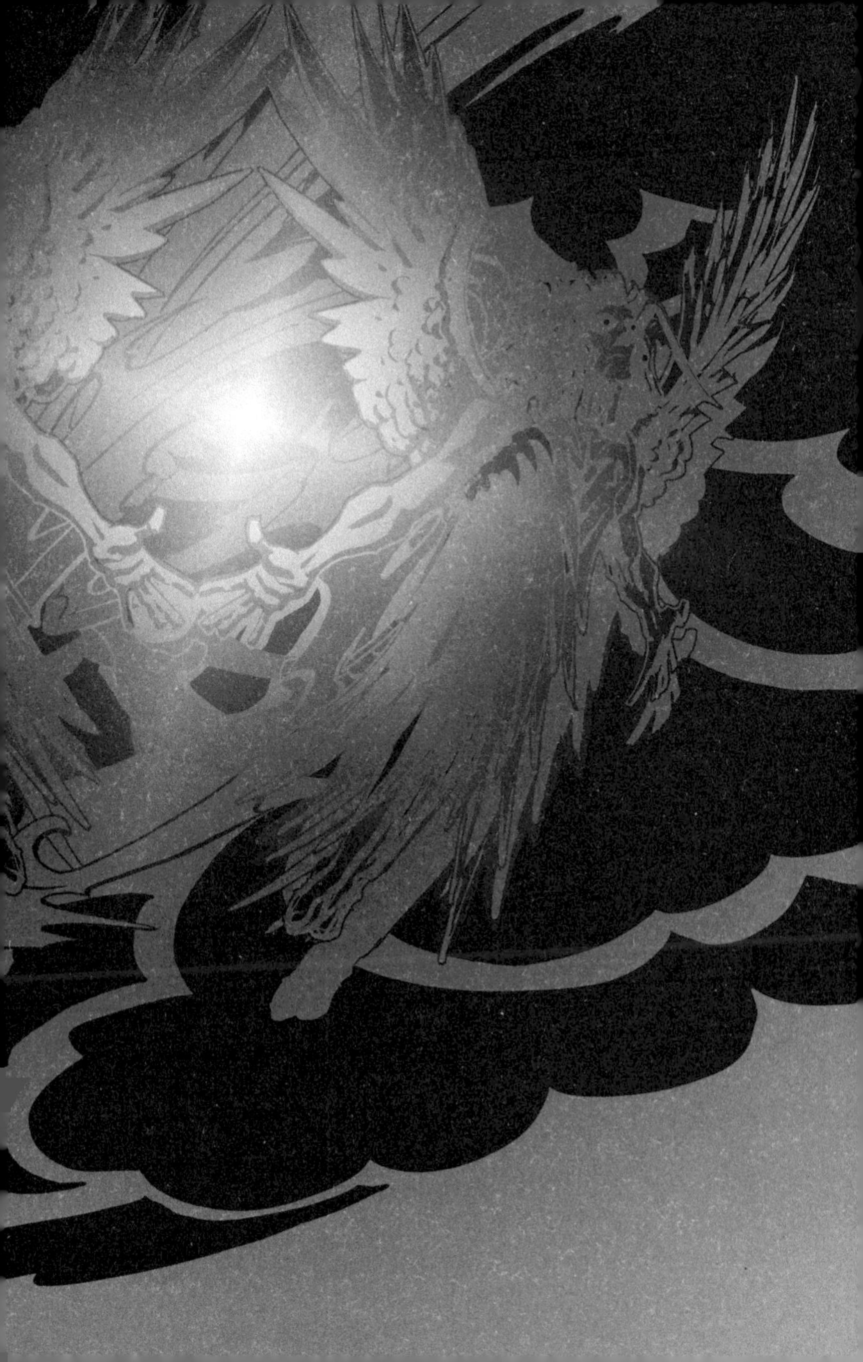

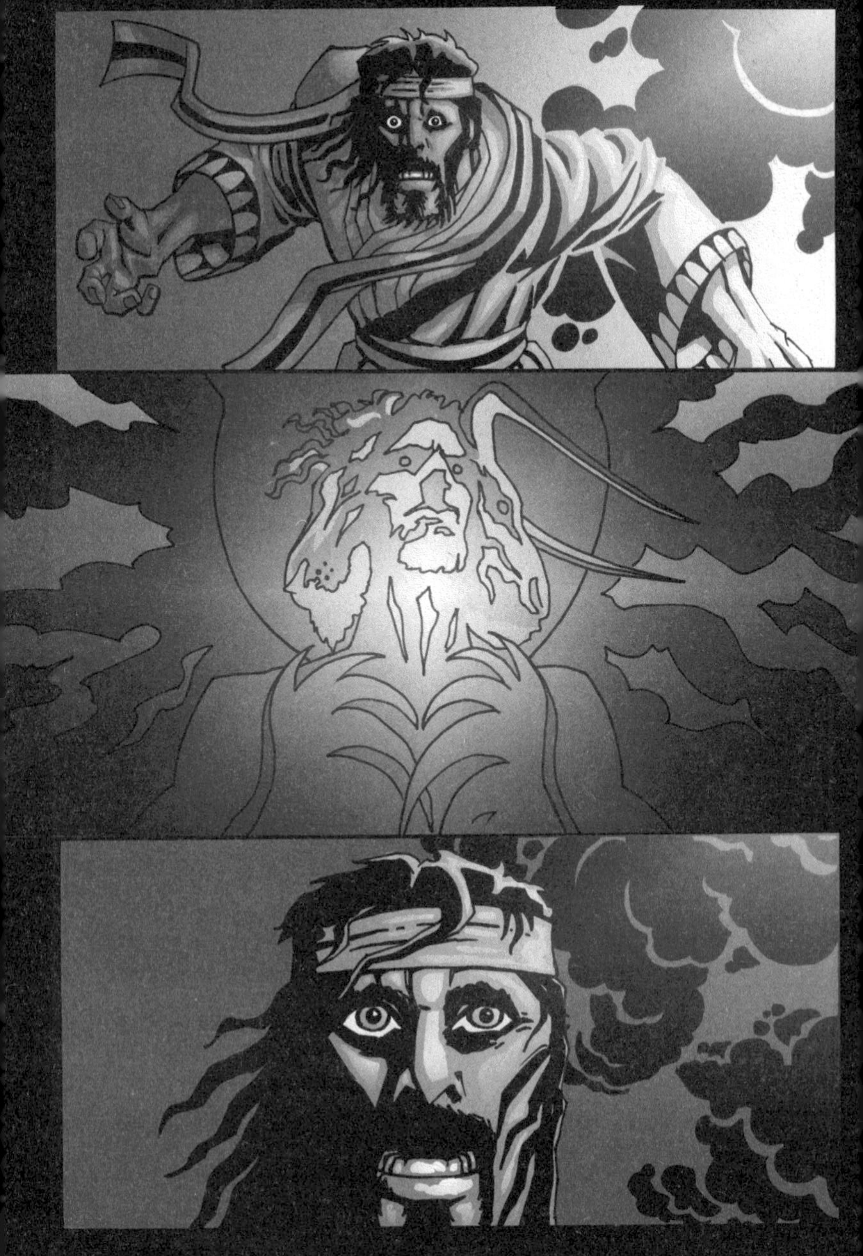

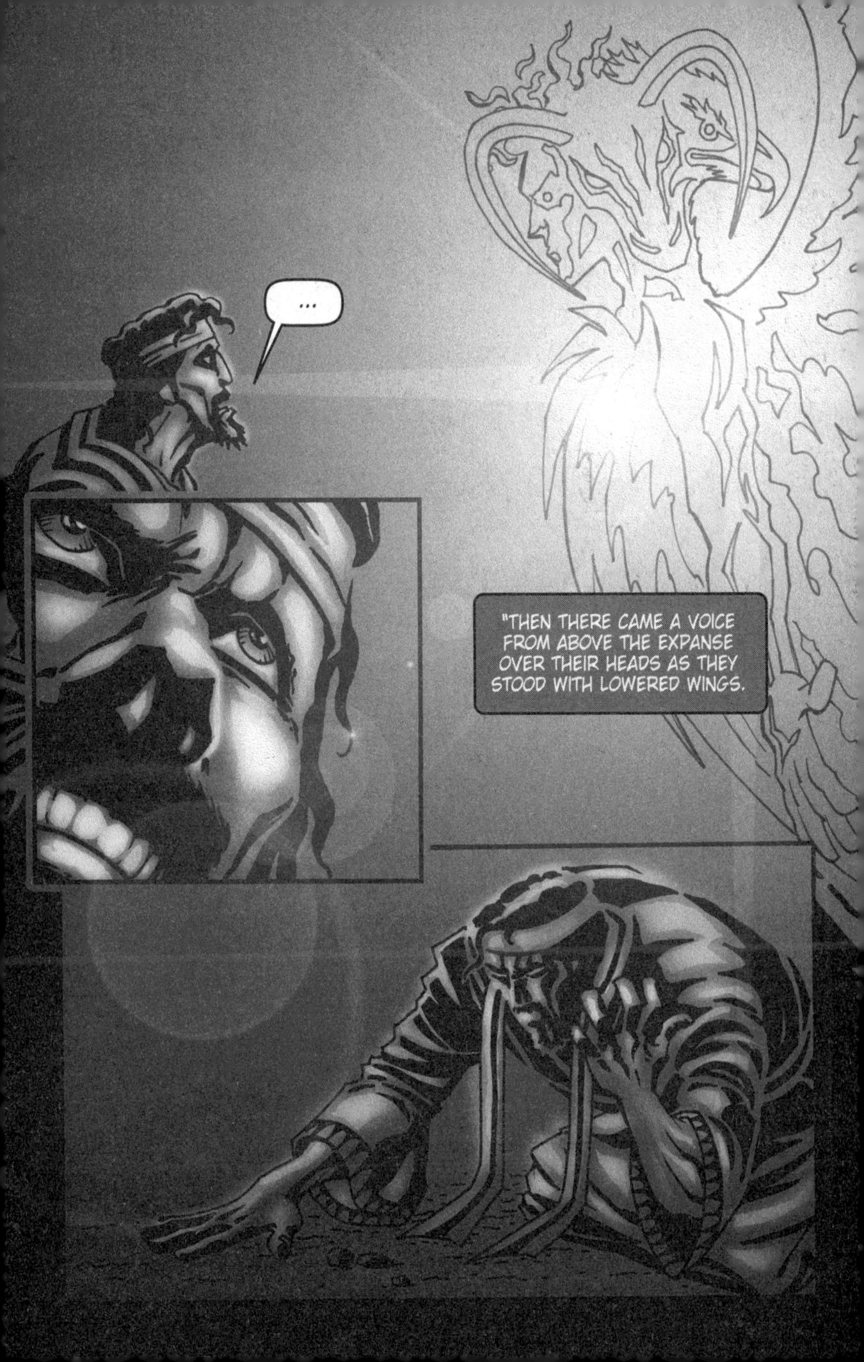
...
"THEN THERE CAME A VOICE FROM ABOVE THE EXPANSE OVER THEIR HEADS AS THEY STOOD WITH LOWERED WINGS.

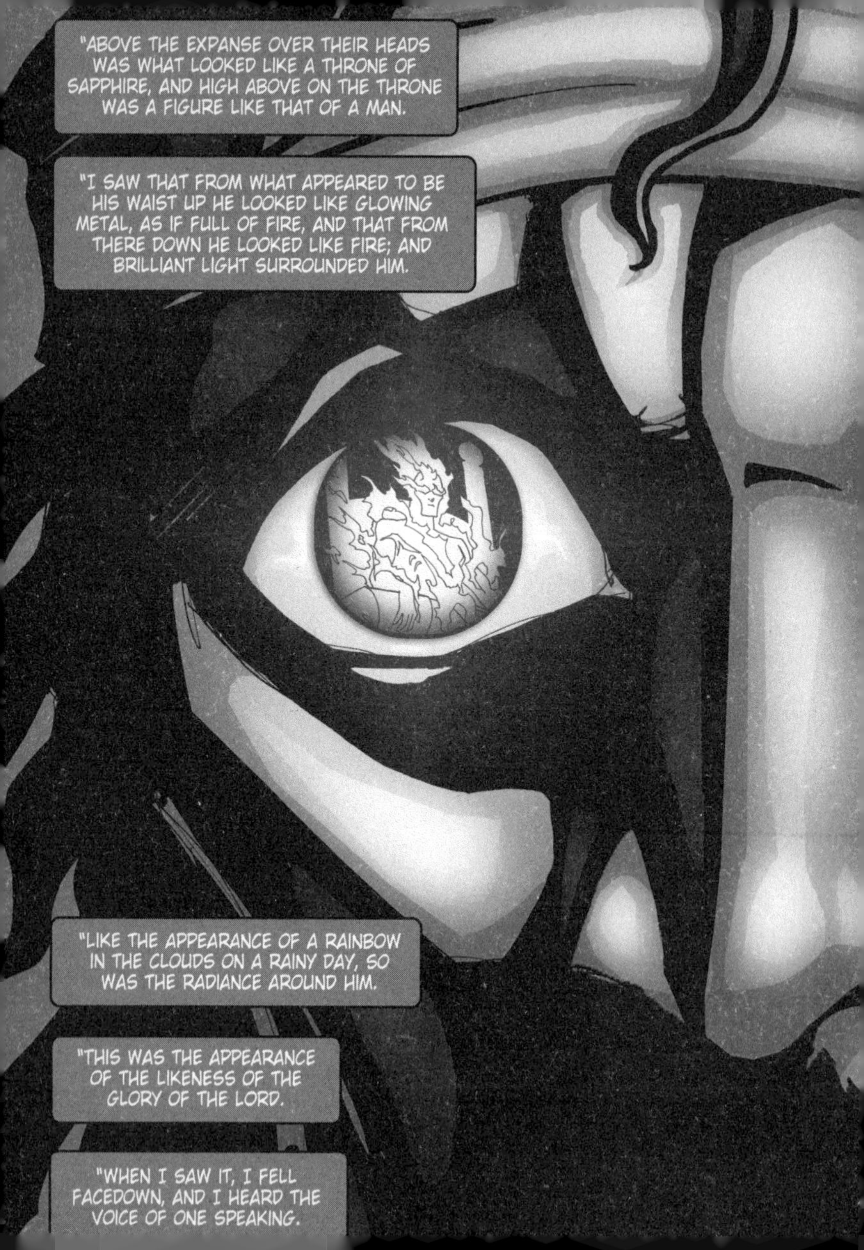
"ABOVE THE EXPANSE OVER THEIR HEADS WAS WHAT LOOKED LIKE A THRONE OF SAPPHIRE, AND HIGH ABOVE ON THE THRONE WAS A FIGURE LIKE THAT OF A MAN.
"I SAW THAT FROM WHAT APPEARED TO BE HIS WAIST UP HE LOOKED LIKE GLOWING METAL, AS IF FULL OF FIRE, AND THAT FROM THERE DOWN HE LOOKED LIKE FIRE; AND BRILLIANT LIGHT SURROUNDED HIM.
"LIKE THE APPEARANCE OF A RAINBOW IN THE CLOUDS ON A RAINY DAY, SO WAS THE RADIANCE AROUND HIM.
"THIS WAS THE APPEARANCE OF THE LIKENESS OF THE GLORY OF THE LORD.
"WHEN I SAW IT, I FELL FACEDOWN, AND I HEARD THE VOICE OF ONE SPEAKING.

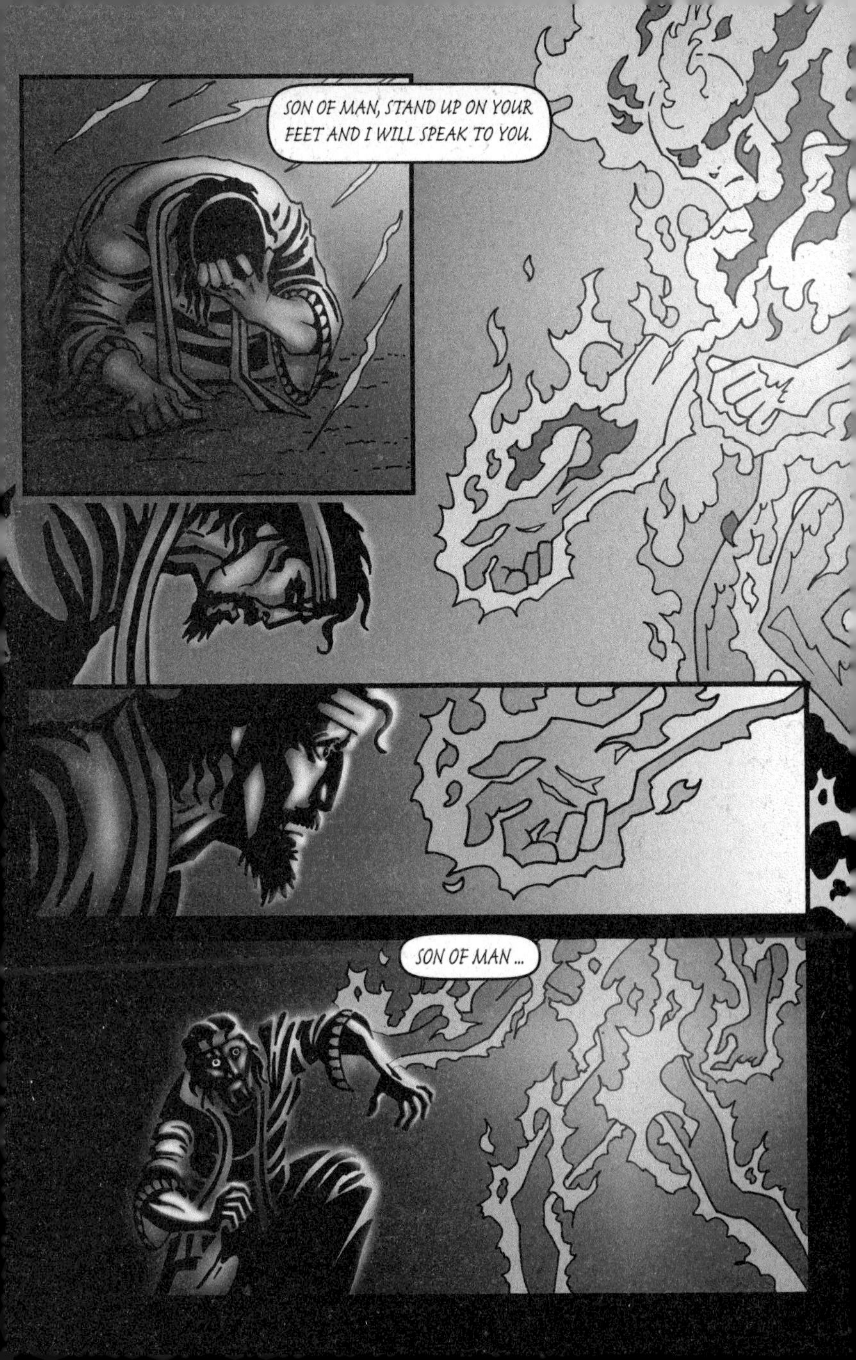
SON OF MAN, STAND UP ON YOUR FEET AND I WILL SPEAK TO YOU.
SON OF MAN ...

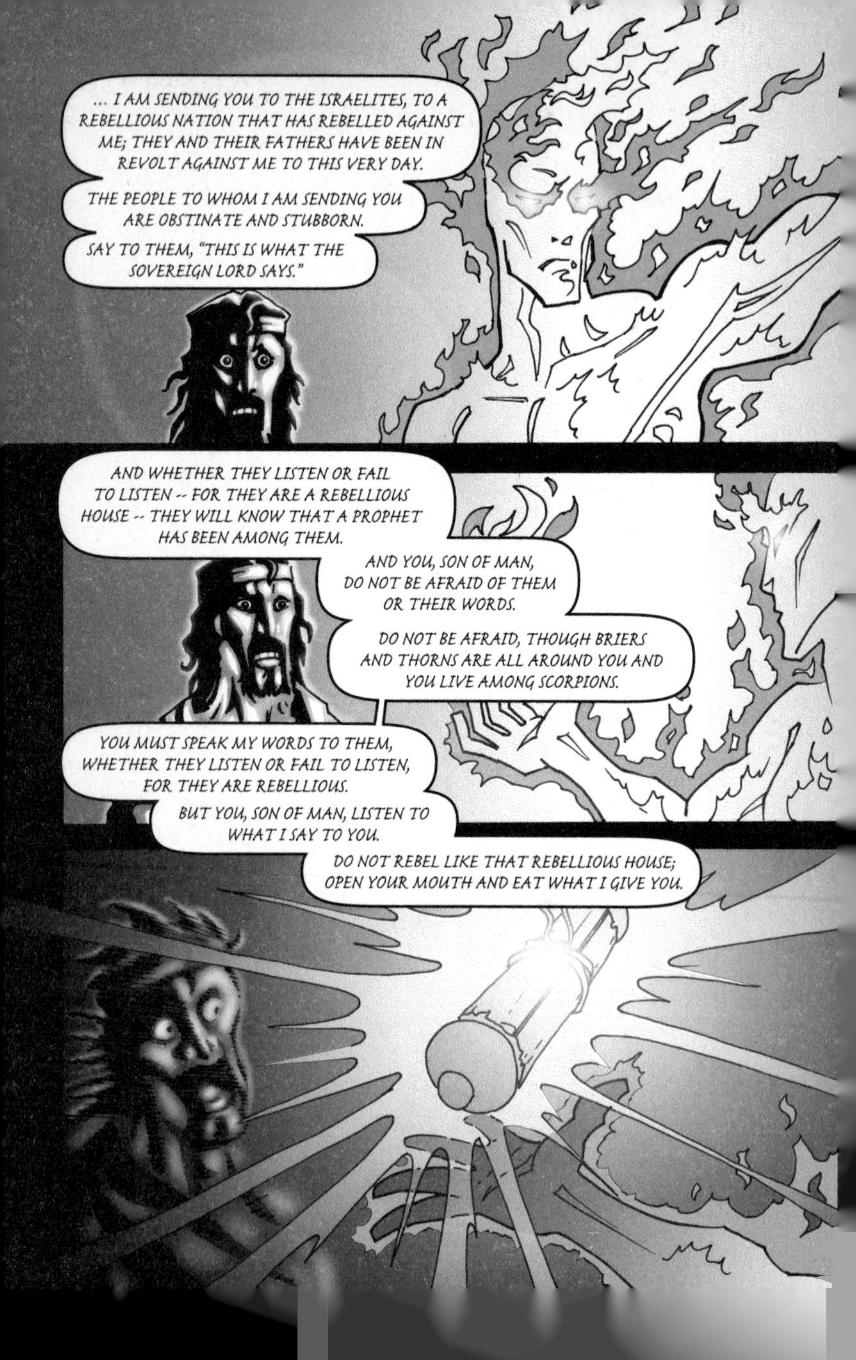
... I AM SENDING YOU TO THE ISRAELITES, TO A REBELLIOUS NATION THAT HAS REBELLED AGAINST ME; THEY AND THEIR FATHERS HAVE BEEN IN REVOLT AGAINST ME TO THIS VERY DAY.
THE PEOPLE TO WHOM I AM SENDING YOU ARE OBSTINATE AND STUBBORN.
SAY TO THEM, "THIS IS WHAT THE SOVEREIGN LORD SAYS."
AND WHETHER THEY LISTEN OR FAIL TO LISTEN -- FOR THEY ARE A REBELLIOUS HOUSE -- THEY WILL KNOW THAT A PROPHET HAS BEEN AMONG THEM.
AND YOU, SON OF MAN, DO NOT BE AFRAID OF THEM OR THEIR WORDS.
DO NOT BE AFRAID, THOUGH BRIERS AND THORNS ARE ALL AROUND YOU AND YOU LIVE AMONG SCORPIONS.
YOU MUST SPEAK MY WORDS TO THEM, WHETHER THEY LISTEN OR FAIL TO LISTEN, FOR THEY ARE REBELLIOUS.
BUT YOU, SON OF MAN, LISTEN TO WHAT I SAY TO YOU.
DO NOT REBEL LIKE THAT REBELLIOUS HOUSE; OPEN YOUR MOUTH AND EAT WHAT I GIVE YOU.

"ON BOTH SIDES OF THE SCROLL WERE WRITTEN WORDS OF LAMENT AND MOURNING AND WOE.
SON OF MAN, EAT WHAT IS BEFORE YOU, EAT THIS SCROLL.
THEN GO AND SPEAK TO THE HOUSE OF ISRAEL.

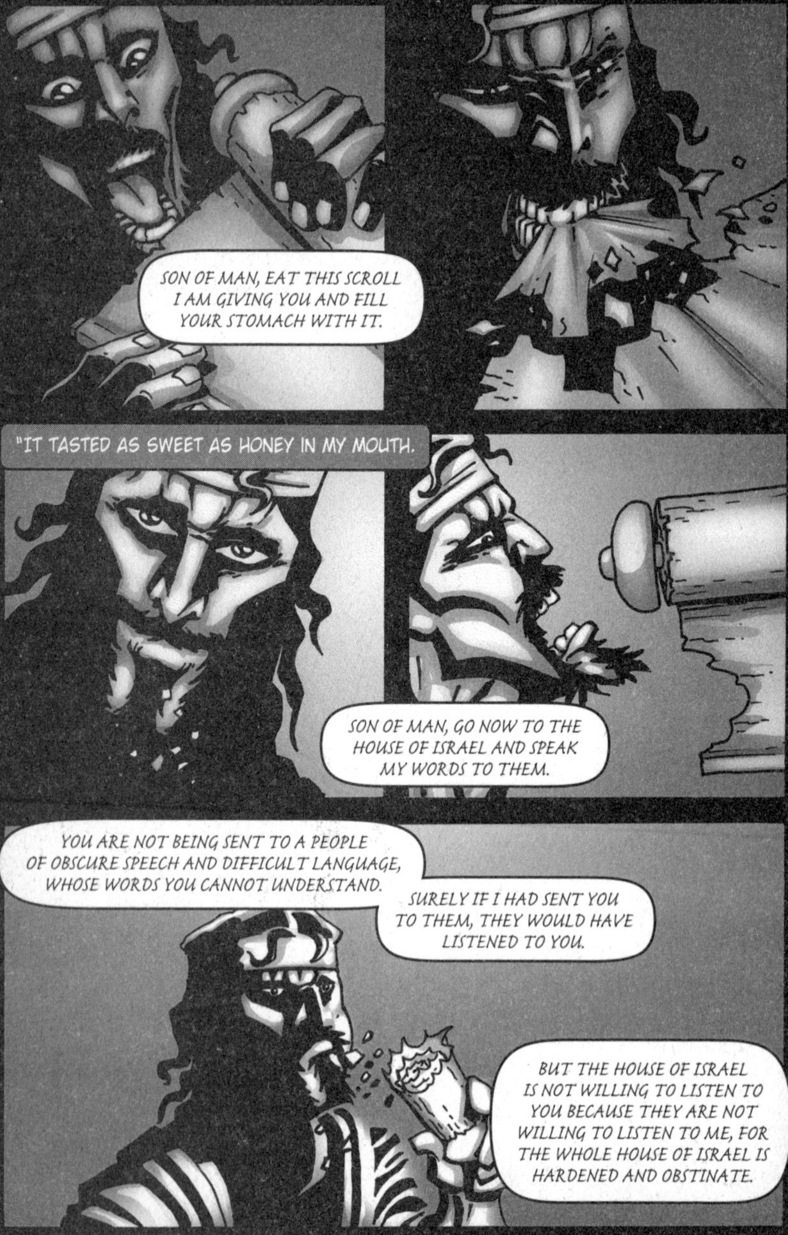
SON OF MAN, EAT THIS SCROLL I AM GIVING YOU AND FILL YOUR STOMACH WITH IT.
"IT TASTED AS SWEET AS HONEY IN MY MOUTH.
SON OF MAN, GO NOW TO THE HOUSE OF ISRAEL AND SPEAK MY WORDS TO THEM.
YOU ARE NOT BEING SENT TO A PEOPLE OF OBSCURE SPEECH AND DIFFICULT LANGUAGE, WHOSE WORDS YOU CANNOT UNDERSTAND.
SURELY IF I HAD SENT YOU TO THEM, THEY WOULD HAVE LISTENED TO YOU.
BUT THE HOUSE OF ISRAEL IS NOT WILLING TO LISTEN TO YOU BECAUSE THEY ARE NOT WILLING TO LISTEN TO ME, FOR THE WHOLE HOUSE OF ISRAEL IS HARDENED AND OBSTINATE.

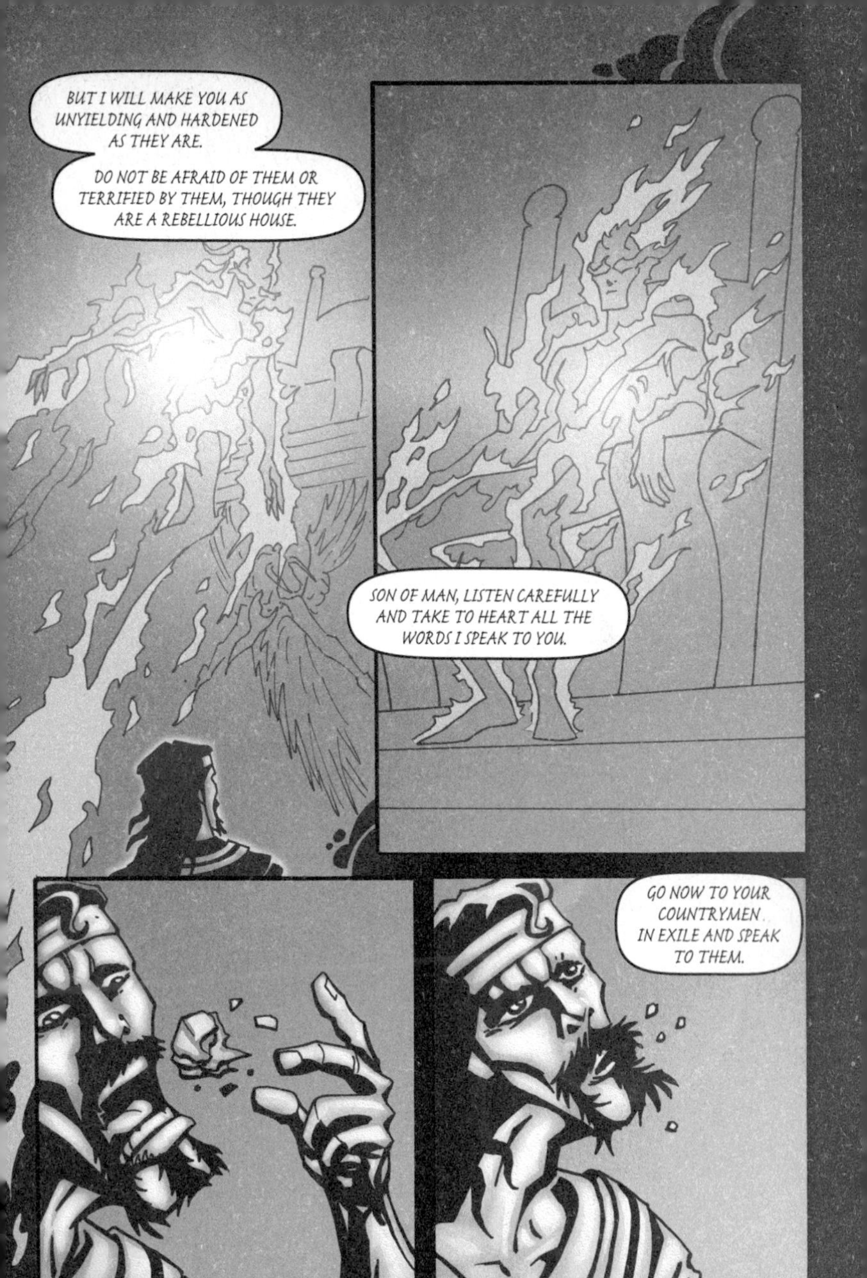
BUT I WILL MAKE YOU AS UNYIELDING AND HARDENED AS THEY ARE.
DO NOT BE AFRAID OF THEM OR TERRIFIED BY THEM, THOUGH THEY ARE A REBELLIOUS HOUSE.
SON OF MAN, LISTEN CAREFULLY AND TAKE TO HEART ALL THE WORDS I SPEAK TO YOU.
GO NOW TO YOUR COUNTRYMEN IN EXILE AND SPEAK TO THEM.

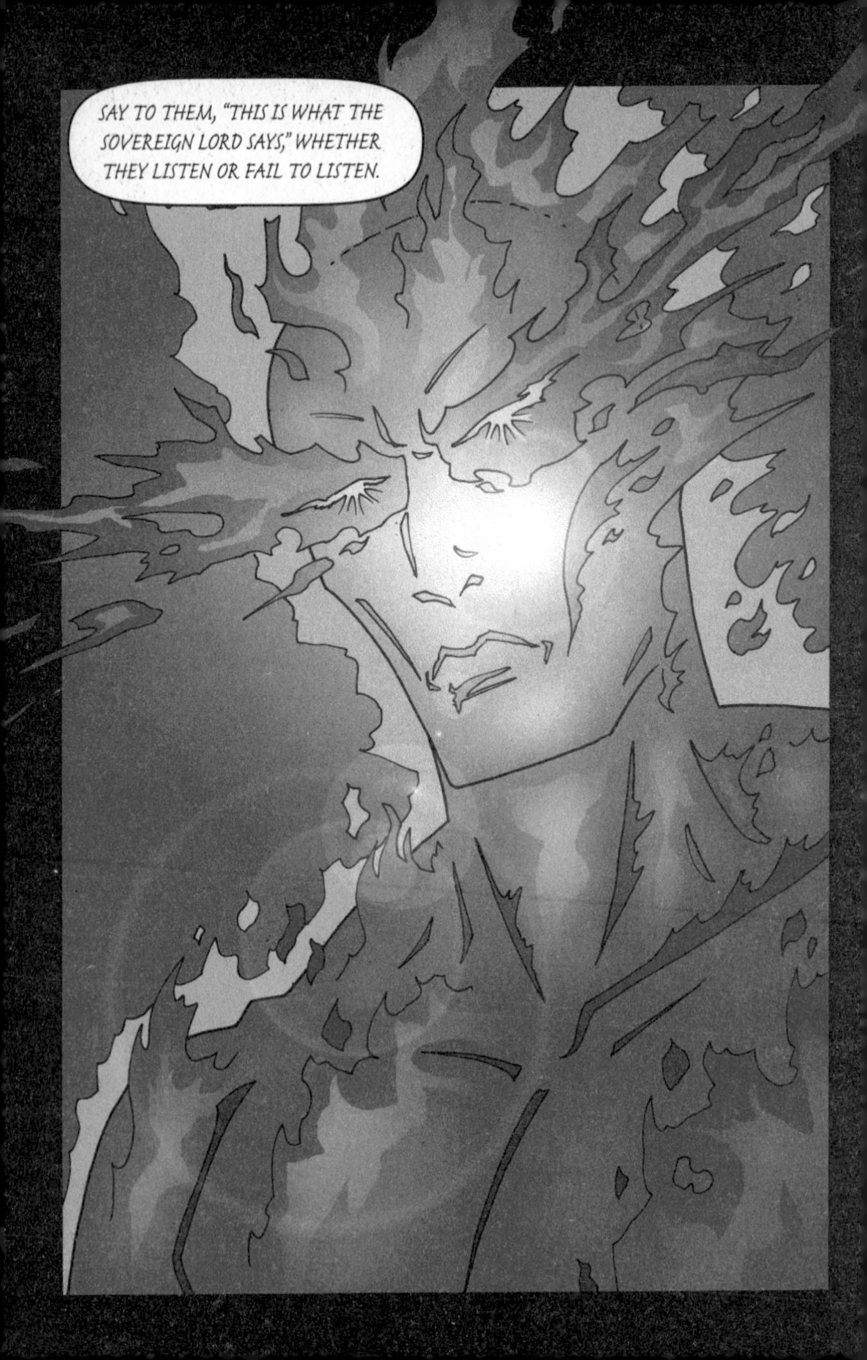
SAY TO THEM, "THIS IS WHAT THE SOVEREIGN LORD SAYS," WHETHER THEY LISTEN OR FAIL TO LISTEN.

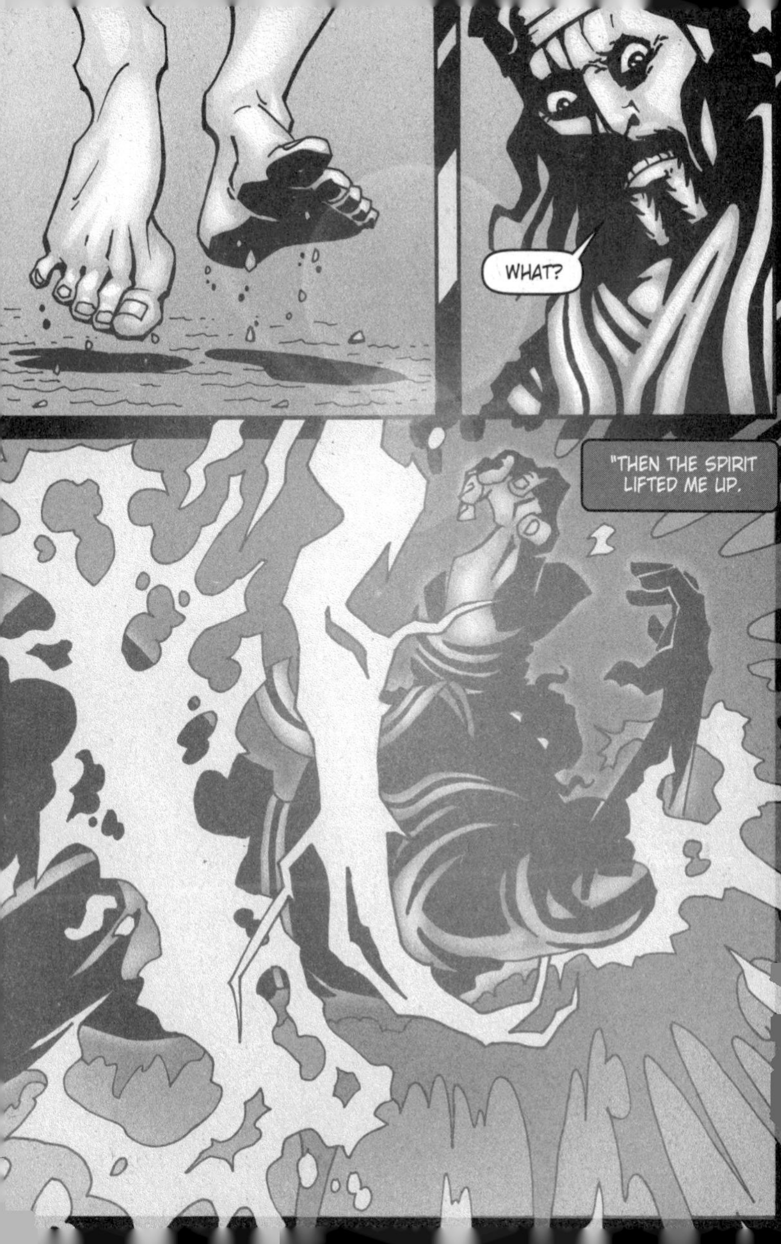
WHAT?
"THEN THE SPIRIT LIFTED ME UP.

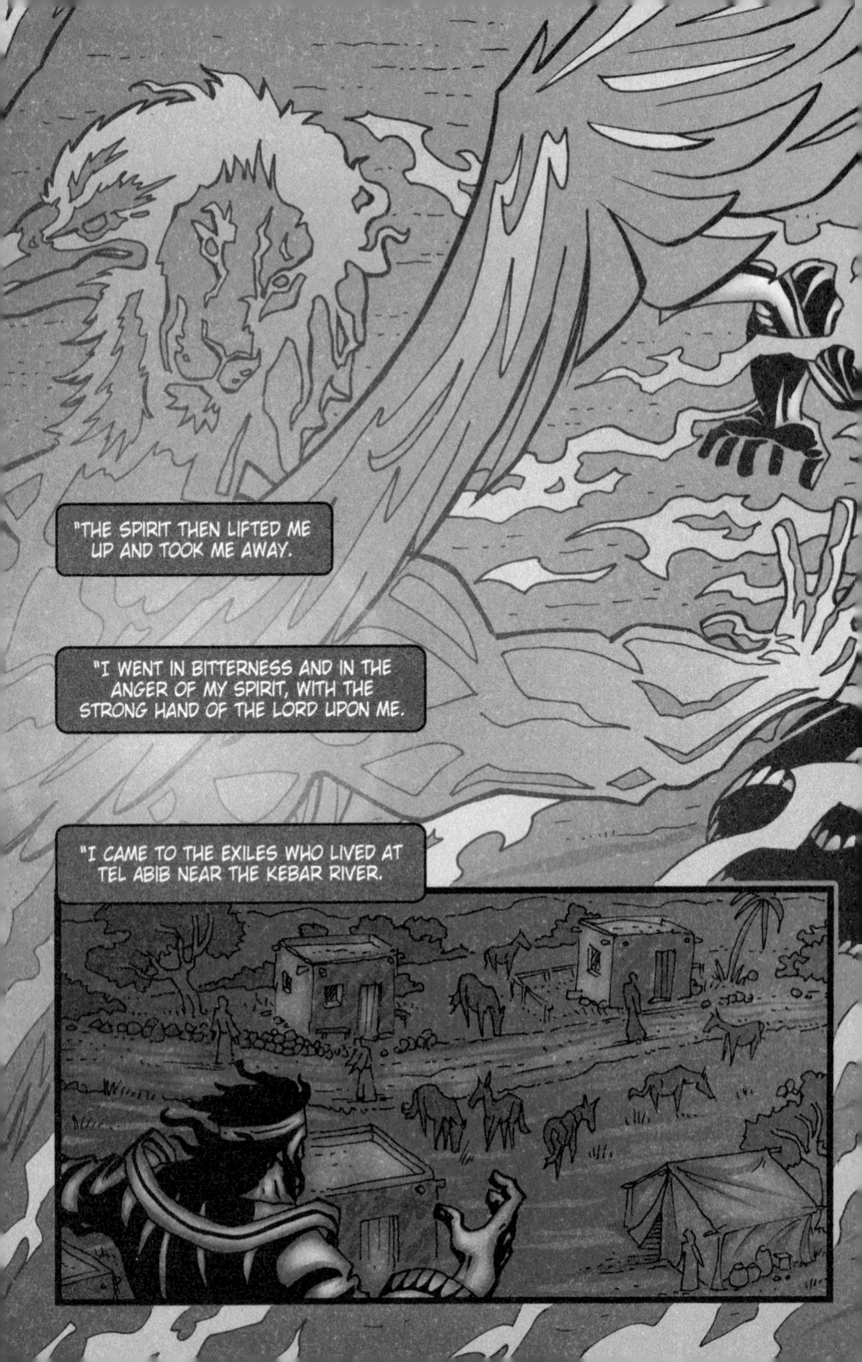
"THE SPIRIT THEN LIFTED ME UP AND TOOK ME AWAY.
"I WENT IN BITTERNESS AND IN THE ANGER OF MY SPIRIT, WITH THE STRONG HAND OF THE LORD UPON ME.
"I CAME TO THE EXILES WHO LIVED AT TEL ABIB NEAR THE KEBAR RIVER.

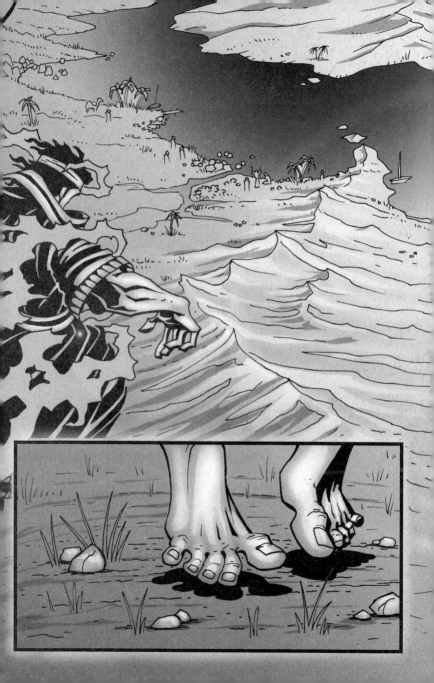

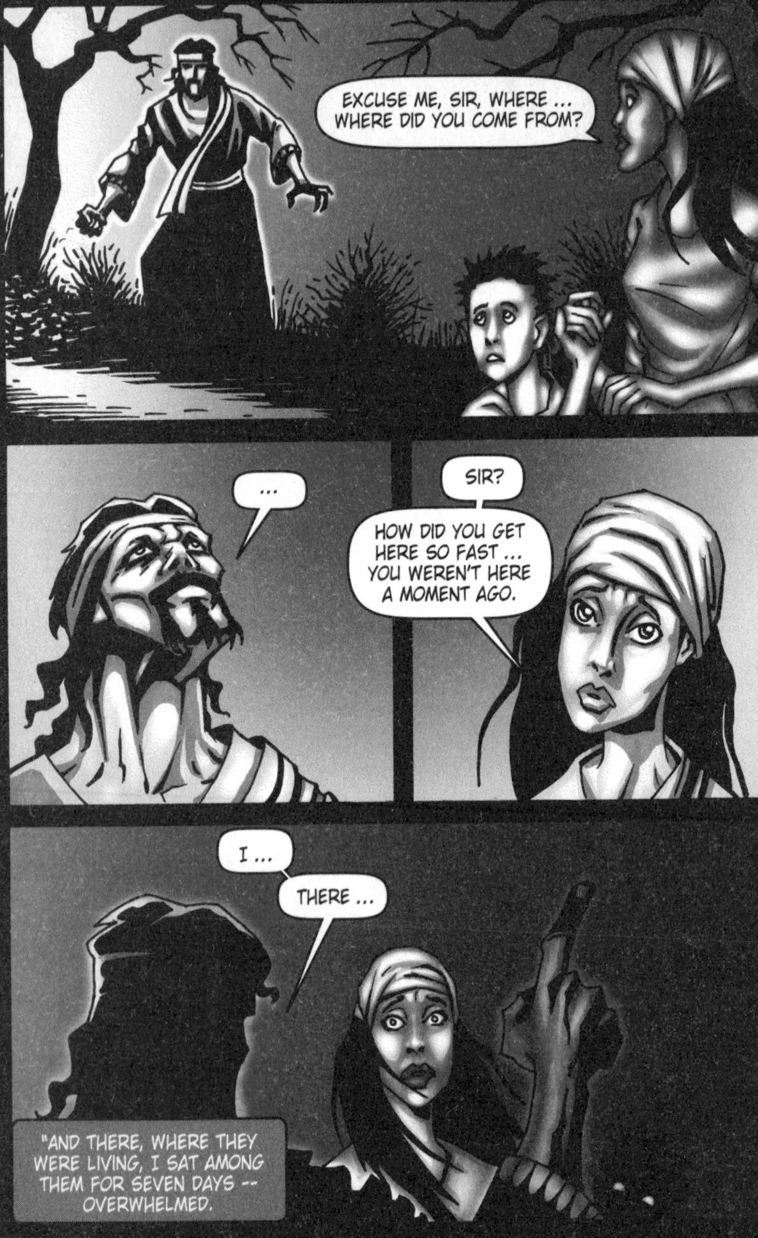
EXCUSE ME, SIR, WHERE ... WHERE DID YOU COME FROM?
...
SIR?
HOW DID YOU GET HERE SO FAST ... YOU WEREN'T HERE A MOMENT AGO.
I ...
THERE ...
"AND THERE, WHERE THEY WERE LIVING, I SAT AMONG THEM FOR SEVEN DAYS -- OVERWHELMED.

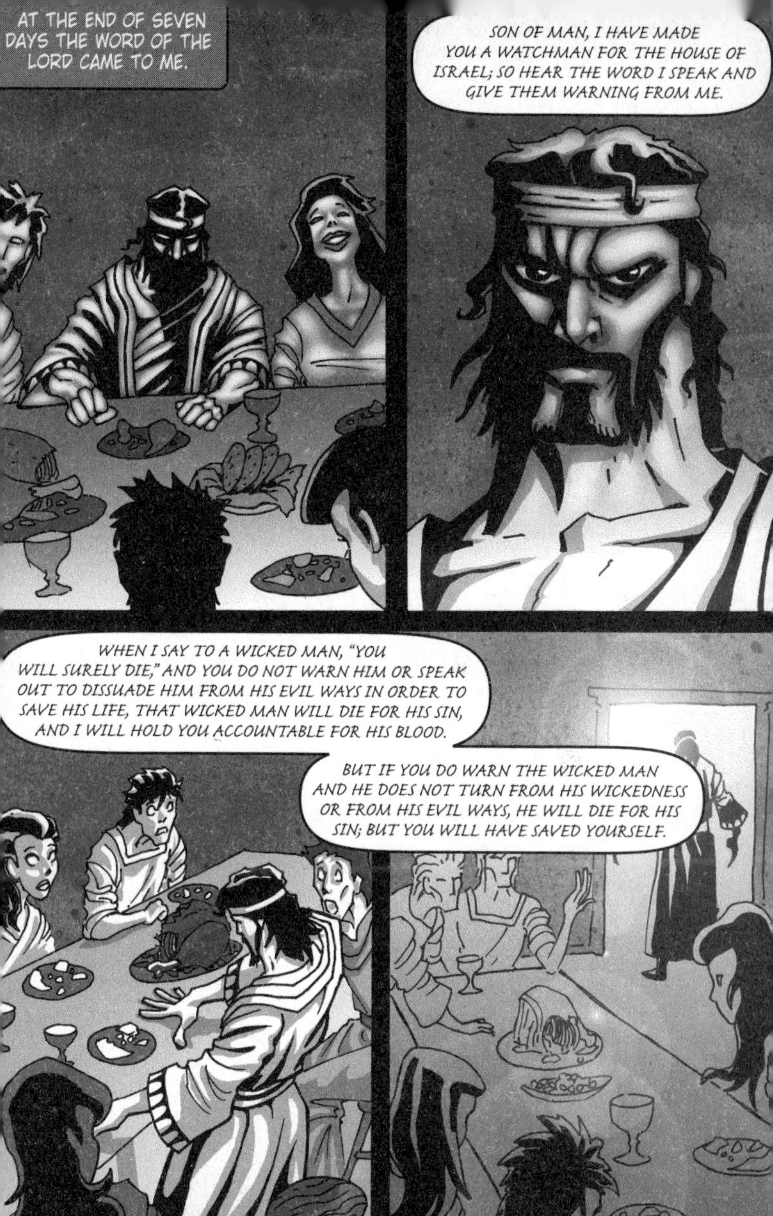
AT THE END OF SEVEN DAYS THE WORD OF THE LORD CAME TO ME.
SON OF MAN, I HAVE MADE YOU A WATCHMAN FOR THE HOUSE OF ISRAEL; SO HEAR THE WORD I SPEAK AND GIVE THEM WARNING FROM ME.
WHEN I SAY TO A WICKED MAN, "YOU WILL SURELY DIE," AND YOU DO NOT WARN HIM OR SPEAK OUT TO DISSUADE HIM FROM HIS EVIL WAYS IN ORDER TO SAVE HIS LIFE, THAT WICKED MAN WILL DIE FOR HIS SIN, AND I WILL HOLD YOU ACCOUNTABLE FOR HIS BLOOD.
BUT IF YOU DO WARN THE WICKED MAN AND HE DOES NOT TURN FROM HIS WICKEDNESS OR FROM HIS EVIL WAYS, HE WILL DIE FOR HIS SIN; BUT YOU WILL HAVE SAVED YOURSELF.

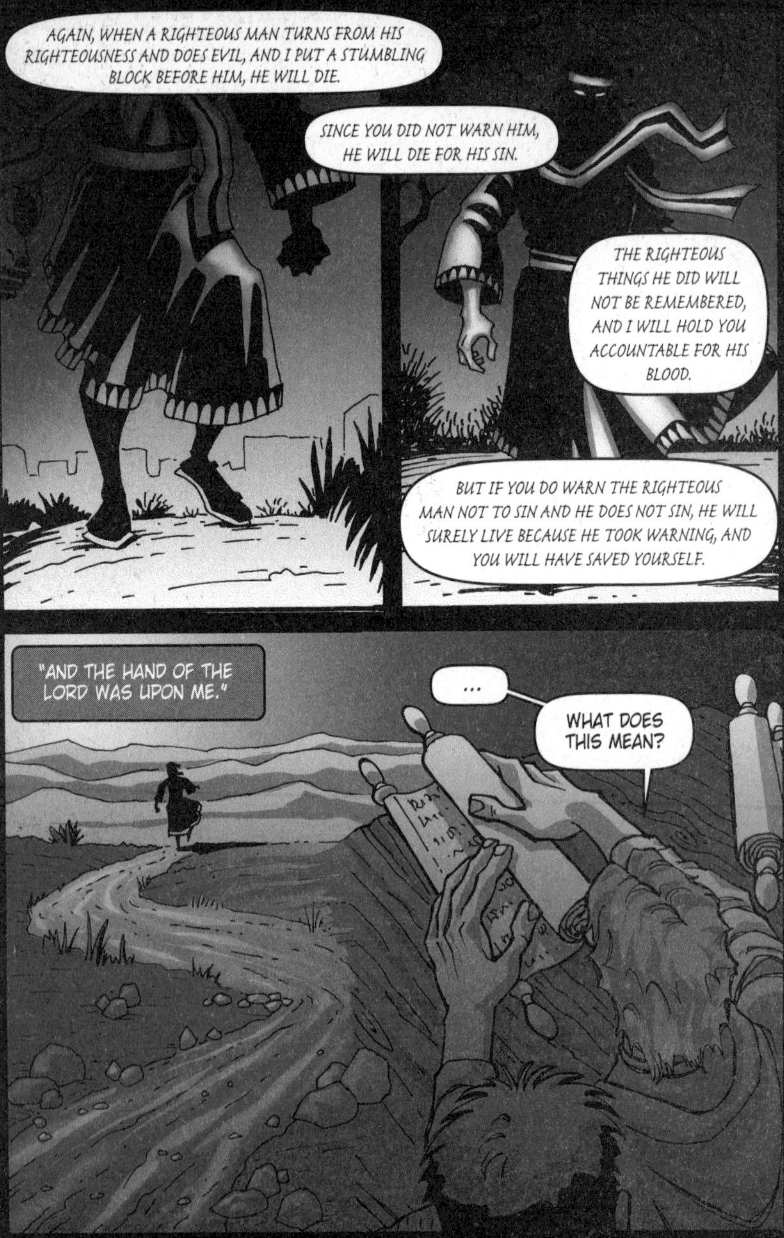
AGAIN, WHEN A RIGHTEOUS MAN TURNS FROM HIS RIGHTEOUSNESS AND DOES EVIL, AND I PUT A STUMBLING BLOCK BEFORE HIM, HE WILL DIE.
SINCE YOU DID NOT WARN HIM, HE WILL DIE FOR HIS SIN.
THE RIGHTEOUS THINGS HE DID WILL NOT BE REMEMBERED, AND I WILL HOLD YOU ACCOUNTABLE FOR HIS BLOOD.
BUT IF YOU DO WARN THE RIGHTEOUS MAN NOT TO SIN AND HE DOES NOT SIN, HE WILL SURELY LIVE BECAUSE HE TOOK WARNING, AND YOU WILL HAVE SAVED YOURSELF.
"AND THE HAND OF THE LORD WAS UPON ME."
...
WHAT DOES THIS MEAN?

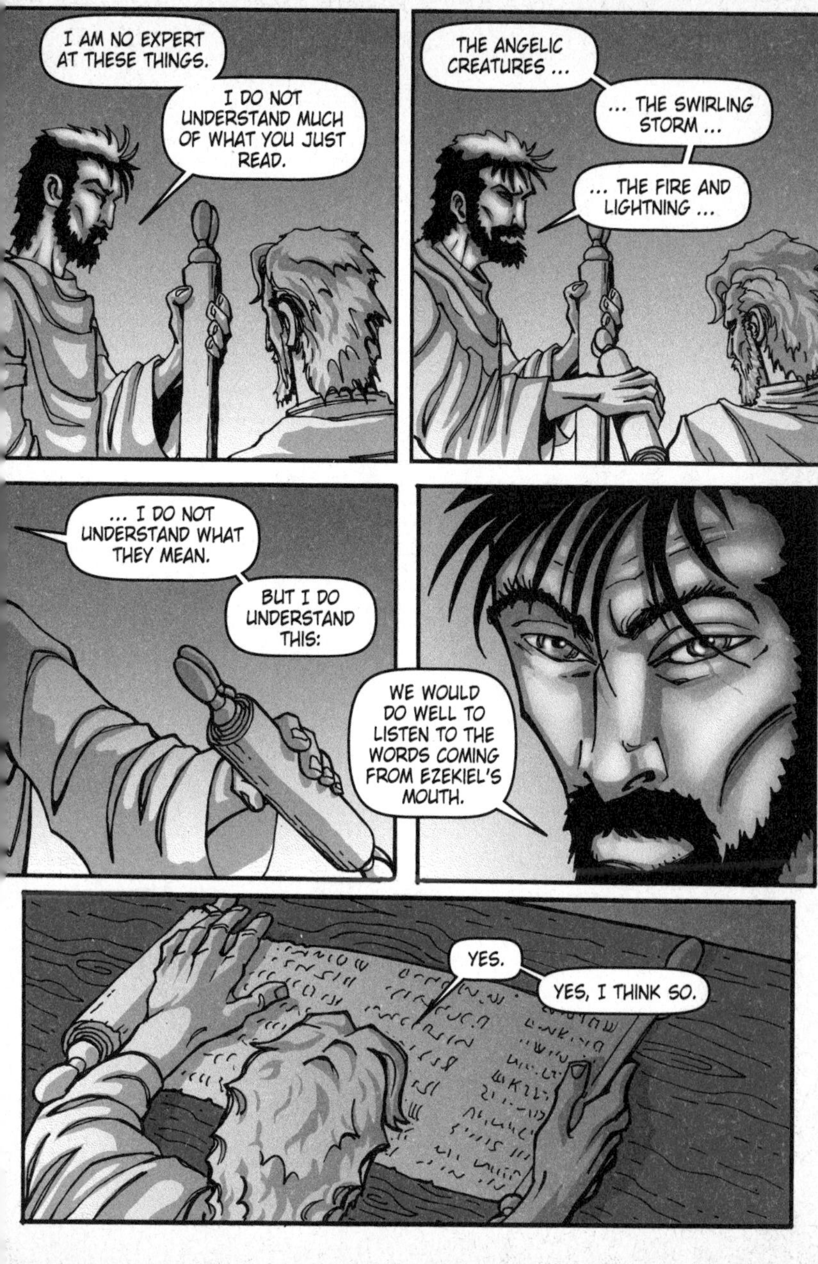
I AM NO EXPERT AT THESE THINGS.
I DO NOT UNDERSTAND MUCH OF WHAT YOU JUST READ.
THE ANGELIC CREATURES ...
... THE SWIRLING STORM ...
... THE FIRE AND LIGHTNING ...
... I DO NOT UNDERSTAND WHAT THEY MEAN.
BUT I DO UNDERSTAND THIS:
WE WOULD DO WELL TO LISTEN TO THE WORDS COMING FROM EZEKIEL'S MOUTH.
YES.
YES, I THINK SO.

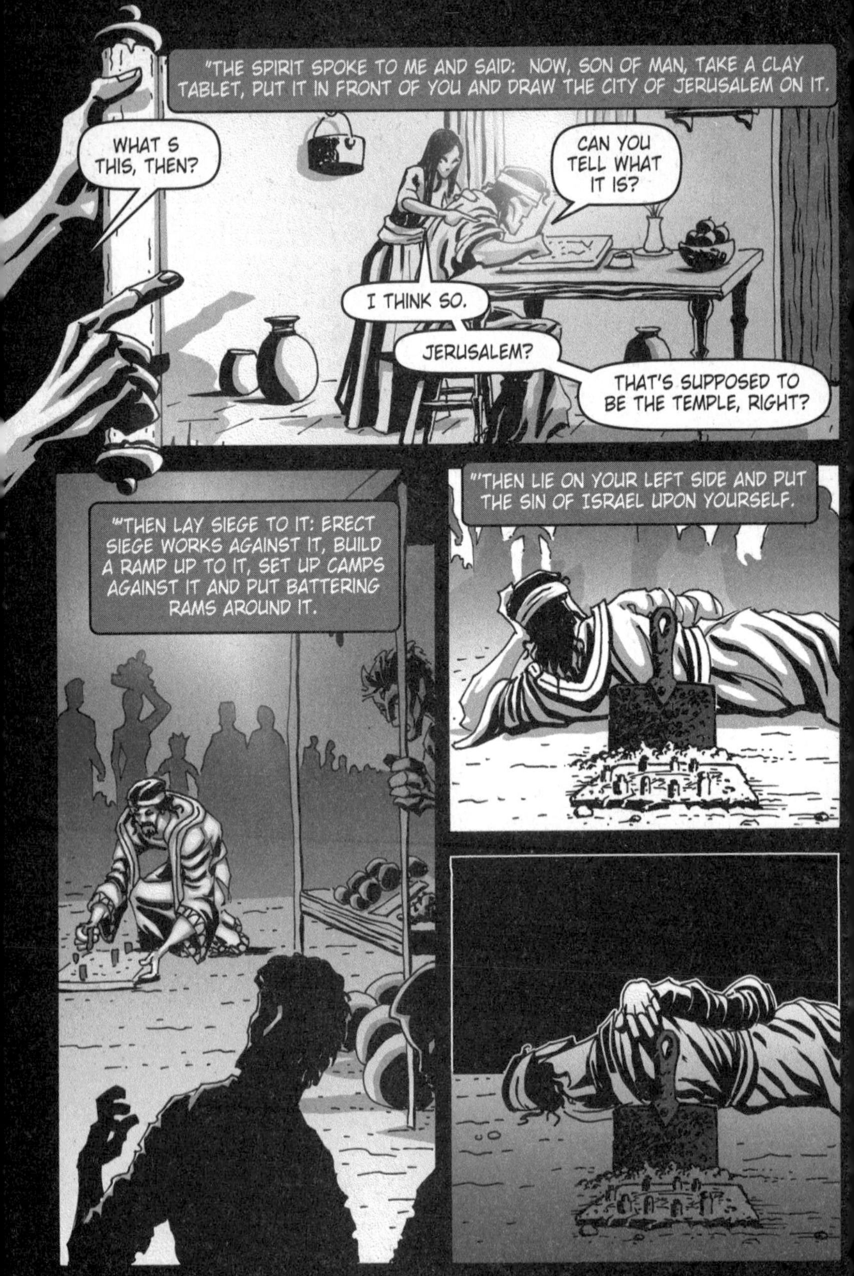
"THE SPIRIT SPOKE TO ME AND SAID: NOW, SON OF MAN, TAKE A CLAY TABLET, PUT IT IN FRONT OF YOU AND DRAW THE CITY OF JERUSALEM ON IT.
WHAT S THIS, THEN?
CAN YOU TELL WHAT IT IS?
I THINK SO.
JERUSALEM?
THAT'S SUPPOSED TO BE THE TEMPLE, RIGHT?
"'THEN LAY SIEGE TO IT: ERECT SIEGE WORKS AGAINST IT, BUILD A RAMP UP TO IT, SET UP CAMPS AGAINST IT AND PUT BATTERING RAMS AROUND IT.
"'THEN LIE ON YOUR LEFT SIDE AND PUT THE SIN OF ISRAEL UPON YOURSELF.

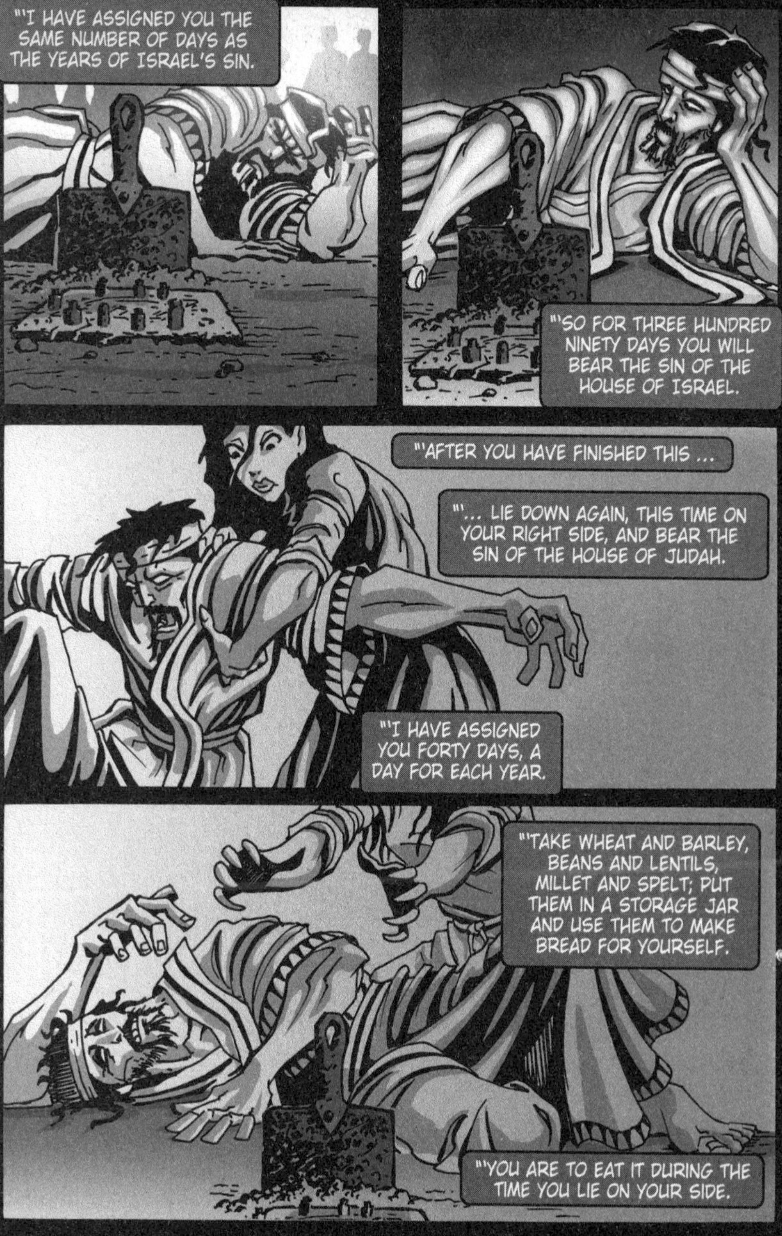
"'I HAVE ASSIGNED YOU THE SAME NUMBER OF DAYS AS THE YEARS OF ISRAEL'S SIN.
"'SO FOR THREE HUNDRED NINETY DAYS YOU WILL BEAR THE SIN OF THE HOUSE OF ISRAEL.
"'AFTER YOU HAVE FINISHED THIS ...
"'... LIE DOWN AGAIN, THIS TIME ON YOUR RIGHT SIDE, AND BEAR THE SIN OF THE HOUSE OF JUDAH.
"'I HAVE ASSIGNED YOU FORTY DAYS, A DAY FOR EACH YEAR.
"'TAKE WHEAT AND BARLEY, BEANS AND LENTILS, MILLET AND SPELT; PUT THEM IN A STORAGE JAR AND USE THEM TO MAKE BREAD FOR YOURSELF.
"'YOU ARE TO EAT IT DURING THE TIME YOU LIE ON YOUR SIDE.

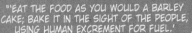

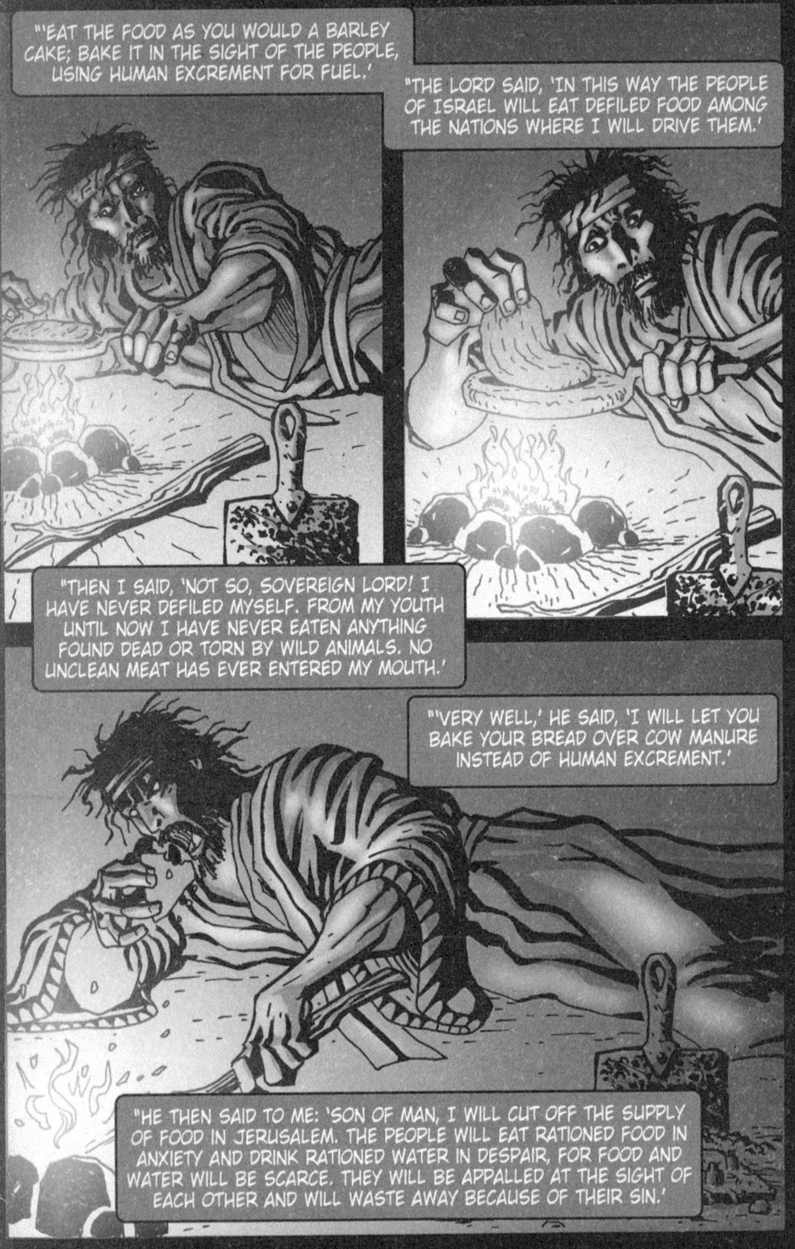

"'EAT THE FOOD AS YOU WOULD A BARLEY CAKE; BAKE IT IN THE SIGHT OF THE PEOPLE, USING HUMAN EXCREMENT FOR FUEL.'

"THE LORD SAID, 'IN THIS WAY THE PEOPLE OF ISRAEL WILL EAT DEFILED FOOD AMONG THE NATIONS WHERE I WILL DRIVE THEM.'

"THEN I SAID, 'NOT SO, SOVEREIGN LORD! I HAVE NEVER DEFILED MYSELF. FROM MY YOUTH UNTIL NOW I HAVE NEVER EATEN ANYTHING FOUND DEAD OR TORN BY WILD ANIMALS. NO UNCLEAN MEAT HAS EVER ENTERED MY MOUTH.'

"'VERY WELL,' HE SAID, 'I WILL LET YOU BAKE YOUR BREAD OVER COW MANURE INSTEAD OF HUMAN EXCREMENT.'

"HE THEN SAID TO ME: 'SON OF MAN, I WILL CUT OFF THE SUPPLY OF FOOD IN JERUSALEM. THE PEOPLE WILL EAT RATIONED FOOD IN ANXIETY AND DRINK RATIONED WATER IN DESPAIR, FOR FOOD AND WATER WILL BE SCARCE. THEY WILL BE APPALLED AT THE SIGHT OF EACH OTHER AND WILL WASTE AWAY BECAUSE OF THEIR SIN.'

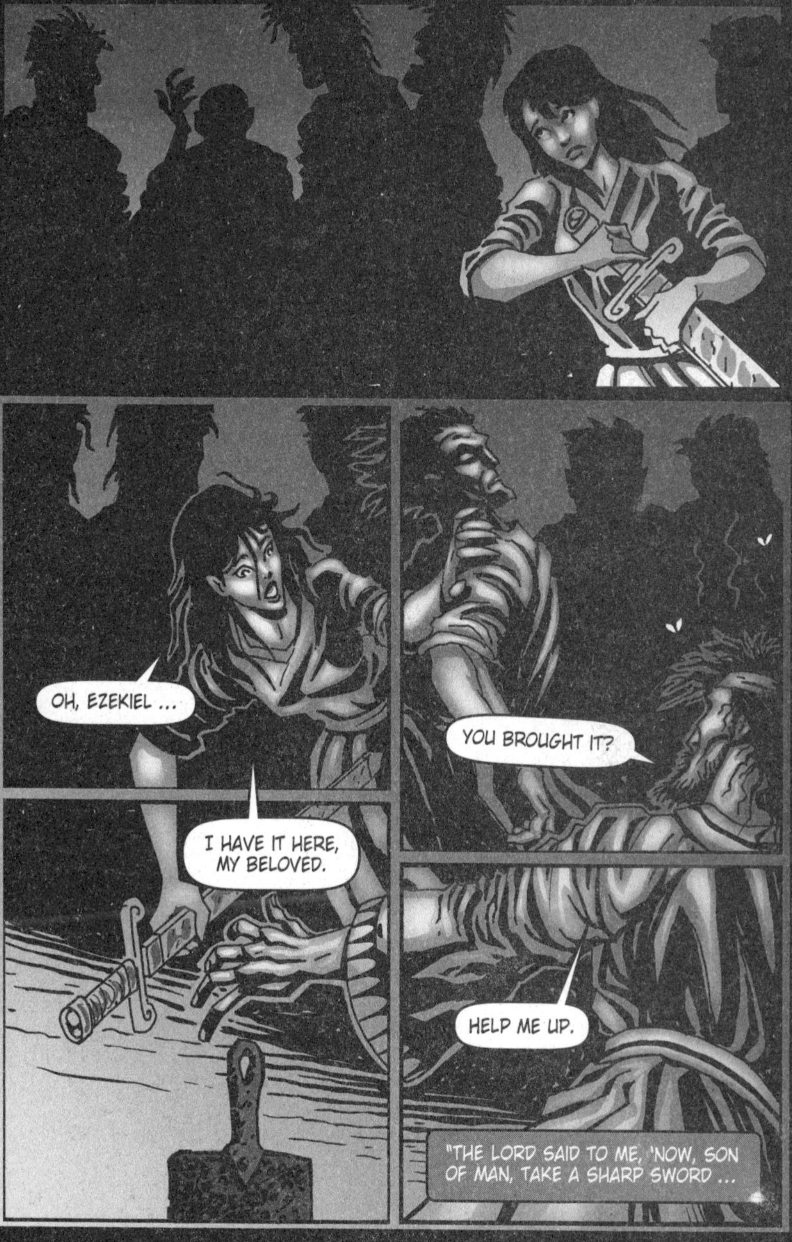
OH, EZEKIEL ...
YOU BROUGHT IT?
I HAVE IT HERE, MY BELOVED.
HELP ME UP.
"THE LORD SAID TO ME, 'NOW, SON OF MAN, TAKE A SHARP SWORD ...

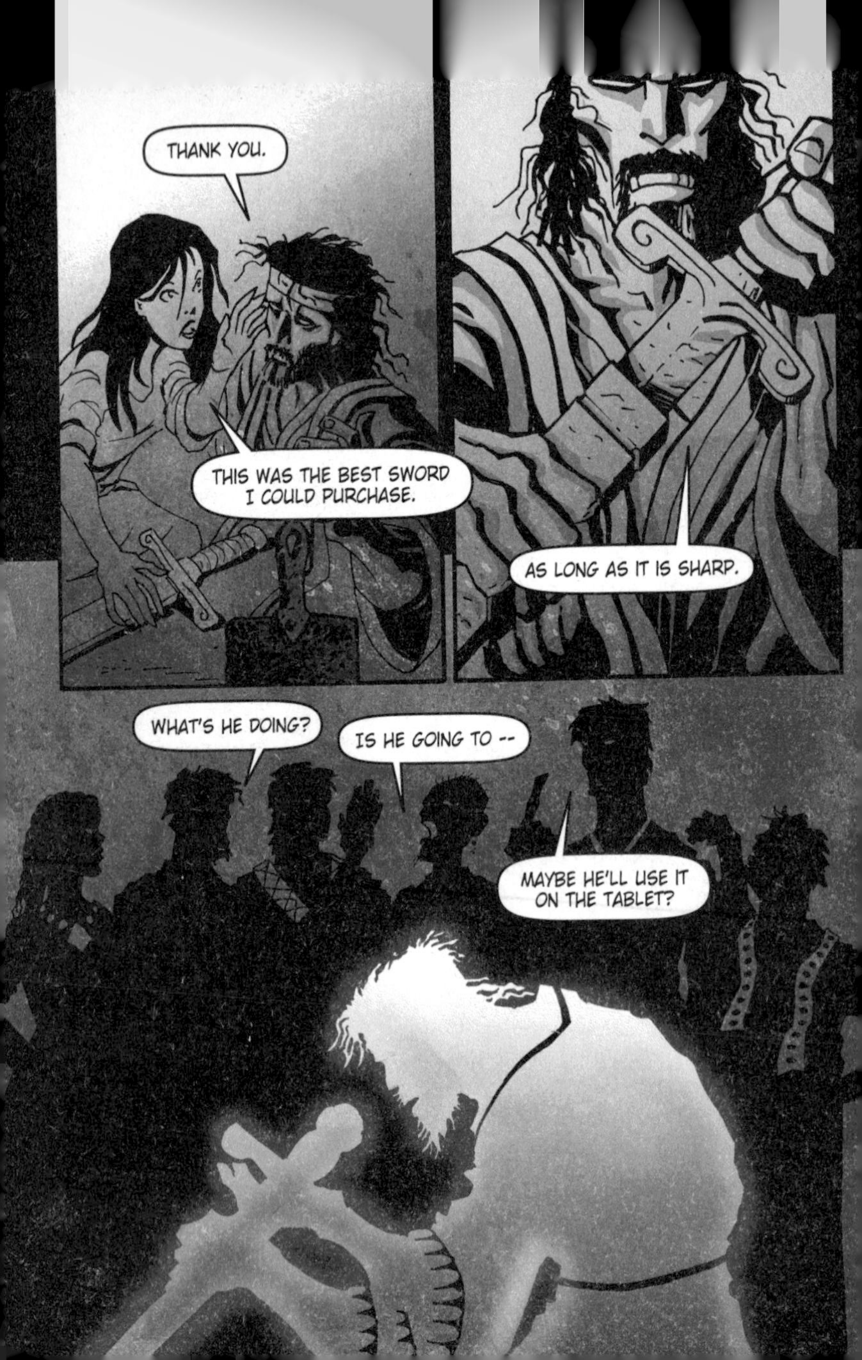
THANK YOU.
THIS WAS THE BEST SWORD I COULD PURCHASE.
AS LONG AS IT IS SHARP.
WHAT'S HE DOING?
IS HE GOING TO --
MAYBE HE'LL USE IT ON THE TABLET?

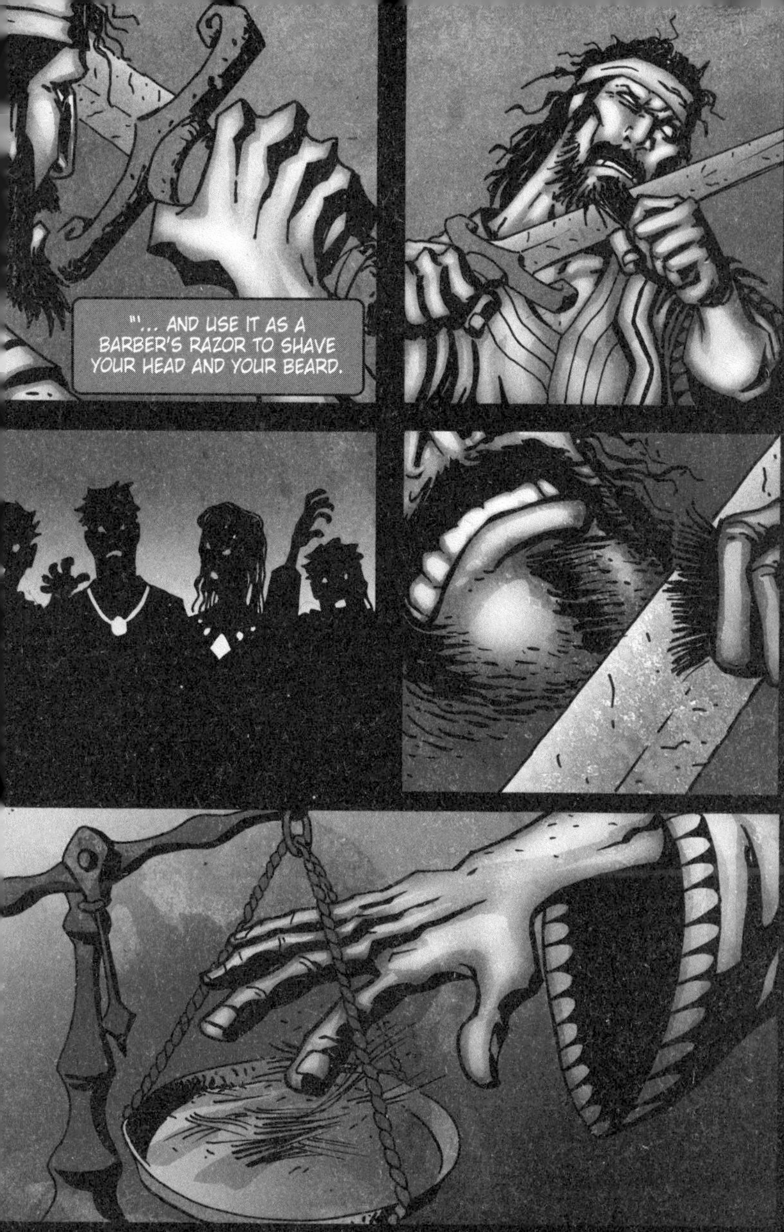
"'... AND USE IT AS A BARBER'S RAZOR TO SHAVE YOUR HEAD AND YOUR BEARD.

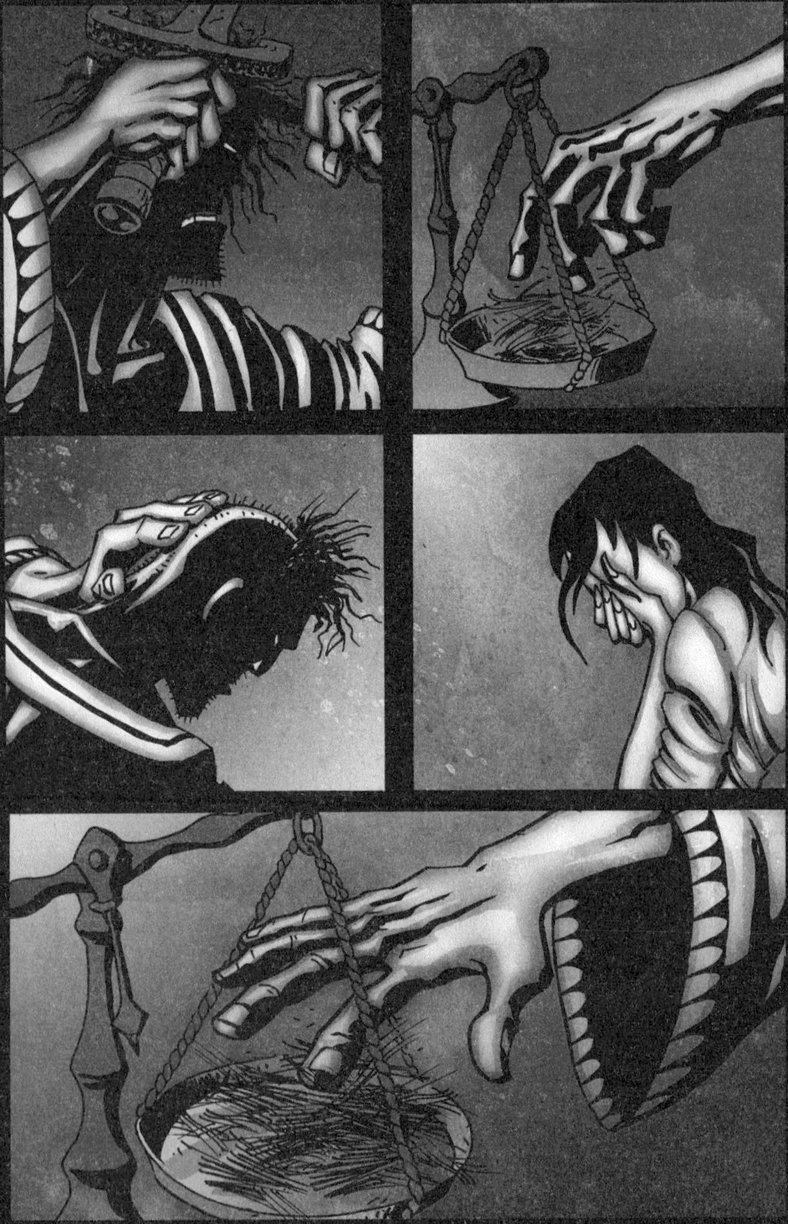

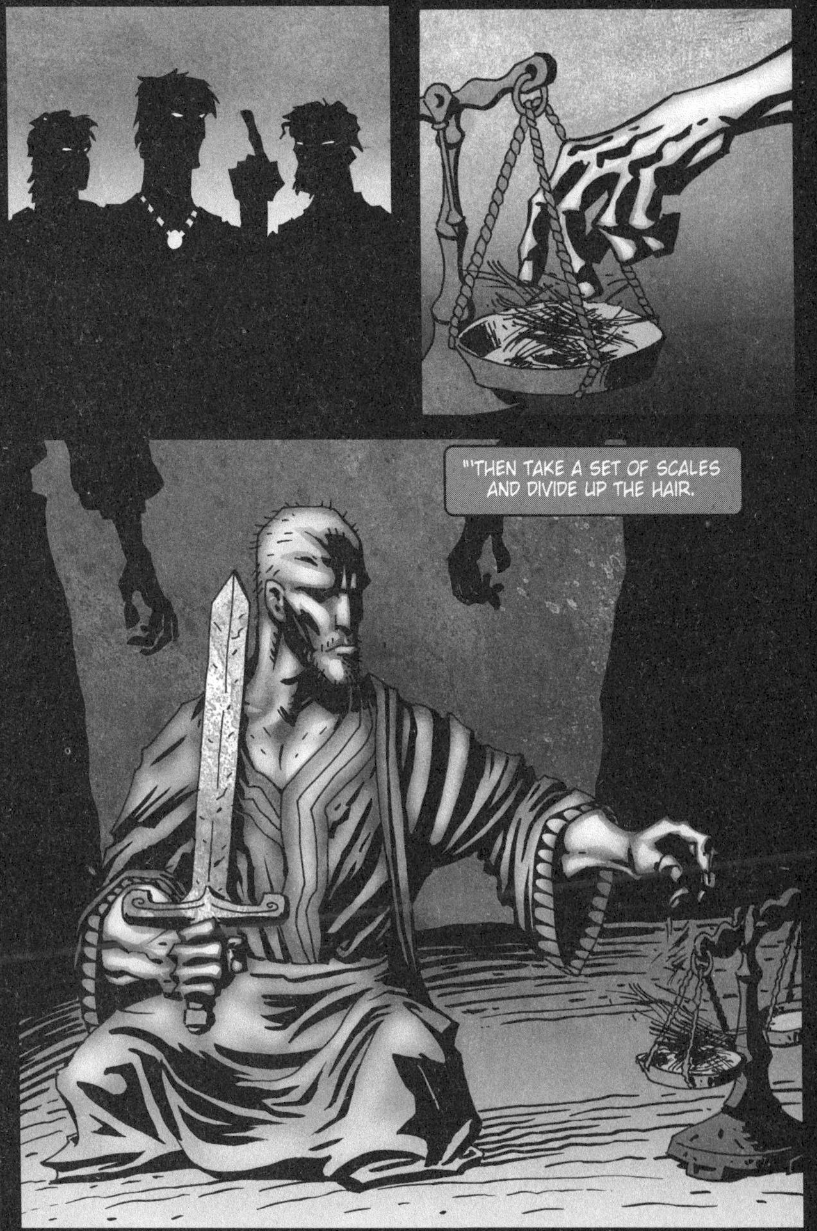
"'THEN TAKE A SET OF SCALES AND DIVIDE UP THE HAIR.

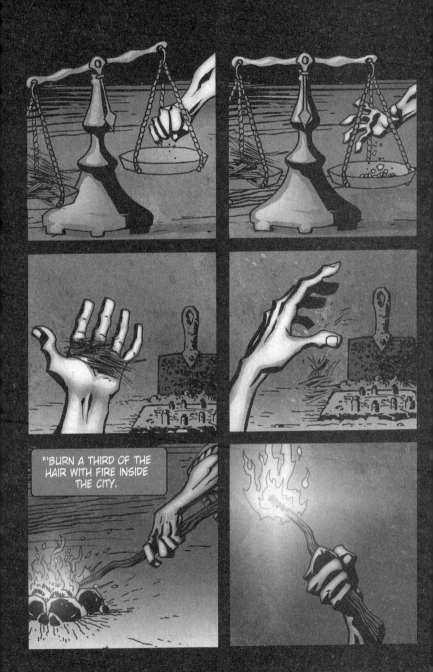

"'BURN A THIRD OF THE HAIR WITH FIRE INSIDE THE CITY.

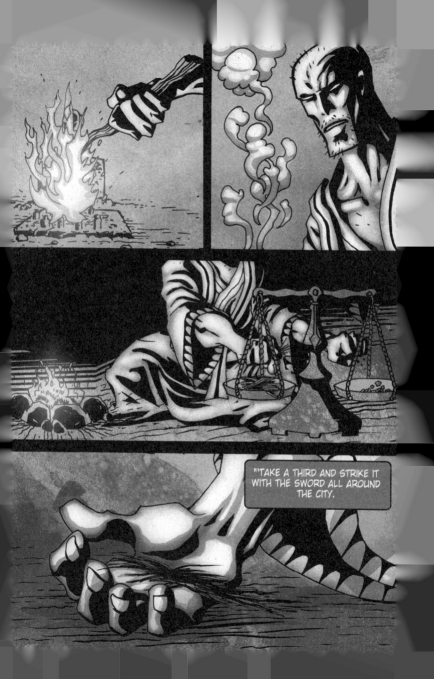

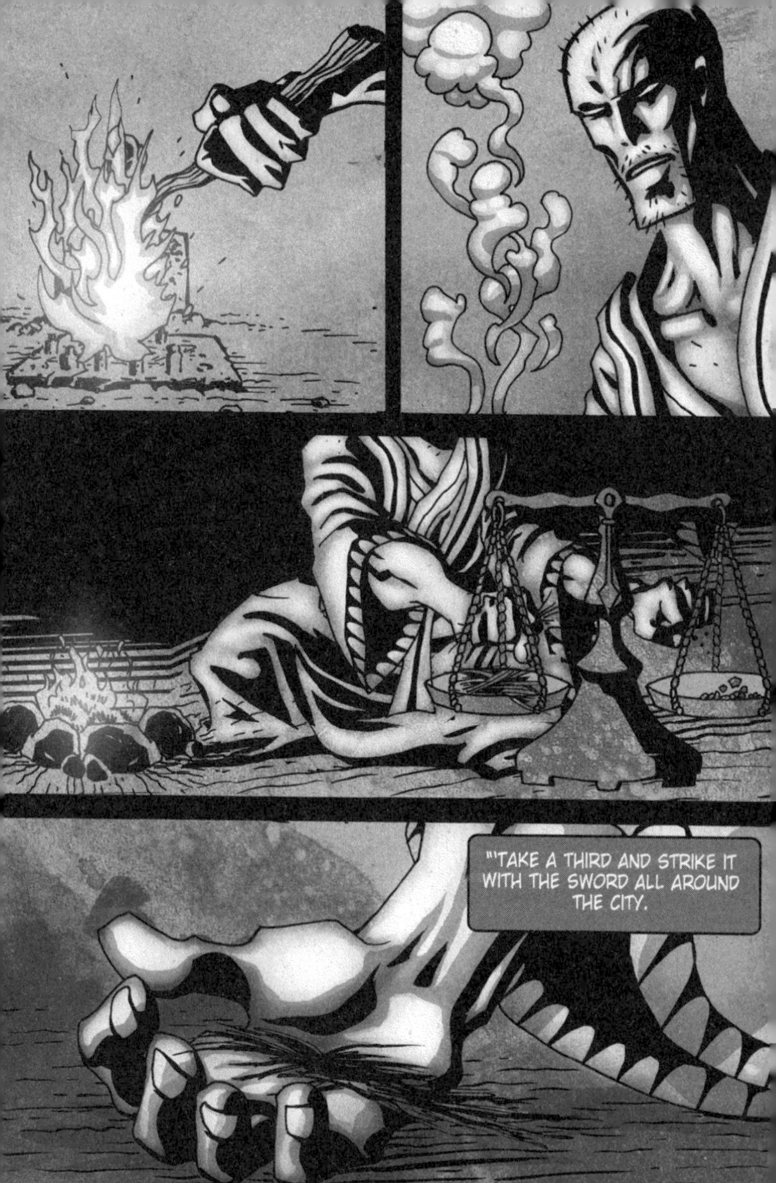
"'TAKE A THIRD AND STRIKE IT WITH THE SWORD ALL AROUND THE CITY.

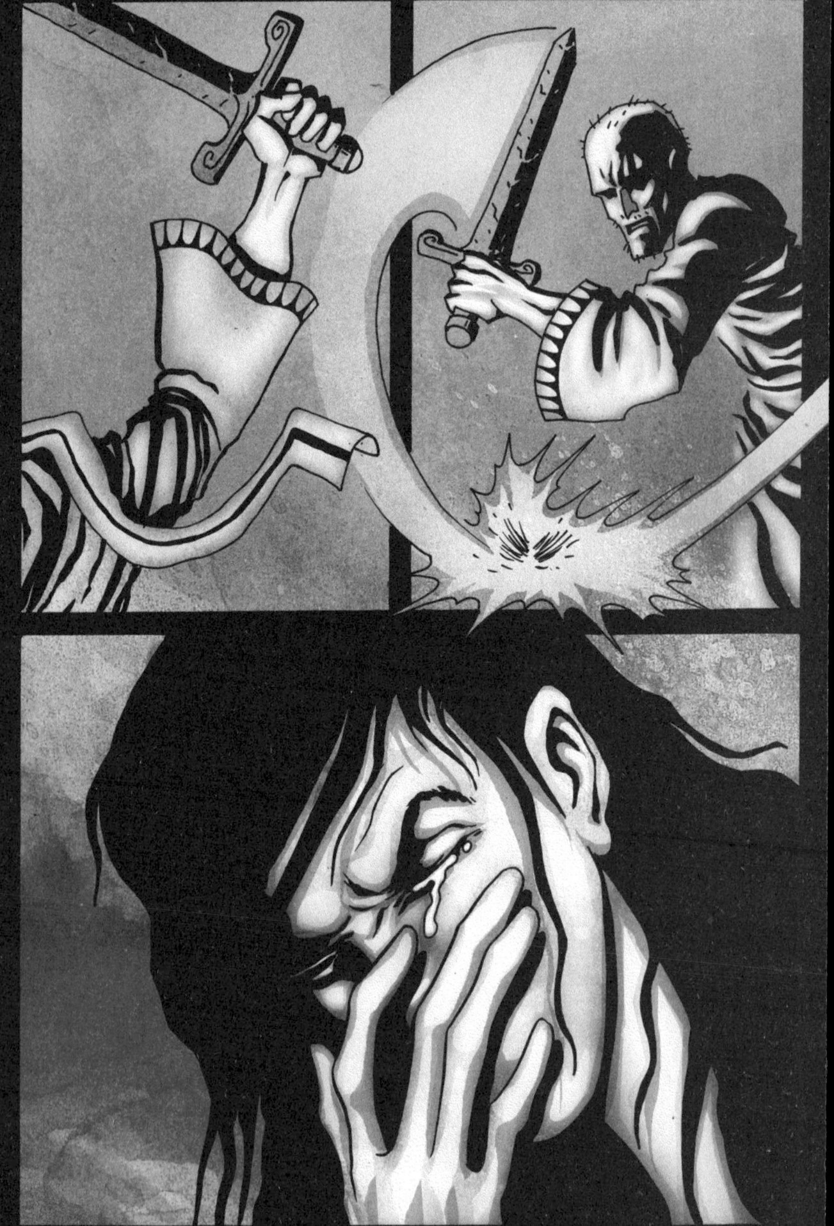

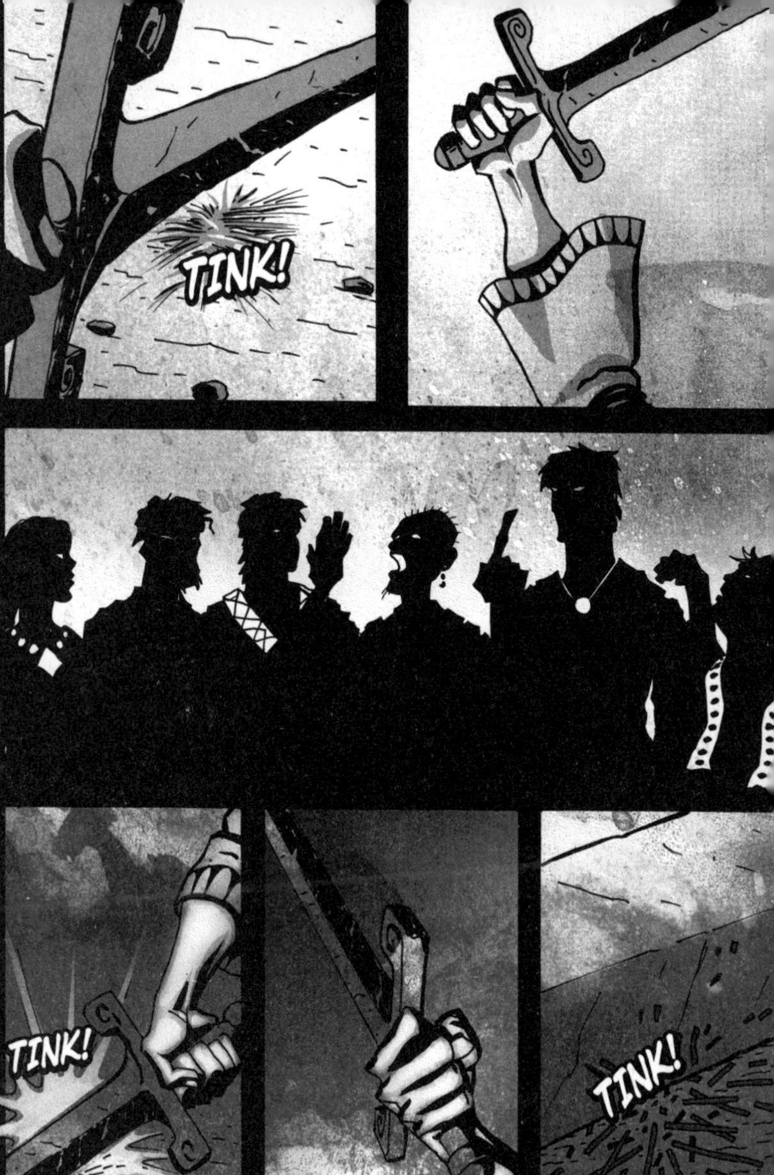
TINK!
TINK!
TINK!

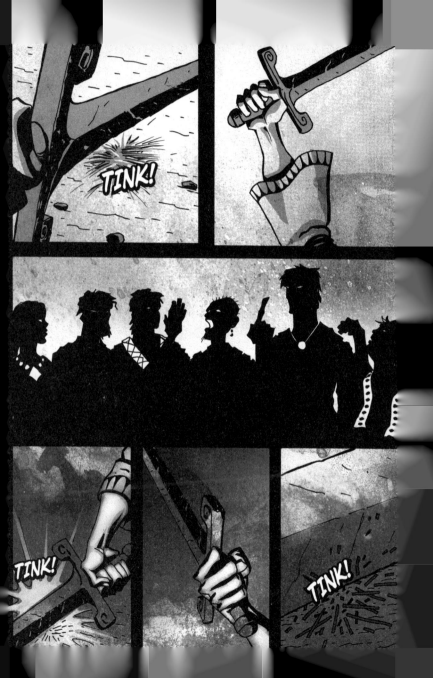

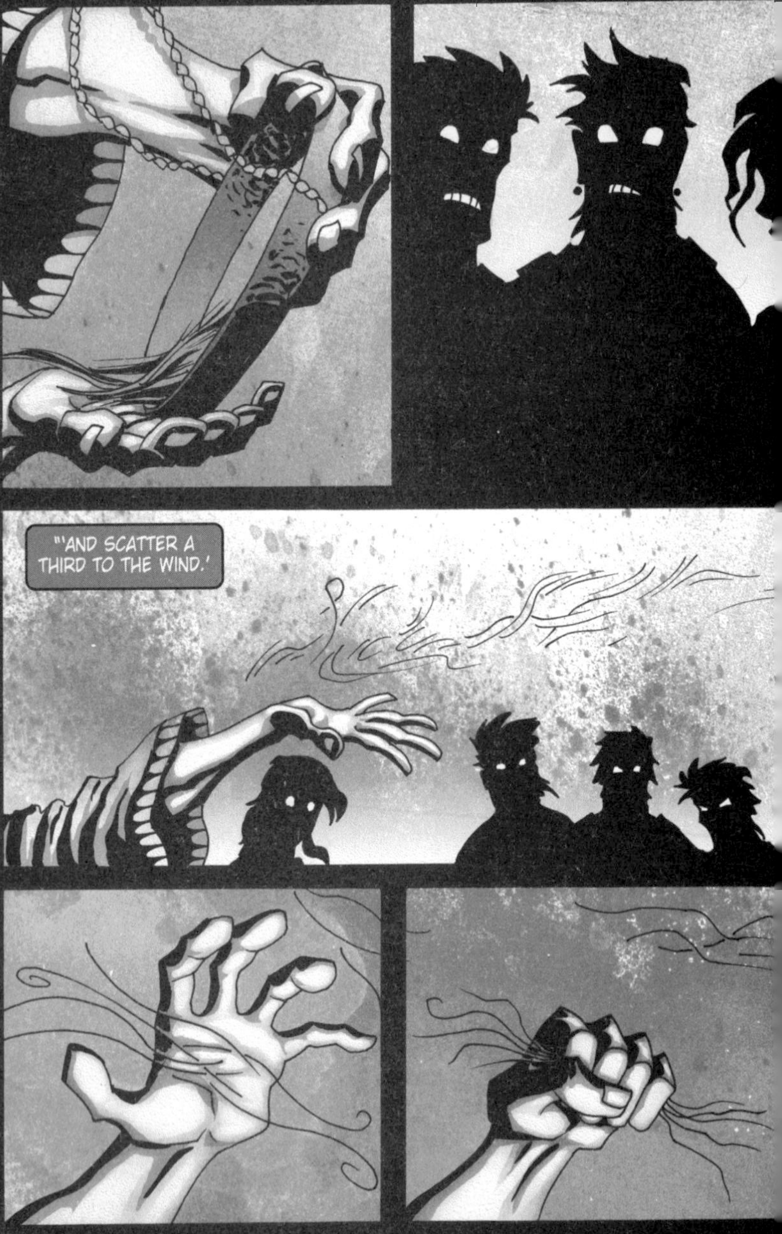
"'AND SCATTER A THIRD TO THE WIND.'

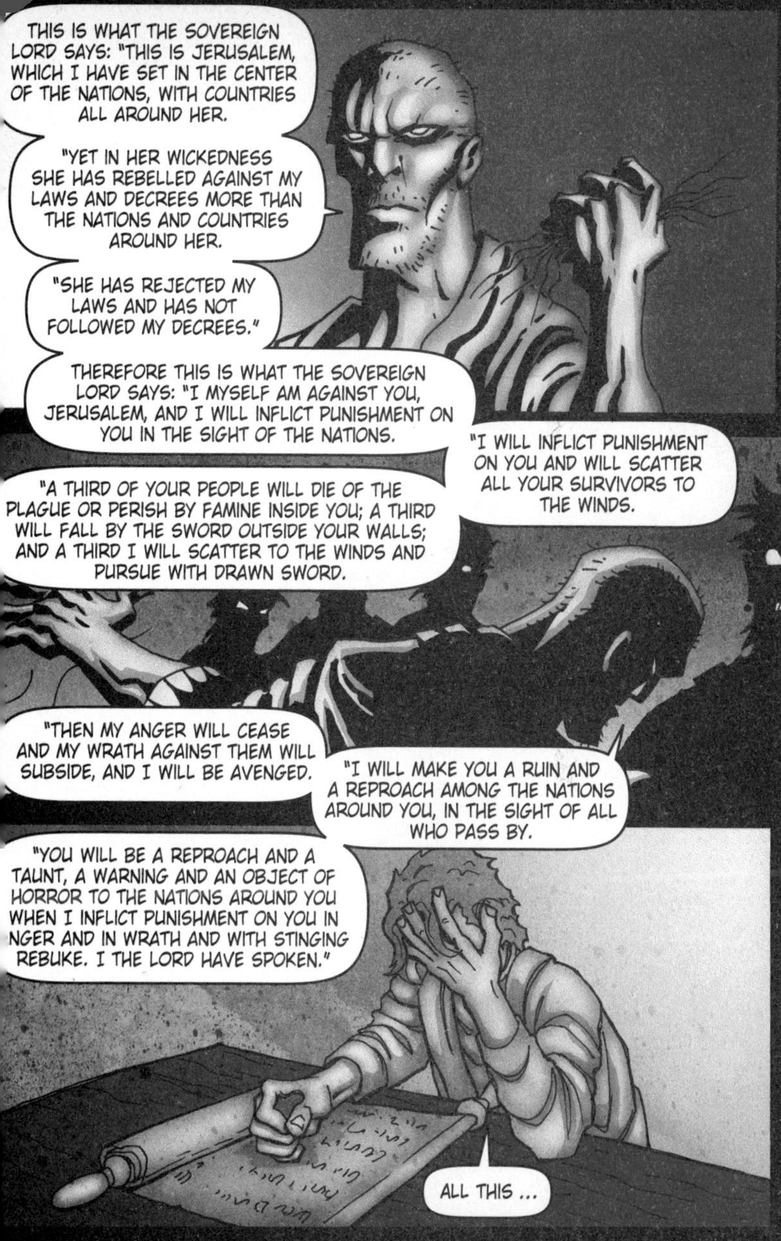
THIS IS WHAT THE SOVEREIGN LORD SAYS: "THIS IS JERUSALEM, WHICH I HAVE SET IN THE CENTER OF THE NATIONS, WITH COUNTRIES ALL AROUND HER.
"YET IN HER WICKEDNESS SHE HAS REBELLED AGAINST MY LAWS AND DECREES MORE THAN THE NATIONS AND COUNTRIES AROUND HER.
"SHE HAS REJECTED MY LAWS AND HAS NOT FOLLOWED MY DECREES."
THEREFORE THIS IS WHAT THE SOVEREIGN LORD SAYS: "I MYSELF AM AGAINST YOU, JERUSALEM, AND I WILL INFLICT PUNISHMENT ON YOU IN THE SIGHT OF THE NATIONS.
"I WILL INFLICT PUNISHMENT ON YOU AND WILL SCATTER ALL YOUR SURVIVORS TO THE WINDS.
"A THIRD OF YOUR PEOPLE WILL DIE OF THE PLAGUE OR PERISH BY FAMINE INSIDE YOU; A THIRD WILL FALL BY THE SWORD OUTSIDE YOUR WALLS; AND A THIRD I WILL SCATTER TO THE WINDS AND PURSUE WITH DRAWN SWORD.
"THEN MY ANGER WILL CEASE AND MY WRATH AGAINST THEM WILL SUBSIDE, AND I WILL BE AVENGED.
"I WILL MAKE YOU A RUIN AND A REPROACH AMONG THE NATIONS AROUND YOU, IN THE SIGHT OF ALL WHO PASS BY.
"YOU WILL BE A REPROACH AND A TAUNT, A WARNING AND AN OBJECT OF HORROR TO THE NATIONS AROUND YOU WHEN I INFLICT PUNISHMENT ON YOU IN NGER AND IN WRATH AND WITH STINGING REBUKE. I THE LORD HAVE SPOKEN."
ALL THIS ...

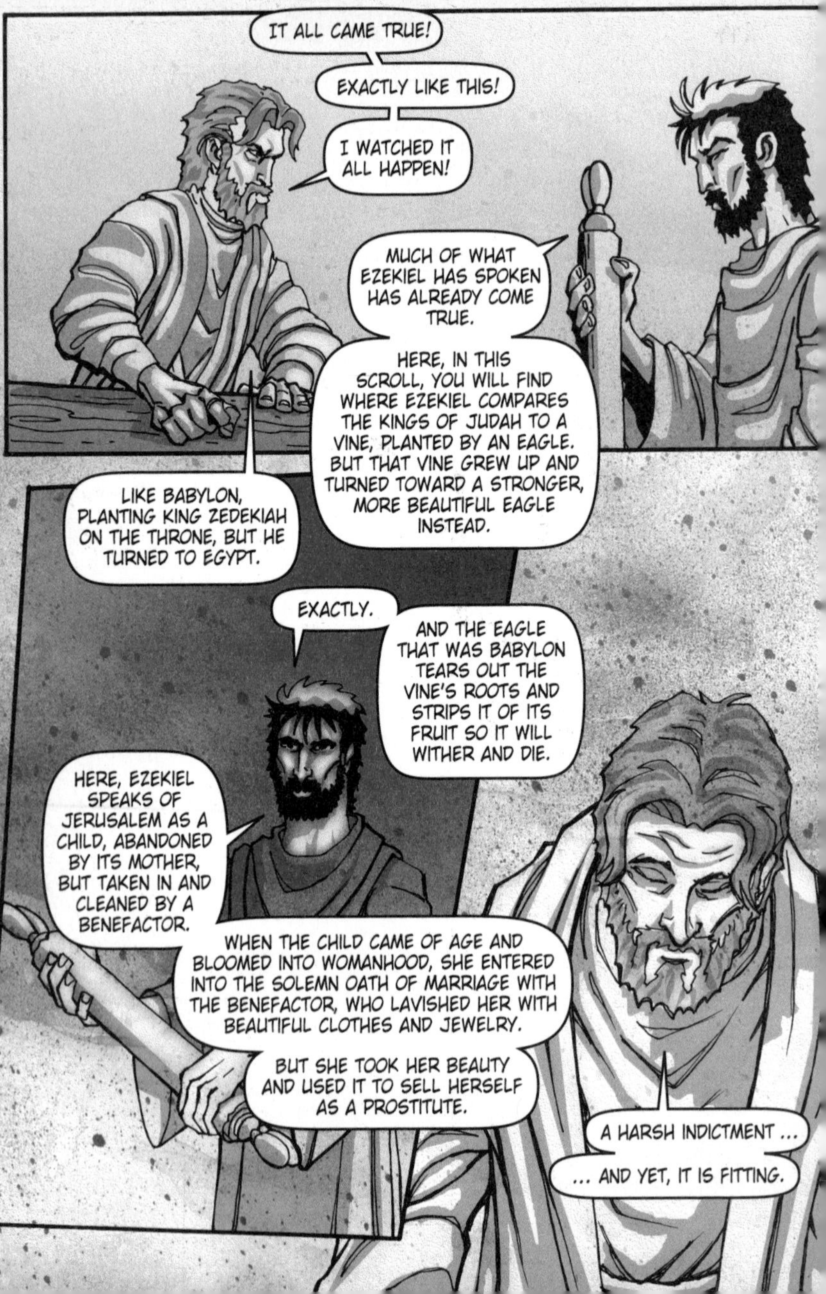
IT ALL CAME TRUE!
EXACTLY LIKE THIS!
I WATCHED IT ALL HAPPEN!
MUCH OF WHAT EZEKIEL HAS SPOKEN HAS ALREADY COME TRUE.
HERE, IN THIS SCROLL, YOU WILL FIND WHERE EZEKIEL COMPARES THE KINGS OF JUDAH TO A VINE, PLANTED BY AN EAGLE. BUT THAT VINE GREW UP AND TURNED TOWARD A STRONGER, MORE BEAUTIFUL EAGLE INSTEAD.
LIKE BABYLON, PLANTING KING ZEDEKIAH ON THE THRONE, BUT HE TURNED TO EGYPT.
EXACTLY.
AND THE EAGLE THAT WAS BABYLON TEARS OUT THE VINE'S ROOTS AND STRIPS IT OF ITS FRUIT SO IT WILL WITHER AND DIE.
HERE, EZEKIEL SPEAKS OF JERUSALEM AS A CHILD, ABANDONED BY ITS MOTHER, BUT TAKEN IN AND CLEANED BY A BENEFACTOR.
WHEN THE CHILD CAME OF AGE AND BLOOMED INTO WOMANHOOD, SHE ENTERED INTO THE SOLEMN OATH OF MARRIAGE WITH THE BENEFACTOR, WHO LAVISHED HER WITH BEAUTIFUL CLOTHES AND JEWELRY.
BUT SHE TOOK HER BEAUTY AND USED IT TO SELL HERSELF AS A PROSTITUTE.
A HARSH INDICTMENT ...
... AND YET, IT IS FITTING.

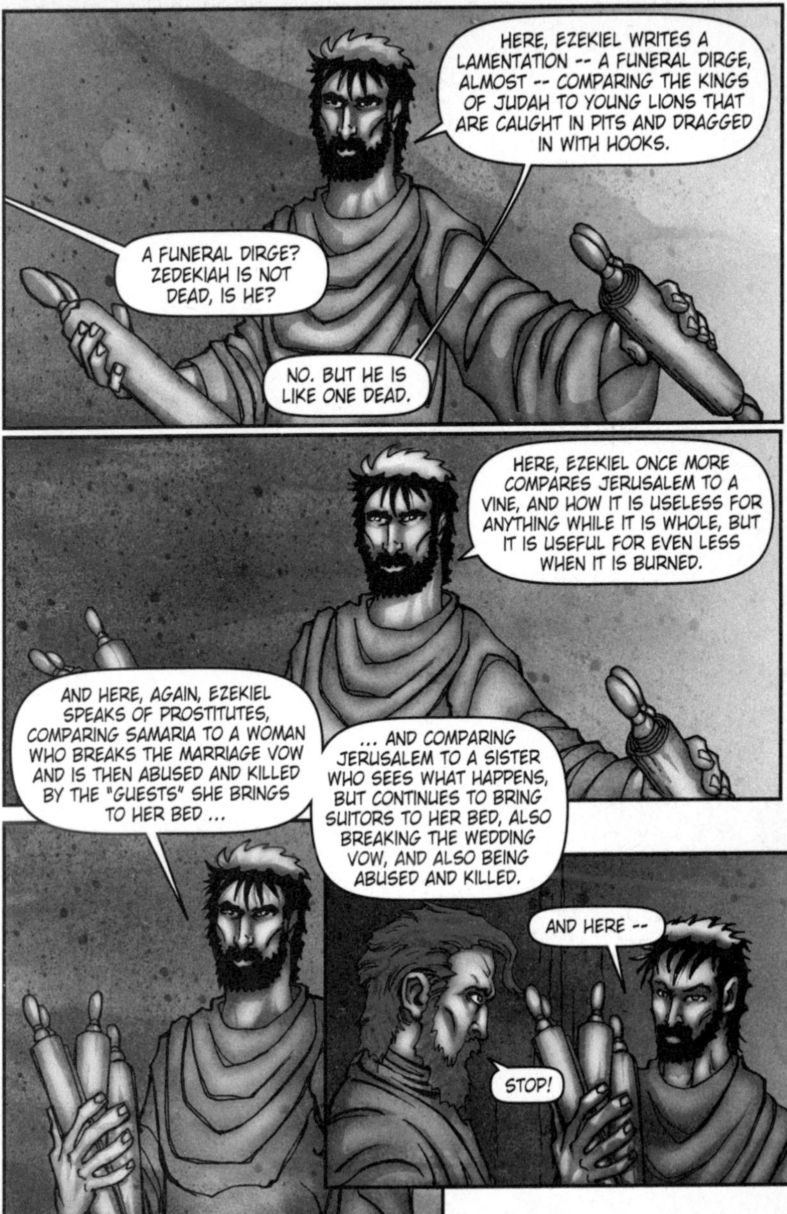
HERE, EZEKIEL WRITES A LAMENTATION -- A FUNERAL DIRGE, ALMOST -- COMPARING THE KINGS OF JUDAH TO YOUNG LIONS THAT ARE CAUGHT IN PITS AND DRAGGED IN WITH HOOKS.
A FUNERAL DIRGE? ZEDEKIAH IS NOT DEAD, IS HE?
NO. BUT HE IS LIKE ONE DEAD.
HERE, EZEKIEL ONCE MORE COMPARES JERUSALEM TO A VINE, AND HOW IT IS USELESS FOR ANYTHING WHILE IT IS WHOLE, BUT IT IS USEFUL FOR EVEN LESS WHEN IT IS BURNED.
AND HERE, AGAIN, EZEKIEL SPEAKS OF PROSTITUTES, COMPARING SAMARIA TO A WOMAN WHO BREAKS THE MARRIAGE VOW AND IS THEN ABUSED AND KILLED BY THE "GUESTS" SHE BRINGS TO HER BED ...
... AND COMPARING JERUSALEM TO A SISTER WHO SEES WHAT HAPPENS, BUT CONTINUES TO BRING SUITORS TO HER BED, ALSO BREAKING THE WEDDING VOW, AND ALSO BEING ABUSED AND KILLED.
AND HERE --
STOP!

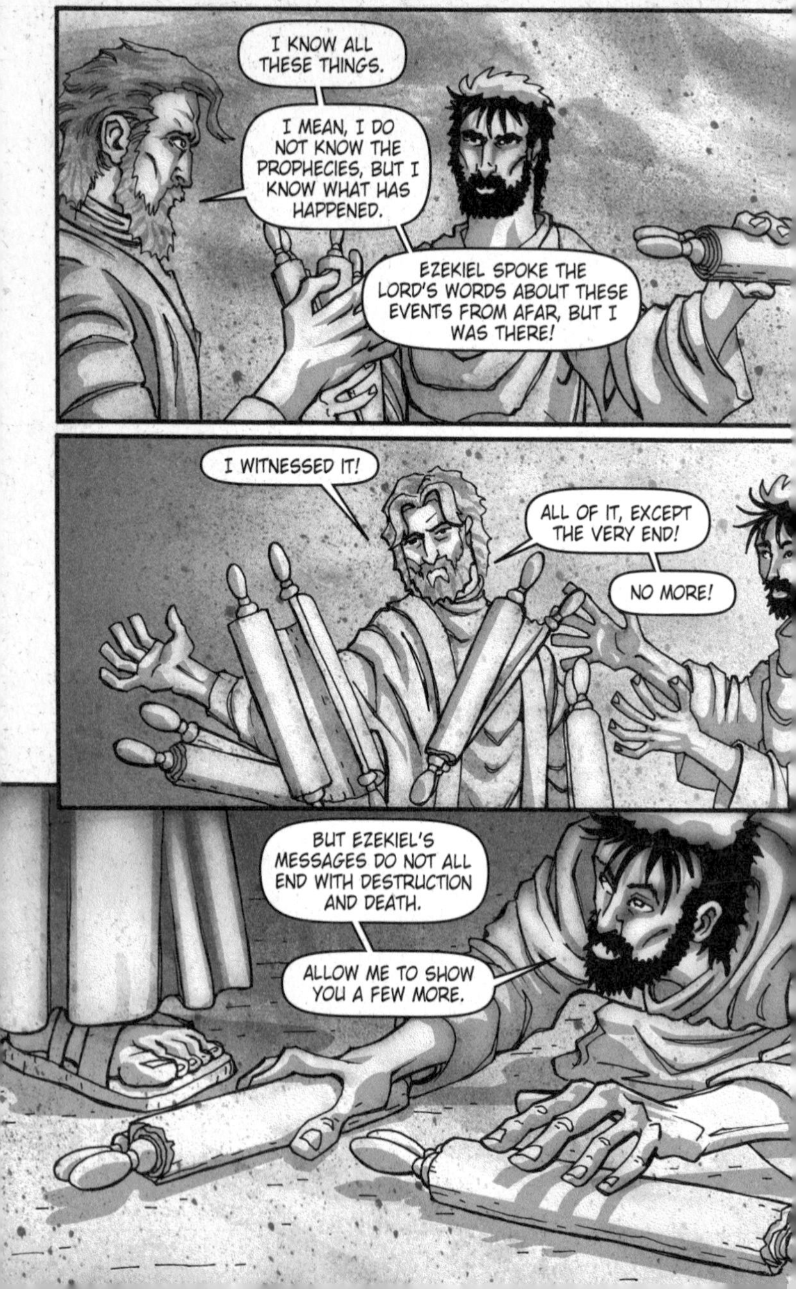
I KNOW ALL THESE THINGS.
I MEAN, I DO NOT KNOW THE PROPHECIES, BUT I KNOW WHAT HAS HAPPENED.
EZEKIEL SPOKE THE LORD'S WORDS ABOUT THESE EVENTS FROM AFAR, BUT I WAS THERE!
I WITNESSED IT!
ALL OF IT, EXCEPT THE VERY END!
NO MORE!
BUT EZEKIEL'S MESSAGES DO NOT ALL END WITH DESTRUCTION AND DEATH.
ALLOW ME TO SHOW YOU A FEW MORE.

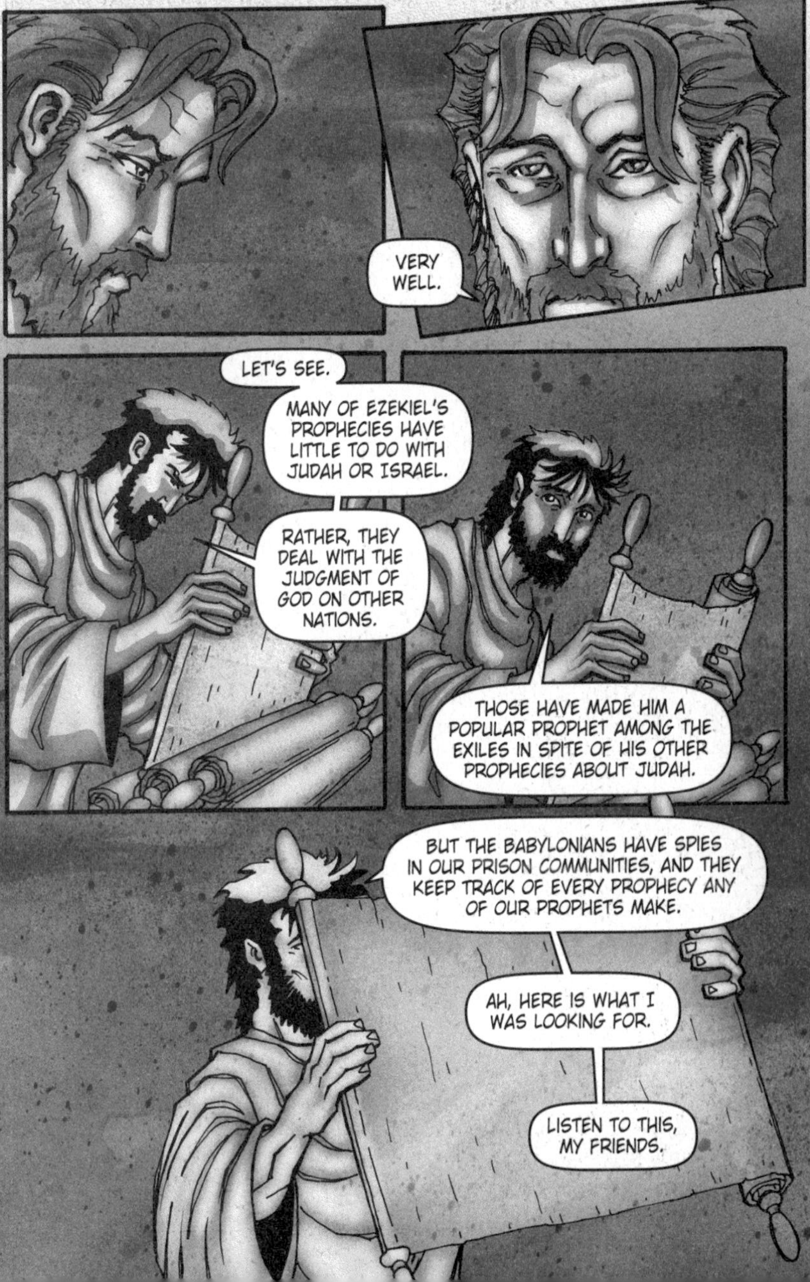
VERY WELL.
LET'S SEE.
MANY OF EZEKIEL'S PROPHECIES HAVE LITTLE TO DO WITH JUDAH OR ISRAEL.
RATHER, THEY DEAL WITH THE JUDGMENT OF GOD ON OTHER NATIONS.
THOSE HAVE MADE HIM A POPULAR PROPHET AMONG THE EXILES IN SPITE OF HIS OTHER PROPHECIES ABOUT JUDAH.
BUT THE BABYLONIANS HAVE SPIES IN OUR PRISON COMMUNITIES, AND THEY KEEP TRACK OF EVERY PROPHECY ANY OF OUR PROPHETS MAKE.
AH, HERE IS WHAT I WAS LOOKING FOR.
LISTEN TO THIS, MY FRIENDS.

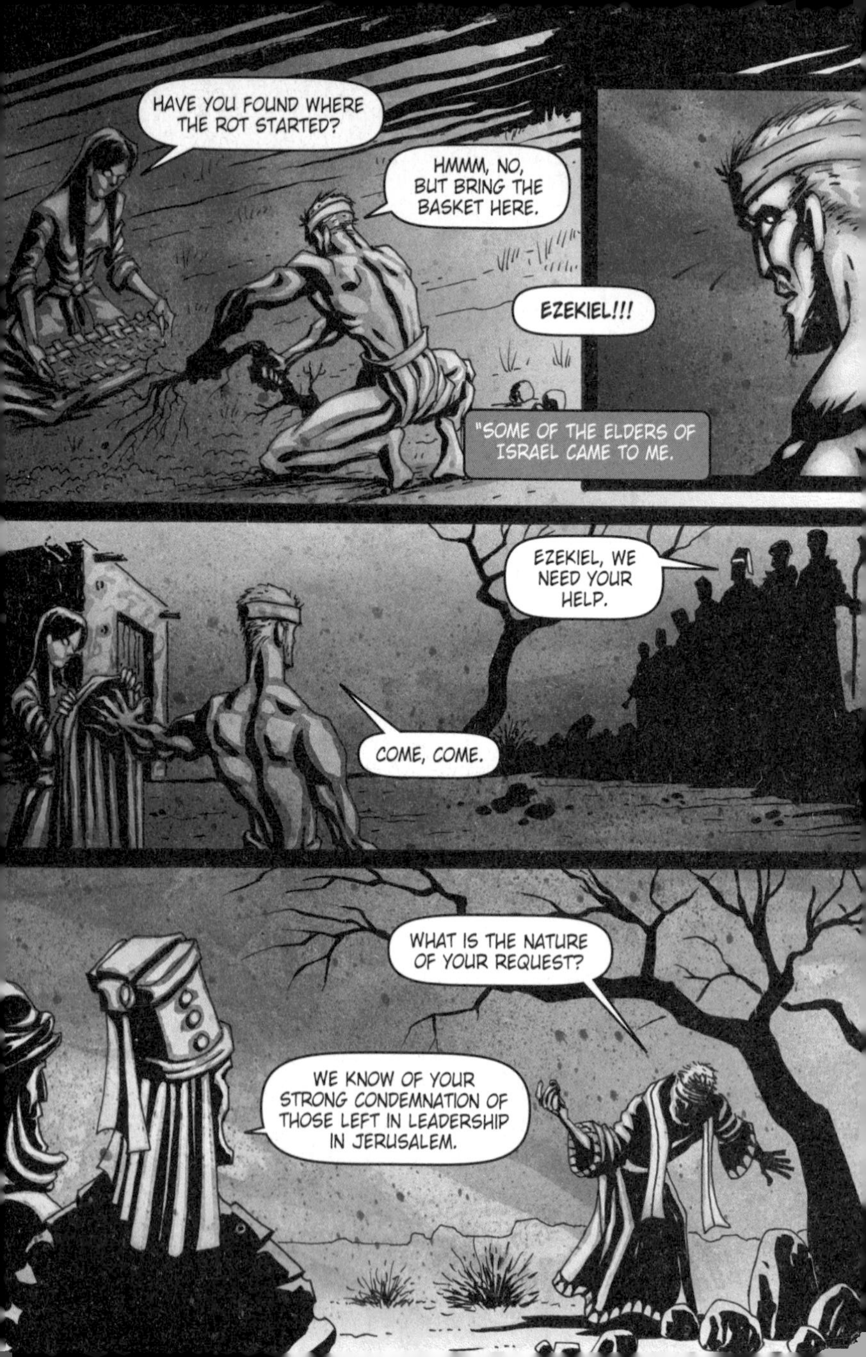
HAVE YOU FOUND WHERE THE ROT STARTED?
HMMM, NO, BUT BRING THE BASKET HERE.
EZEKIEL!!!
"SOME OF THE ELDERS OF ISRAEL CAME TO ME.
EZEKIEL, WE NEED YOUR HELP.
COME, COME.
WHAT IS THE NATURE OF YOUR REQUEST?
WE KNOW OF YOUR STRONG CONDEMNATION OF THOSE LEFT IN LEADERSHIP IN JERUSALEM.

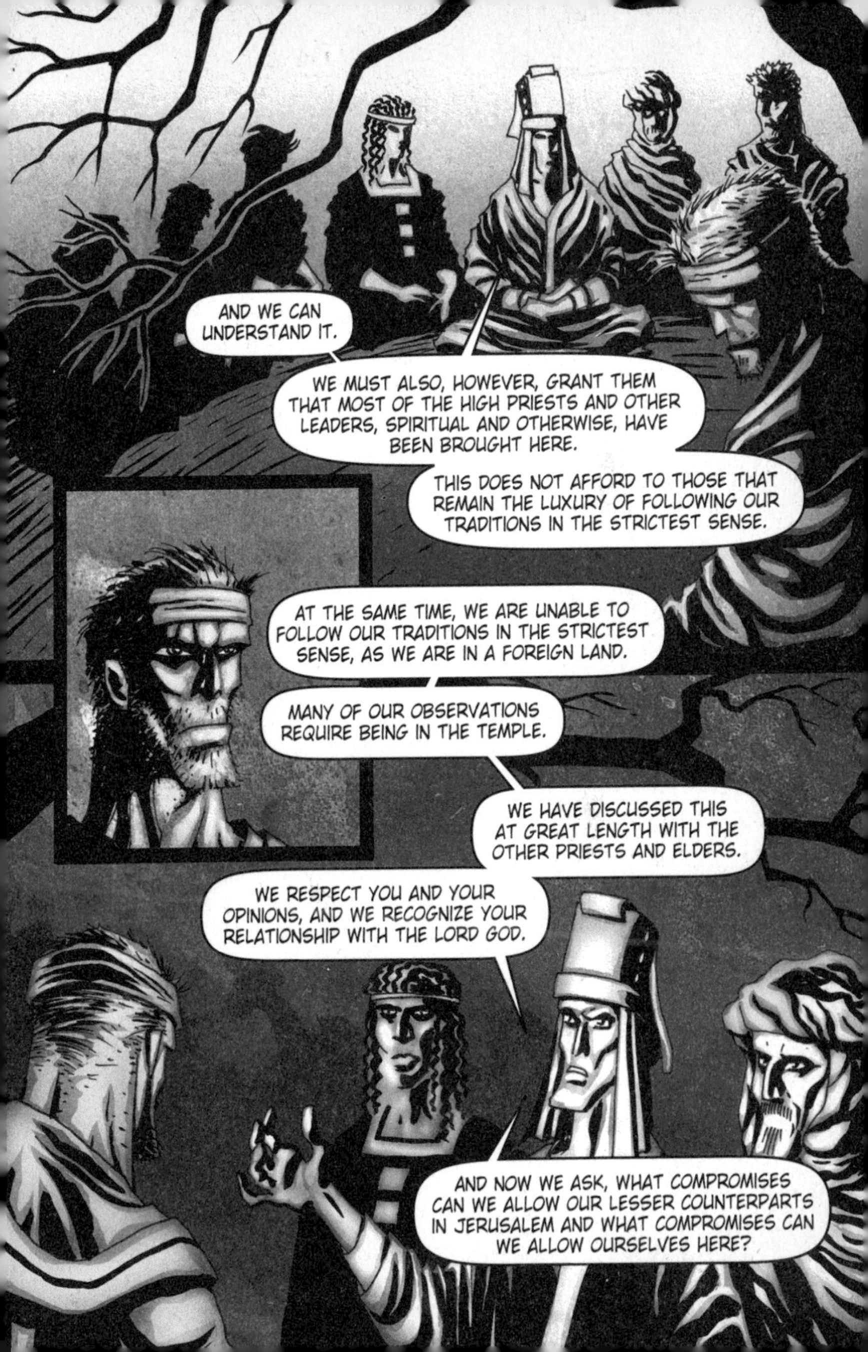
AND WE CAN UNDERSTAND IT.
WE MUST ALSO, HOWEVER, GRANT THEM THAT MOST OF THE HIGH PRIESTS AND OTHER LEADERS, SPIRITUAL AND OTHERWISE, HAVE BEEN BROUGHT HERE.
THIS DOES NOT AFFORD TO THOSE THAT REMAIN THE LUXURY OF FOLLOWING OUR TRADITIONS IN THE STRICTEST SENSE.
AT THE SAME TIME, WE ARE UNABLE TO FOLLOW OUR TRADITIONS IN THE STRICTEST SENSE, AS WE ARE IN A FOREIGN LAND.
MANY OF OUR OBSERVATIONS REQUIRE BEING IN THE TEMPLE.
WE HAVE DISCUSSED THIS AT GREAT LENGTH WITH THE OTHER PRIESTS AND ELDERS.
WE RESPECT YOU AND YOUR OPINIONS, AND WE RECOGNIZE YOUR RELATIONSHIP WITH THE LORD GOD.
AND NOW WE ASK, WHAT COMPROMISES CAN WE ALLOW OUR LESSER COUNTERPARTS IN JERUSALEM AND WHAT COMPROMISES CAN WE ALLOW OURSELVES HERE?

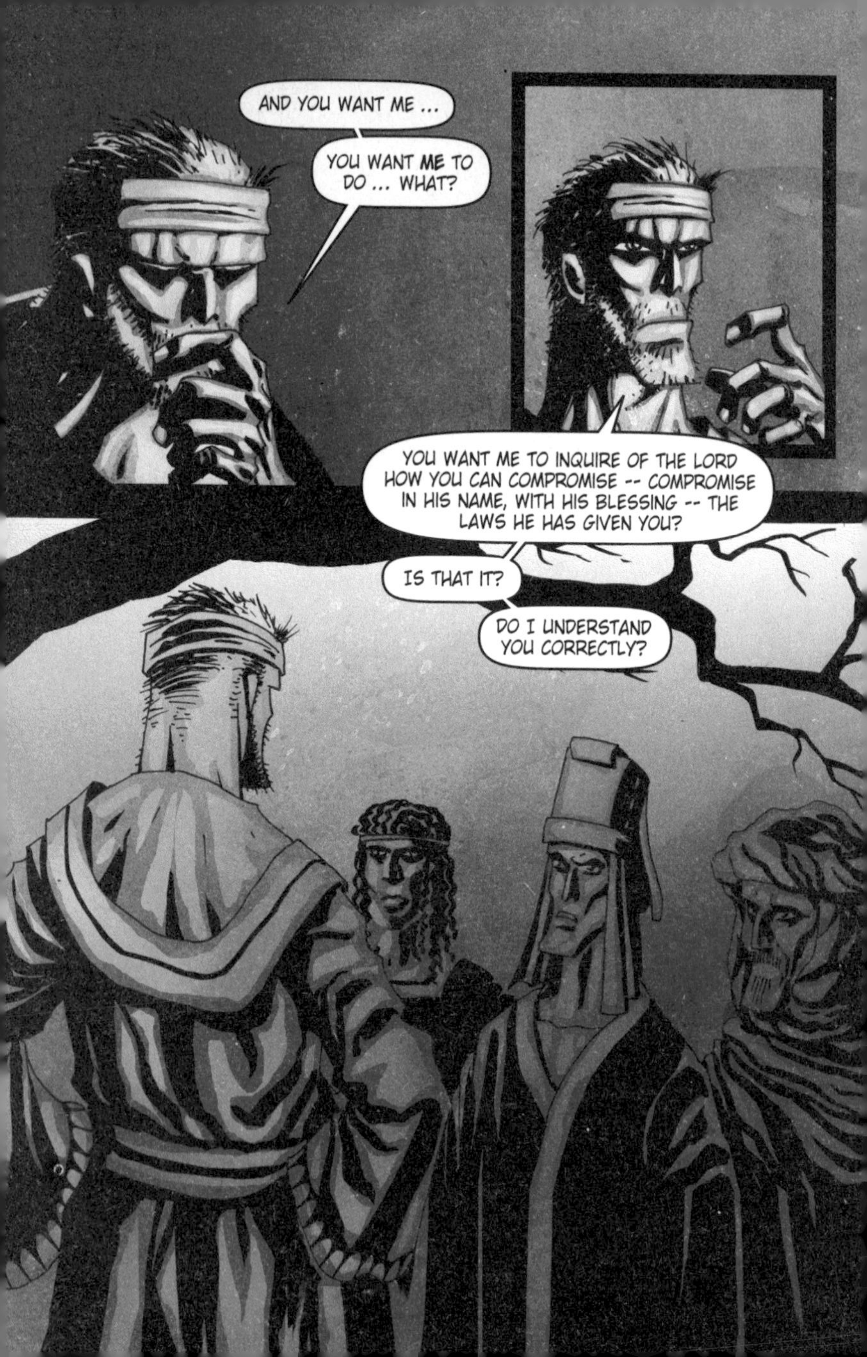
AND YOU WANT ME ...
YOU WANT ME TO DO ... WHAT?
YOU WANT ME TO INQUIRE OF THE LORD HOW YOU CAN COMPROMISE -- COMPROMISE IN HIS NAME, WITH HIS BLESSING -- THE LAWS HE HAS GIVEN YOU?
IS THAT IT?
DO I UNDERSTAND YOU CORRECTLY?

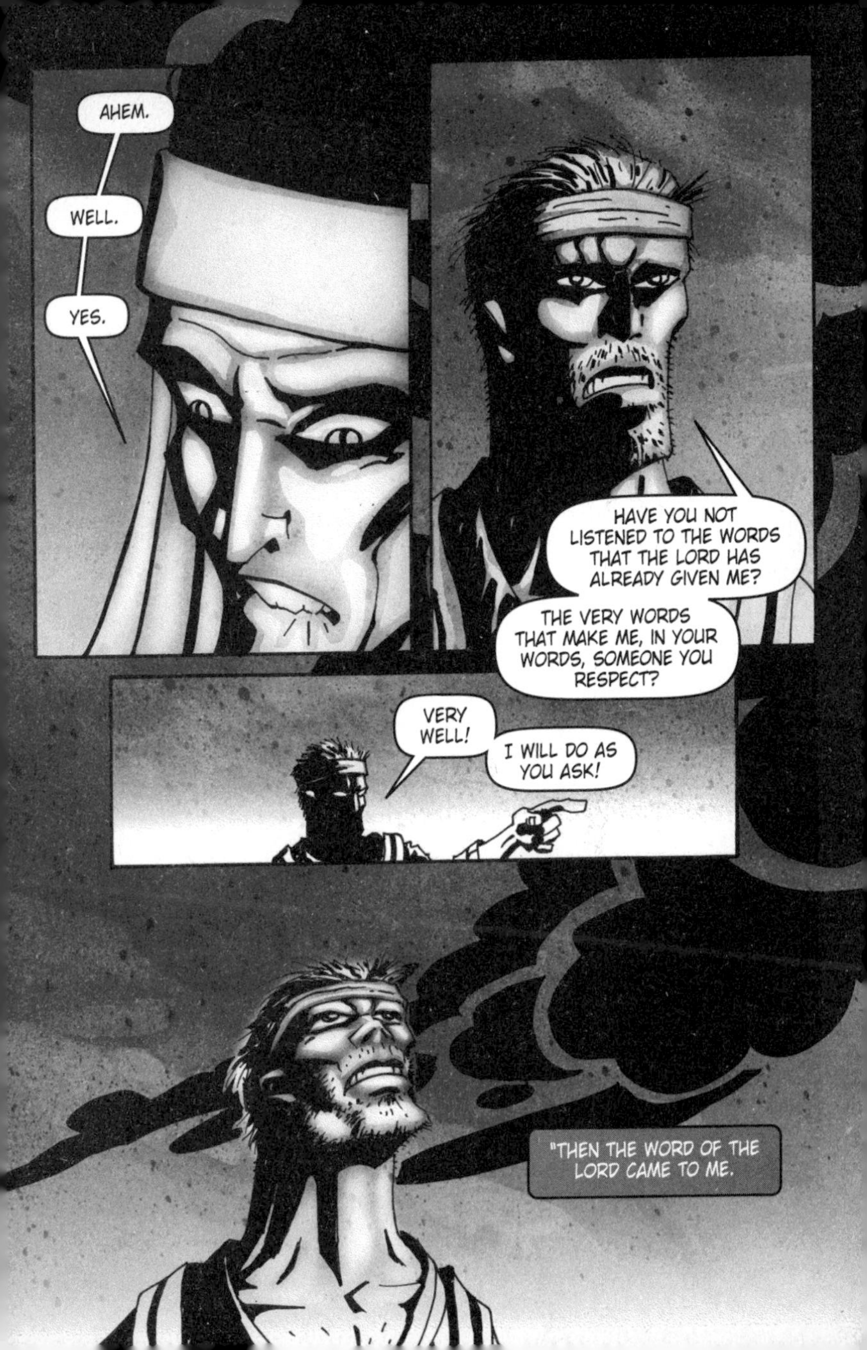
AHEM.
WELL.
YES.
HAVE YOU NOT LISTENED TO THE WORDS THAT THE LORD HAS ALREADY GIVEN ME?
THE VERY WORDS THAT MAKE ME, IN YOUR WORDS, SOMEONE YOU RESPECT?
VERY WELL!
I WILL DO AS YOU ASK!
"THEN THE WORD OF THE LORD CAME TO ME.

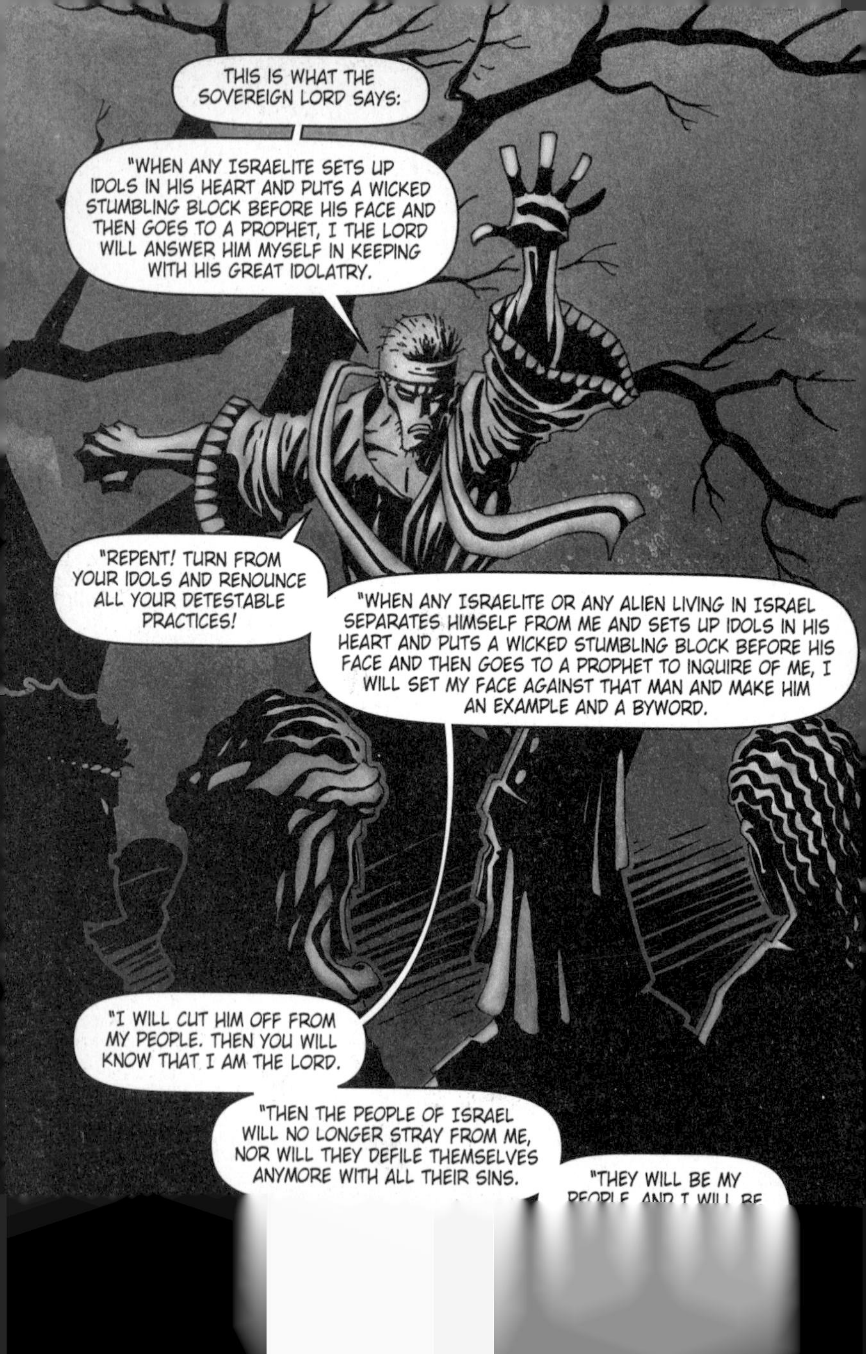
THIS IS WHAT THE SOVEREIGN LORD SAYS:
"WHEN ANY ISRAELITE SETS UP IDOLS IN HIS HEART AND PUTS A WICKED STUMBLING BLOCK BEFORE HIS FACE AND THEN GOES TO A PROPHET, I THE LORD WILL ANSWER HIM MYSELF IN KEEPING WITH HIS GREAT IDOLATRY.
"REPENT! TURN FROM YOUR IDOLS AND RENOUNCE ALL YOUR DETESTABLE PRACTICES!
"WHEN ANY ISRAELITE OR ANY ALIEN LIVING IN ISRAEL SEPARATES HIMSELF FROM ME AND SETS UP IDOLS IN HIS HEART AND PUTS A WICKED STUMBLING BLOCK BEFORE HIS FACE AND THEN GOES TO A PROPHET TO INQUIRE OF ME, I WILL SET MY FACE AGAINST THAT MAN AND MAKE HIM AN EXAMPLE AND A BYWORD.
"I WILL CUT HIM OFF FROM MY PEOPLE. THEN YOU WILL KNOW THAT I AM THE LORD.
"THEN THE PEOPLE OF ISRAEL WILL NO LONGER STRAY FROM ME, NOR WILL THEY DEFILE THEMSELVES ANYMORE WITH ALL THEIR SINS.
"THEY WILL BE MY

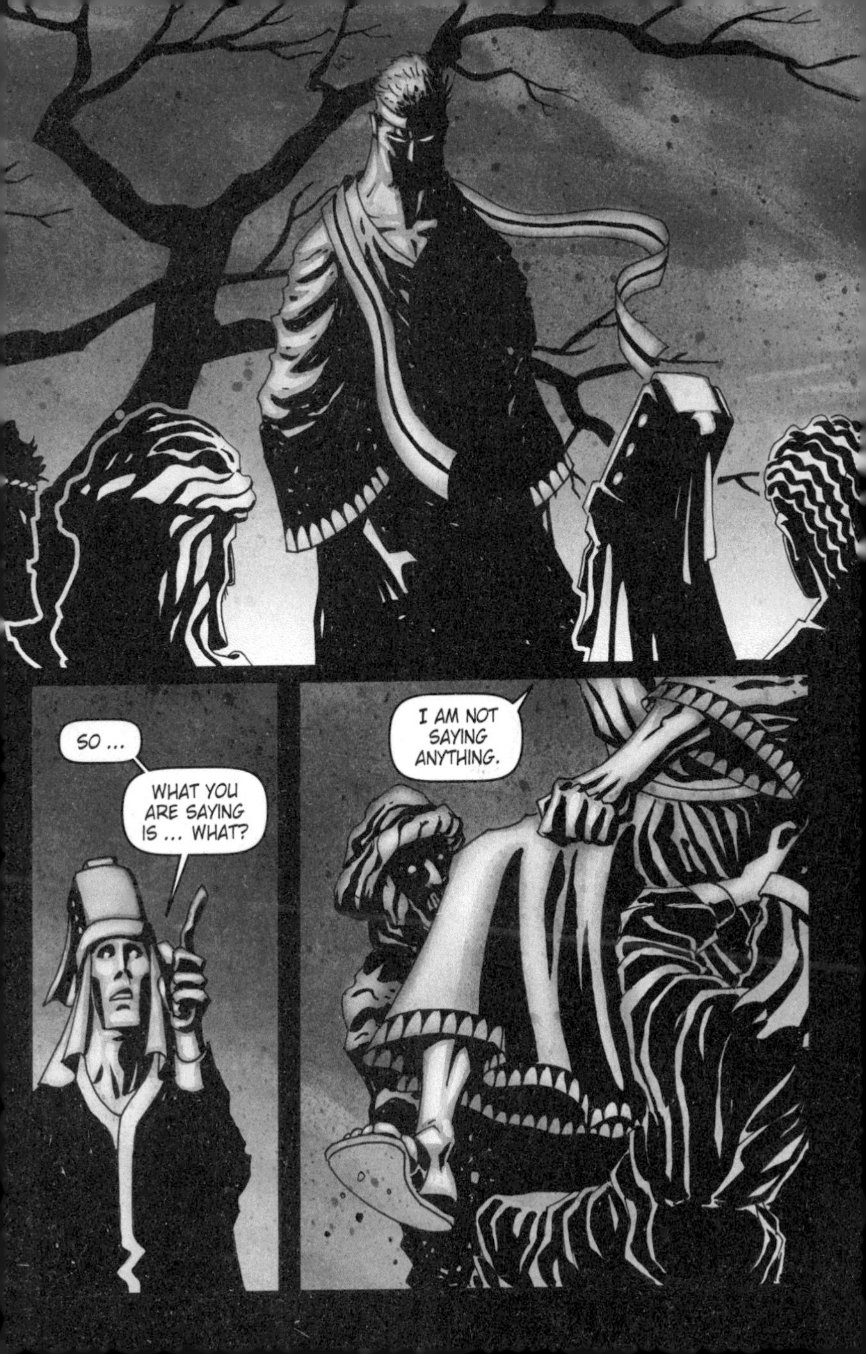
SO ...
WHAT YOU ARE SAYING IS ... WHAT?
I AM NOT SAYING ANYTHING.

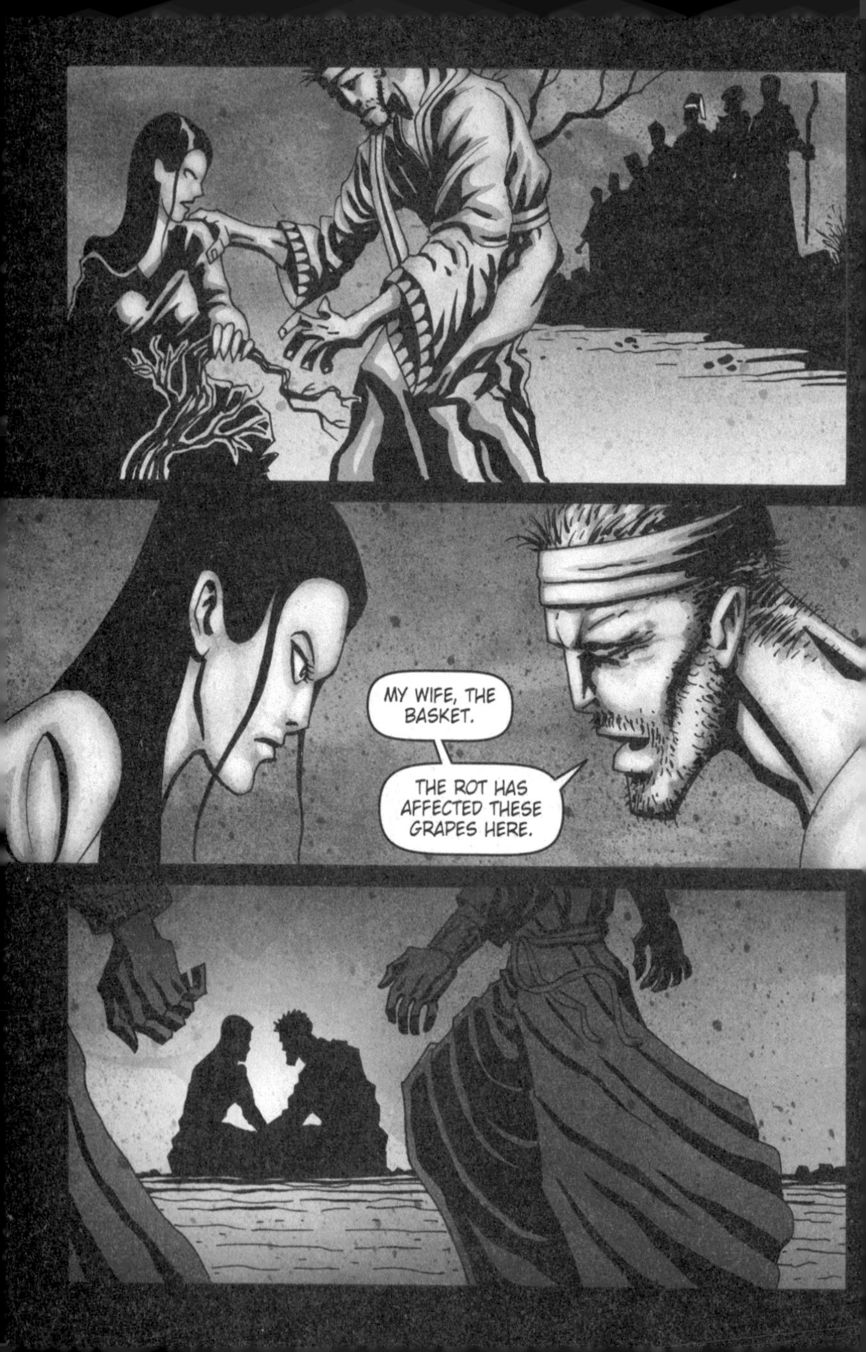
MY WIFE, THE BASKET.
THE ROT HAS AFFECTED THESE GRAPES HERE.

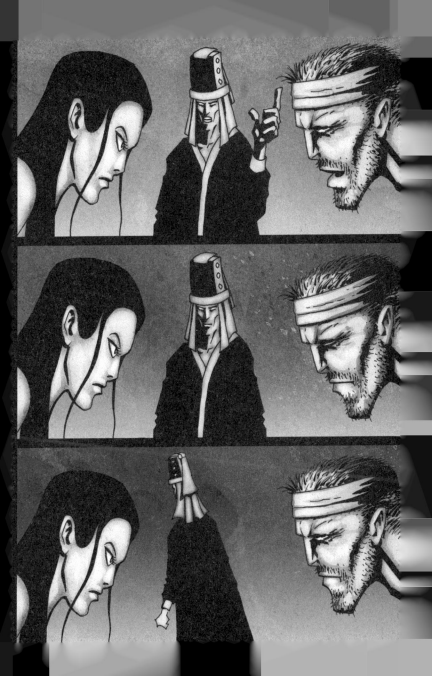

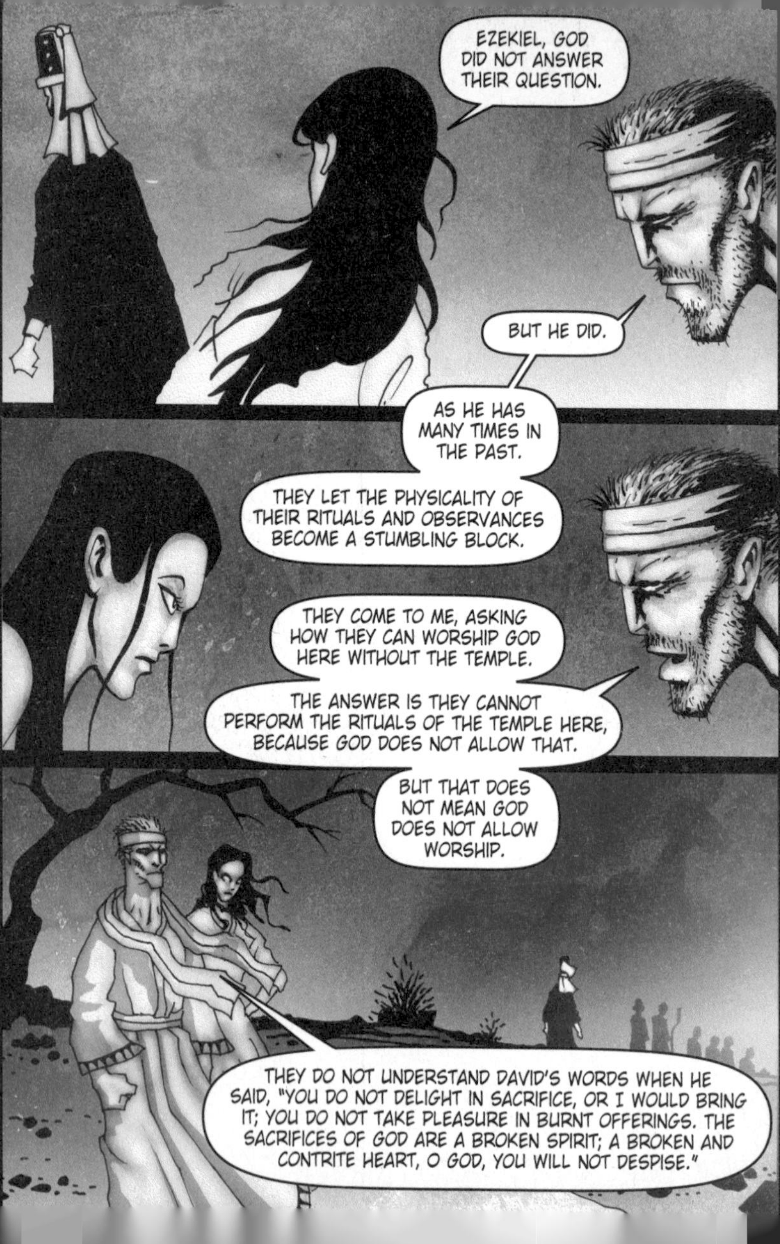
EZEKIEL, GOD DID NOT ANSWER THEIR QUESTION.
BUT HE DID.
AS HE HAS MANY TIMES IN THE PAST.
THEY LET THE PHYSICALITY OF THEIR RITUALS AND OBSERVANCES BECOME A STUMBLING BLOCK.
THEY COME TO ME, ASKING HOW THEY CAN WORSHIP GOD HERE WITHOUT THE TEMPLE.
THE ANSWER IS THEY CANNOT PERFORM THE RITUALS OF THE TEMPLE HERE, BECAUSE GOD DOES NOT ALLOW THAT.
BUT THAT DOES NOT MEAN GOD DOES NOT ALLOW WORSHIP.
THEY DO NOT UNDERSTAND DAVID'S WORDS WHEN HE SAID, "YOU DO NOT DELIGHT IN SACRIFICE, OR I WOULD BRING IT; YOU DO NOT TAKE PLEASURE IN BURNT OFFERINGS. THE SACRIFICES OF GOD ARE A BROKEN SPIRIT; A BROKEN AND CONTRITE HEART, O GOD, YOU WILL NOT DESPISE."

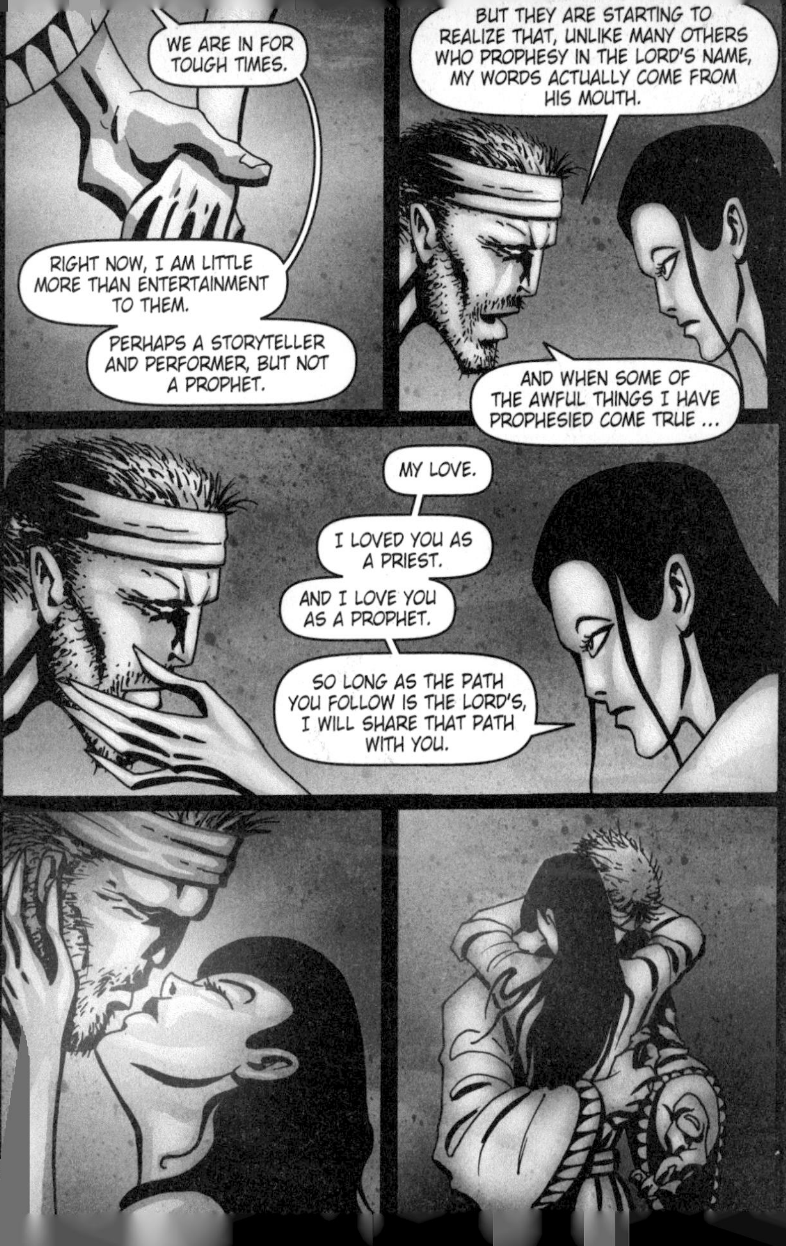
WE ARE IN FOR TOUGH TIMES.
RIGHT NOW, I AM LITTLE MORE THAN ENTERTAINMENT TO THEM.
PERHAPS A STORYTELLER AND PERFORMER, BUT NOT A PROPHET.
BUT THEY ARE STARTING TO REALIZE THAT, UNLIKE MANY OTHERS WHO PROPHESY IN THE LORD'S NAME, MY WORDS ACTUALLY COME FROM HIS MOUTH.
AND WHEN SOME OF THE AWFUL THINGS I HAVE PROPHESIED COME TRUE ...
MY LOVE.
I LOVED YOU AS A PRIEST.
AND I LOVE YOU AS A PROPHET.
SO LONG AS THE PATH YOU FOLLOW IS THE LORD'S, I WILL SHARE THAT PATH WITH YOU.

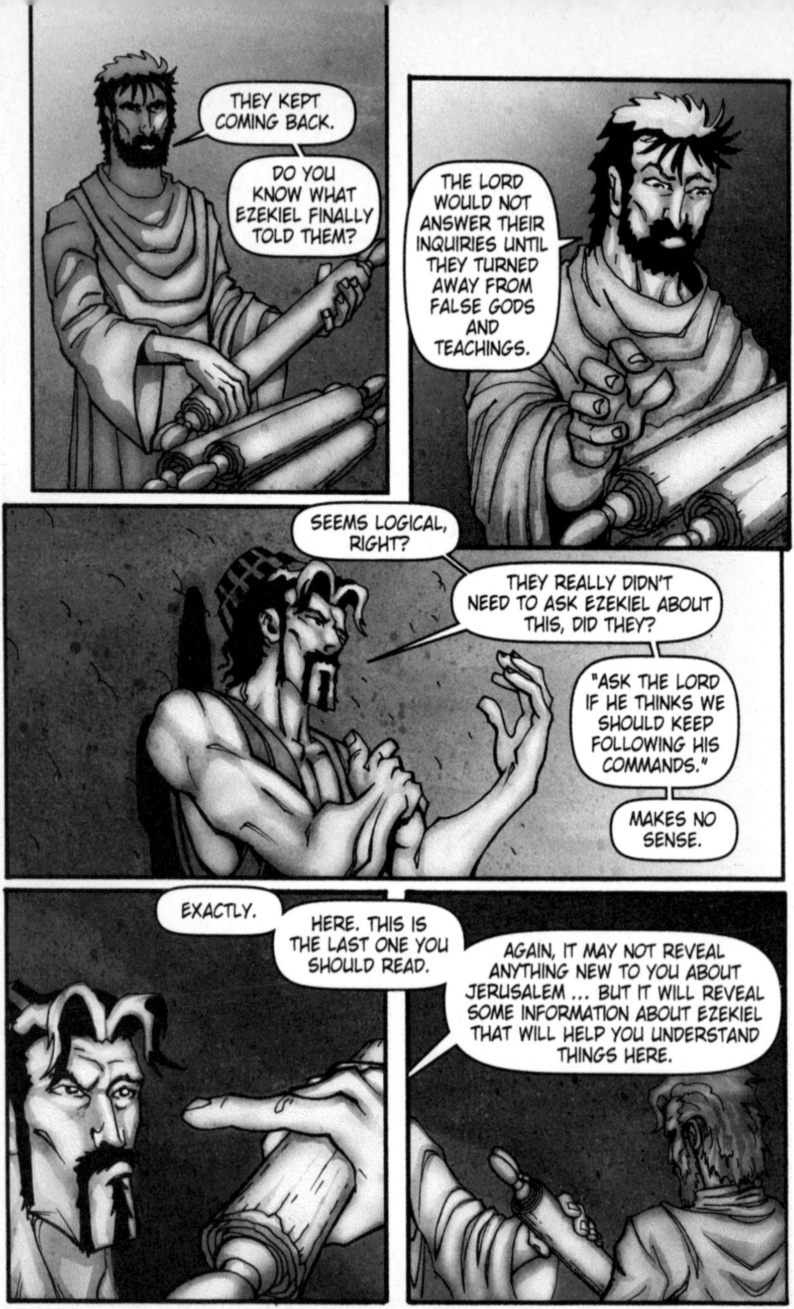
THEY KEPT COMING BACK.
DO YOU KNOW WHAT EZEKIEL FINALLY TOLD THEM?
THE LORD WOULD NOT ANSWER THEIR INQUIRIES UNTIL THEY TURNED AWAY FROM FALSE GODS AND TEACHINGS.
SEEMS LOGICAL, RIGHT?
THEY REALLY DIDN'T NEED TO ASK EZEKIEL ABOUT THIS, DID THEY?
"ASK THE LORD IF HE THINKS WE SHOULD KEEP FOLLOWING HIS COMMANDS."
MAKES NO SENSE.
EXACTLY.
HERE. THIS IS THE LAST ONE YOU SHOULD READ.
AGAIN, IT MAY NOT REVEAL ANYTHING NEW TO YOU ABOUT JERUSALEM ... BUT IT WILL REVEAL SOME INFORMATION ABOUT EZEKIEL THAT WILL HELP YOU UNDERSTAND THINGS HERE.

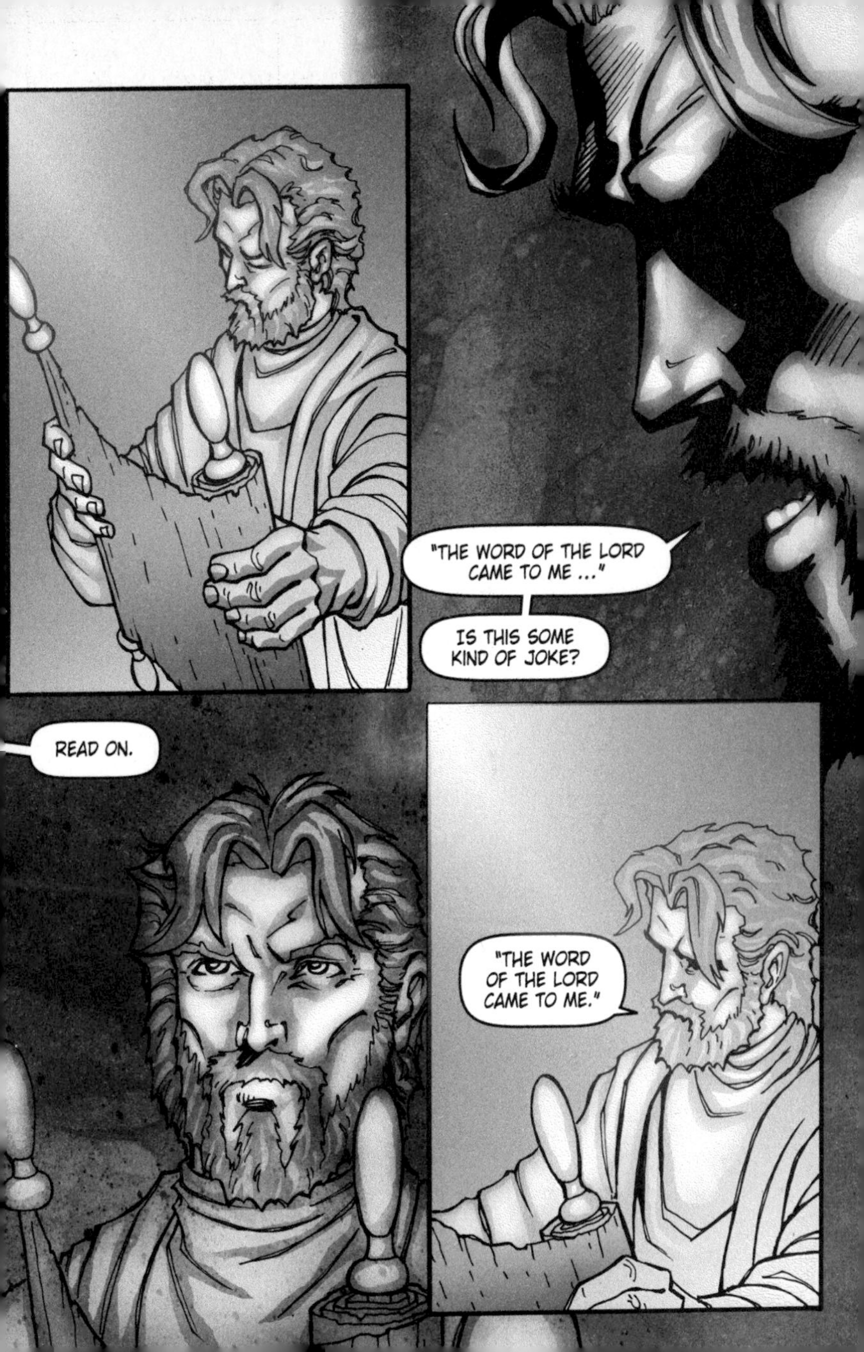
"THE WORD OF THE LORD CAME TO ME ..."
IS THIS SOME KIND OF JOKE?
READ ON.
"THE WORD OF THE LORD CAME TO ME."

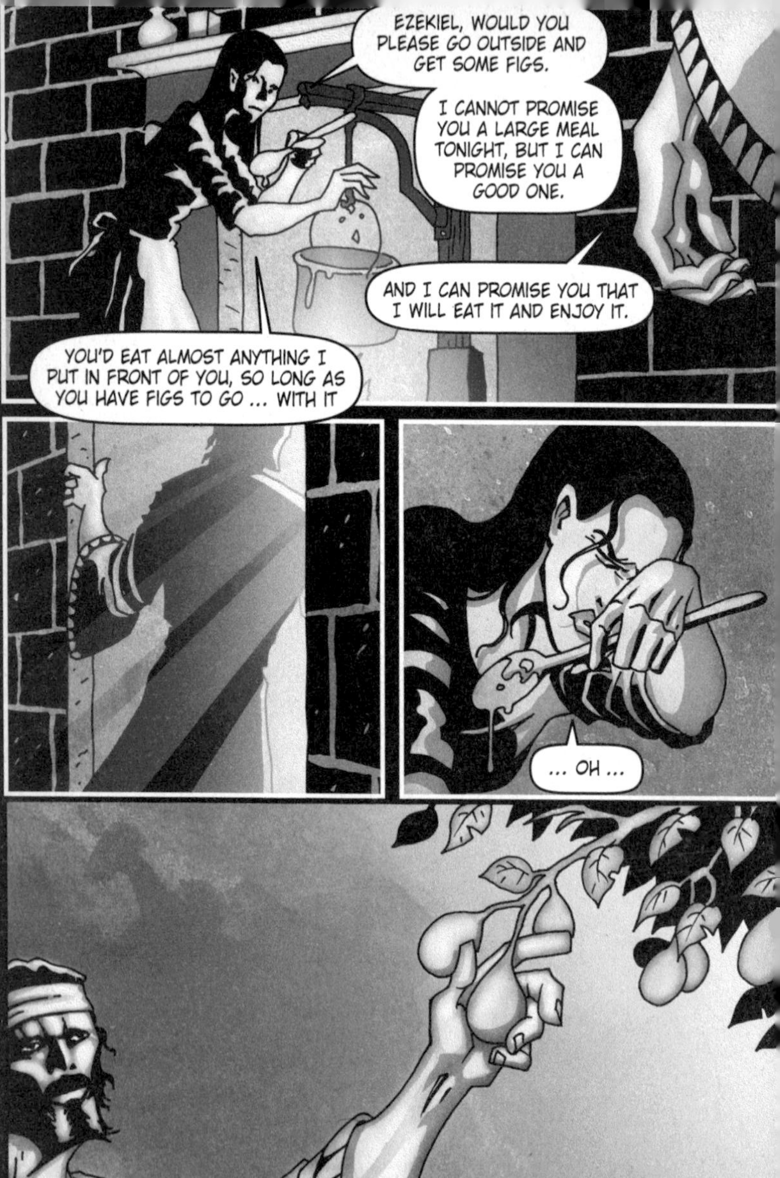
EZEKIEL, WOULD YOU PLEASE GO OUTSIDE AND GET SOME FIGS.
I CANNOT PROMISE YOU A LARGE MEAL TONIGHT, BUT I CAN PROMISE YOU A GOOD ONE.
AND I CAN PROMISE YOU THAT I WILL EAT IT AND ENJOY IT.
YOU'D EAT ALMOST ANYTHING I PUT IN FRONT OF YOU, SO LONG AS YOU HAVE FIGS TO GO ... WITH IT
... OH ...

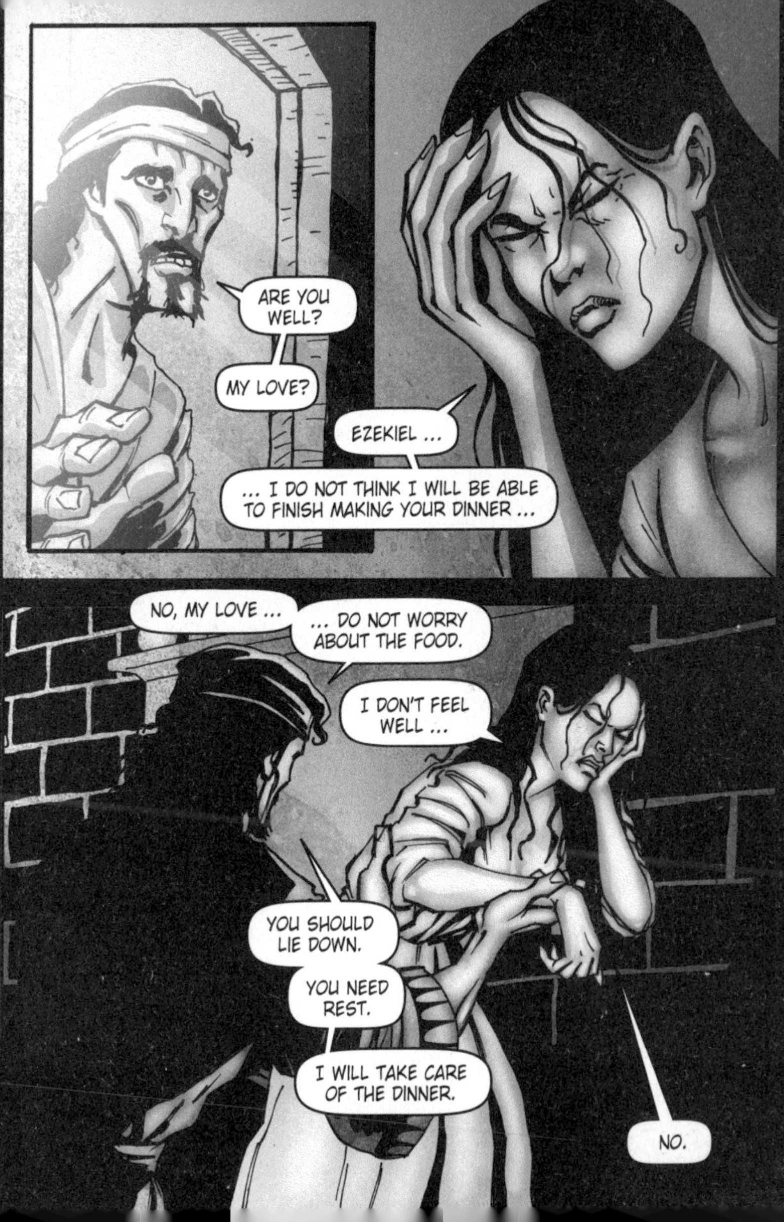
ARE YOU WELL?
MY LOVE?
EZEKIEL ...
... I DO NOT THINK I WILL BE ABLE TO FINISH MAKING YOUR DINNER ...
NO, MY LOVE ...
... DO NOT WORRY ABOUT THE FOOD.
I DON'T FEEL WELL ...
YOU SHOULD LIE DOWN.
YOU NEED REST.
I WILL TAKE CARE OF THE DINNER.
NO.

YOU HAD BETTER NOT ... PREPARE DINNER ...
... NO NEED FOR ... US BOTH TO BE ... ILL ...
JUST LIE DOWN HERE.
REST, MY LOVE. REST.
THANK YOU ... MY ... LOVE ...
WHY?
WHY TAKE HER?

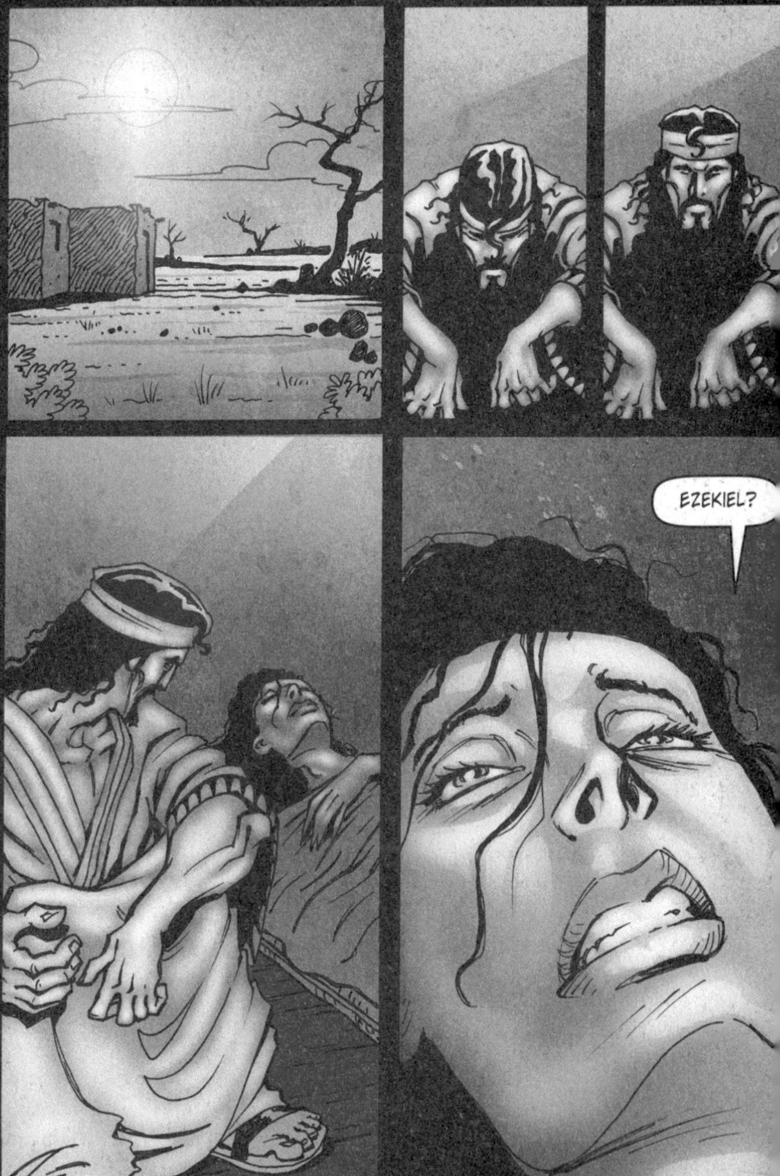
EZEKIEL?

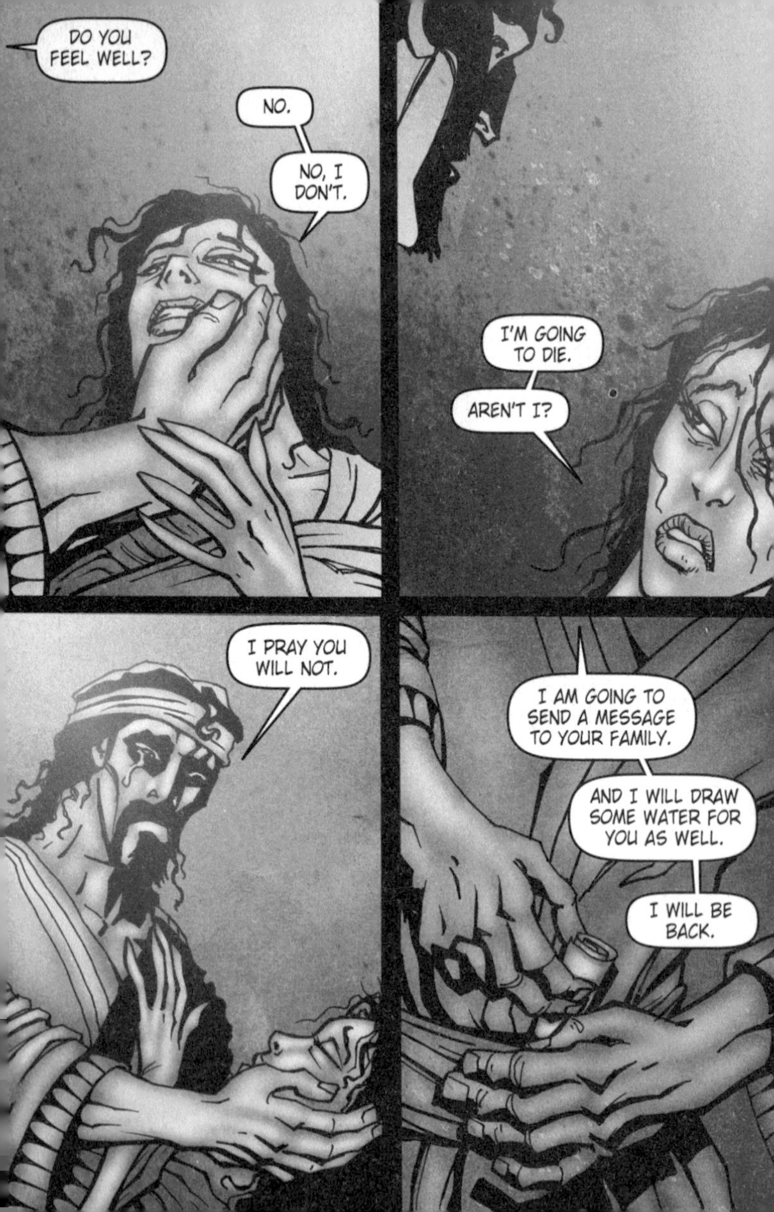
DO YOU FEEL WELL?
NO.
NO, I DON'T.
I'M GOING TO DIE.
AREN'T I?
I PRAY YOU WILL NOT.
I AM GOING TO SEND A MESSAGE TO YOUR FAMILY.
AND I WILL DRAW SOME WATER FOR YOU AS WELL.
I WILL BE BACK.

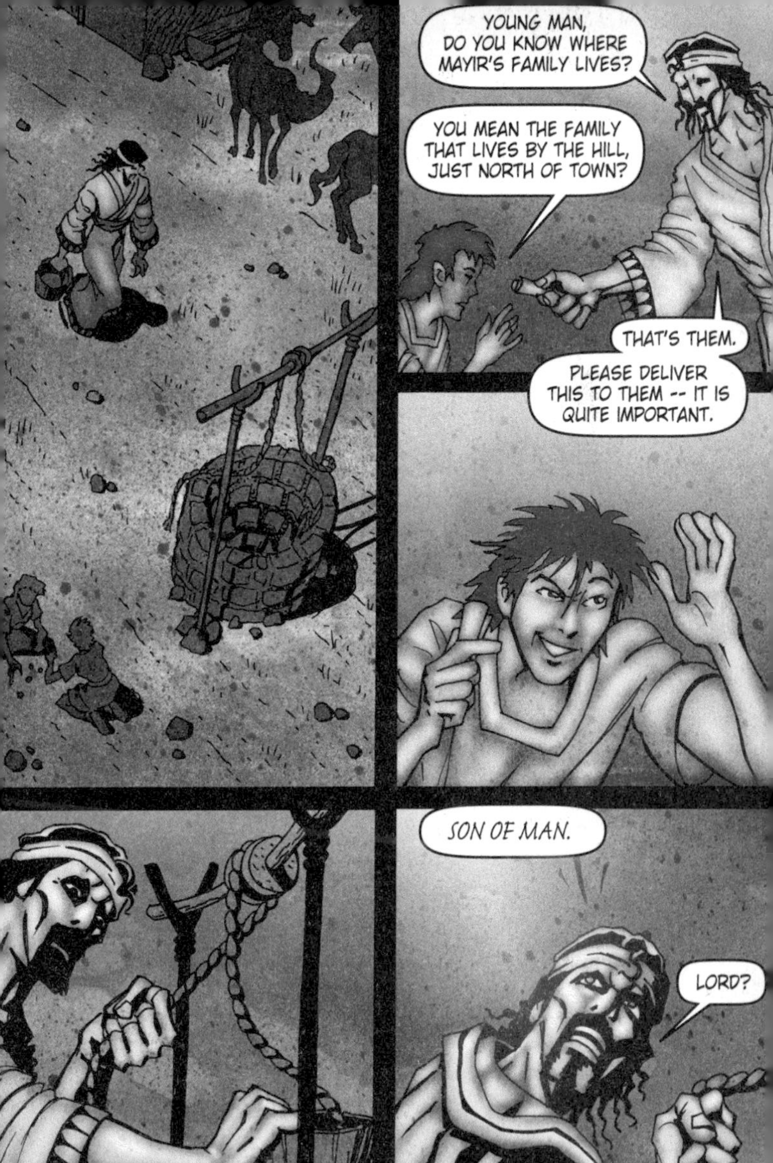
YOUNG MAN, DO YOU KNOW WHERE MAYIR'S FAMILY LIVES?
YOU MEAN THE FAMILY THAT LIVES BY THE HILL, JUST NORTH OF TOWN?
THAT'S THEM.
PLEASE DELIVER THIS TO THEM -- IT IS QUITE IMPORTANT.
SON OF MAN.
LORD?

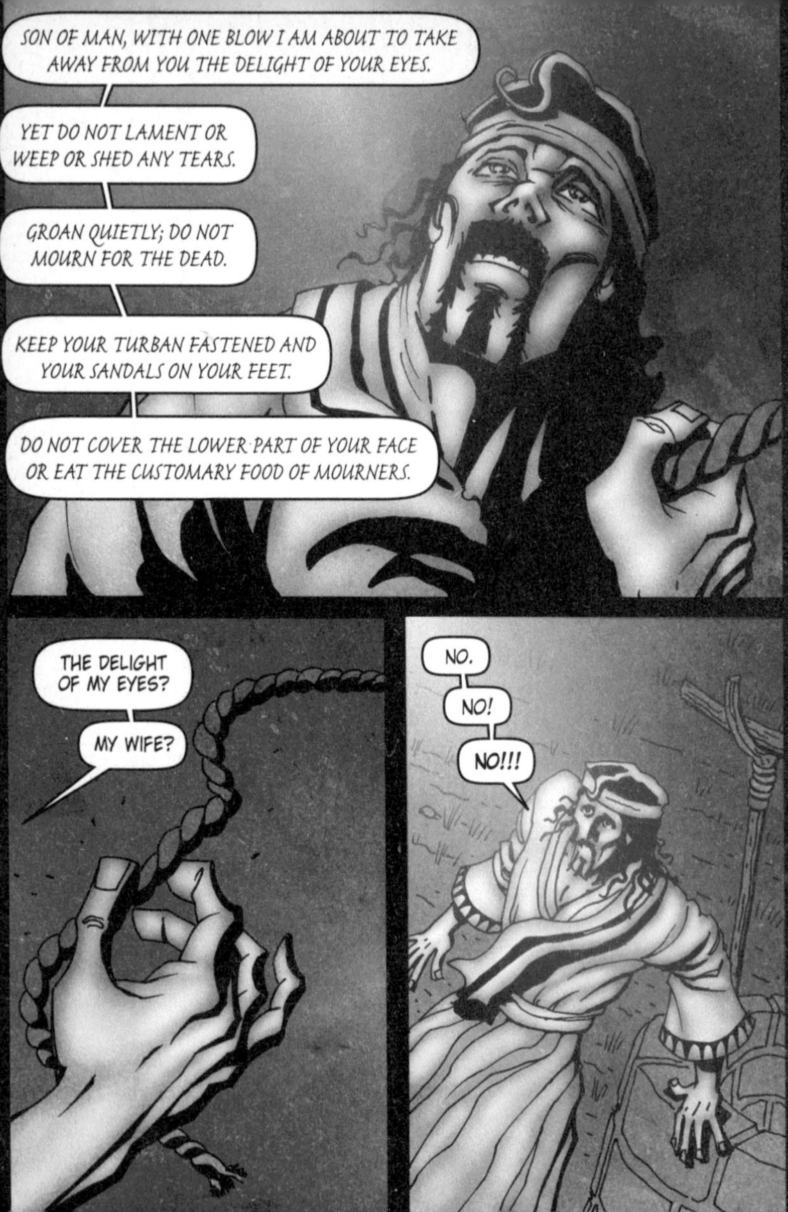
SON OF MAN, WITH ONE BLOW I AM ABOUT TO TAKE AWAY FROM YOU THE DELIGHT OF YOUR EYES.
YET DO NOT LAMENT OR WEEP OR SHED ANY TEARS.
GROAN QUIETLY; DO NOT MOURN FOR THE DEAD.
KEEP YOUR TURBAN FASTENED AND YOUR SANDALS ON YOUR FEET.
DO NOT COVER THE LOWER PART OF YOUR FACE OR EAT THE CUSTOMARY FOOD OF MOURNERS.
THE DELIGHT OF MY EYES?
MY WIFE?
NO.
NO!
NO!!!

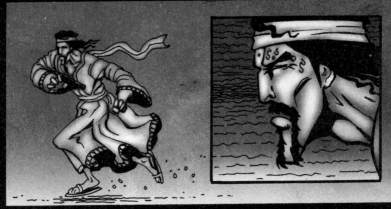

HUHN?

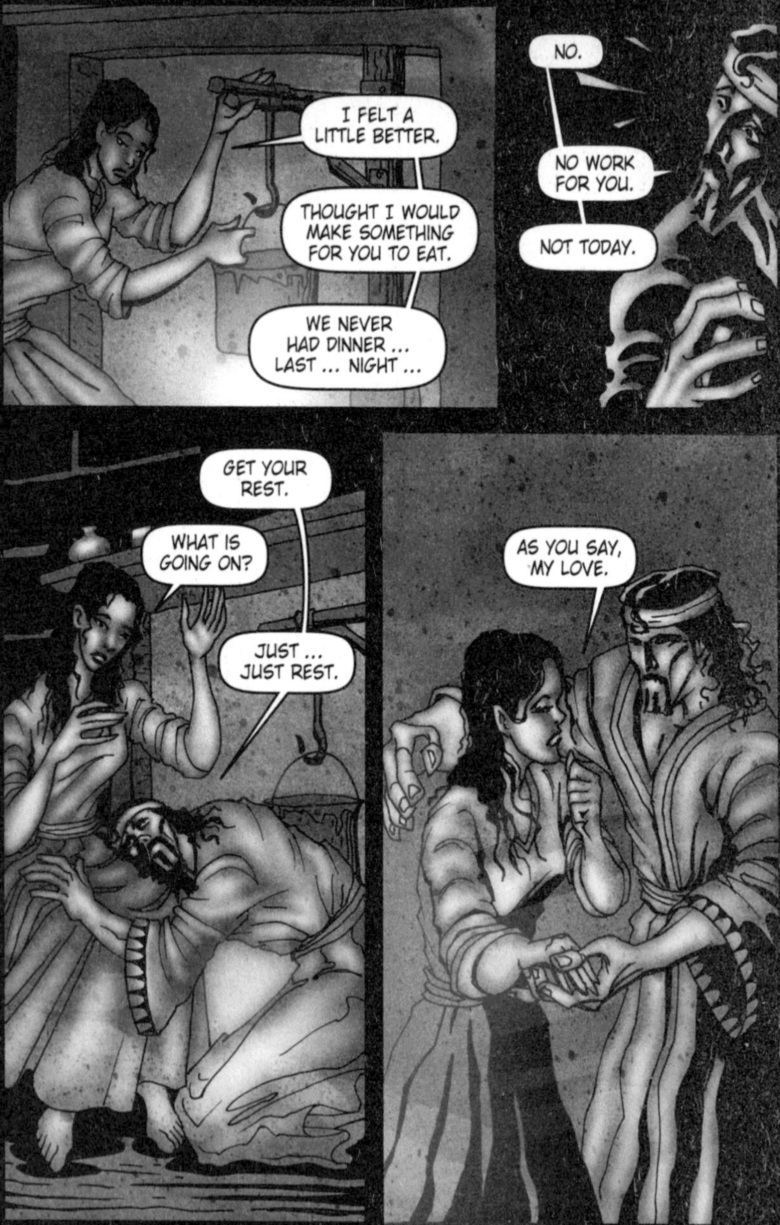
I FELT A LITTLE BETTER.
THOUGHT I WOULD MAKE SOMETHING FOR YOU TO EAT.
WE NEVER HAD DINNER ... LAST ... NIGHT ...
NO.
NO WORK FOR YOU.
NOT TODAY.
GET YOUR REST.
WHAT IS GOING ON?
JUST ... JUST REST.
AS YOU SAY, MY LOVE.

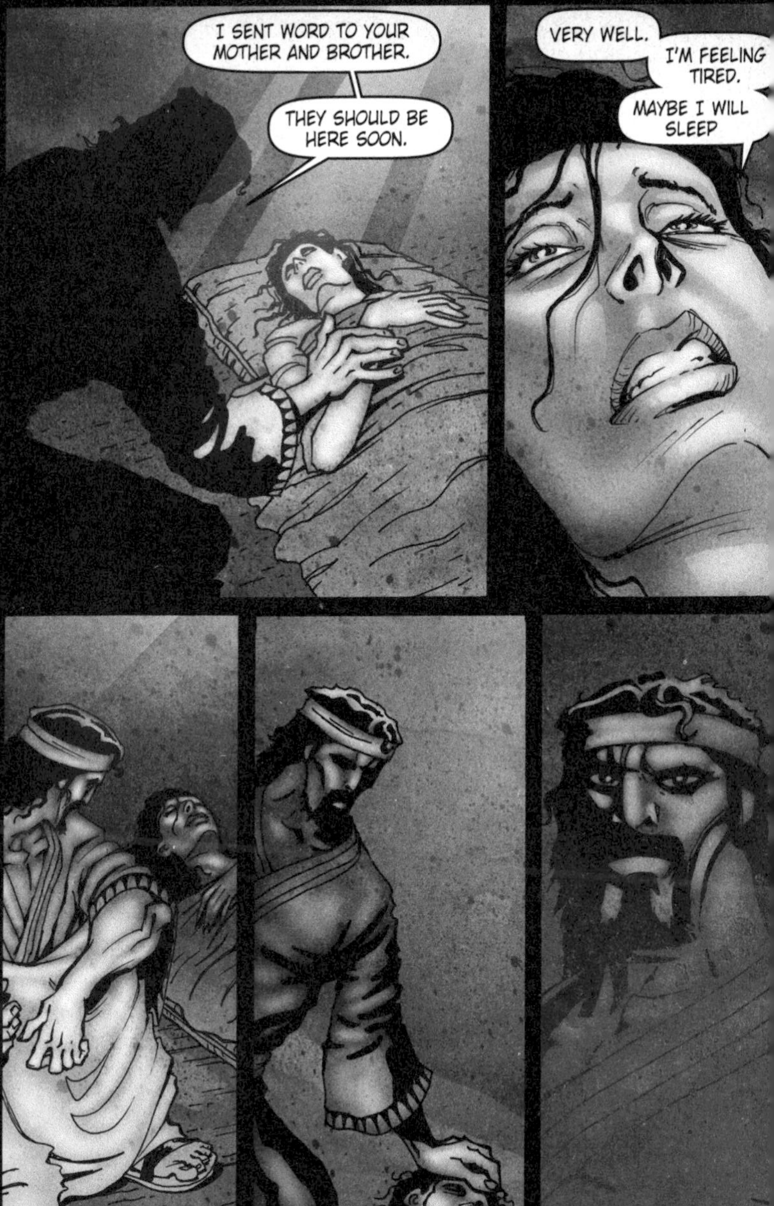
I SENT WORD TO YOUR MOTHER AND BROTHER.
THEY SHOULD BE HERE SOON.
VERY WELL.
I'M FEELING TIRED.
MAYBE I WILL SLEEP

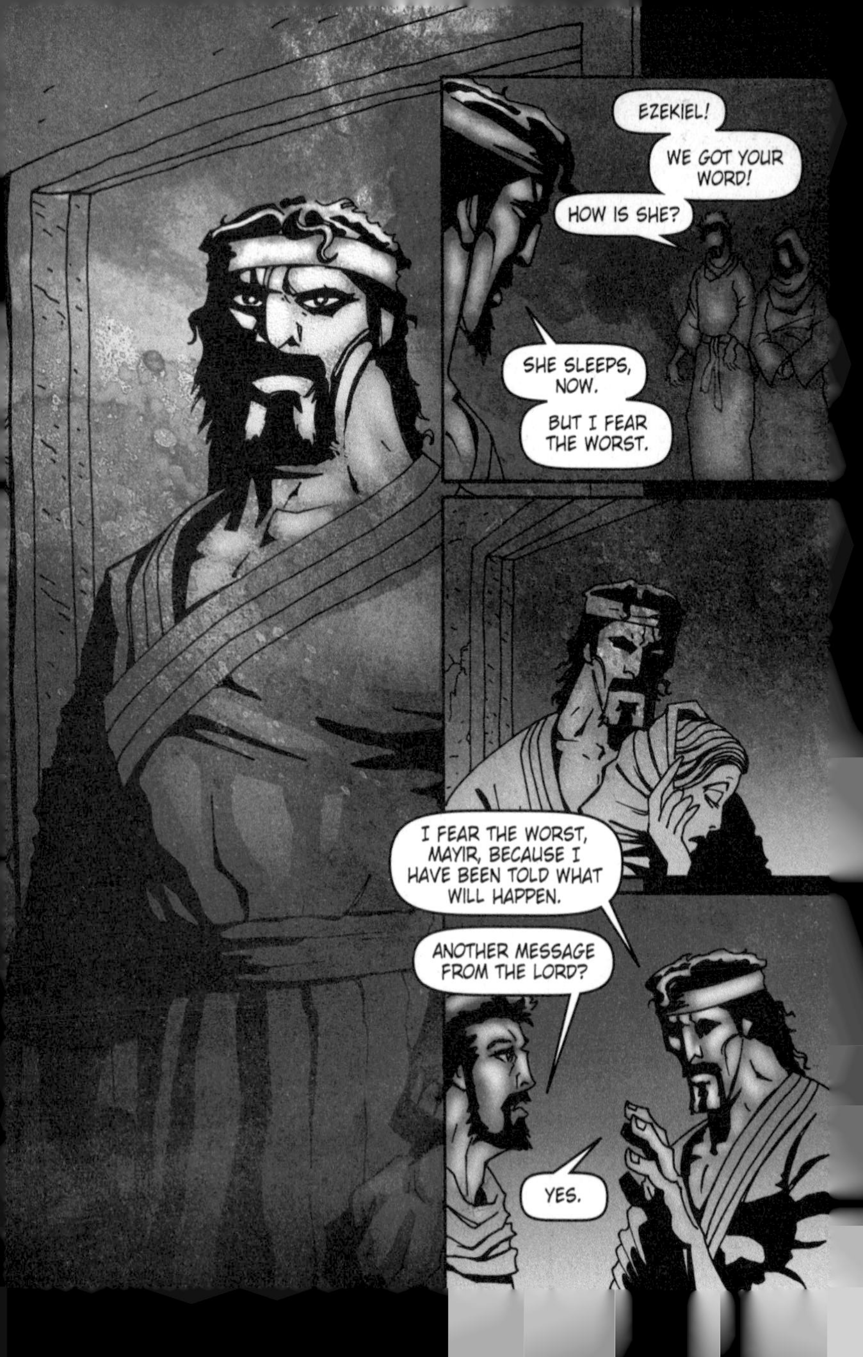
EZEKIEL!
WE GOT YOUR WORD!
HOW IS SHE?
SHE SLEEPS, NOW.
BUT I FEAR THE WORST.
I FEAR THE WORST, MAYIR, BECAUSE I HAVE BEEN TOLD WHAT WILL HAPPEN.
ANOTHER MESSAGE FROM THE LORD?
YES.

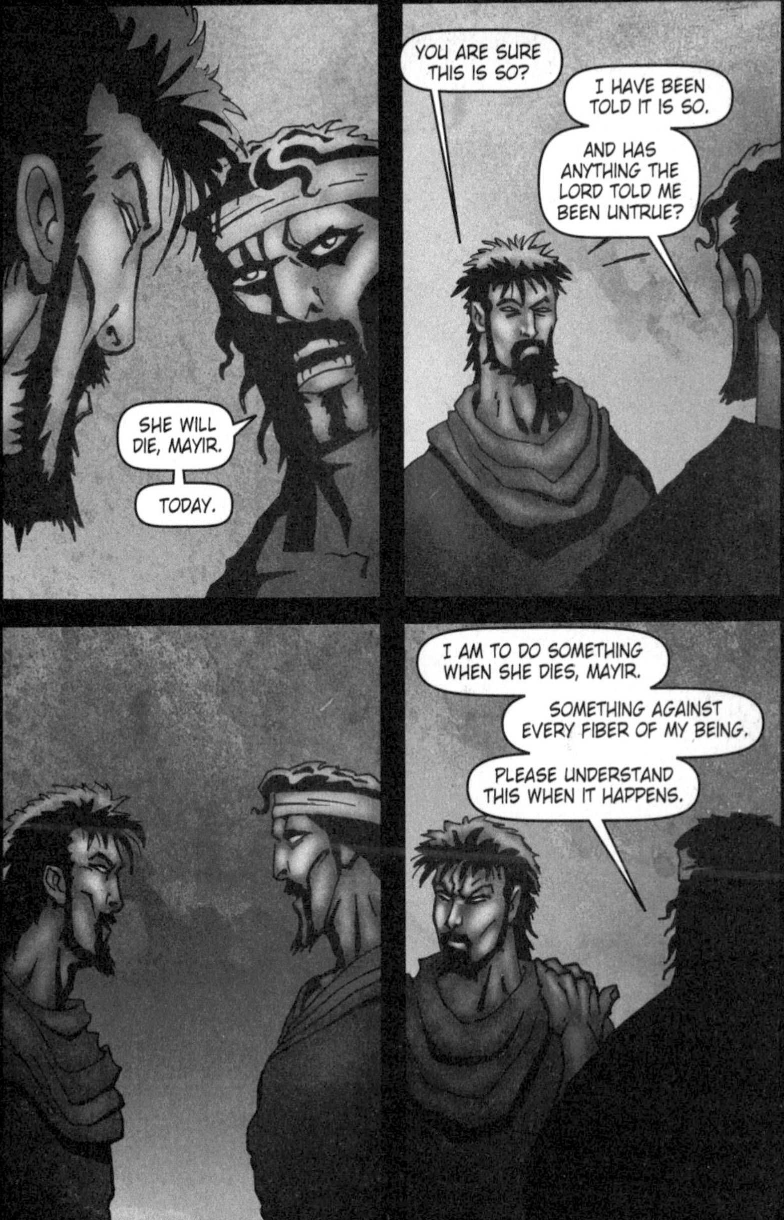
SHE WILL DIE, MAYIR.
TODAY.
YOU ARE SURE THIS IS SO?
I HAVE BEEN TOLD IT IS SO.
AND HAS ANYTHING THE LORD TOLD ME BEEN UNTRUE?
I AM TO DO SOMETHING WHEN SHE DIES, MAYIR.
SOMETHING AGAINST EVERY FIBER OF MY BEING.
PLEASE UNDERSTAND THIS WHEN IT HAPPENS.

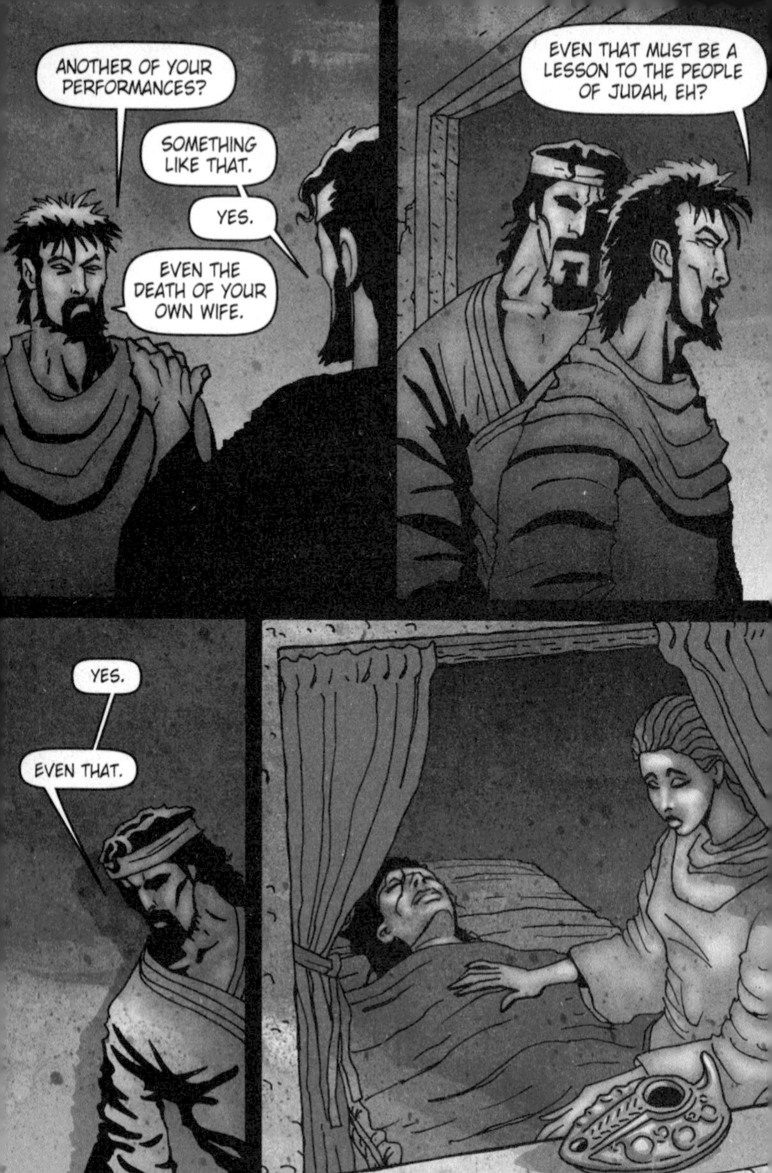
ANOTHER OF YOUR PERFORMANCES?
SOMETHING LIKE THAT.
YES.
EVEN THE DEATH OF YOUR OWN WIFE.
EVEN THAT MUST BE A LESSON TO THE PEOPLE OF JUDAH, EH?
YES.
EVEN THAT.

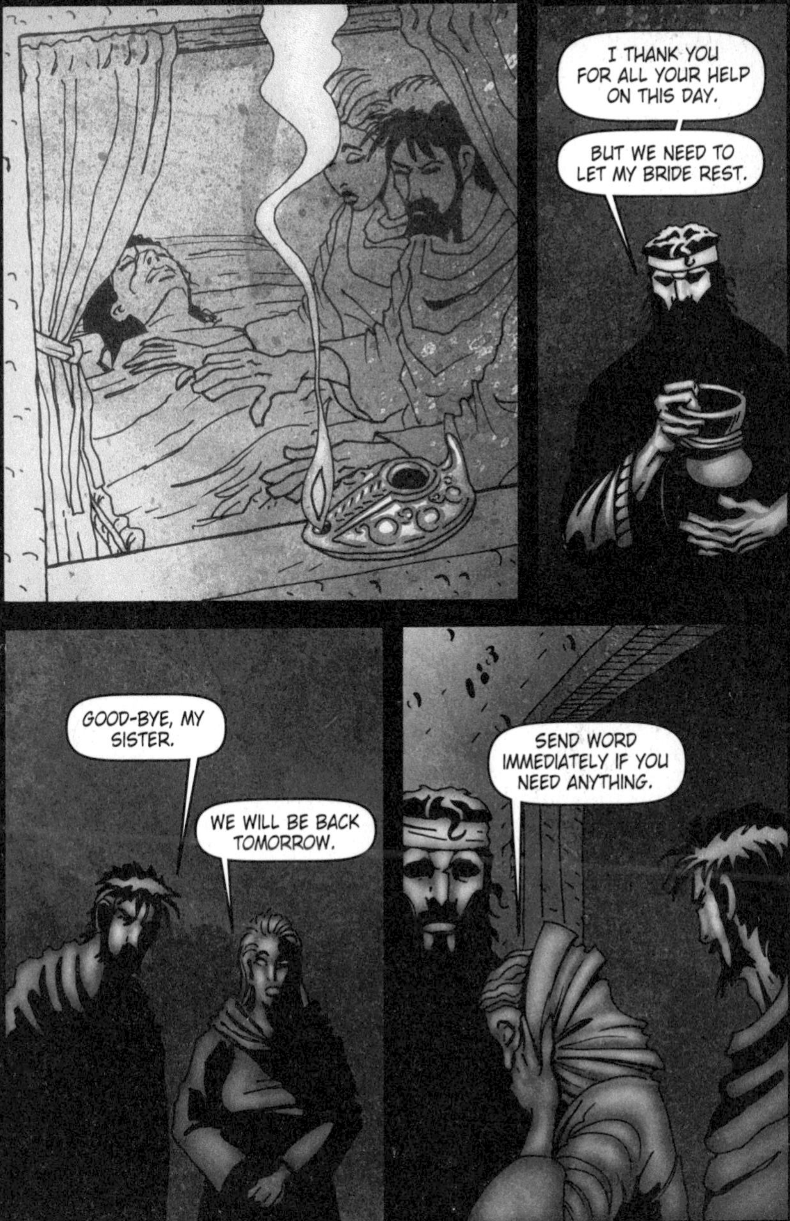
I THANK YOU FOR ALL YOUR HELP ON THIS DAY.
BUT WE NEED TO LET MY BRIDE REST.
GOOD-BYE, MY SISTER.
WE WILL BE BACK TOMORROW.
SEND WORD IMMEDIATELY IF YOU NEED ANYTHING.

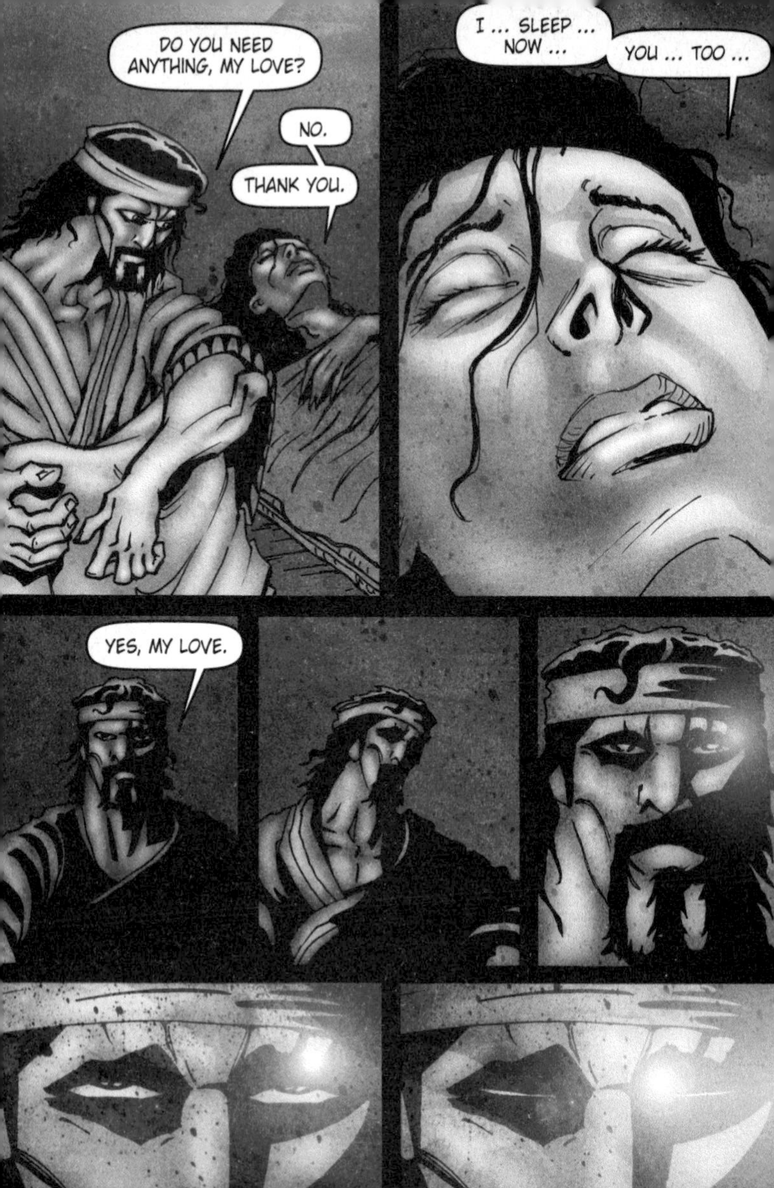
DO YOU NEED ANYTHING, MY LOVE?
NO.
THANK YOU.
I ... SLEEP ... NOW ...
YOU ... TOO ...
YES, MY LOVE.

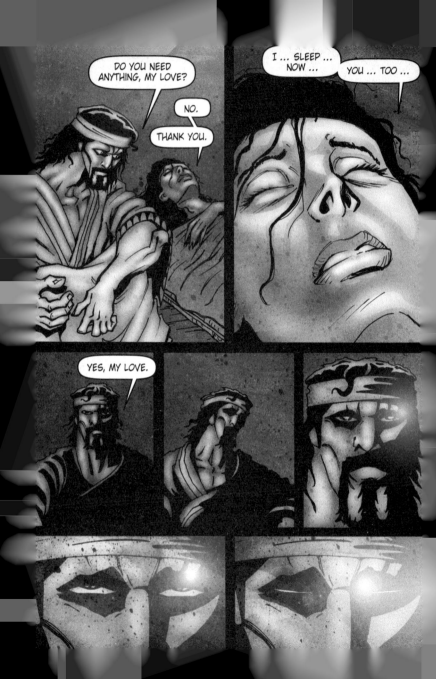

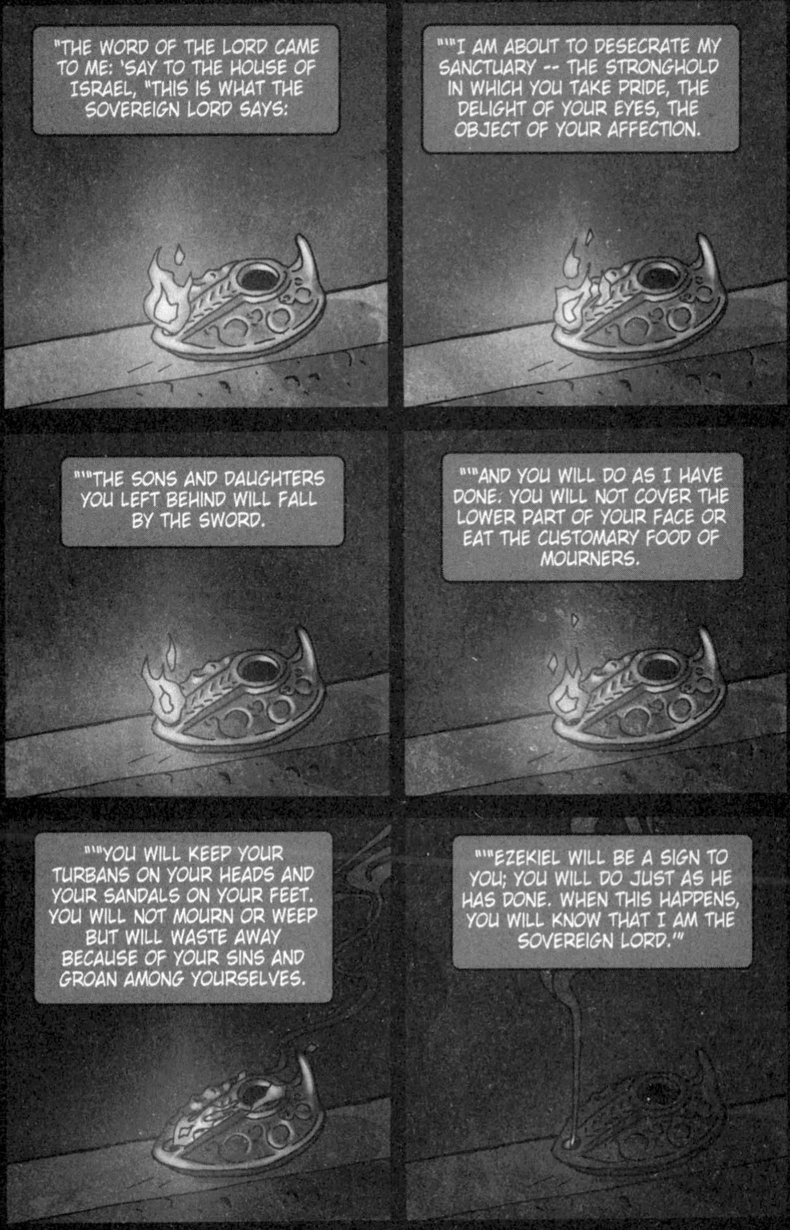
"THE WORD OF THE LORD CAME TO ME: 'SAY TO THE HOUSE OF ISRAEL, "THIS IS WHAT THE SOVEREIGN LORD SAYS:
"'"I AM ABOUT TO DESECRATE MY SANCTUARY -- THE STRONGHOLD IN WHICH YOU TAKE PRIDE, THE DELIGHT OF YOUR EYES, THE OBJECT OF YOUR AFFECTION.
"'"THE SONS AND DAUGHTERS YOU LEFT BEHIND WILL FALL BY THE SWORD.
"'"AND YOU WILL DO AS I HAVE DONE. YOU WILL NOT COVER THE LOWER PART OF YOUR FACE OR EAT THE CUSTOMARY FOOD OF MOURNERS.
"'"YOU WILL KEEP YOUR TURBANS ON YOUR HEADS AND YOUR SANDALS ON YOUR FEET. YOU WILL NOT MOURN OR WEEP BUT WILL WASTE AWAY BECAUSE OF YOUR SINS AND GROAN AMONG YOURSELVES.
"'"EZEKIEL WILL BE A SIGN TO YOU; YOU WILL DO JUST AS HE HAS DONE. WHEN THIS HAPPENS, YOU WILL KNOW THAT I AM THE SOVEREIGN LORD.'"

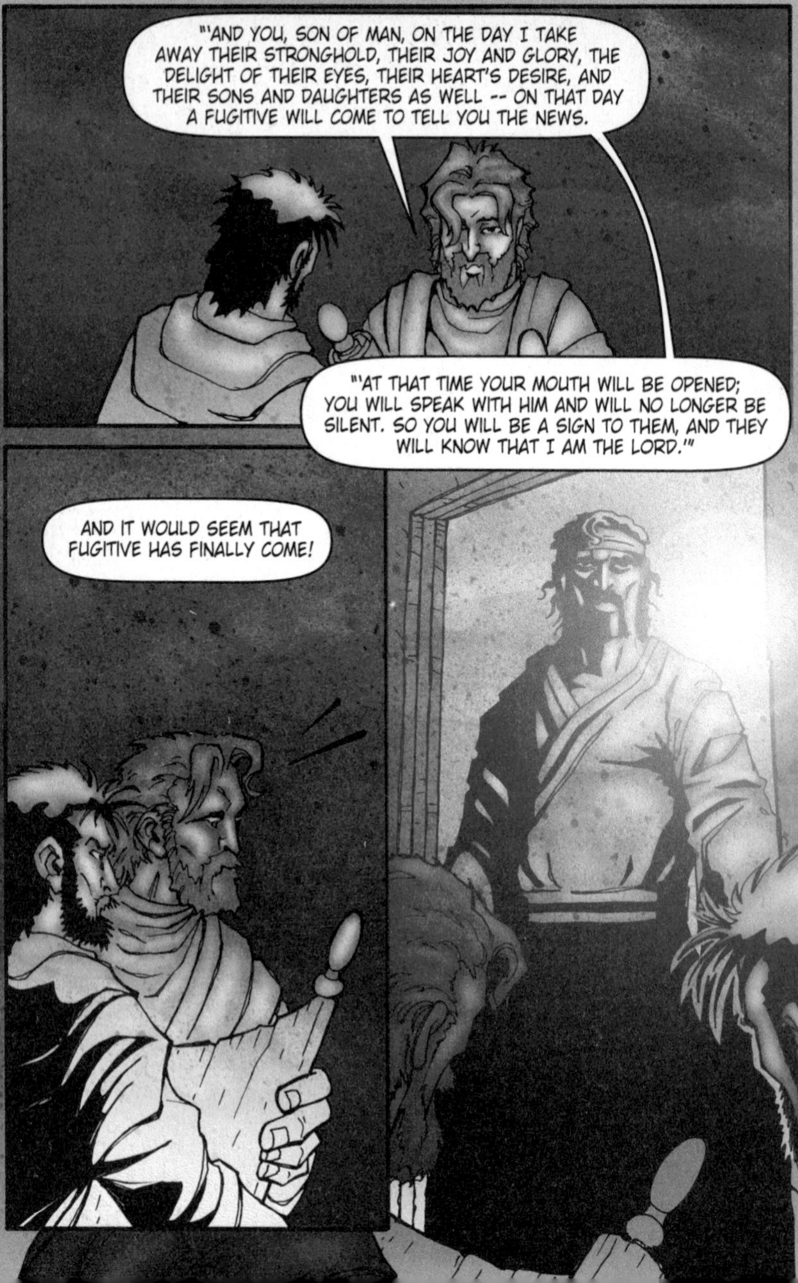
"'AND YOU, SON OF MAN, ON THE DAY I TAKE AWAY THEIR STRONGHOLD, THEIR JOY AND GLORY, THE DELIGHT OF THEIR EYES, THEIR HEART'S DESIRE, AND THEIR SONS AND DAUGHTERS AS WELL -- ON THAT DAY A FUGITIVE WILL COME TO TELL YOU THE NEWS.
"'AT THAT TIME YOUR MOUTH WILL BE OPENED; YOU WILL SPEAK WITH HIM AND WILL NO LONGER BE SILENT. SO YOU WILL BE A SIGN TO THEM, AND THEY WILL KNOW THAT I AM THE LORD.'"
AND IT WOULD SEEM THAT FUGITIVE HAS FINALLY COME!

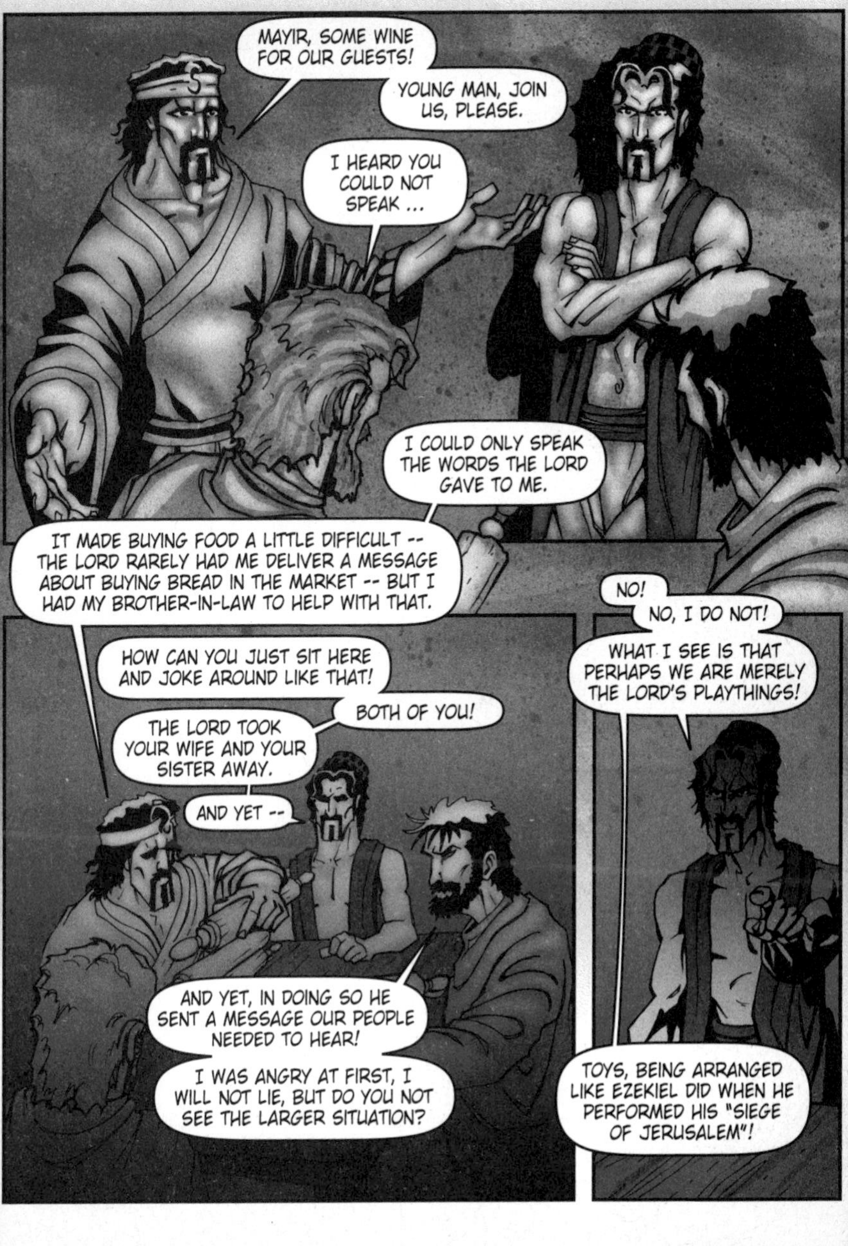
MAYIR, SOME WINE FOR OUR GUESTS!
YOUNG MAN, JOIN US, PLEASE.
I HEARD YOU COULD NOT SPEAK ...
I COULD ONLY SPEAK THE WORDS THE LORD GAVE TO ME.
IT MADE BUYING FOOD A LITTLE DIFFICULT -- THE LORD RARELY HAD ME DELIVER A MESSAGE ABOUT BUYING BREAD IN THE MARKET -- BUT I HAD MY BROTHER-IN-LAW TO HELP WITH THAT.
HOW CAN YOU JUST SIT HERE AND JOKE AROUND LIKE THAT!
BOTH OF YOU!
THE LORD TOOK YOUR WIFE AND YOUR SISTER AWAY.
AND YET --
AND YET, IN DOING SO HE SENT A MESSAGE OUR PEOPLE NEEDED TO HEAR!
I WAS ANGRY AT FIRST, I WILL NOT LIE, BUT DO YOU NOT SEE THE LARGER SITUATION?
NO!
NO, I DO NOT!
WHAT I SEE IS THAT PERHAPS WE ARE MERELY THE LORD'S PLAYTHINGS!
TOYS, BEING ARRANGED LIKE EZEKIEL DID WHEN HE PERFORMED HIS "SIEGE OF JERUSALEM"!

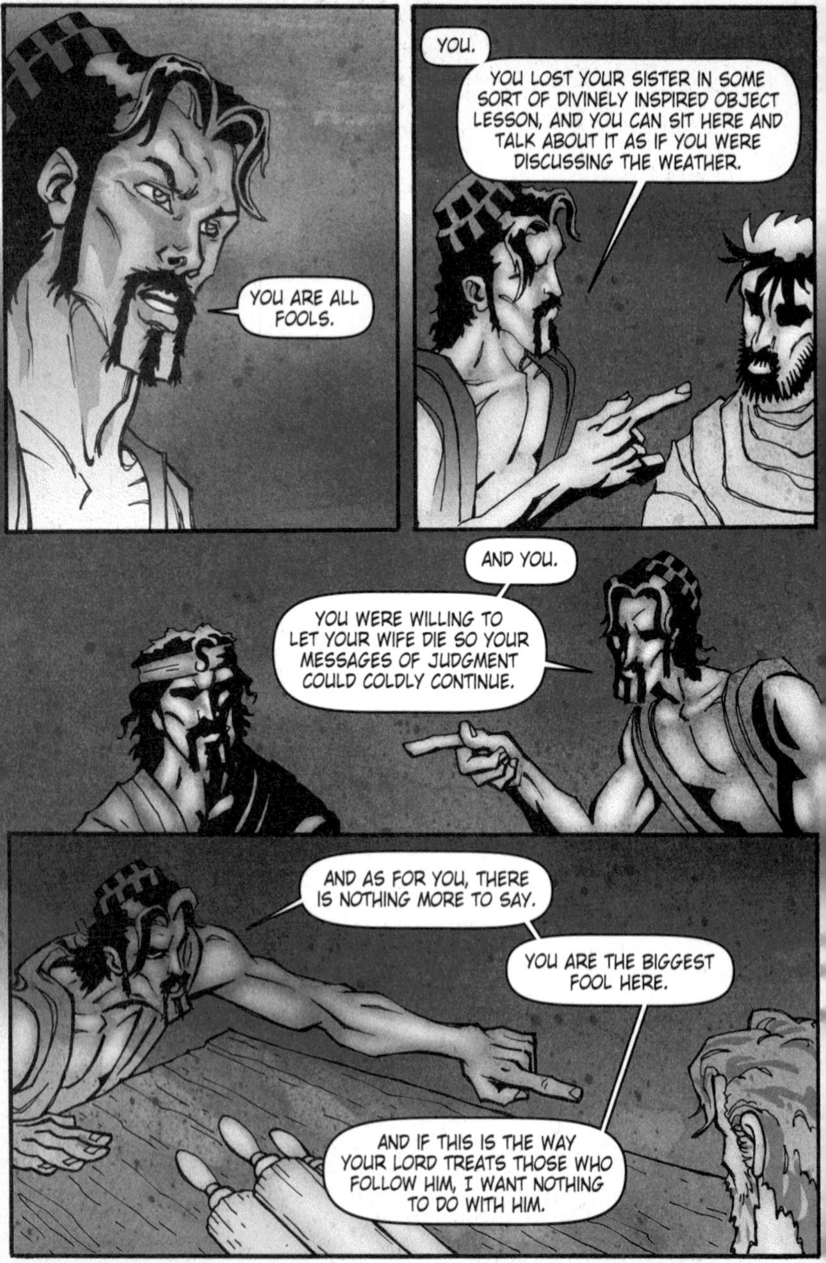
YOU ARE ALL FOOLS.
YOU.
YOU LOST YOUR SISTER IN SOME SORT OF DIVINELY INSPIRED OBJECT LESSON, AND YOU CAN SIT HERE AND TALK ABOUT IT AS IF YOU WERE DISCUSSING THE WEATHER.
AND YOU.
YOU WERE WILLING TO LET YOUR WIFE DIE SO YOUR MESSAGES OF JUDGMENT COULD COLDLY CONTINUE.
AND AS FOR YOU, THERE IS NOTHING MORE TO SAY.
YOU ARE THE BIGGEST FOOL HERE.
AND IF THIS IS THE WAY YOUR LORD TREATS THOSE WHO FOLLOW HIM, I WANT NOTHING TO DO WITH HIM.

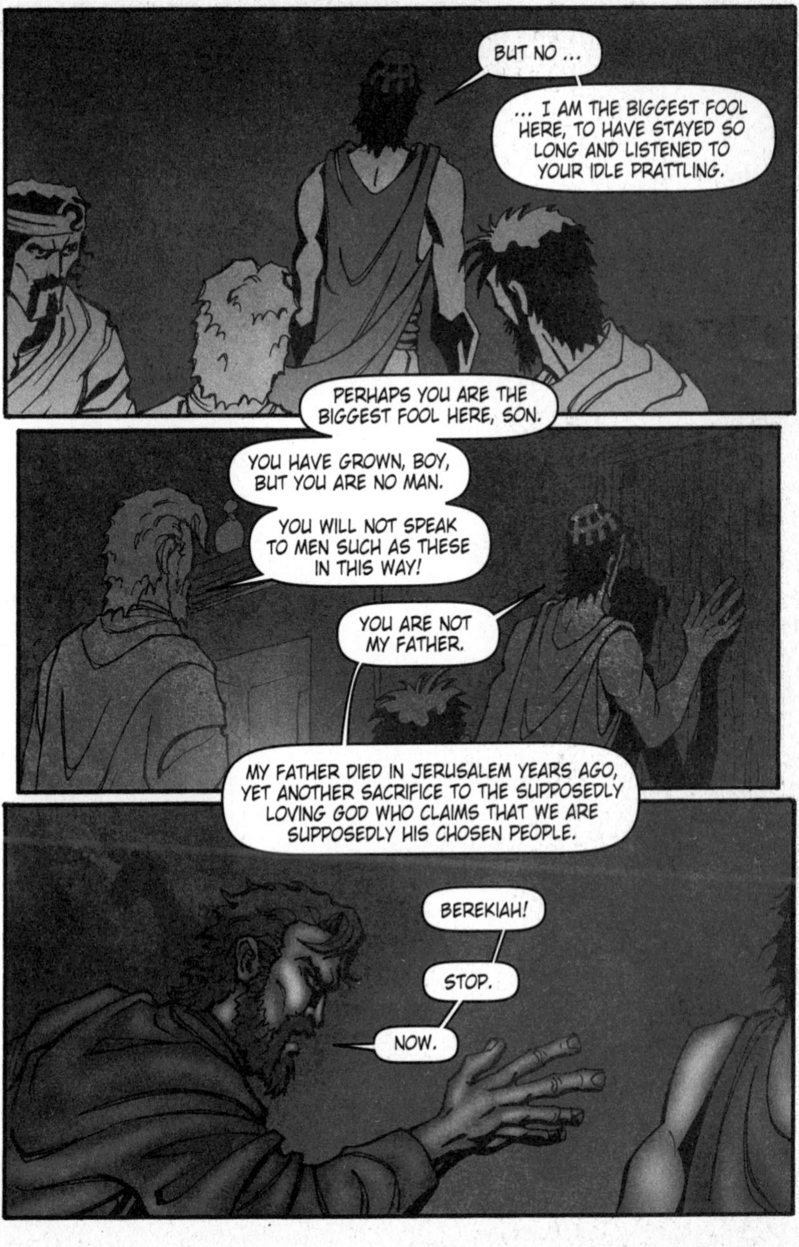
BUT NO ...
... I AM THE BIGGEST FOOL HERE, TO HAVE STAYED SO LONG AND LISTENED TO YOUR IDLE PRATTLING.
PERHAPS YOU ARE THE BIGGEST FOOL HERE, SON.
YOU HAVE GROWN, BOY, BUT YOU ARE NO MAN.
YOU WILL NOT SPEAK TO MEN SUCH AS THESE IN THIS WAY!
YOU ARE NOT MY FATHER.
MY FATHER DIED IN JERUSALEM YEARS AGO, YET ANOTHER SACRIFICE TO THE SUPPOSEDLY LOVING GOD WHO CLAIMS THAT WE ARE SUPPOSEDLY HIS CHOSEN PEOPLE.
BEREKIAH!
STOP.
NOW.

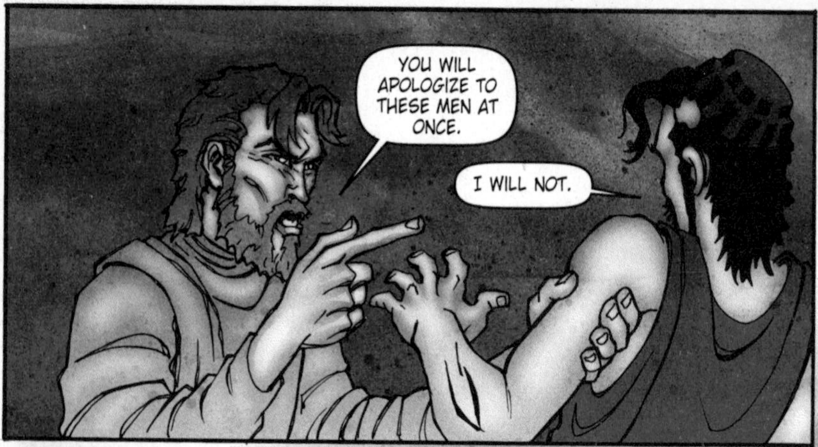
YOU WILL APOLOGIZE TO THESE MEN AT ONCE.
I WILL NOT.
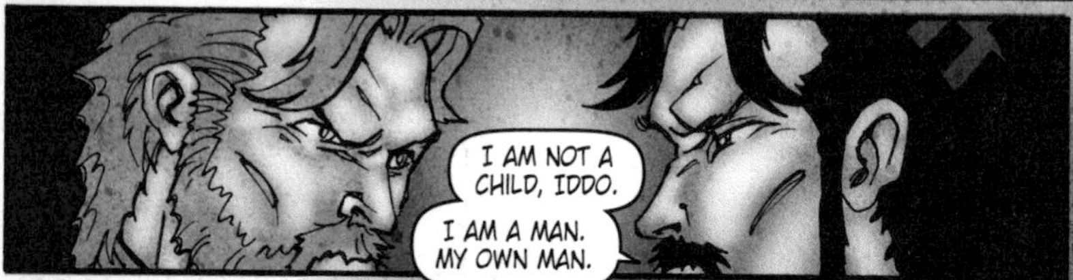
I AM NOT A CHILD, IDDO.
I AM A MAN. MY OWN MAN.
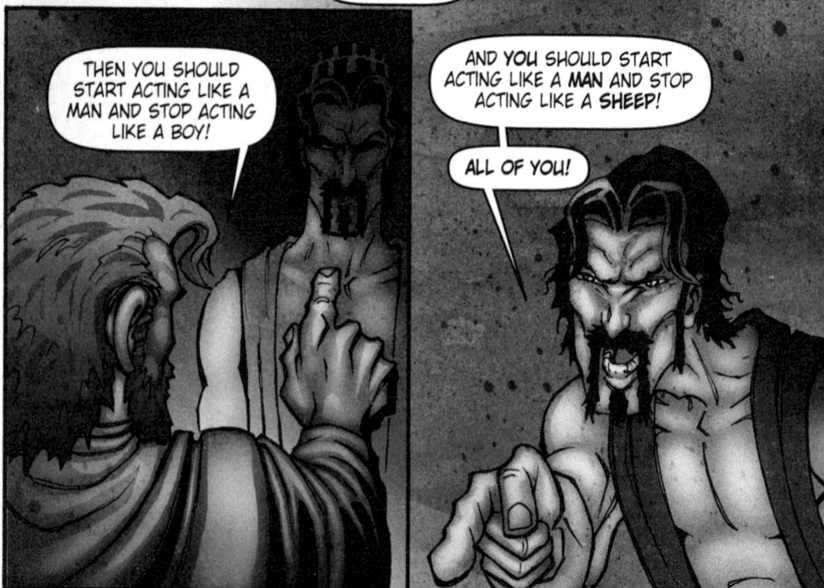
THEN YOU SHOULD START ACTING LIKE A MAN AND STOP ACTING LIKE A BOY!
AND YOU SHOULD START ACTING LIKE A MAN AND STOP ACTING LIKE A SHEEP!
ALL OF YOU!

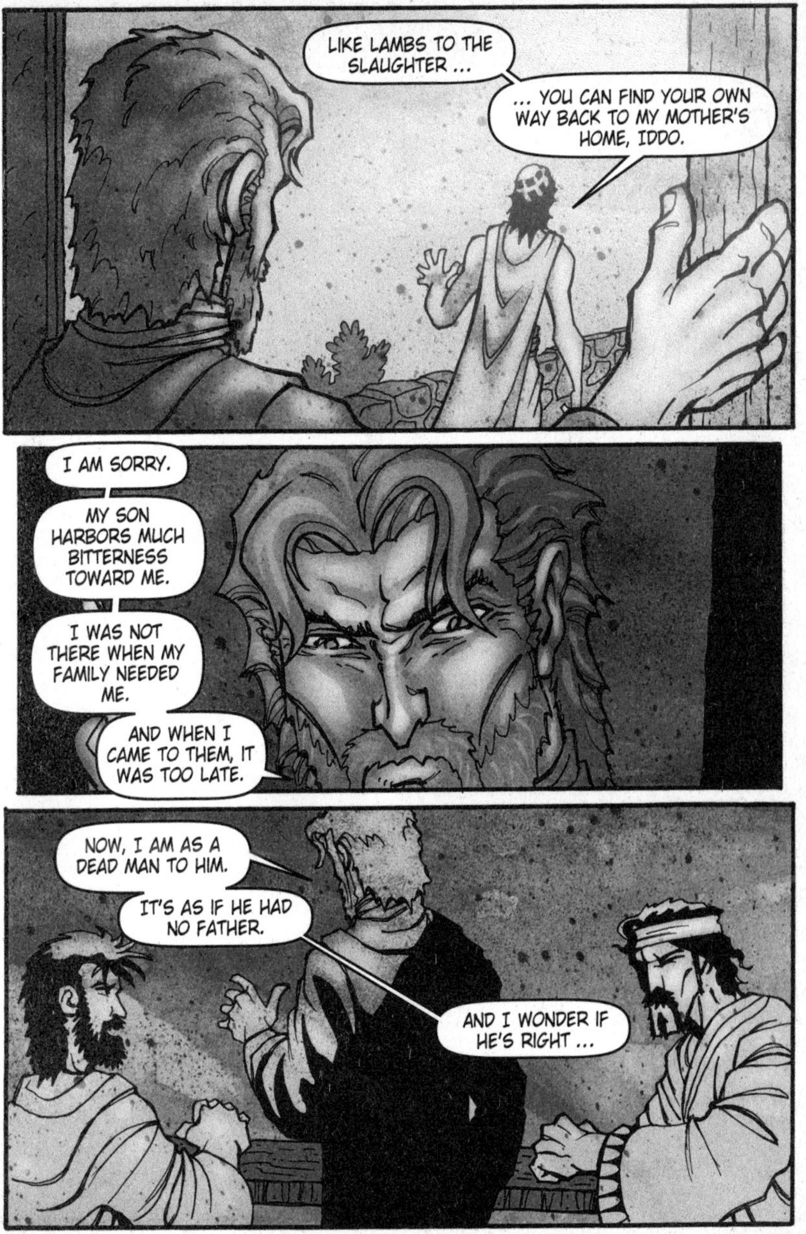
LIKE LAMBS TO THE SLAUGHTER ...
... YOU CAN FIND YOUR OWN WAY BACK TO MY MOTHER'S HOME, IDDO.
I AM SORRY.
MY SON HARBORS MUCH BITTERNESS TOWARD ME.
I WAS NOT THERE WHEN MY FAMILY NEEDED ME.
AND WHEN I CAME TO THEM, IT WAS TOO LATE.
NOW, I AM AS A DEAD MAN TO HIM.
IT'S AS IF HE HAD NO FATHER.
AND I WONDER IF HE'S RIGHT ...

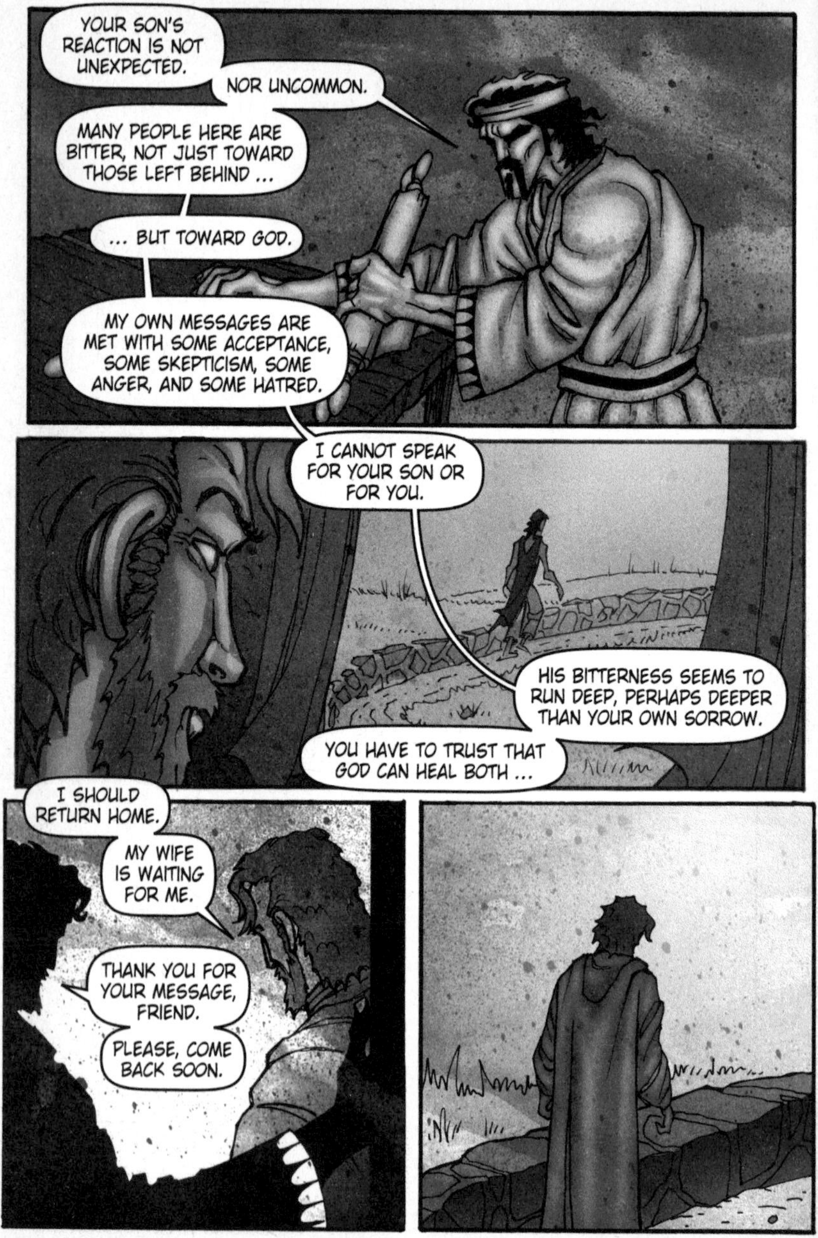
YOUR SON'S REACTION IS NOT UNEXPECTED.
NOR UNCOMMON.
MANY PEOPLE HERE ARE BITTER, NOT JUST TOWARD THOSE LEFT BEHIND ...
... BUT TOWARD GOD.
MY OWN MESSAGES ARE MET WITH SOME ACCEPTANCE, SOME SKEPTICISM, SOME ANGER, AND SOME HATRED.
I CANNOT SPEAK FOR YOUR SON OR FOR YOU.
HIS BITTERNESS SEEMS TO RUN DEEP, PERHAPS DEEPER THAN YOUR OWN SORROW.
YOU HAVE TO TRUST THAT GOD CAN HEAL BOTH ...
I SHOULD RETURN HOME.
MY WIFE IS WAITING FOR ME.
THANK YOU FOR YOUR MESSAGE, FRIEND.
PLEASE, COME BACK SOON.

CHAPTER THREE
"The Valley of Death"

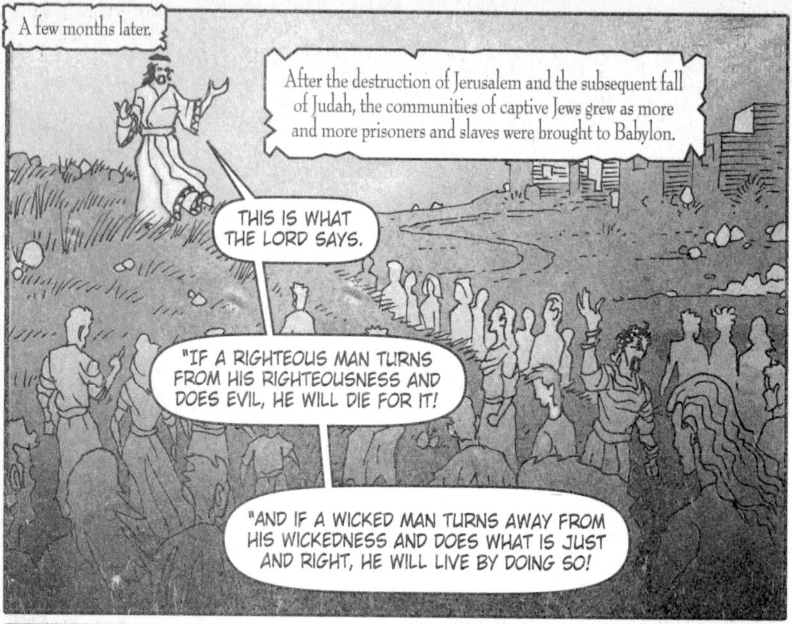
A few months later.
After the destruction of Jerusalem and the subsequent fall of Judah, the communities of captive Jews grew as more and more prisoners and slaves were brought to Babylon.
THIS IS WHAT THE LORD SAYS.
"IF A RIGHTEOUS MAN TURNS FROM HIS RIGHTEOUSNESS AND DOES EVIL, HE WILL DIE FOR IT!
"AND IF A WICKED MAN TURNS AWAY FROM HIS WICKEDNESS AND DOES WHAT IS JUST AND RIGHT, HE WILL LIVE BY DOING SO!

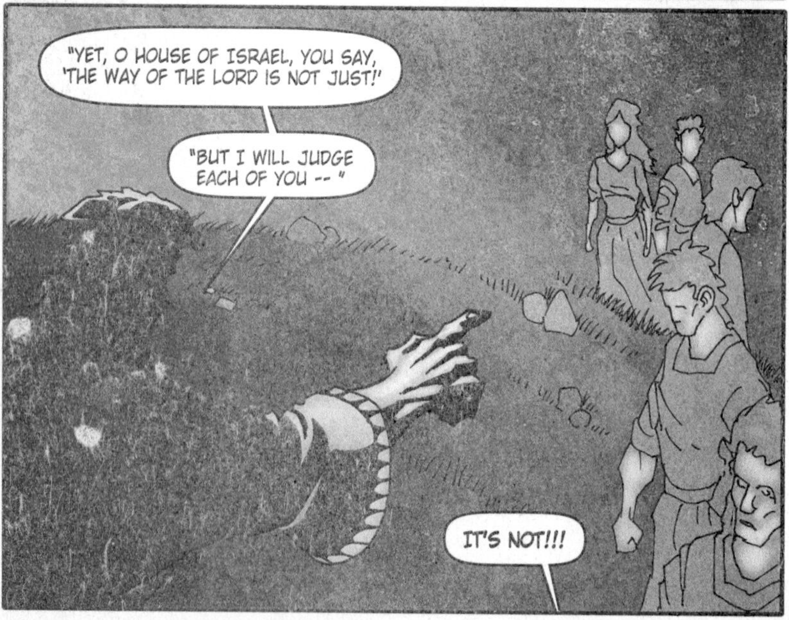
"YET, O HOUSE OF ISRAEL, YOU SAY, 'THE WAY OF THE LORD IS NOT JUST!'
"BUT I WILL JUDGE EACH OF YOU -- "
IT'S NOT!!!

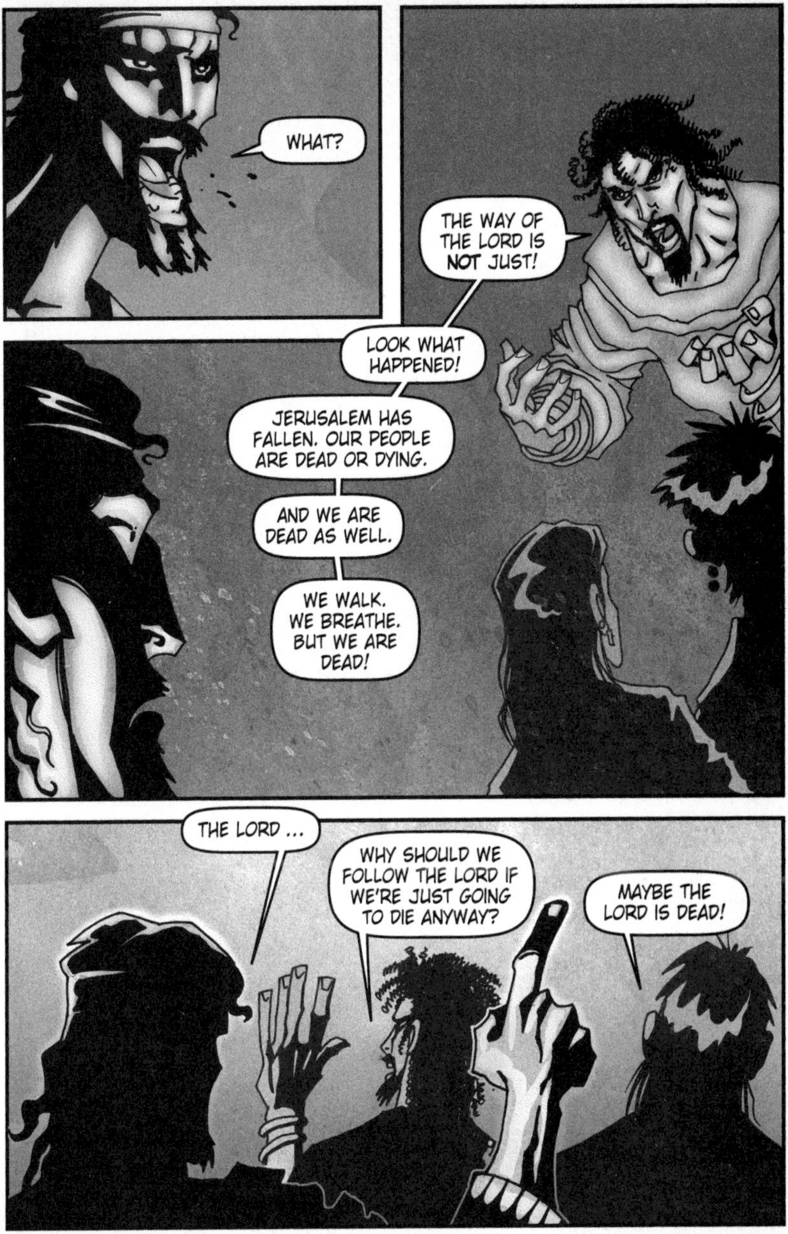
WHAT?
THE WAY OF THE LORD IS NOT JUST!
LOOK WHAT HAPPENED!
JERUSALEM HAS FALLEN. OUR PEOPLE ARE DEAD OR DYING.
AND WE ARE DEAD AS WELL.
WE WALK. WE BREATHE. BUT WE ARE DEAD!
THE LORD ...
WHY SHOULD WE FOLLOW THE LORD IF WE'RE JUST GOING TO DIE ANYWAY?
MAYBE THE LORD IS DEAD!

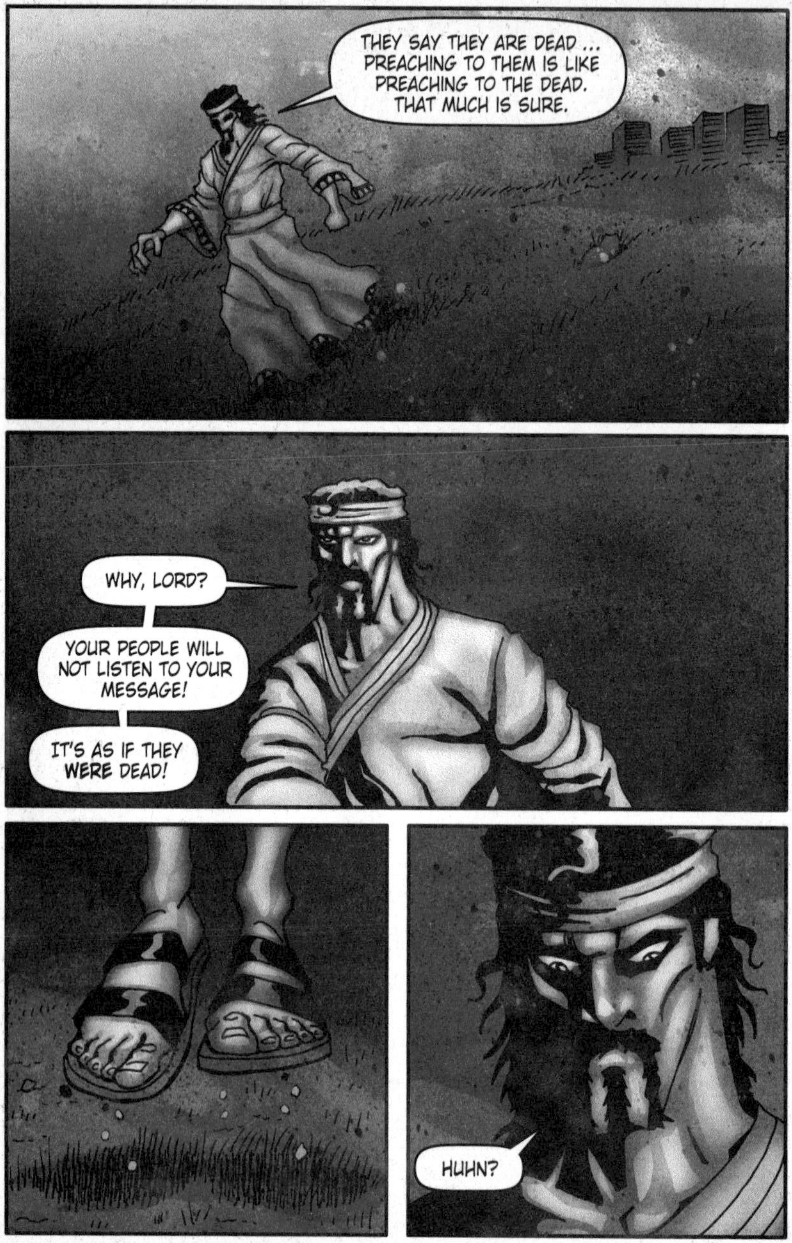
THEY SAY THEY ARE DEAD ... PREACHING TO THEM IS LIKE PREACHING TO THE DEAD. THAT MUCH IS SURE.
WHY, LORD?
YOUR PEOPLE WILL NOT LISTEN TO YOUR MESSAGE!
IT'S AS IF THEY WERE DEAD!
HUHN?

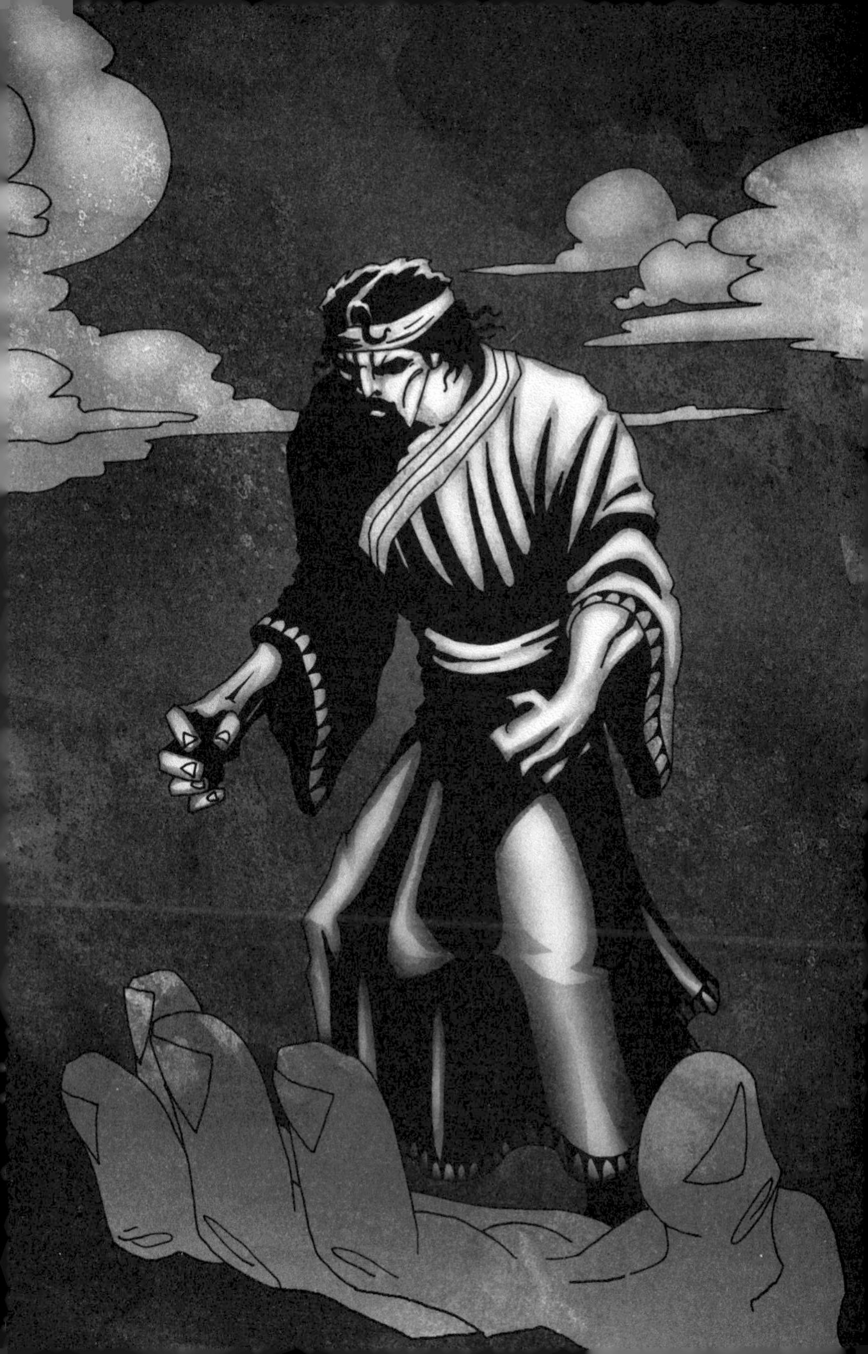

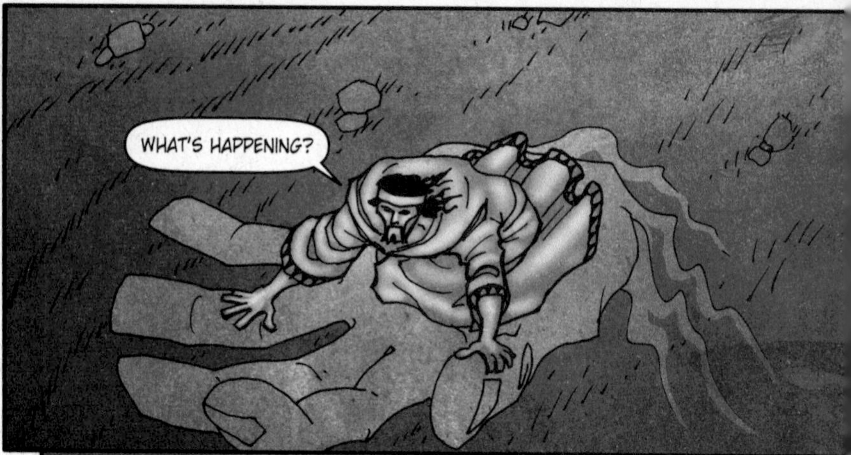
WHAT'S HAPPENING?
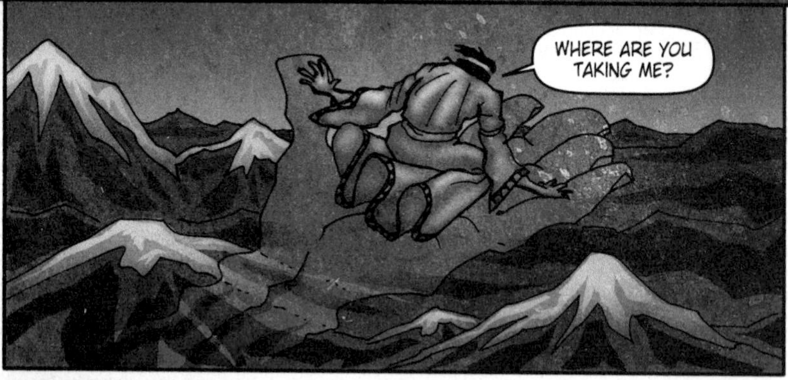
WHERE ARE YOU TAKING ME?
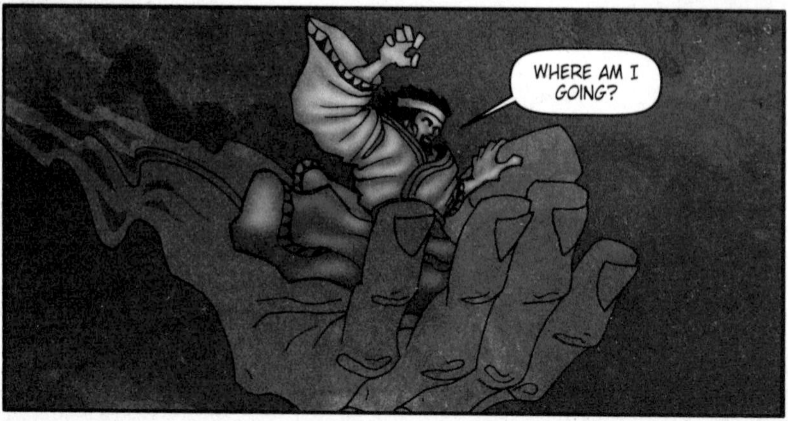
WHERE AM I GOING?

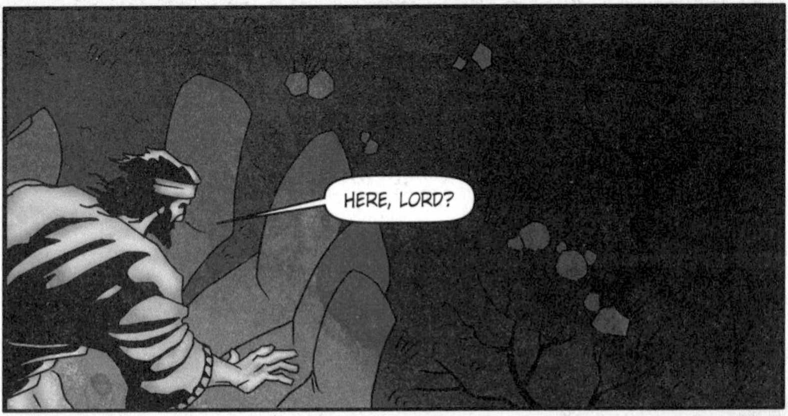
HERE, LORD?
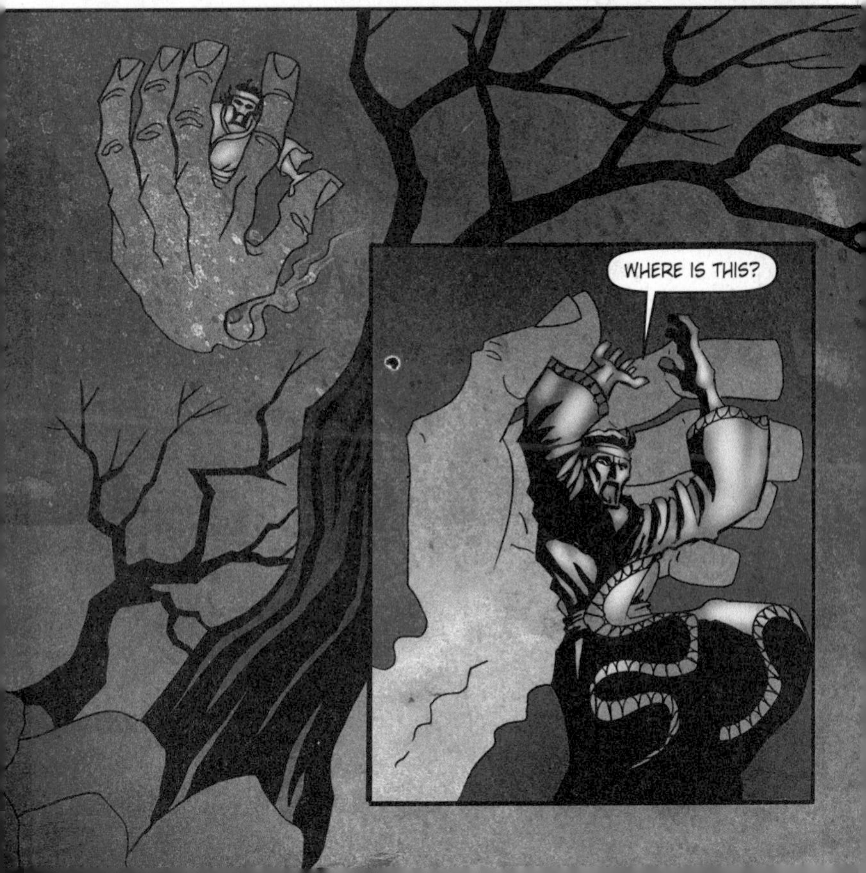
WHERE IS THIS?

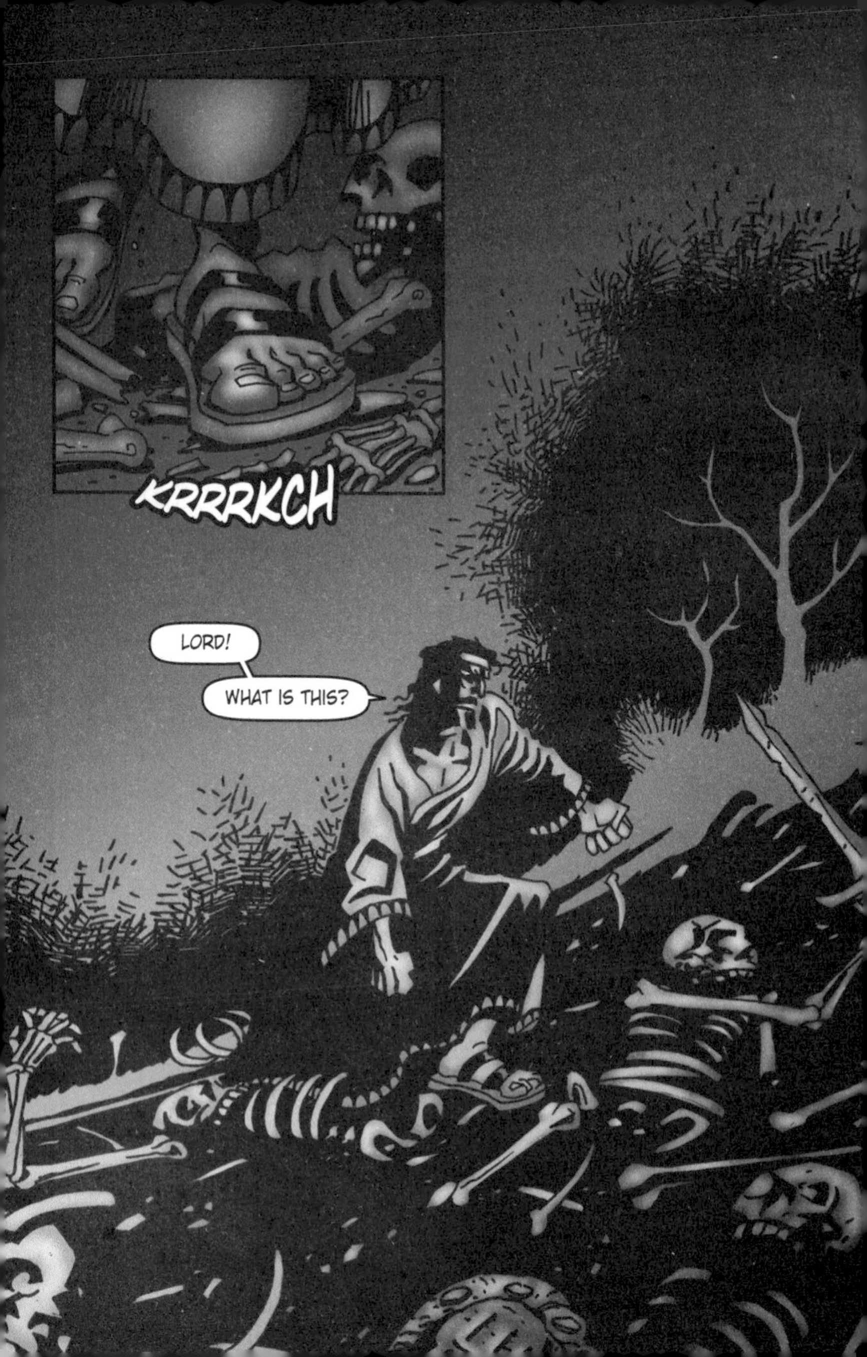
KRRRKCH
LORD!
WHAT IS THIS?

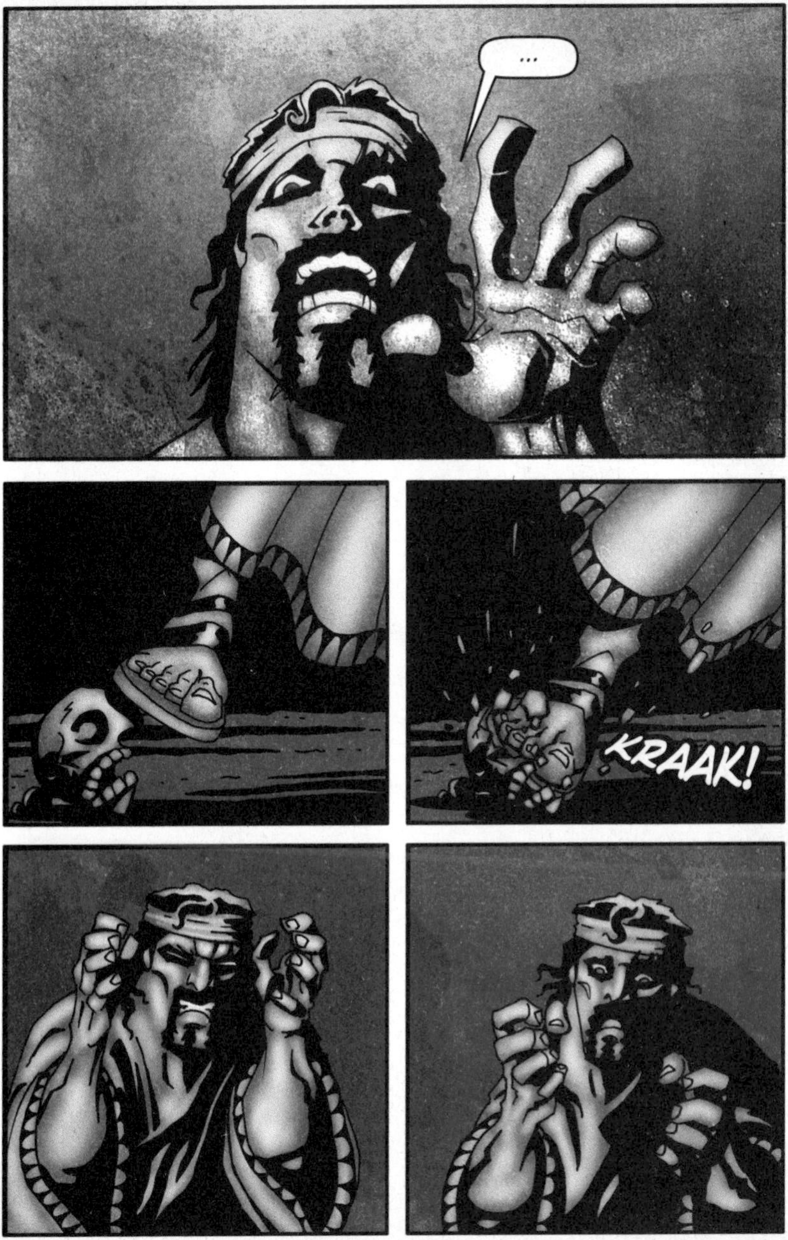
...
KRAAK!

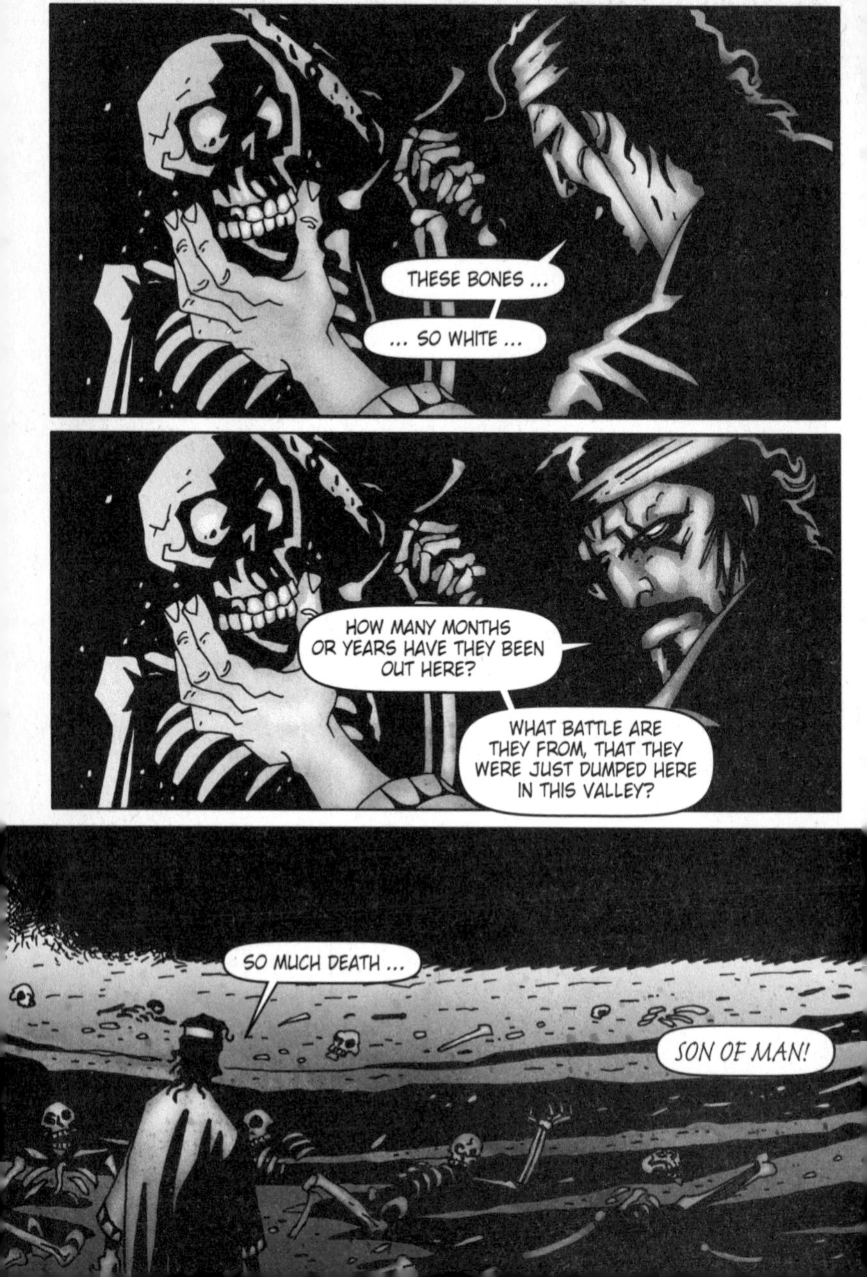
THESE BONES ...
... SO WHITE ...
HOW MANY MONTHS OR YEARS HAVE THEY BEEN OUT HERE?
WHAT BATTLE ARE THEY FROM, THAT THEY WERE JUST DUMPED HERE IN THIS VALLEY?
SO MUCH DEATH ...
SON OF MAN!

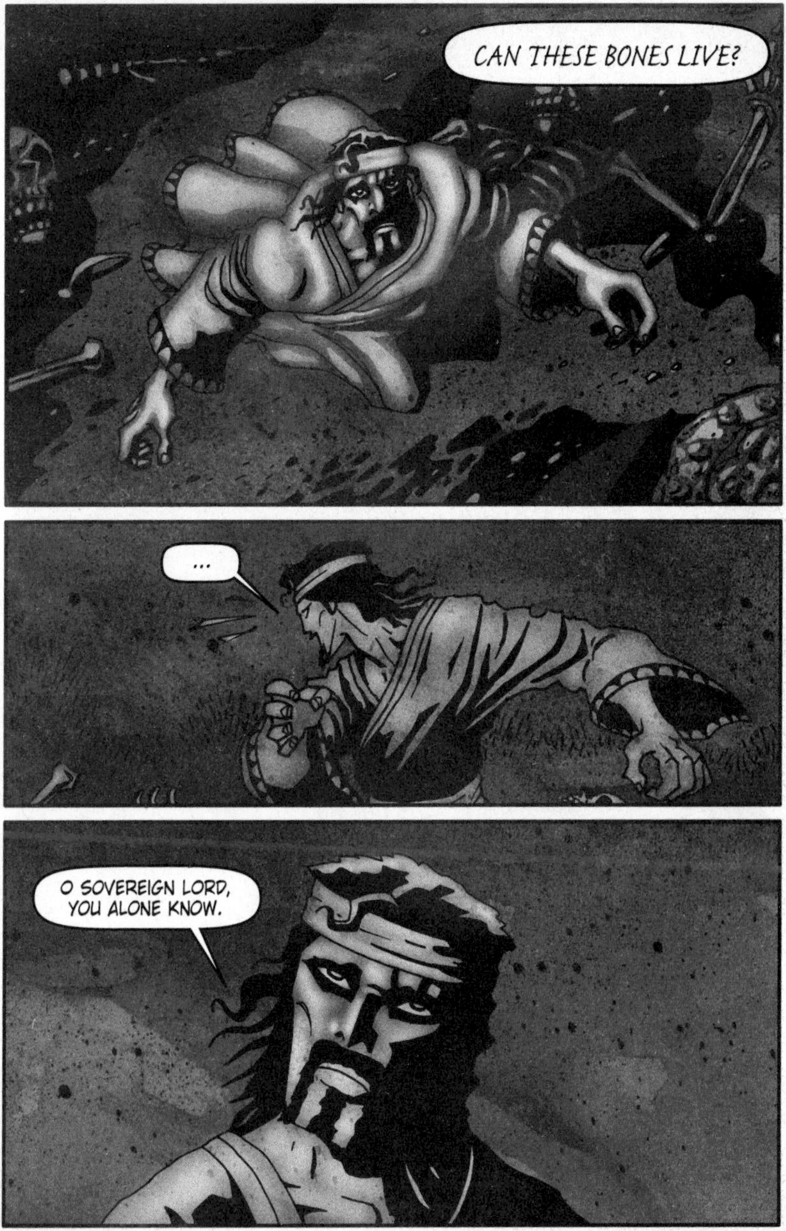
CAN THESE BONES LIVE?
...
O SOVEREIGN LORD,
YOU ALONE KNOW.

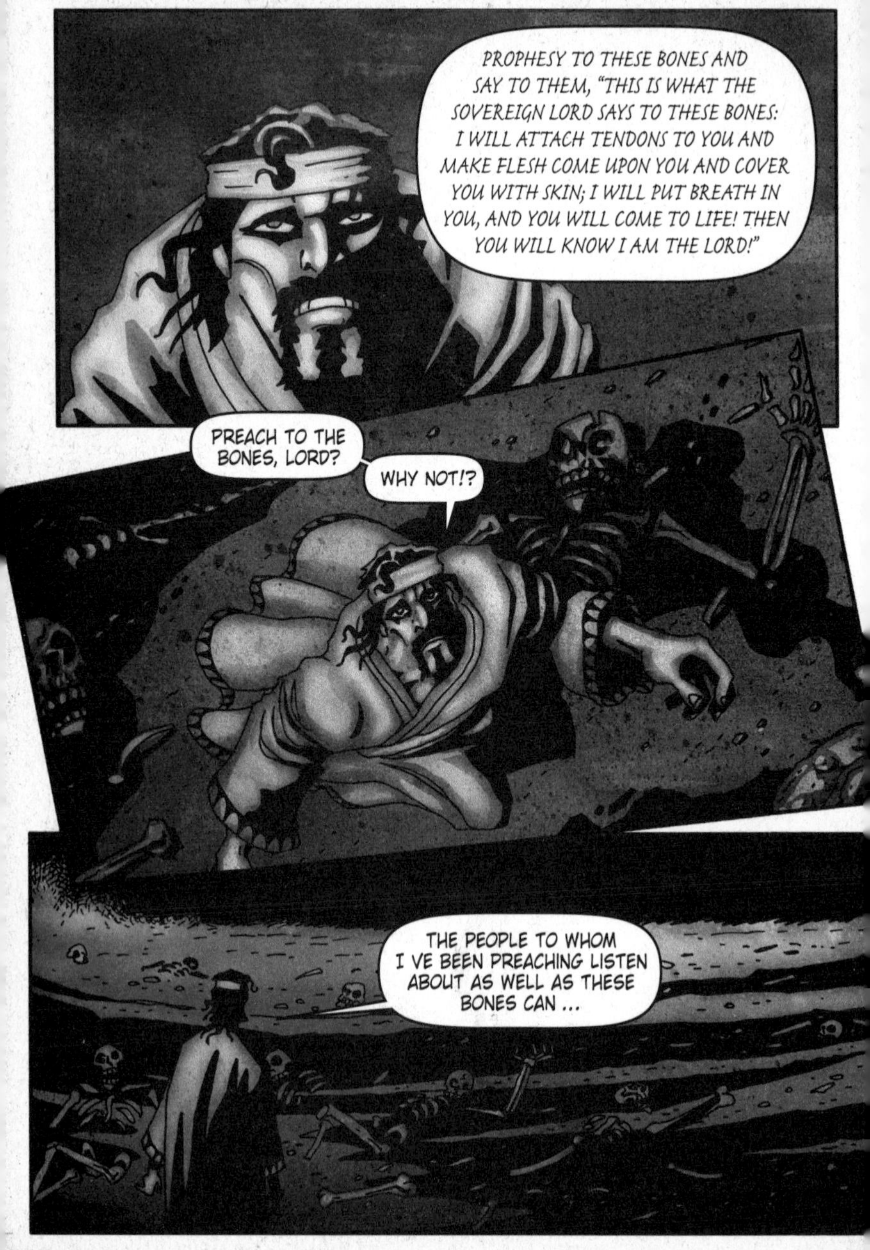
PROPHESY TO THESE BONES AND SAY TO THEM, "THIS IS WHAT THE SOVEREIGN LORD SAYS TO THESE BONES: I WILL ATTACH TENDONS TO YOU AND MAKE FLESH COME UPON YOU AND COVER YOU WITH SKIN; I WILL PUT BREATH IN YOU, AND YOU WILL COME TO LIFE! THEN YOU WILL KNOW I AM THE LORD!"
PREACH TO THE BONES, LORD?
WHY NOT!?
THE PEOPLE TO WHOM I VE BEEN PREACHING LISTEN ABOUT AS WELL AS THESE BONES CAN ...

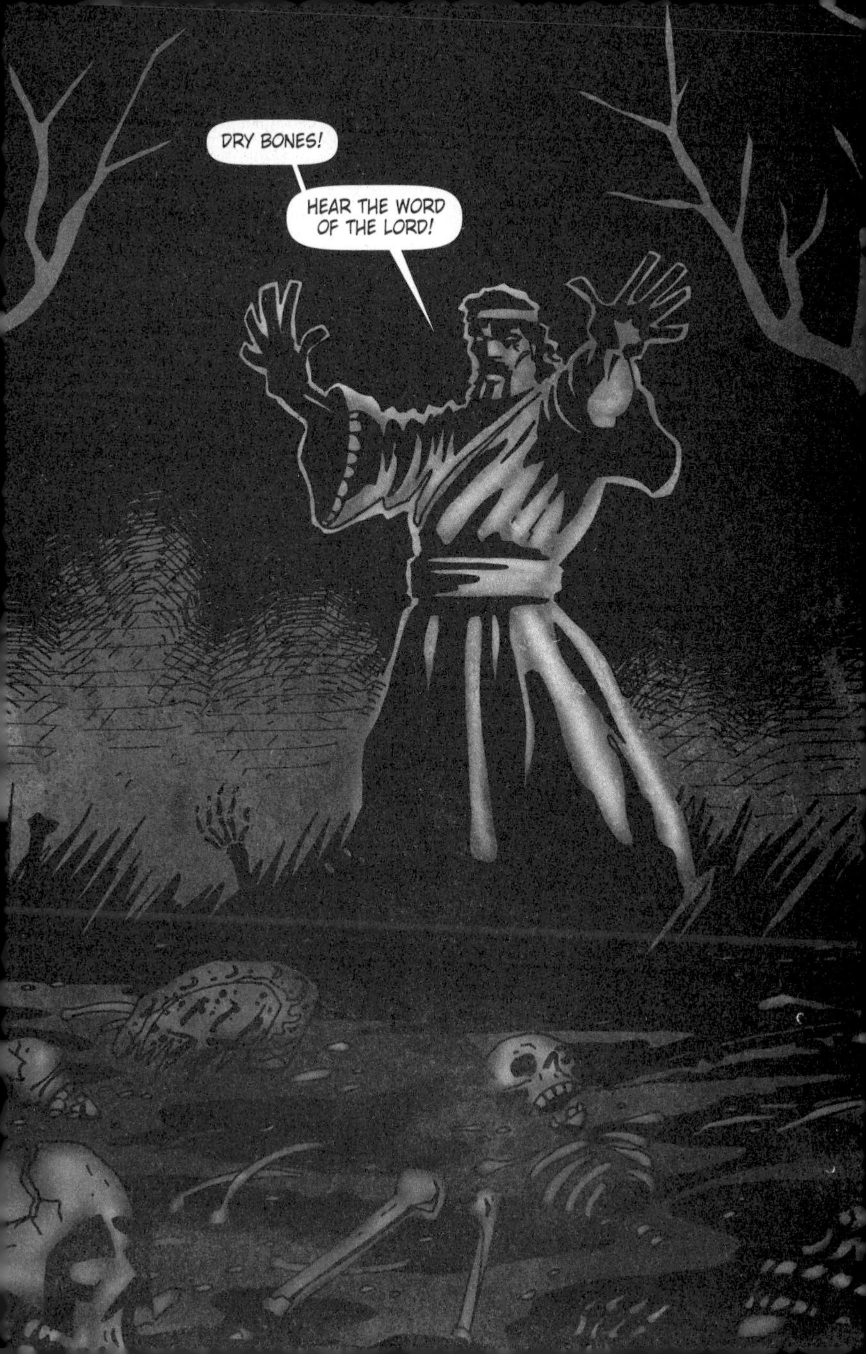
DRY BONES!
HEAR THE WORD OF THE LORD!

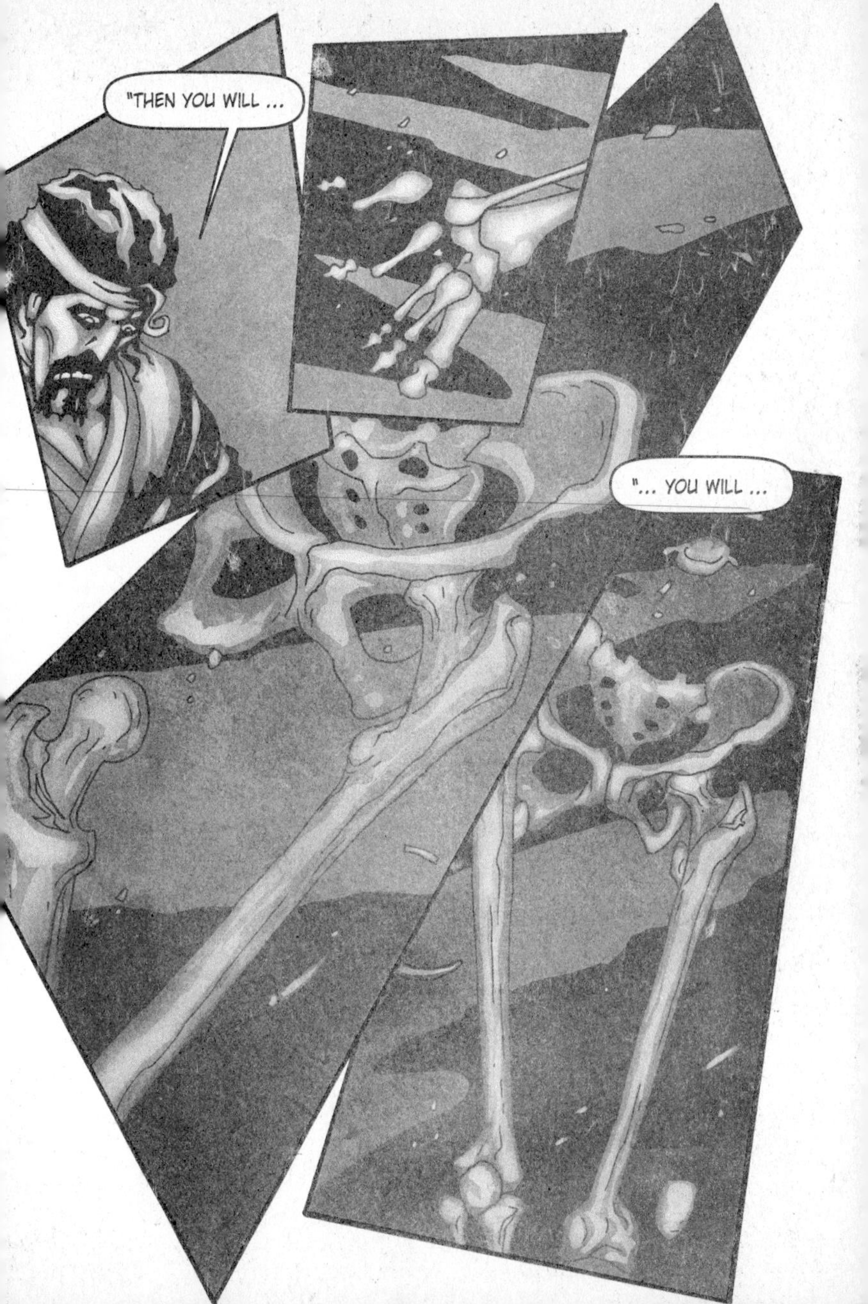
"THEN YOU WILL ...
"... YOU WILL ...

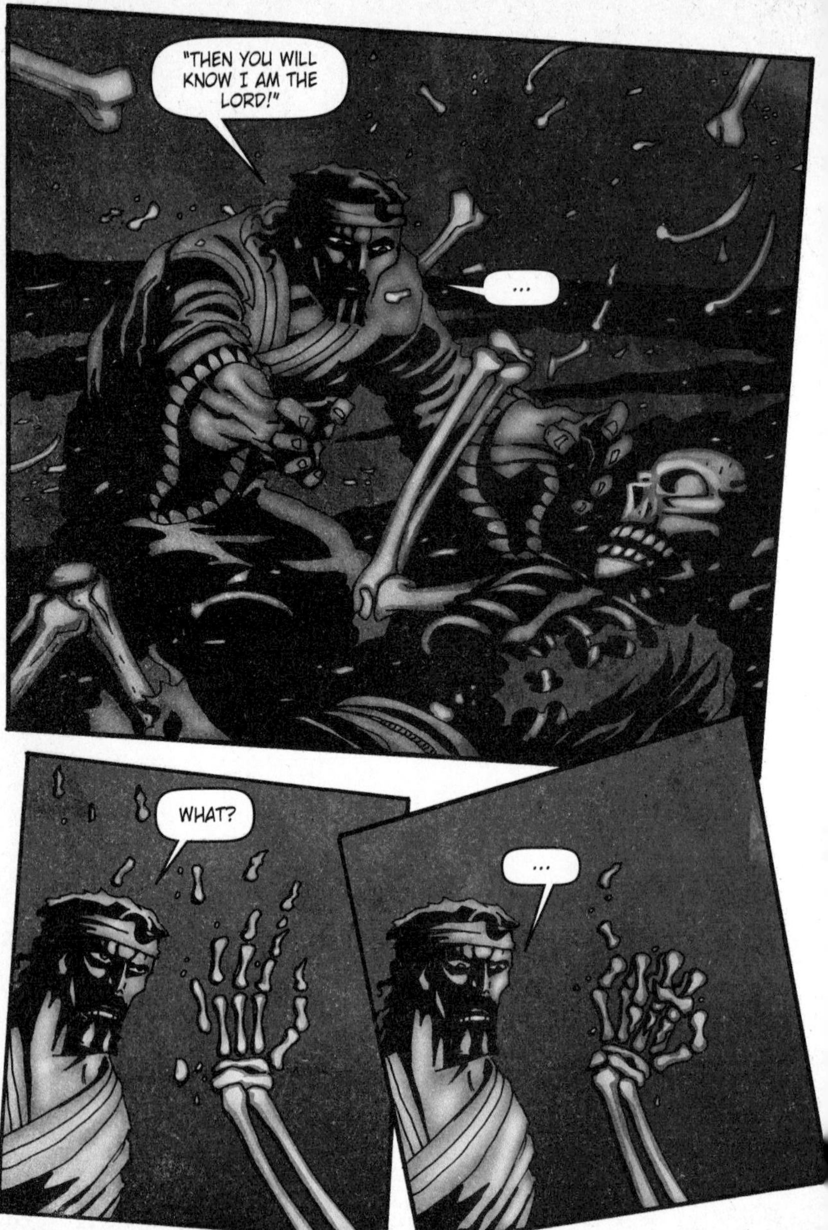
"THEN YOU WILL KNOW I AM THE LORD!"
...
WHAT?
...

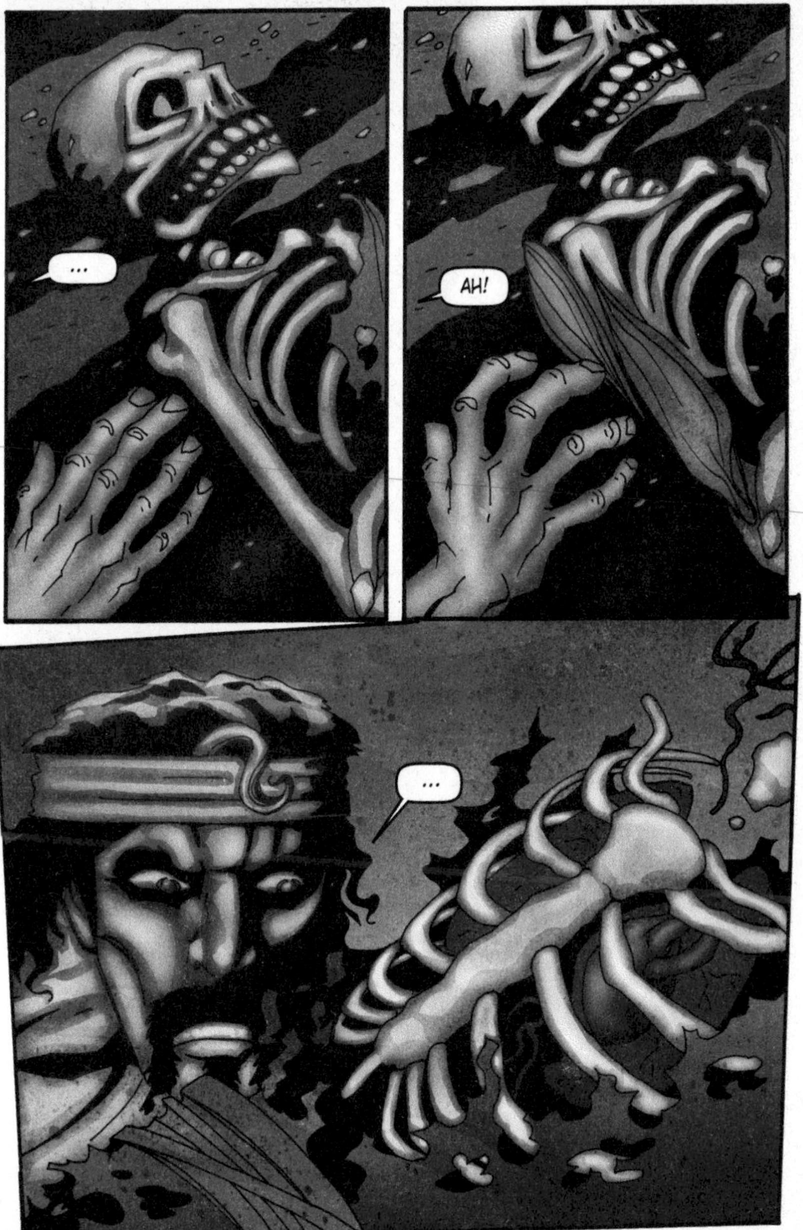
...
AH!
...

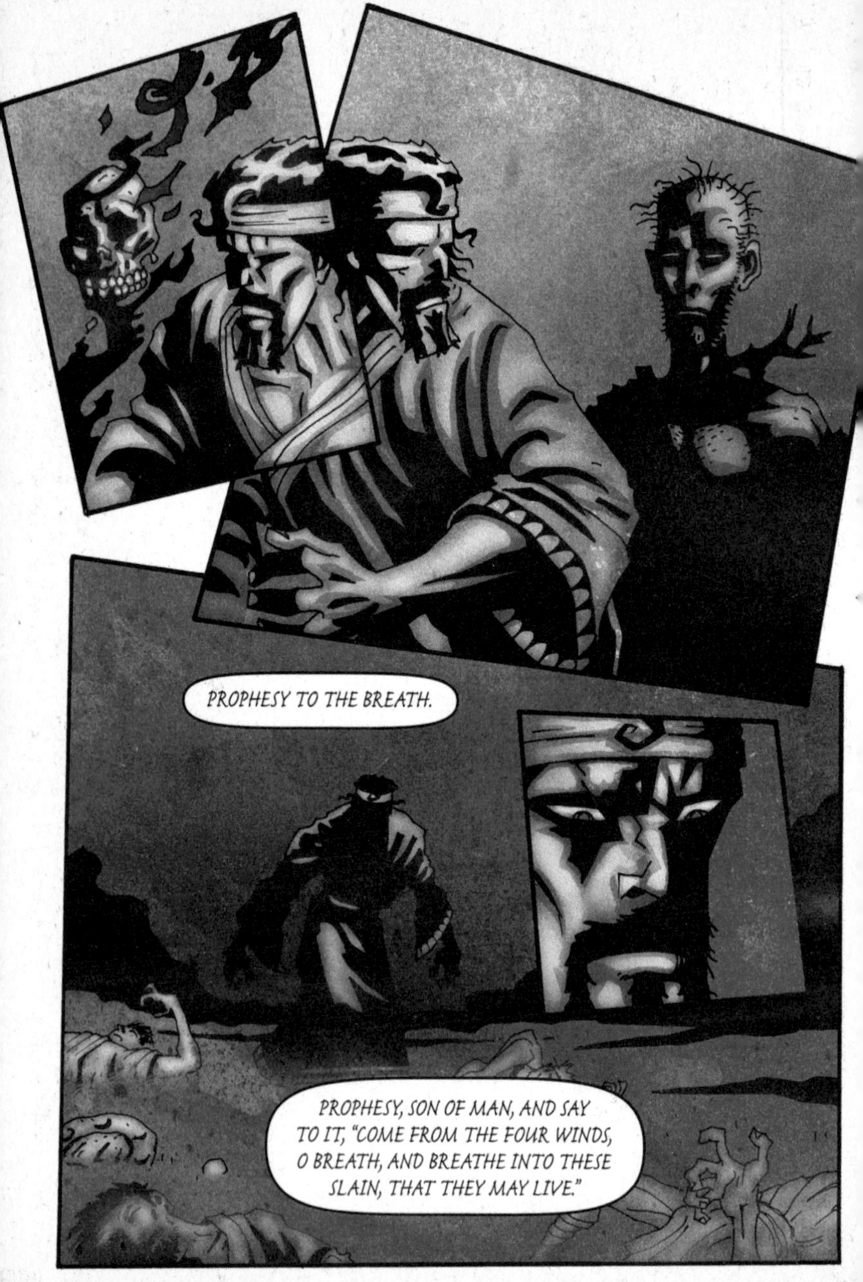
PROPHESY TO THE BREATH.
PROPHESY, SON OF MAN, AND SAY TO IT, "COME FROM THE FOUR WINDS, O BREATH, AND BREATHE INTO THESE SLAIN, THAT THEY MAY LIVE."

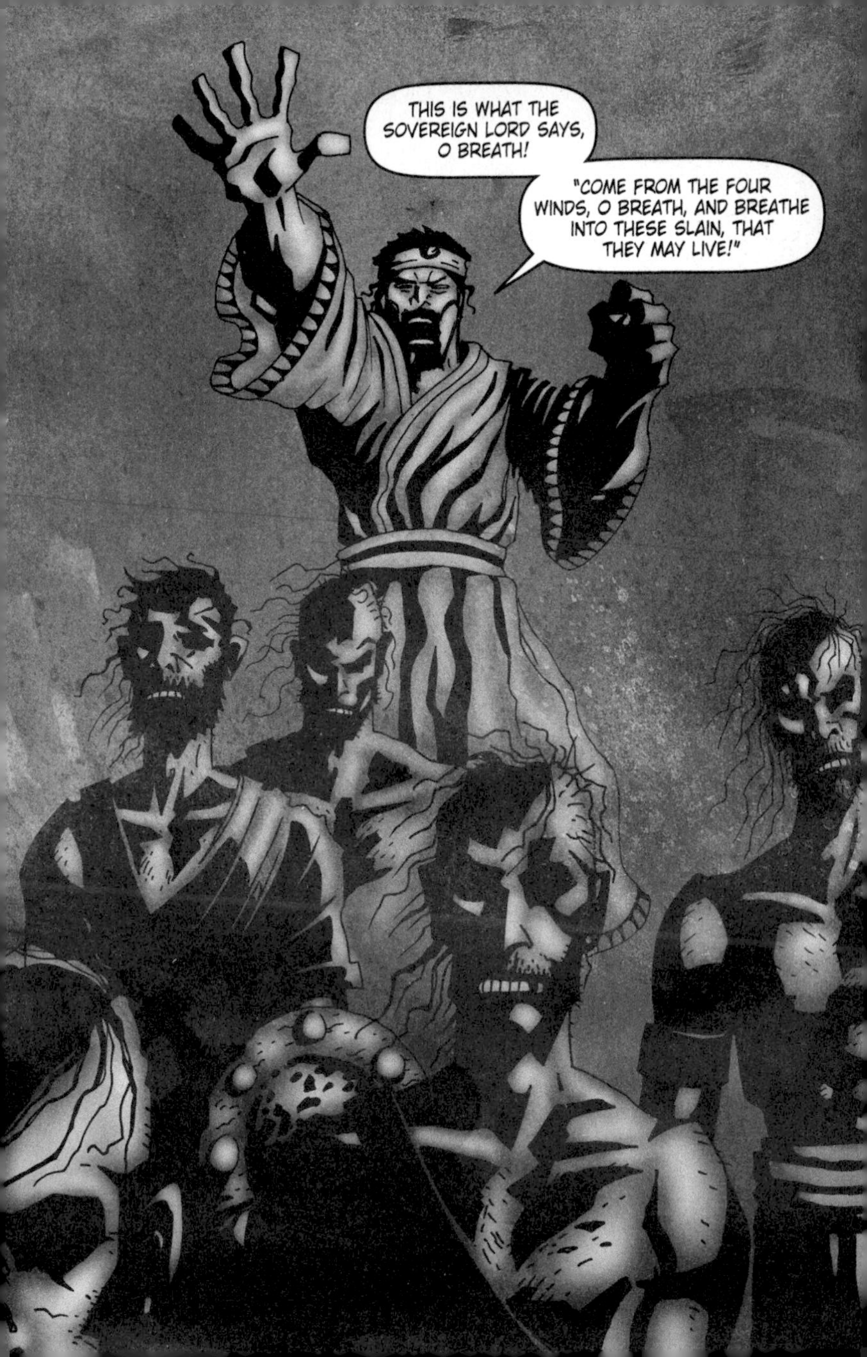
THIS IS WHAT THE SOVEREIGN LORD SAYS, O BREATH!
"COME FROM THE FOUR WINDS, O BREATH, AND BREATHE INTO THESE SLAIN, THAT THEY MAY LIVE!"

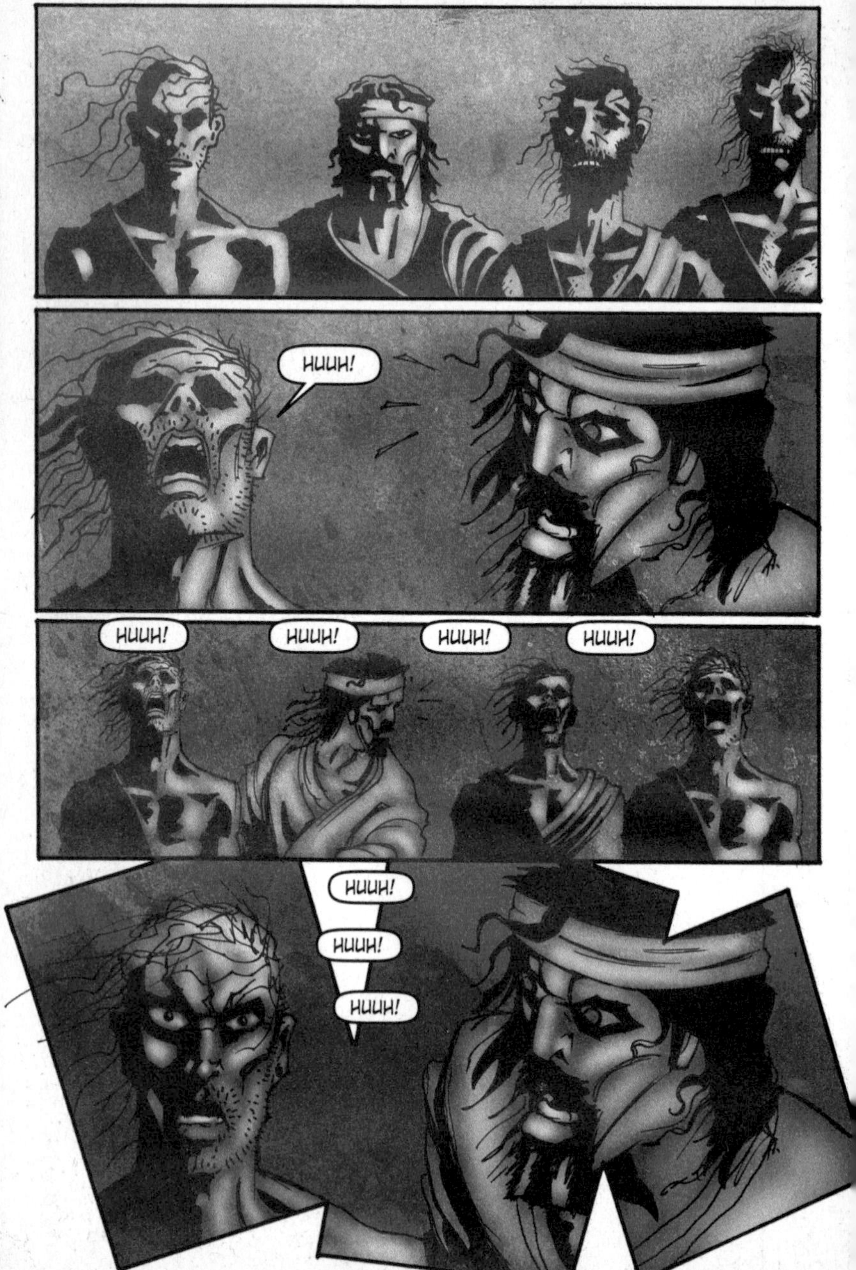
HUUH!
HUUH!
HUUH!
HUUH!
HUUH!
HUUH!
HUUH!
HUUH!

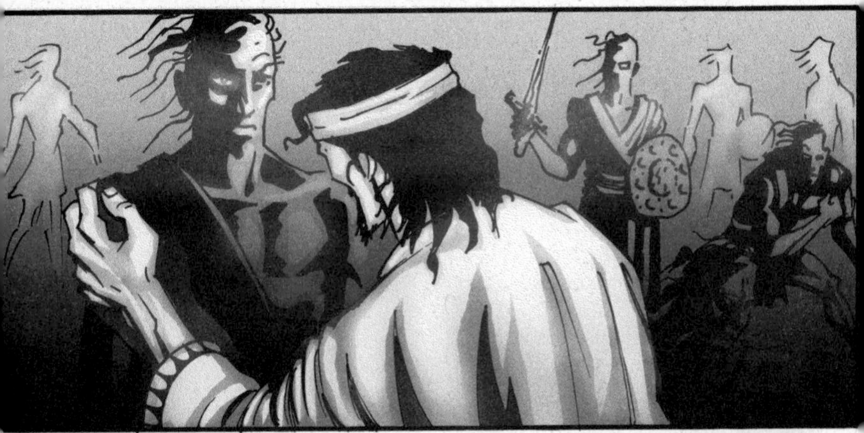
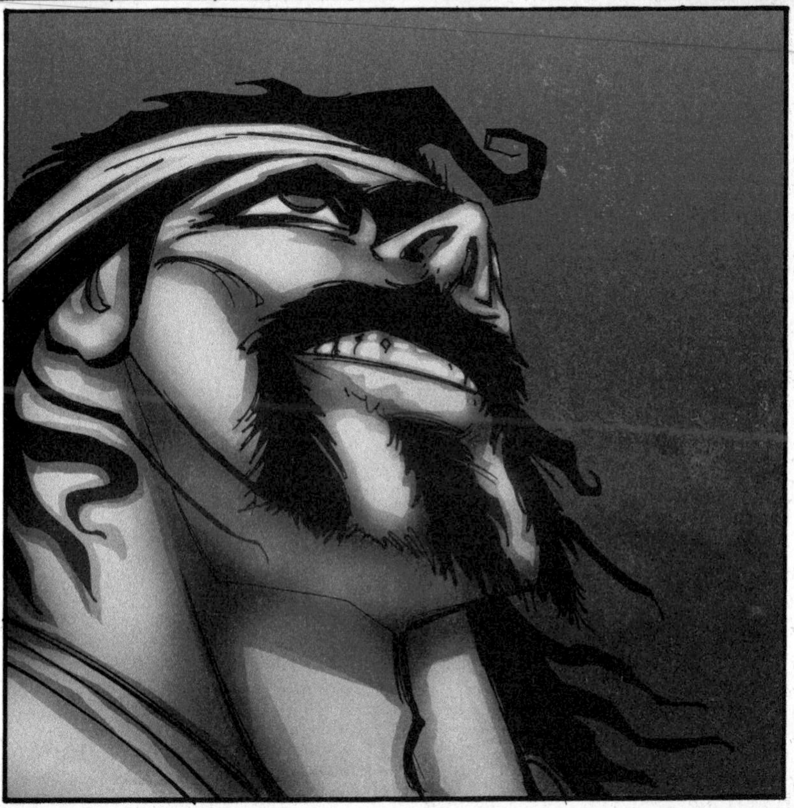

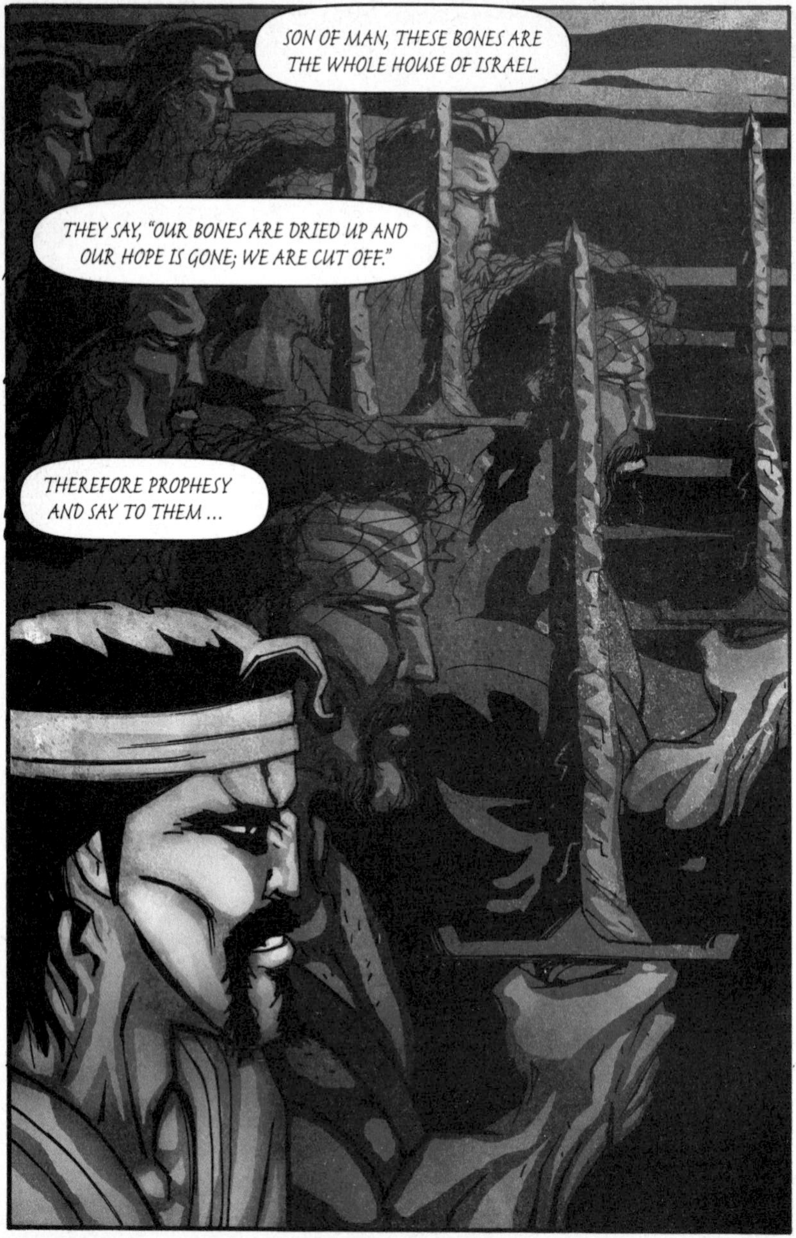
SON OF MAN, THESE BONES ARE THE WHOLE HOUSE OF ISRAEL.
THEY SAY, "OUR BONES ARE DRIED UP AND OUR HOPE IS GONE; WE ARE CUT OFF."
THEREFORE PROPHESY AND SAY TO THEM ...

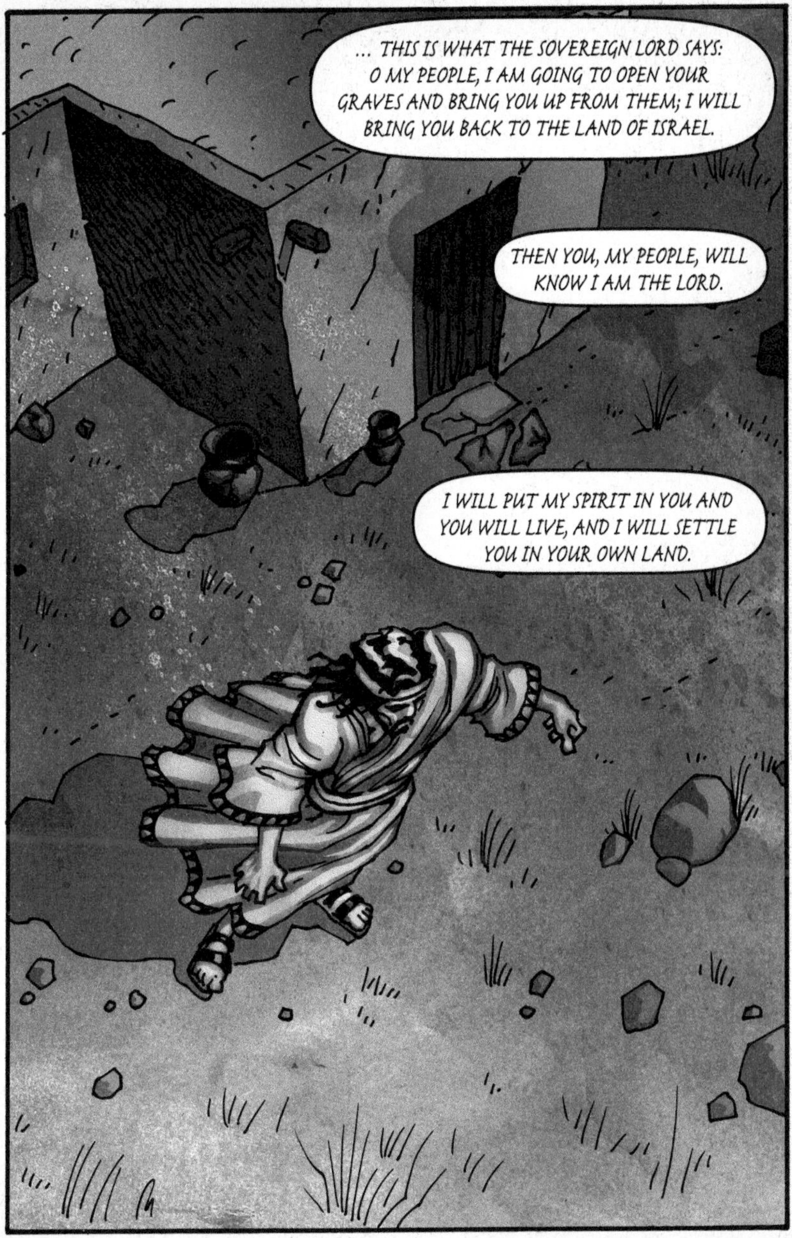
... THIS IS WHAT THE SOVEREIGN LORD SAYS: O MY PEOPLE, I AM GOING TO OPEN YOUR GRAVES AND BRING YOU UP FROM THEM; I WILL BRING YOU BACK TO THE LAND OF ISRAEL.
THEN YOU, MY PEOPLE, WILL KNOW I AM THE LORD.
I WILL PUT MY SPIRIT IN YOU AND YOU WILL LIVE, AND I WILL SETTLE YOU IN YOUR OWN LAND.

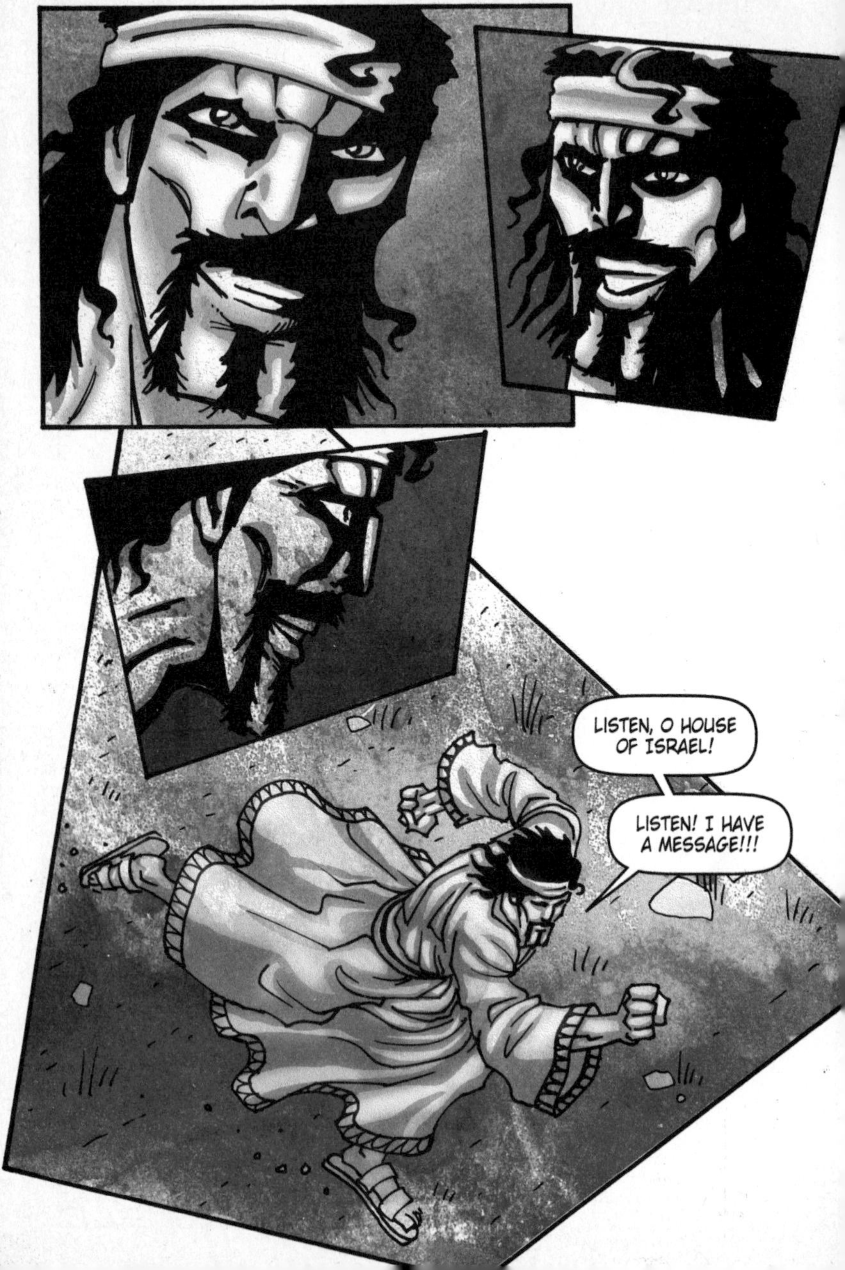
LISTEN, O HOUSE OF ISRAEL!
LISTEN! I HAVE A MESSAGE!!!

CHAPTER FOUR
"River of Life"

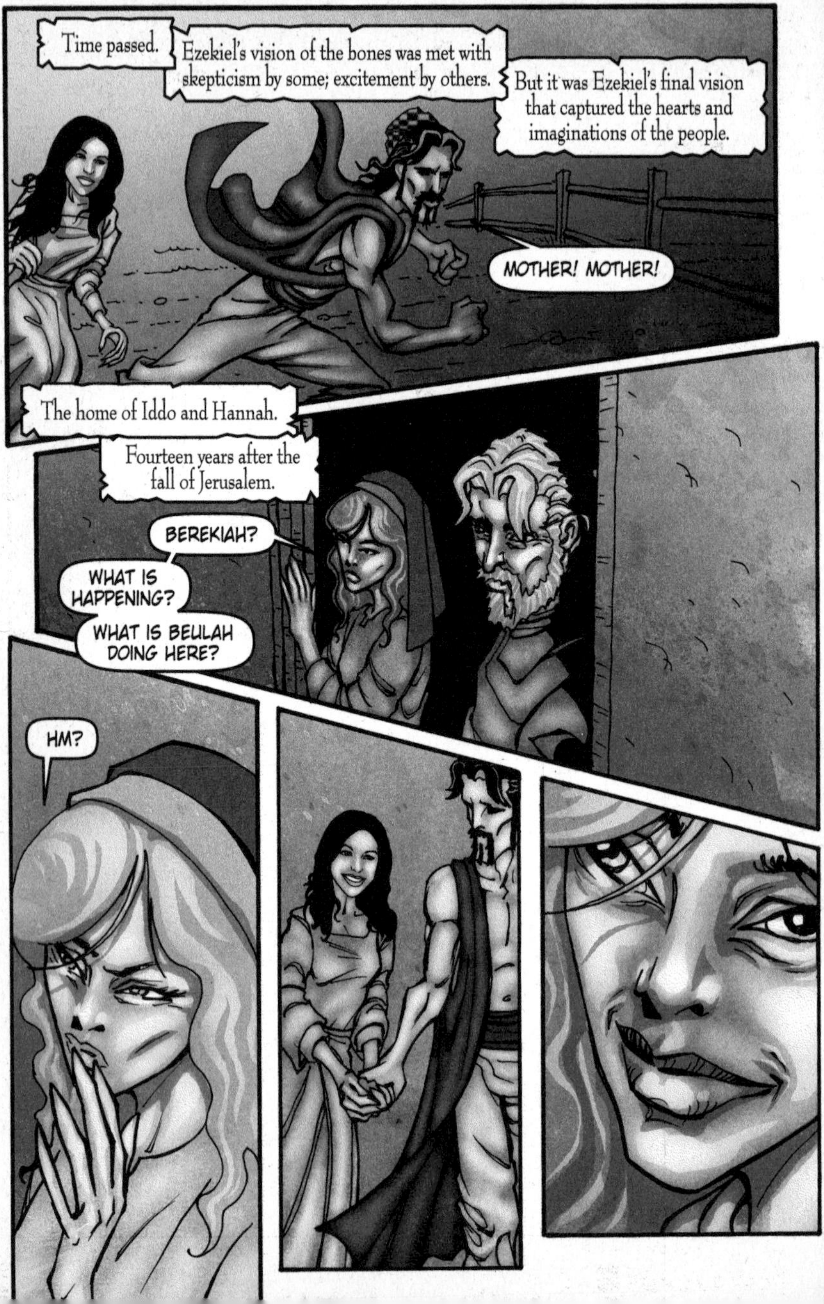
Time passed.
Ezekiel's vision of the bones was met with skepticism by some; excitement by others.
But it was Ezekiel's final vision that captured the hearts and imaginations of the people.
MOTHER! MOTHER!
The home of Iddo and Hannah.
Fourteen years after the fall of Jerusalem.
BEREKIAH?
WHAT IS HAPPENING?
WHAT IS BEULAH DOING HERE?
HM?

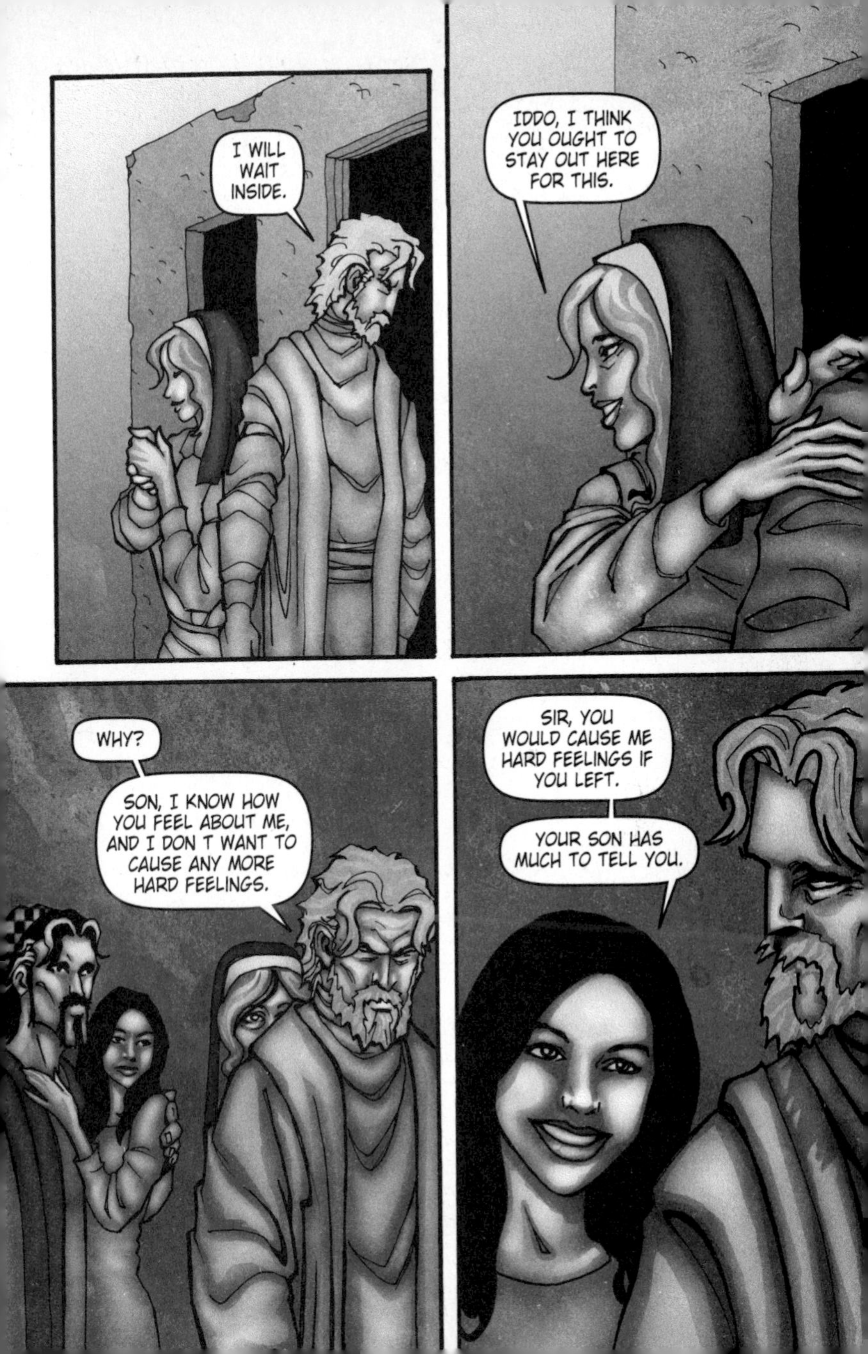
I WILL WAIT INSIDE.
IDDO, I THINK YOU OUGHT TO STAY OUT HERE FOR THIS.
WHY?
SON, I KNOW HOW YOU FEEL ABOUT ME, AND I DON T WANT TO CAUSE ANY MORE HARD FEELINGS.
SIR, YOU WOULD CAUSE ME HARD FEELINGS IF YOU LEFT.
YOUR SON HAS MUCH TO TELL YOU.

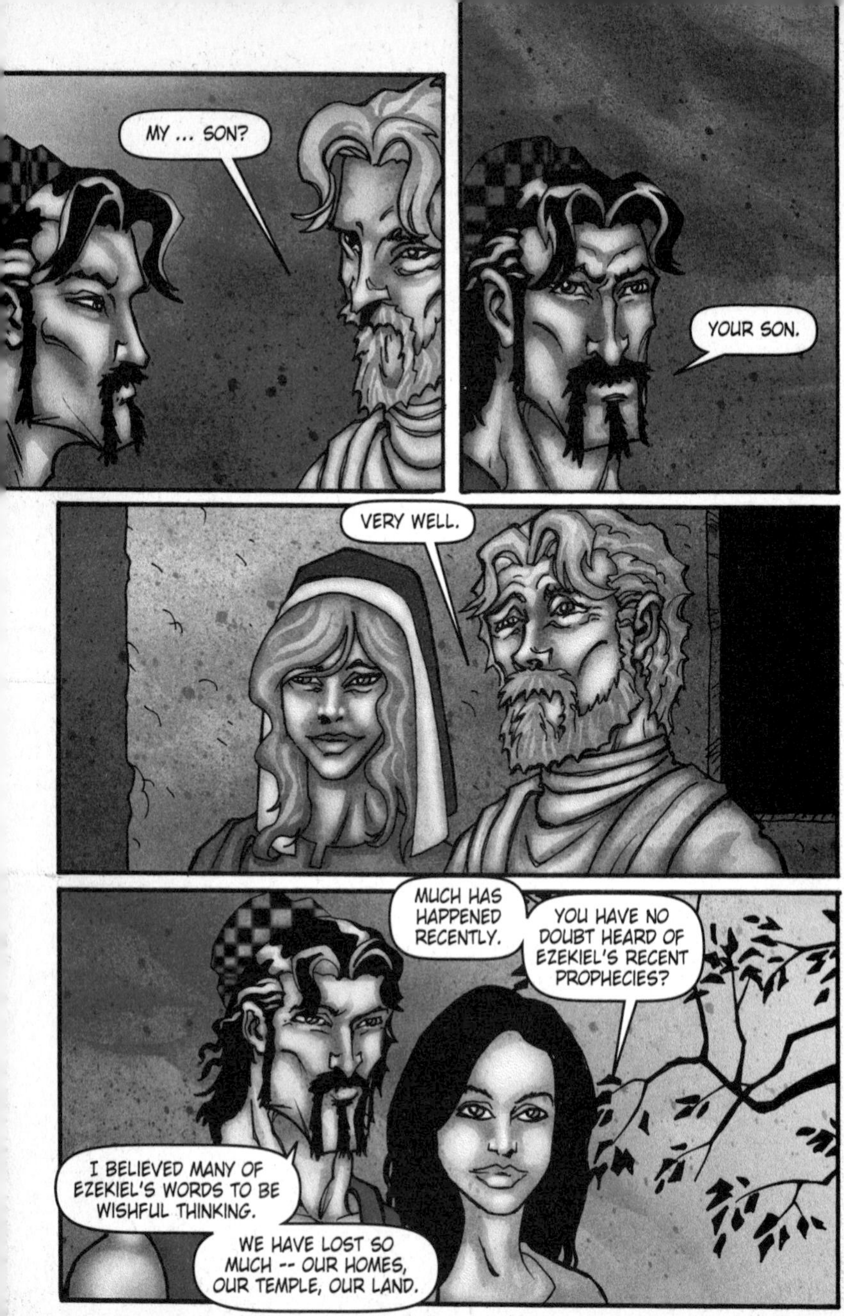
MY ... SON?
YOUR SON.
VERY WELL.
MUCH HAS HAPPENED RECENTLY.
YOU HAVE NO DOUBT HEARD OF EZEKIEL'S RECENT PROPHECIES?
I BELIEVED MANY OF EZEKIEL'S WORDS TO BE WISHFUL THINKING.
WE HAVE LOST SO MUCH -- OUR HOMES, OUR TEMPLE, OUR LAND.

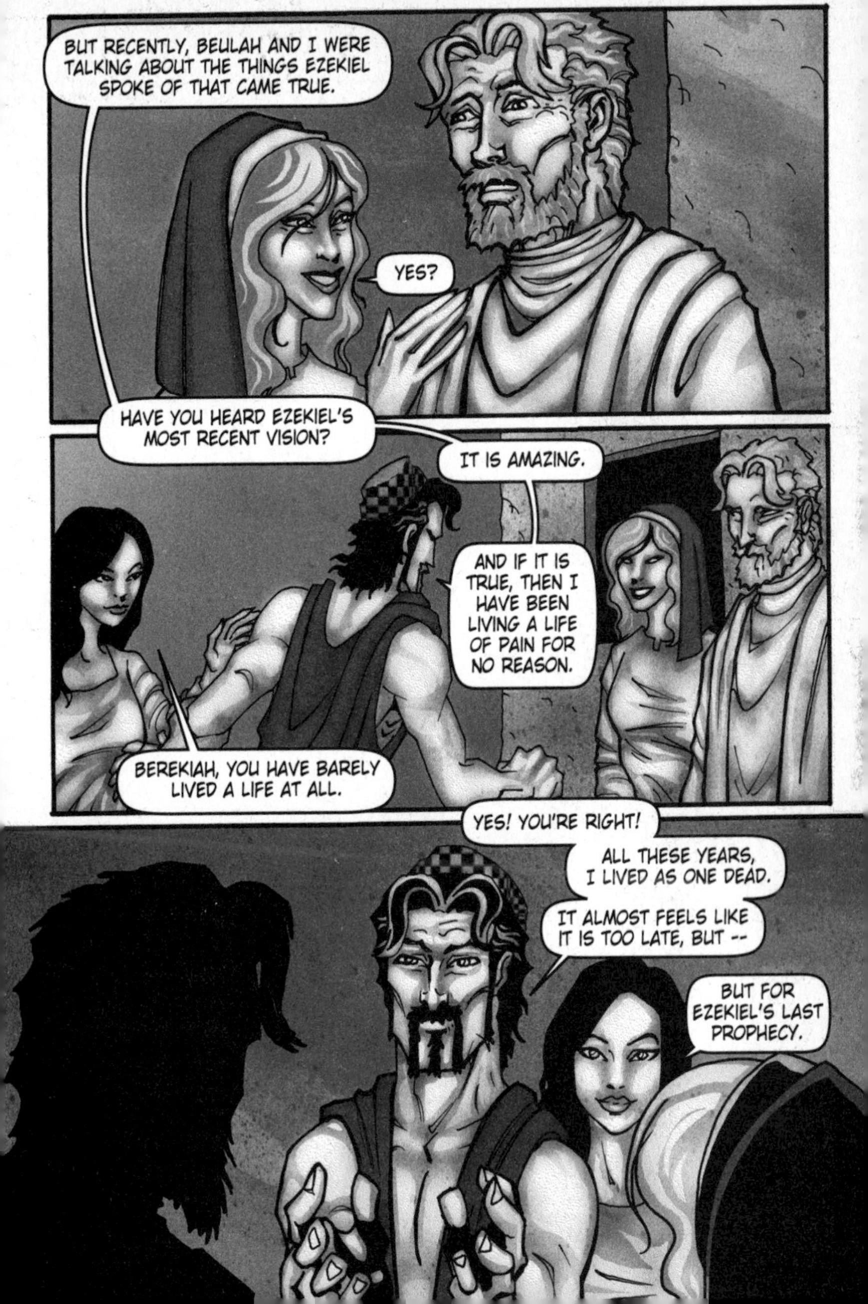
BUT RECENTLY, BEULAH AND I WERE TALKING ABOUT THE THINGS EZEKIEL SPOKE OF THAT CAME TRUE.
YES?
HAVE YOU HEARD EZEKIEL'S MOST RECENT VISION?
IT IS AMAZING.
AND IF IT IS TRUE, THEN I HAVE BEEN LIVING A LIFE OF PAIN FOR NO REASON.
BEREKIAH, YOU HAVE BARELY LIVED A LIFE AT ALL.
YES! YOU'RE RIGHT!
ALL THESE YEARS, I LIVED AS ONE DEAD.
IT ALMOST FEELS LIKE IT IS TOO LATE, BUT --
BUT FOR EZEKIEL'S LAST PROPHECY.

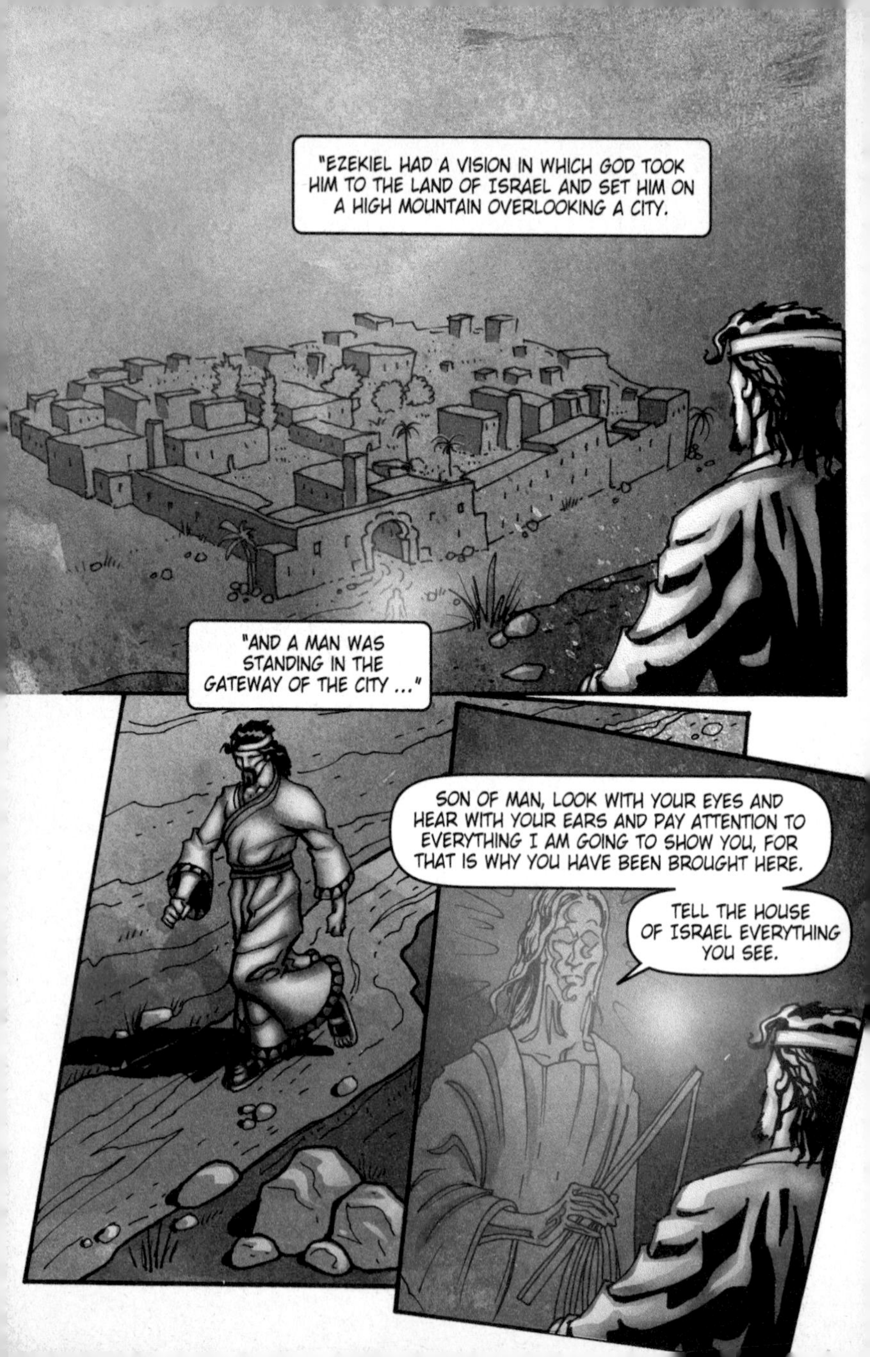
"EZEKIEL HAD A VISION IN WHICH GOD TOOK HIM TO THE LAND OF ISRAEL AND SET HIM ON A HIGH MOUNTAIN OVERLOOKING A CITY.
"AND A MAN WAS STANDING IN THE GATEWAY OF THE CITY ..."
SON OF MAN, LOOK WITH YOUR EYES AND HEAR WITH YOUR EARS AND PAY ATTENTION TO EVERYTHING I AM GOING TO SHOW YOU, FOR THAT IS WHY YOU HAVE BEEN BROUGHT HERE.
TELL THE HOUSE OF ISRAEL EVERYTHING YOU SEE.

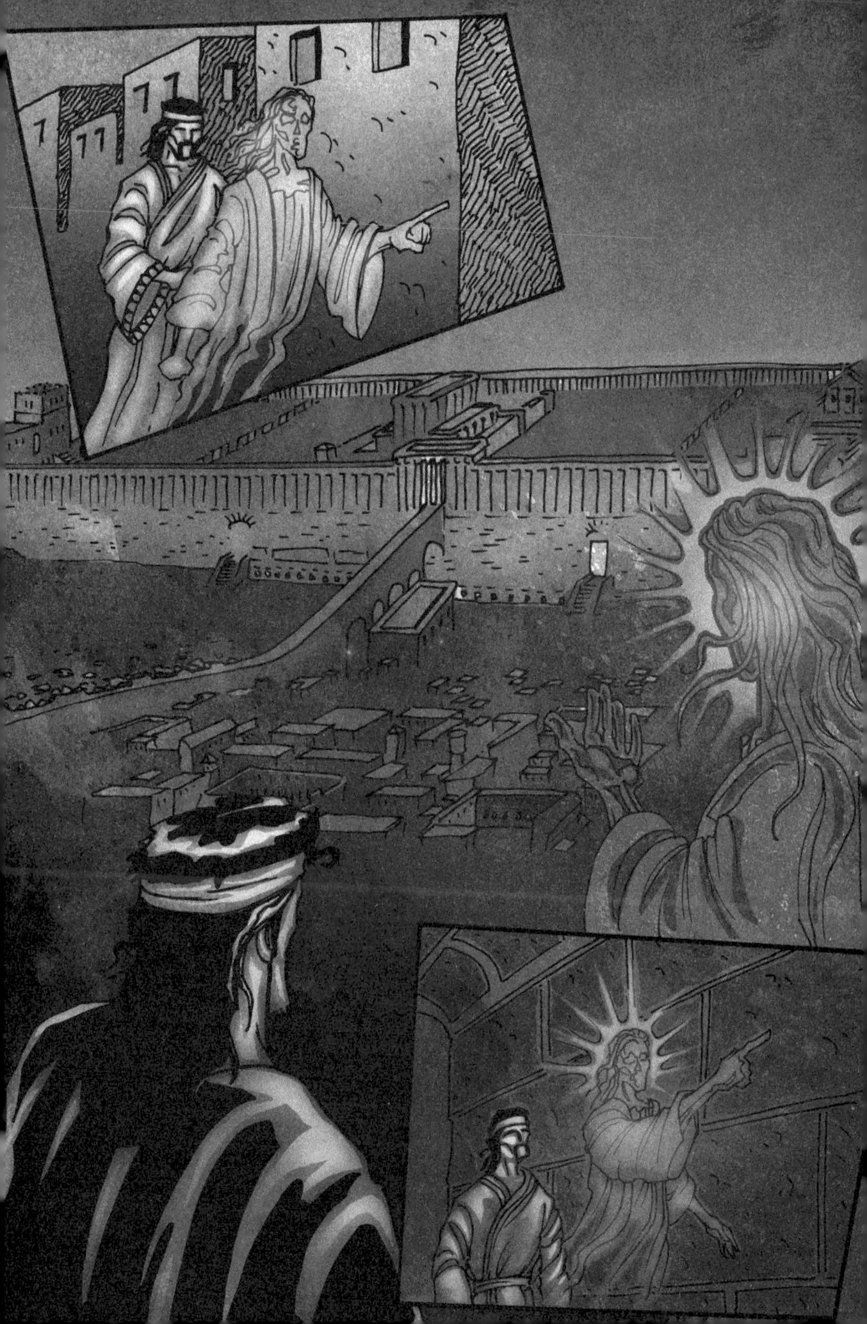

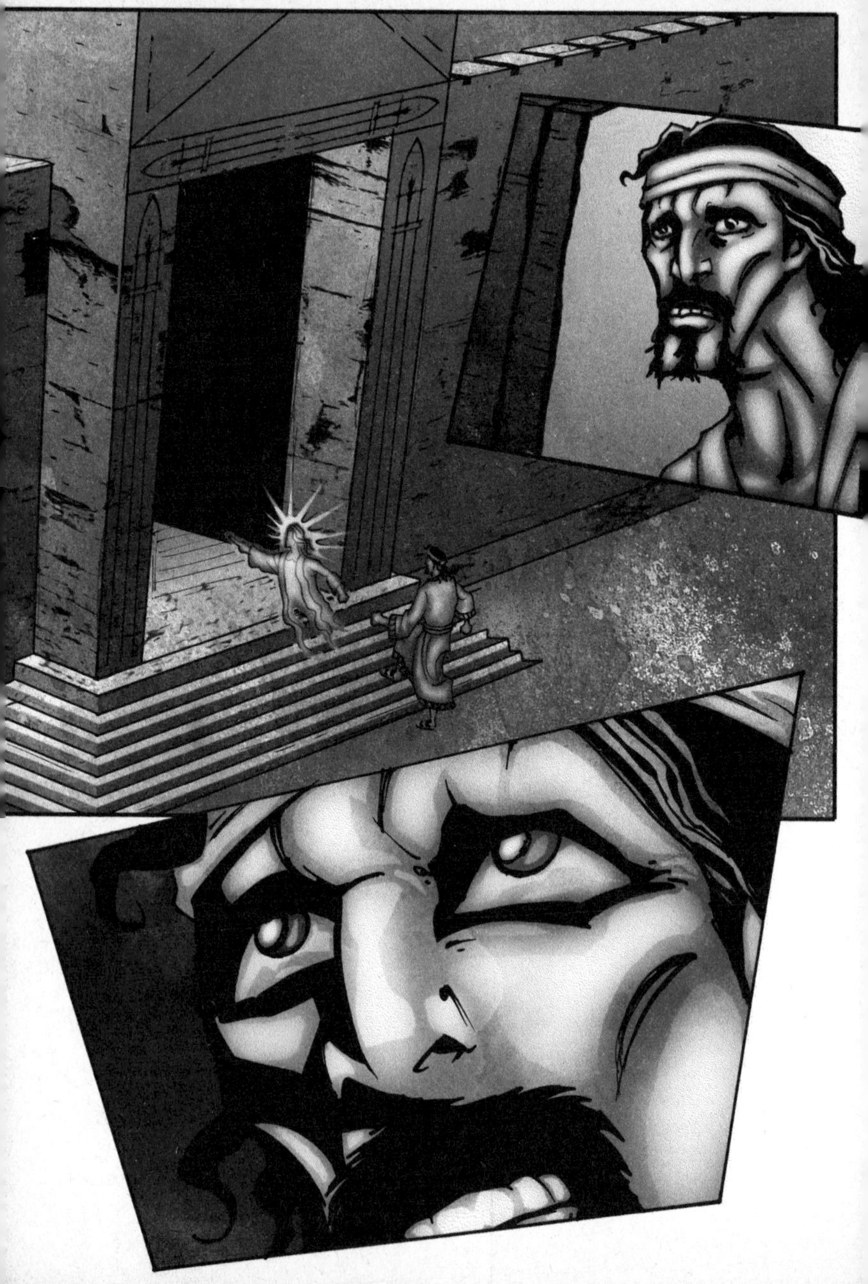

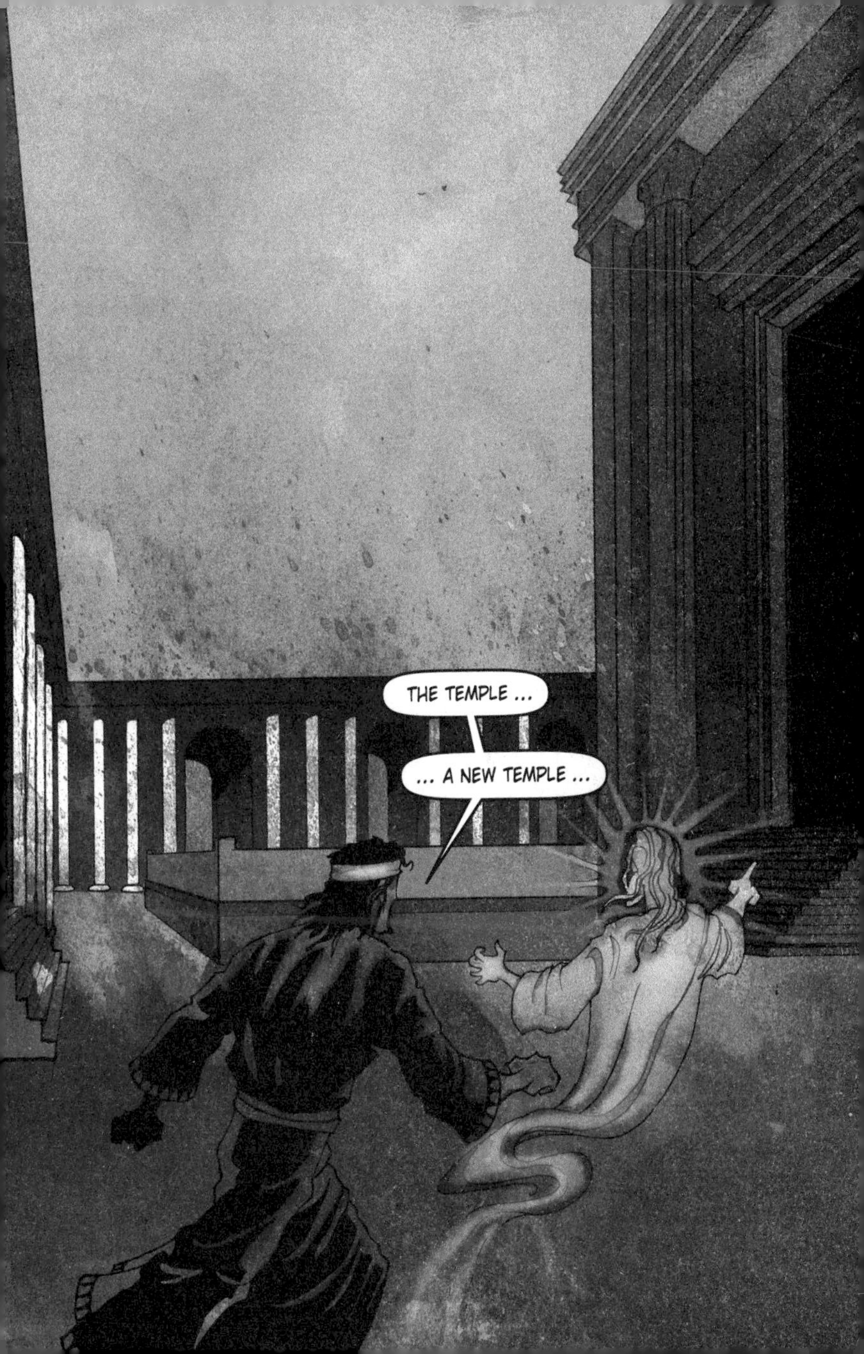
THE TEMPLE ...
... A NEW TEMPLE ...

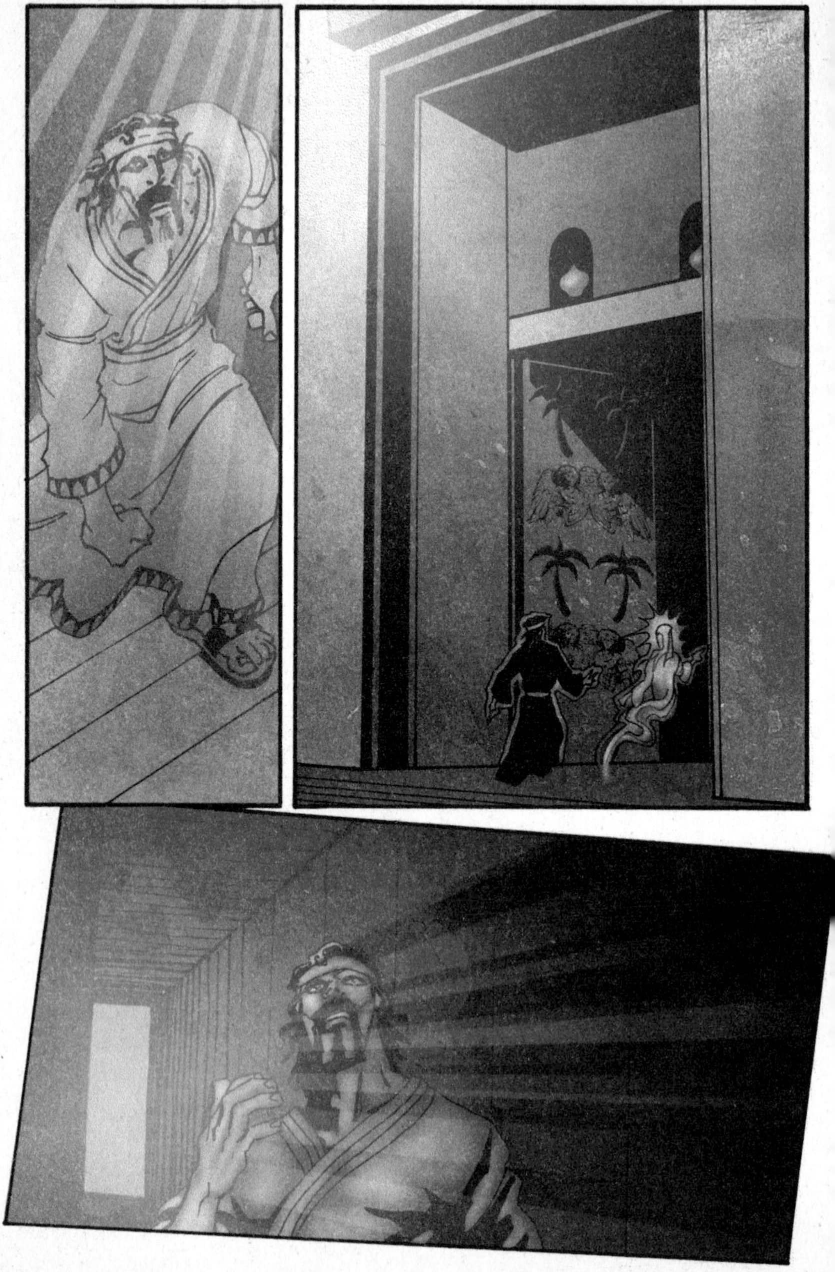

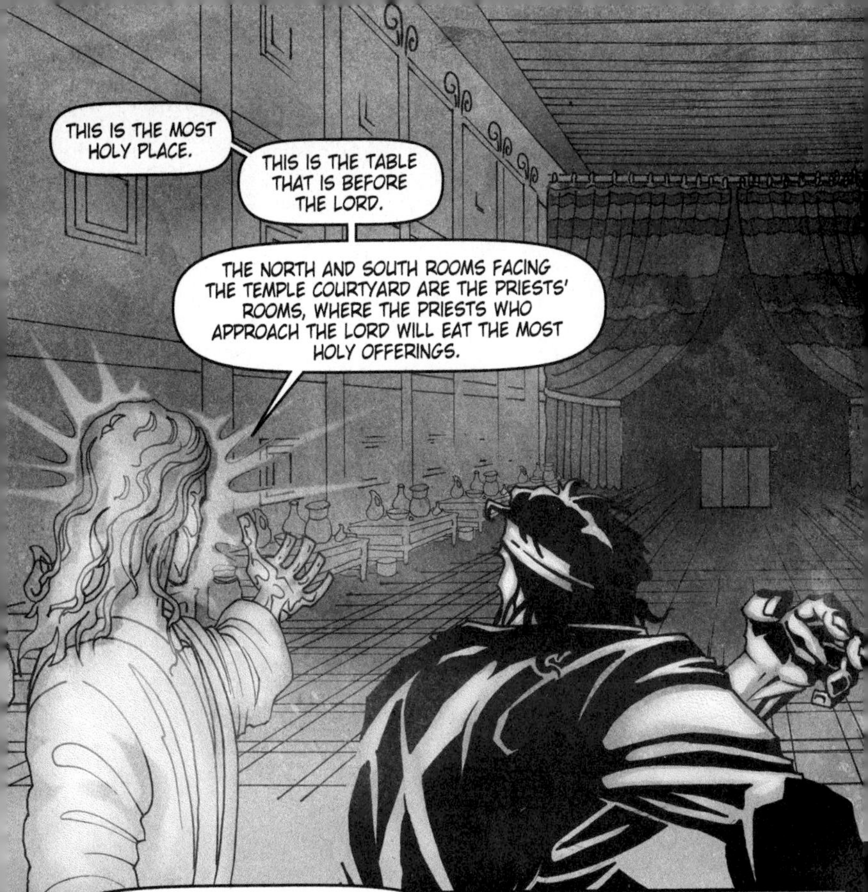
THIS IS THE MOST HOLY PLACE.
THIS IS THE TABLE THAT IS BEFORE THE LORD.
THE NORTH AND SOUTH ROOMS FACING THE TEMPLE COURTYARD ARE THE PRIESTS' ROOMS, WHERE THE PRIESTS WHO APPROACH THE LORD WILL EAT THE MOST HOLY OFFERINGS.

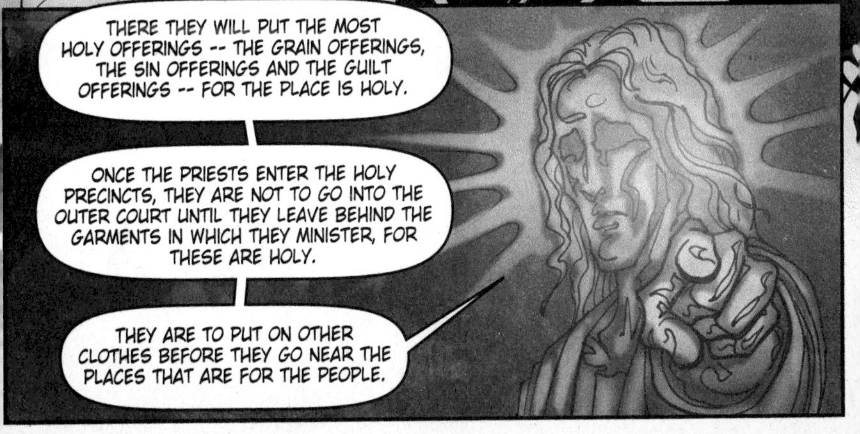
THERE THEY WILL PUT THE MOST HOLY OFFERINGS -- THE GRAIN OFFERINGS, THE SIN OFFERINGS AND THE GUILT OFFERINGS -- FOR THE PLACE IS HOLY.
ONCE THE PRIESTS ENTER THE HOLY PRECINCTS, THEY ARE NOT TO GO INTO THE OUTER COURT UNTIL THEY LEAVE BEHIND THE GARMENTS IN WHICH THEY MINISTER, FOR THESE ARE HOLY.
THEY ARE TO PUT ON OTHER CLOTHES BEFORE THEY GO NEAR THE PLACES THAT ARE FOR THE PEOPLE.

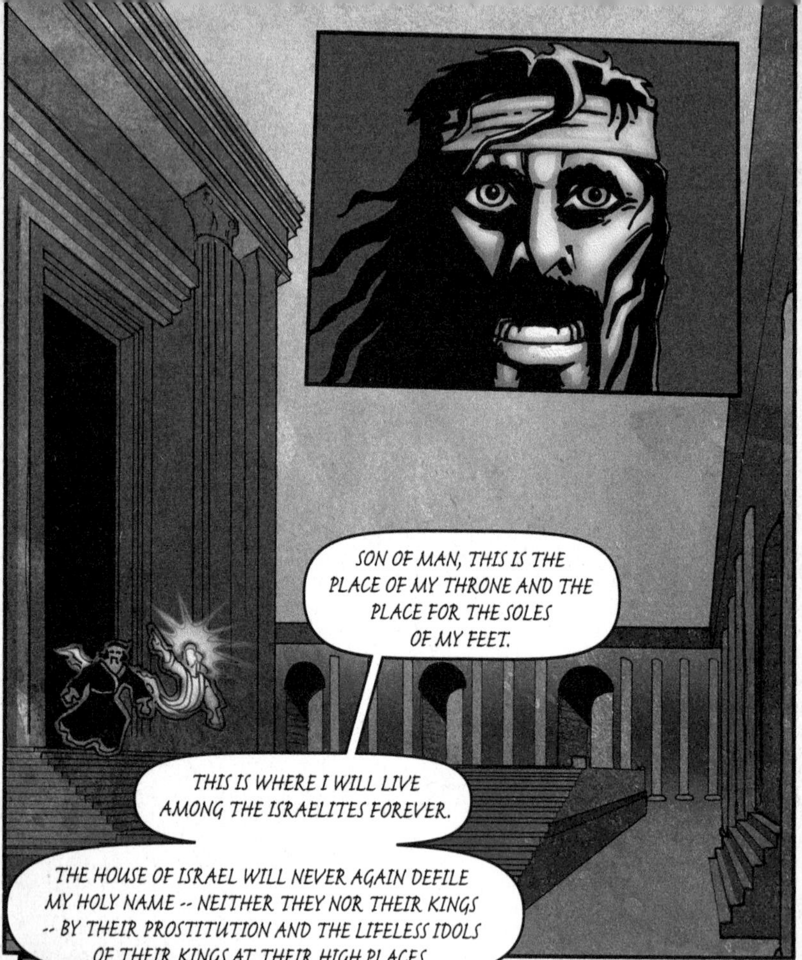
SON OF MAN, THIS IS THE PLACE OF MY THRONE AND THE PLACE FOR THE SOLES OF MY FEET.
THIS IS WHERE I WILL LIVE AMONG THE ISRAELITES FOREVER.
THE HOUSE OF ISRAEL WILL NEVER AGAIN DEFILE MY HOLY NAME -- NEITHER THEY NOR THEIR KINGS -- BY THEIR PROSTITUTION AND THE LIFELESS IDOLS OF THEIR KINGS AT THEIR HIGH PLACES.
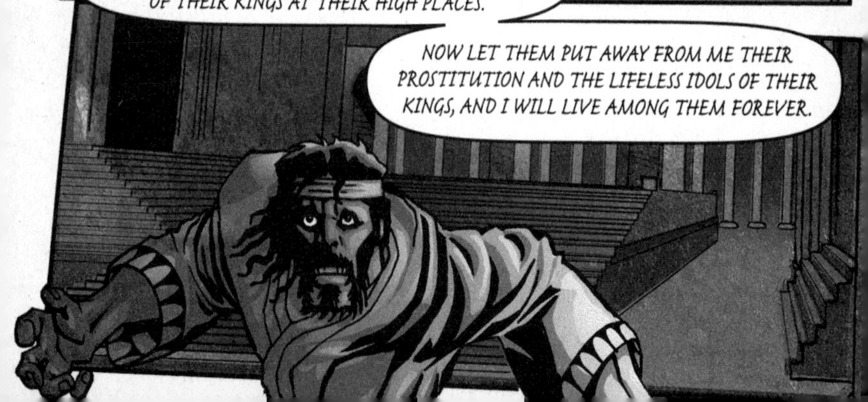
NOW LET THEM PUT AWAY FROM ME THEIR PROSTITUTION AND THE LIFELESS IDOLS OF THEIR KINGS, AND I WILL LIVE AMONG THEM FOREVER.

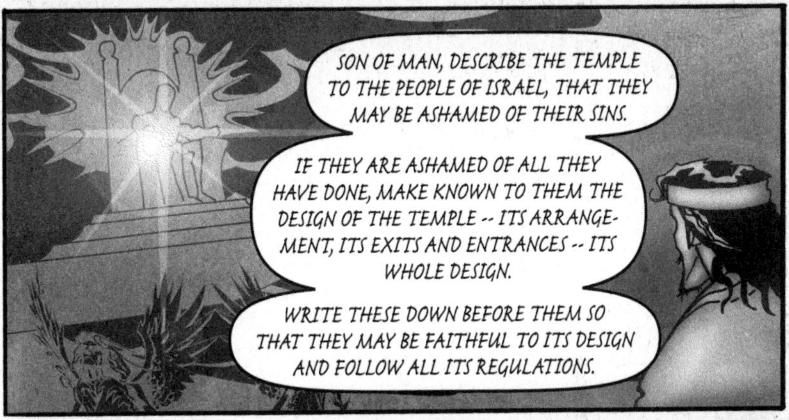
SON OF MAN, DESCRIBE THE TEMPLE TO THE PEOPLE OF ISRAEL, THAT THEY MAY BE ASHAMED OF THEIR SINS.
IF THEY ARE ASHAMED OF ALL THEY HAVE DONE, MAKE KNOWN TO THEM THE DESIGN OF THE TEMPLE -- ITS ARRANGE-MENT, ITS EXITS AND ENTRANCES -- ITS WHOLE DESIGN.
WRITE THESE DOWN BEFORE THEM SO THAT THEY MAY BE FAITHFUL TO ITS DESIGN AND FOLLOW ALL ITS REGULATIONS.
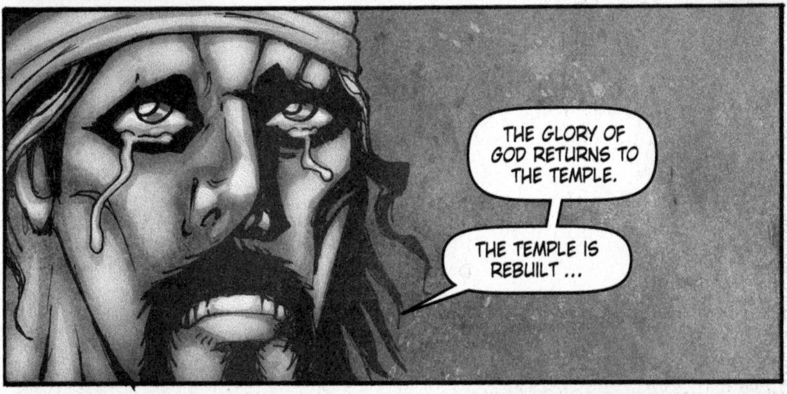
THE GLORY OF GOD RETURNS TO THE TEMPLE.
THE TEMPLE IS REBUILT ...
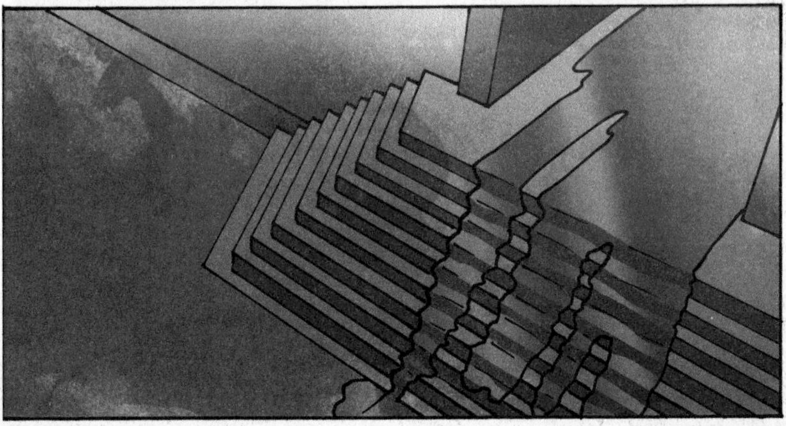

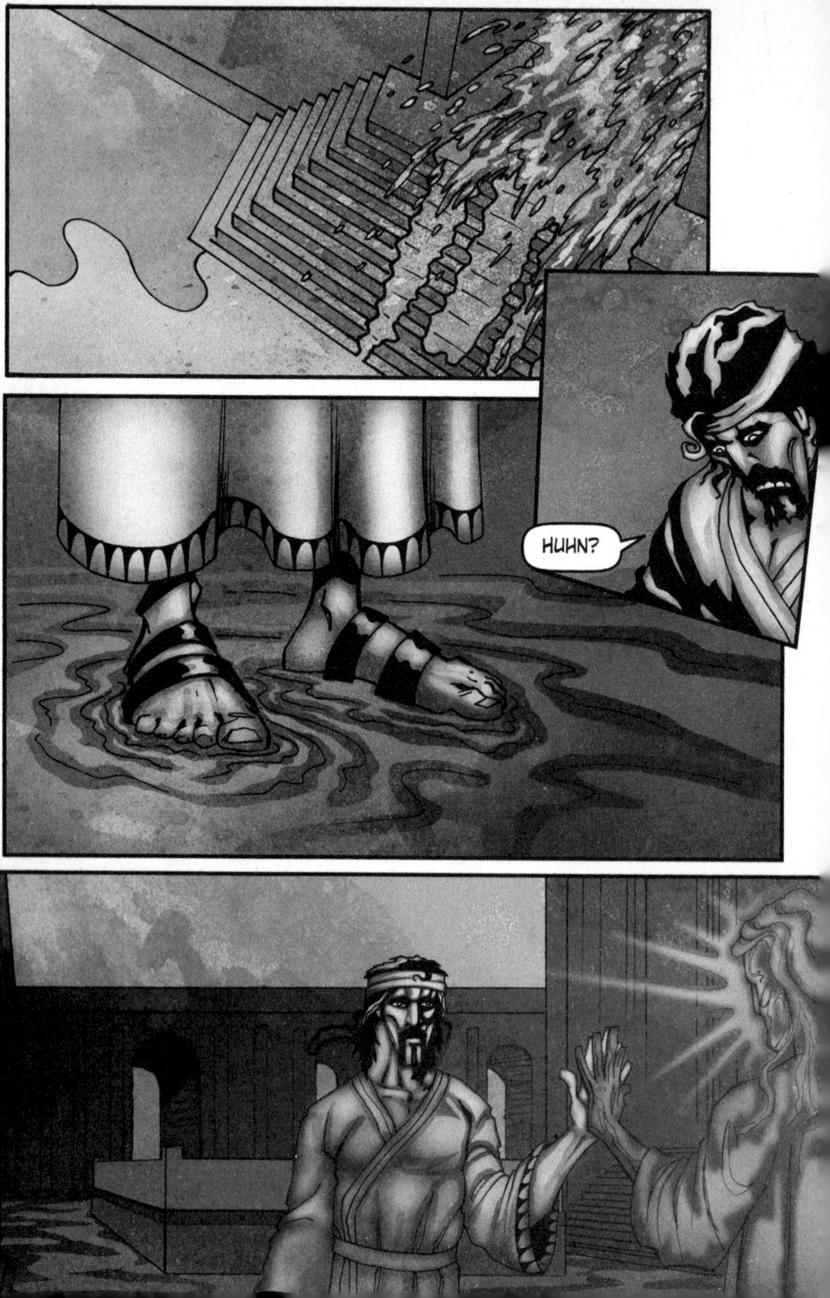
HUHN?

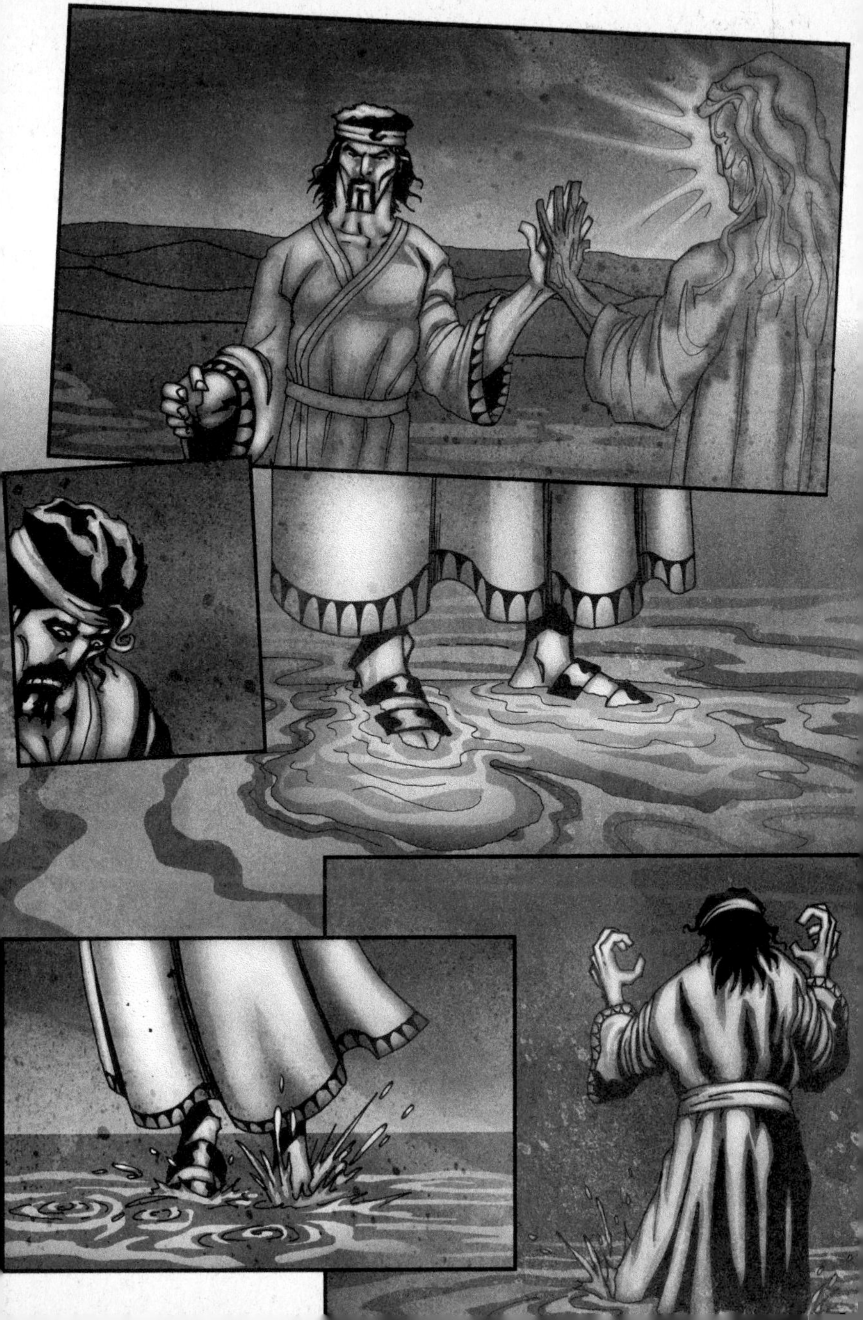

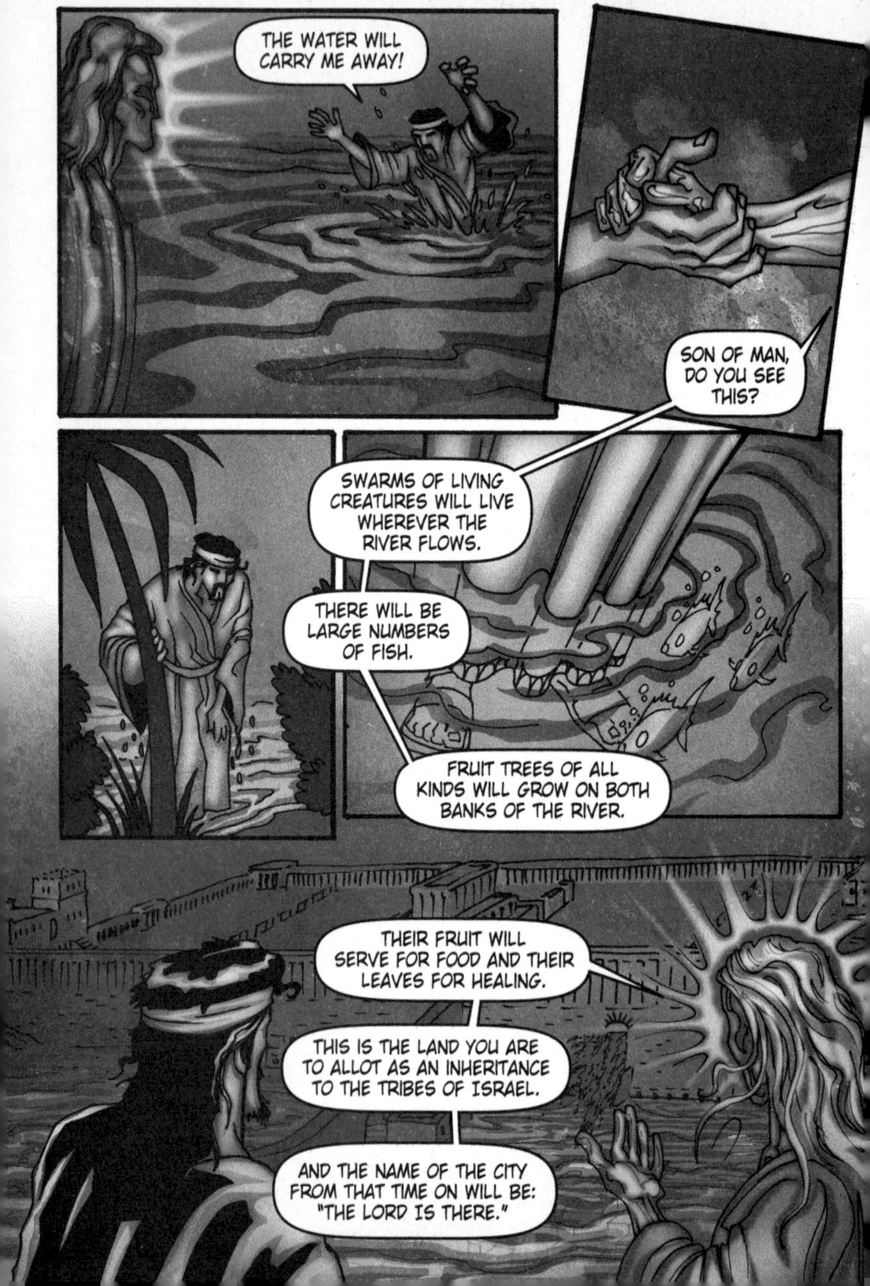
THE WATER WILL CARRY ME AWAY!
SON OF MAN, DO YOU SEE THIS?
SWARMS OF LIVING CREATURES WILL LIVE WHEREVER THE RIVER FLOWS.
THERE WILL BE LARGE NUMBERS OF FISH.
FRUIT TREES OF ALL KINDS WILL GROW ON BOTH BANKS OF THE RIVER.
THEIR FRUIT WILL SERVE FOR FOOD AND THEIR LEAVES FOR HEALING.
THIS IS THE LAND YOU ARE TO ALLOT AS AN INHERITANCE TO THE TRIBES OF ISRAEL.
AND THE NAME OF THE CITY FROM THAT TIME ON WILL BE: "THE LORD IS THERE."

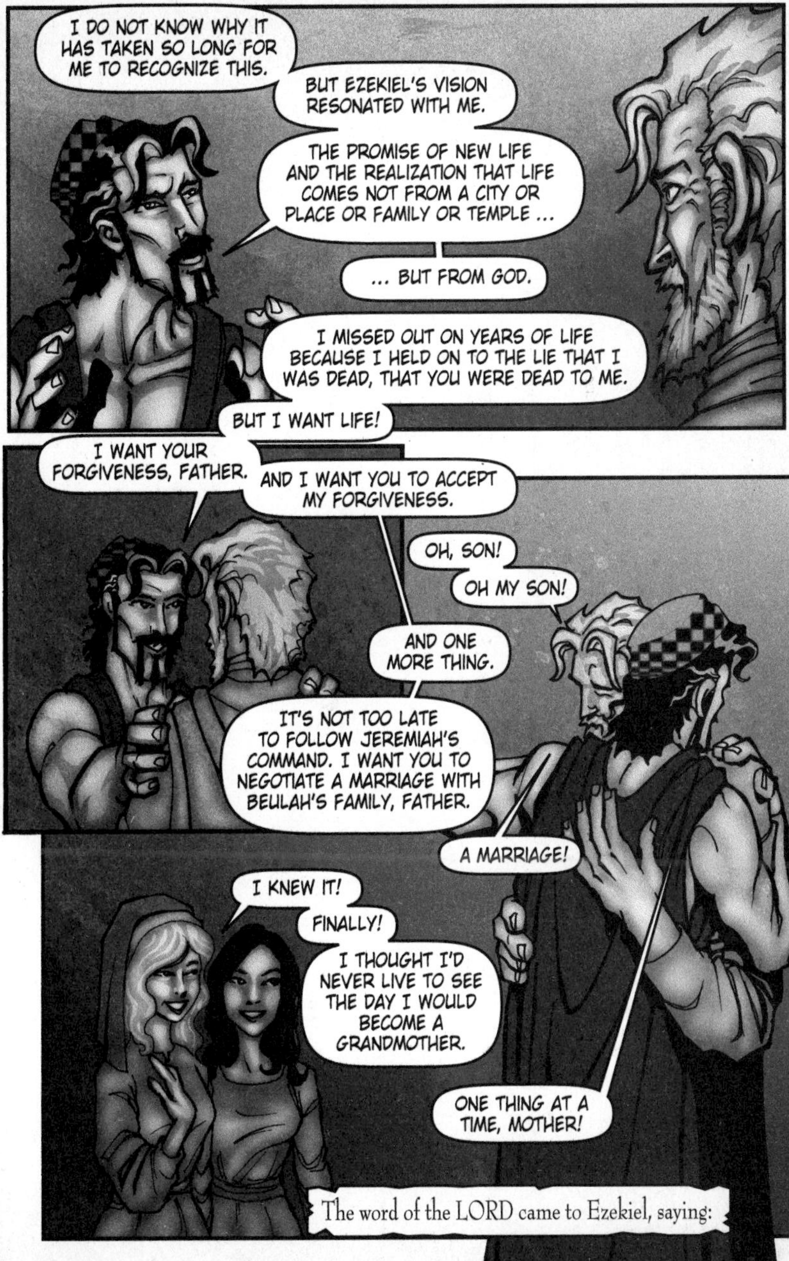
I DO NOT KNOW WHY IT HAS TAKEN SO LONG FOR ME TO RECOGNIZE THIS.
BUT EZEKIEL'S VISION RESONATED WITH ME.
THE PROMISE OF NEW LIFE AND THE REALIZATION THAT LIFE COMES NOT FROM A CITY OR PLACE OR FAMILY OR TEMPLE ...
... BUT FROM GOD.
I MISSED OUT ON YEARS OF LIFE BECAUSE I HELD ON TO THE LIE THAT I WAS DEAD, THAT YOU WERE DEAD TO ME.
BUT I WANT LIFE!
I WANT YOUR FORGIVENESS, FATHER.
AND I WANT YOU TO ACCEPT MY FORGIVENESS.
OH, SON!
OH MY SON!
AND ONE MORE THING.
IT'S NOT TOO LATE TO FOLLOW JEREMIAH'S COMMAND. I WANT YOU TO NEGOTIATE A MARRIAGE WITH BEULAH'S FAMILY, FATHER.
A MARRIAGE!
I KNEW IT!
FINALLY!
I THOUGHT I'D NEVER LIVE TO SEE THE DAY I WOULD BECOME A GRANDMOTHER.
ONE THING AT A TIME, MOTHER!
The word of the LORD came to Ezekiel, saying:

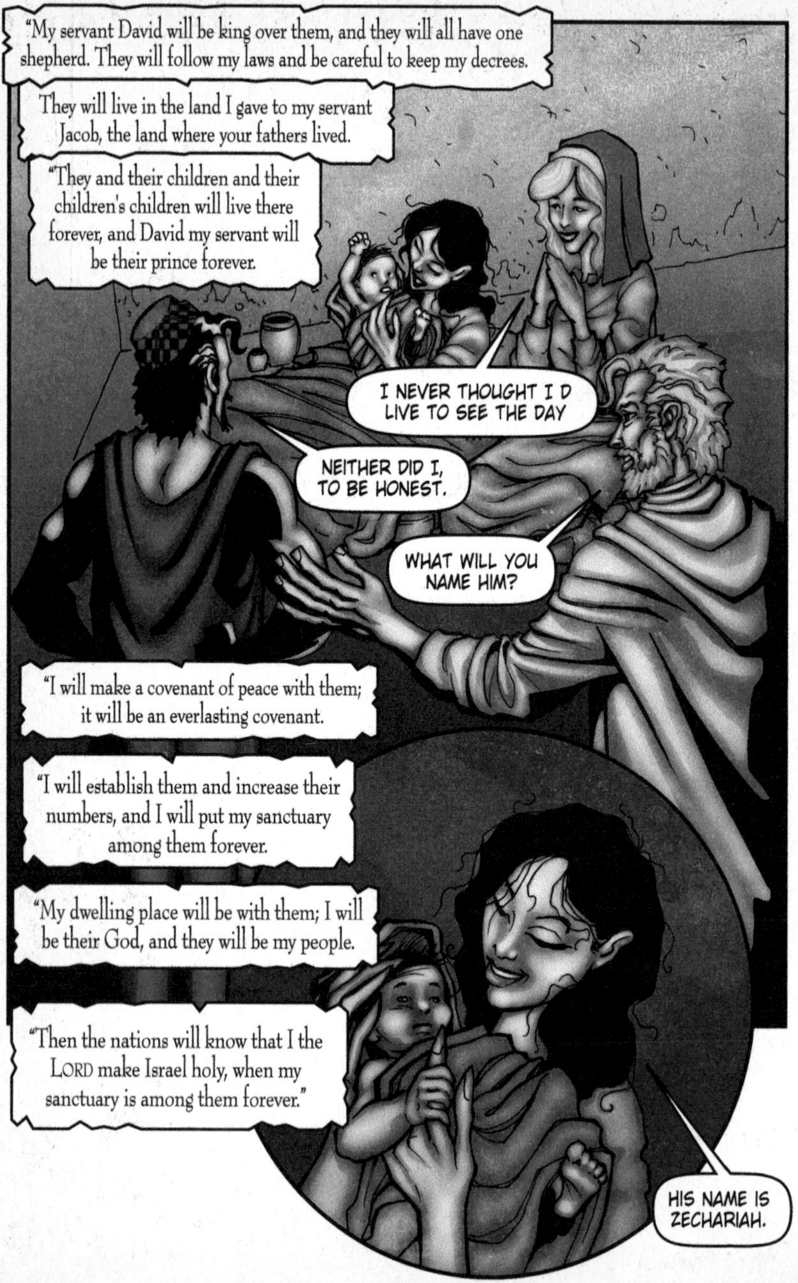
"My servant David will be king over them, and they will all have one shepherd. They will follow my laws and be careful to keep my decrees.
They will live in the land I gave to my servant Jacob, the land where your fathers lived.
"They and their children and their children's children will live there forever, and David my servant will be their prince forever.
I NEVER THOUGHT I D LIVE TO SEE THE DAY
NEITHER DID I, TO BE HONEST.
WHAT WILL YOU NAME HIM?
"I will make a covenant of peace with them; it will be an everlasting covenant.
"I will establish them and increase their numbers, and I will put my sanctuary among them forever.
"My dwelling place will be with them; I will be their God, and they will be my people.
"Then the nations will know that I the LORD make Israel holy, when my sanctuary is among them forever."
HIS NAME IS ZECHARIAH.

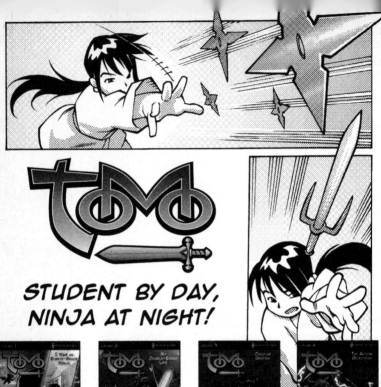

ZONDERVAN®

We want to hear from you. Please send your comments
about this book to us in care of zreview@zondervan.com. Thank you.

Grand Rapids, MI 49530
www.zonderkidz.com

ZONDERVAN.com/
AUTHORTRACKER
follow your favorite authors